Praise for *Believe The Magic*

"Believe the Magic is a wonderful story to read, effortlessly taking you away from your world and into another. A lot of action kept this story moving forward at a fast pace....If you are looking for a different twist to magic and a heroine you can sympathies with, make sure you check out Believe the Magic." ~ *Stacey Brutger, The Road to Romance*

"BELIEVE THE MAGIC is action-packed from the very beginning. With its acerbic wit and the most unlikely of heroines, readers will delight in the escapades of Ella...Due to the imagination of Melani Blazer, readers will BELIEVE IN MAGIC thanks to a charming leading lady and an adventurous love story!" ~ *Courtney Michelle, Romance Reviews Today*

"Believe The Magic is a roller coaster ride of emotion. One moment I found myself laughing and the next crying. Ella has a witty sense of humor and I enjoyed being carried away with her and Quentin through space and time. The relationship that develops between Ella and Quentin is engaging and full of deep emotion. The supporting relationships are also interesting and kept me entertained and excitedly waiting to see what would happen next. With certainty, Melanie Blazer has written a winner!" ~*Kerin, Euroreviews.eu*

Believe the Magic

Melani Blazer

A Samhain Publishing, Ltd. publication.

Samhain Publishing, Ltd.
2932 Ross Clark Circle, #384
Dothan, AL 36301

Believe The Magic

Cover by Scott Carpenter
Print ISBN: 1-59998-211-0
ISBN: 1-59998-007-X
www.samhainpublishing.com

First Samhain Publishing, Ltd. electronic publication: April 2006
First Samhain Publishing, Ltd. print publication: July 2006

Dedication

For the magic of friendship and those who believe in me. Jaci, Shan, Mandy and Angie, you all give me strength, support me and refuse to let a day go by without making me feel loved. May all the magic of love find you.

Chapter One

I am a sucker when someone needs my help.

I'd gotten better about being talked into doing "favors" for other people, but in this case, I couldn't let my niece down. It was Halloween and she decided, last minute of course, that she wanted to be a gypsy. Since I was the one escorting her on her trick-or-treat dash, she asked me to help her put the costume together.

I agreed. After all, how hard was it to dart into the antique shop around the corner from where I work and grab some gaudy costume jewelry? At this point in my life, my sister and her kids were all I had for a family. My job certainly wasn't something I'd call a career—it was something I did to pay the bills until a better option came along. Days like today made me philosophical about approaching thirty and having little direction in my life. That, in turn, made me a little cranky.

I'd never been in this place before, but someone had dropped off a few fliers at the office a week or so ago announcing the store was under new management. The advertisement said they had Halloween costumes and props, so here I was.

The overhead bell announced me as a customer as I pushed open the squeaky door. The tiny storefront was jam-packed with stuff. It probably all had names and places associated with it, but I'd never gotten into old furniture. I was busy staring at a very strange looking green chair, trying to figure out *why* someone would consider it valuable when a man stepped into my line of view.

He wore a cloak, a long one that immediately made me think of a magician or a wizard. He didn't say anything, not right away, just stared at me.

Too weird. I blinked and shook my head. When I opened my eyes, the same man stood there, but the cloak was gone. He looked like a respectable enough shop owner, dressed in a perfectly normal burgundy sweater and gray pleated slacks. And he was looking at *me* with a raised eyebrow as if *I* was crazy.

"Needing a costume, eh?"

"Oh, s-sorry," I stuttered. I wondered if I had spoken out loud while trying to figure out why I thought he was wearing a cloak. "Um, no. Not exactly."

"It's Halloween. That's been what everyone wants today." He swept his hands wide. A holographic image of a waterfall and well...paradise, appeared between his fingers. The backdrop to this weird vision was the brown cloak. Was he wearing it or wasn't he? But just like that he dropped his hands and the image faded and the robe disappeared.

What was going on here? "Huh?" I blinked, and then blinked again. It was the same man, the same store. He wasn't wearing this cloak my mind insisted on imagining. Heck, I was really seeing things. Was I sick? Ill? Allergic to antiques to the point of having hallucinations?

"Sam Nelson, proprietor. Tell me then, if not a costume, what's your fancy today?" He led me along with a hand at my elbow. In truth it felt more like he had me in a headlock. He didn't give me the choice to smile and take three steps backward, then turn and run.

"Uh, jewelry. Costume jewelry. But not for me. My niece wants to be a gypsy." *Do it for Jess. Don't let her down.*

"Gypsy? Well, I've got some nice scarves and a belt you might want to look at for her. But I've got something for you, too. One should be rewarded for doing favors for others."

His blue-jean eyes faded to black and back again before he turned and disappeared behind a rainbow-colored curtain.

"Bizarre," I muttered, prowling through the banged up furniture and moth-eaten tapestries. This was a mistake. Or else this guy was way into Halloween and making people's eyes bug out.

I nearly jumped out of my skin when I caught movement to my right. When I turned, I saw myself in a half-hidden mirror. Instead of the jeans and T-shirt I'd worn into the store, I was dressed as an Indian. With braided hair, painted face, buckskin, feathers and beads. I had it all.

"No way," I said. I saw mine—hers—*someone's* lips move. Oh God, that was me. I shook my head, closed my eyes, and counted to five. And checked again. There stood plain ole Ella. With an Indian headdress in the background. My imagination was obviously on overload. Or else I needed a vacation worse than I thought.

"Ah, there you are. Finding yourself around okay?"

Why did he say it like that? This Sam guy was getting odder by the moment. The way he watched me, intently studying my reaction, made me feel way too self-conscious, like I was being sized up or something. I needed to get out of this place. "Uh, yeah, just waiting on you."

Sam passed over a half-dozen or so silky scarves. They looked about as antique as my college sweatshirt. And I wasn't that old. Yet.

"Buck for two. And here's some wide hoop earrings and a belt." Now the belt I liked. Had to have it, even if it was just for me. Gold, wide-linked chain, not too far from the kind that holds a screen door from flying off the hinges. The links held charms and bells. I loved the bells.

I snaked out two red and blue scarves and snagged the belt. "That's it."

"You don't want the earrings?"

I studied them again. They looked more like bracelets. "She's twelve."

"Ah." He snatched them back.

I dug out my wallet and presented him with my debit card.

He waved me off. "Cash or check only. But I haven't given you what's yours."

I glanced at my watch and jammed my wallet back in my oversize bag. I rummaged through the collection of receipts, bills, my notepad, my cell phone with eternally dead battery and two paperbacks I'd started but never finished, looking for the checkbook that was undoubtedly lying next to the phone on my dresser. Geez, I was running so late. "I don't have time to shop for me. No offense, but I've never really understood the appeal of antiques."

I looked up to find Sam again dressed in that wizard's get up, holding out a strange necklace. I swear to God, he floated over the table and fastened it around my neck before my tongue hit the roof of my mouth to say, "No, I'm not interested."

I could stake money all he did was tie the choker-looking necklace on—he didn't even touch me—but I felt different—all the way through. Almost energized. Was this some new fangled drug seeping in through my skin? "How did you do that? And *what* did you do to me? You can't just go around looping nooses around your customer's necks. They won't come back."

He tilted his head as if I was the crazy one. "I gave you a necklace. No charge."

With even more desperation, I rooted around in my purse until my hand connected with my checkbook. Thank God. I scribbled out the check as quickly as I could. I was coming down with the flu or something because I was totally hallucinating some strange things. No, I didn't see myself as an Indian in that mirror. No, he wasn't wearing a weird cloak and he couldn't have floated over the table. Speaking of, whatever he'd stuck around my neck was coming off, I decided. As soon as my butt hit the seat of my car this "free" choker would be gone.

"I wouldn't do that if I were you."

"Do what?" I frowned. One hand held the checkbook, the other the torn off check and a ballpoint pen. My feet were solidly on the ground and my bag wasn't threatening to sweep precious breakables from a shelf. So what wasn't I supposed to do?

"Take the necklace off."

I slid my checkbook into my purse before I reached up to do just that. And was promptly rewarded with a violent shock. "A freaking shock collar? You've given me a shock collar? Is this your idea of a joke?" I slid the check onto the desk and scooped up my purchases, tossing them in my bag. "Trick or treat, right? Funny trick." I wasn't laughing.

I'd concede my life was pretty dull and I had been looking for a way to spice things up. This, however, was *not* what I had in mind. And despite my attempt to be utterly disgusted, a little charge of excitement raced through my veins. Or was it the necklace causing that?

So instead of threatening to call in the vice squad, bomb squad and the National Guard, I chalked this up to one of those "You'll never guess what happened to me today," moments and planned to get home and rip it off. Frankly, I was scared to stay here another moment, even if it was for him to take the necklace off. I could handle the removal.

Maybe. If I could find the "off" switch.

"The pair of gems will protect you. Others will try to remove them, or use them. They are very valuable and powerful. You will learn about their secrets later. Do not try to take them off. You wouldn't want to find out what happens if they fall into the wrong hands."

"Candid Camera, right? You're gonna turn around and point out the camera and tell me I'm the subject of a real humorous practical joke."

Not a twitch on his face. His steady stare made me shudder. Scared? More like creeped out. No way would I set foot in this store again. Ever.

"Sorry buddy, I just don't buy it. Thanks for the scarves and the cheap rawhide and glass beads."

I turned and walked out of the store. Heck, I was ready to run, bolt before he had lightning come down and split me in half.

"That could happen," he called after me.

I laughed and kept going without looking back. I wasn't *that* much of a sucker.

In my car, however, I contemplated my choice of words. I'd walked out of that shop with some weird beads around my neck. With them came a strange prophecy I still didn't understand. It being Halloween and all, I might be able to blow off the rest of the very abnormal events I experienced. But something in my gut told me there was a little more to it.

Did I really believe this Sam character bestowed a necklace on every one of his customers? My head didn't feel warm. No fever to blame for thinking he floated. Yes. Floated over the counter. None of it made sense. Especially the warning about the beads, gems, whatever they were.

I reached up and touched the necklace and felt the electricity crackle. Getting shocked while driving was probably not a good idea.

It was nothing more than a trick or treat stunt. I drove toward my sister's house convincing myself of that. I was overanalyzing and certainly over-dramatizing everything because I was having one of my re-assess-where-I-am-in-life-and-not-liking-it moments.

ൡ ൡ ൡ

"Whoa, bitchin' necklace." Jess, the twelve-year-old gypsy wanna-be snagged my offerings to her and reached up to touch the necklace. I'd hoped not to think any more about it and the weird experience at the antique shop, but clearly that wasn't going to happen.

"Is that any way to talk to your aunt?" I handed over the scarves, then pushed past her and dropped my aching body onto the sofa. "Where's your mom?"

"Damnit, Karl, get your shoes on. Jeeeesssss?" Jeannie came rushing out of the room and nearly bowled her daughter over.

"She's right here. Relax, Jeans. I've got her taken care of."

My sis ignored me in standard fashion. I picked up the TV Guide to see how I would be spending my dateless Friday night. After this trick or treating adventure, that is. Jeannie's voice faded to a sound straight out of the Peanuts cartoons when the cover on the mini-magazine started swirling. Sam stood on the cover and smiled up at me.

"What the—" I tried to let go but found it might as well been glued to my fingers.

"Well, still unbelieving aren't you?"

"Oh my God, I've gone and lost my mind." Could I just check myself into the funny farm? No one in this family would doubt the necessity of my stay, I was sure. Telling the doctor about the man on the TV Guide talking to me should guarantee a room for a long visit.

"You aren't crazy. But now you are magic."

"Great. I'll tell them that when they come running at me with the strait jacket."

"Who you talking to, Aunt Ella?" The much too bright adolescent walked over to bust me and my brilliant conversation with a book.

"No one." I caught her eyes with what I thought was a don't-tell-a-soul-or-you-won't-see-thirteen look.

"Aunt Ella's talking to the TV Guide, Mom."

So much for my glare. I couldn't even do that right it seemed. Guess that's why I wasn't a parent. "I was not. I was...um...thinking out loud as I pondered the...uh...outfits these guys are wearing." Where the heck had I seen Sam in the faces of the hottest new boy group?

"Have a long week?" Jeannie wrestled her three-year-old to the ground and twisted on his Winnie-the-Pooh sneakers without breaking the rhythm of her voice. "After five days of Karl in eight hour stretches, I talk back to the TV." She turned to her daughter. "Aunt El's just got some stuff on her mind. She was thinking."

I eyed the gypsy. "You ready?" I didn't regret giving in to Jess's pleadings that I accompany her and her girlfriends on their rounds through the neighborhood. I rather liked the almost-teenager and her sarcastic wit. Plus it was so uncool to walk with Ma and baby brother while trick-or-treating. I liked to be considered the "cool" choice.

I shrugged at my sister. She winked back. I would have my revenge. I'd give birth to twins who'd be spoiled so rotten milk would curdle when they walked in the room. And I'd make her baby-sit them every day while I worked. And I'd feed them Sweet Tarts for breakfast. Just to get back at her for days like this.

"Where's the Joker?" My pet name for her husband. He *was* one, and I didn't mean in a funny way.

"Bowling?" She lifted her shoulder but kept her hands on the wriggling child. I didn't see their marriage lasting six more months. But I'd said that a couple of years after Jess had been born and Jeannie had proven me wrong. Guess she tolerated crap better than me.

"Why aren't you dressing up?" Jess asked me as we pounded down the wooden steps and down her driveway.

I pulled my hair out to the sides and stuck out my tongue. "Dere, dat bedder?"

She giggled and I dropped my hands. Heck, I figured I was dressed up enough; I had clothes on. And makeup. My hair was stick straight so I had limited options. I smoothed it down. "I'm me, that's scary enough, isn't it?"

She rolled her eyes. "So where'd you find these scarves, and this belt? It is so cool." Jess skipped through the door I held open.

"The belt is mine after this, cheeky one." I reached out and pinched her still plump face. She hated when I did that.

"Says who?"

"Says me."

"You gonna let me wear your necklace?"

"This one?" I reached up to touch it. I jerked back as soon as my fingers grazed the beads, but it didn't zap me senseless that time.

"Whoa, El-la, you have got to let me have it."

"What, why? And it's Aunt Ella to you, squirt." I arranged my hair to fall over my shoulders and hide the necklace.

"When you touched it, the beads changed colors. Like it's a mood necklace. That's what it is, right?"

Changed colors? I could have sworn the stones were a milky white when Sam had held it up. "What color are they now?"

"Blue."

"Blue? You sure?"

"Yeah." Her voice was breathy. "And when you touched it, they turned lilac."

"Lilac?" I repeated. Beads that change color? What had that psycho given me anyway? Maybe it was electric—sure would explain the jolt I'd taken earlier.

"Do you know what the colors mean?"

"Not a clue. Now let's find Marisol and Jenny and get this candy snatching show on the road, gypsy girl."

Chapter Two

I was barely awake when I climbed into the shower the next morning. I would have given my eyeteeth to sleep in. As I contemplated if being worn out from traipsing no less than five miles through suburbia qualified as a reasonable excuse for calling off, my fingers connected with something...foreign...on the back of my neck, just under my hairline. I thought a spider had landed on me. I nearly took off soapy and naked to the neighbor's while beating at the back of my head with my loofa.

But after whimpering and clawing at my neck until the worst of the hysterics faded, I kicked up the hot water and hid beneath it. I'd listened long enough in science class to remember insects were cold-blooded. Get them hot enough and they'll explode. Well, I wasn't keen on the idea of spider guts, but I was in the shower, right? Dead bug parts would wash down the drain.

When I reached up again, I realized I must have simply felt the ends of the leather string that had been tied together. I explored the knot with my fingers to make sure that's all it was.

I breathed a sigh of relief and half laughed at my panic. I reached for the razor I must have knocked to the bottom of the tub, but didn't even need to bend down. When my fingers extended for it, the pink disposable just floated up to them.

"No," I said, barely able to breathe. "It didn't just fly. It couldn't have." The shock of thinking arachnids had invaded my apartment had left me unable to digest the impossibility of such...magic. I wondered, if I laid the razor back on the peeling, blue non-skid fishy sticker, could I do it again?

I did, but not until I stared at the razor for a while and felt the necklace burn against my skin. Wowsers.

The feel of power in those beads scared me more than the idea of a spider on my neck. Way more.

My fear, however, was short-lived. I dried off, got dressed and fingered the necklace. What had that goofy guy said about the necklace? Secrets? Power? If...if I thought about believing the concept of a magic necklace, would I also believe I could channel the power? Didn't he say not to *use* it? That implied it was possible. Unbelievable, but possible.

Within ten minutes I had my brush dancing on air and my toothbrush twirling like a live baton.

"You shouldn't toy with the power." Sam stood in the doorway to the bathroom. He put up a hand and stopped the shriek I had opened my mouth to emit. "No matter who you scream for they won't see me unless I want them to."

"Why are you in my house?" I emphasized each syllable, all the while wondering why I didn't have enough guts to throw the contents of the bathroom at him.

"Because my magic is stronger."

I froze and looked at him again. "Huh?"

"You won't try to fight me with your magic because you know mine is stronger. Much more controlled."

"Why are you in my house?" I repeated.

"Because I needed to be sure you don't hurt yourself with the magic."

"Listen, Sam or whatever your name is, you cannot do this to me. I don't want to be some witch and I certainly can't handle you just creeping up on me like this. And this magic stuff?" I shook my head. I couldn't insist I didn't believe, because I was using it, doing it. But I didn't understand it, and didn't want to.

"What if I told you it was me in the bathtub, tickling the back of your neck?"

I screamed.

He laughed. "Just kidding. You felt the ties to the necklace—and I know because I read your thoughts, not because I was there. Now go to the door and tell Bertie you found a spider in the bathtub."

There was a knock at the door. He inclined his head toward it.

I should have passed out, freaked out or demanded he get out.

Well, I'd tried that. I suppose an explanation was equally out of the question. Magic? How? *How?* I really did want to jump up and down screaming at him to show me more, get the damn thing off my neck and tell me what the hell was going on—all at once. But poor Bertie needed to be attended to. "I'm going, I'm going."

"Don't lie. I'm not here." I looked back. He wasn't. What the heck was going on?

I calmed my downstairs neighbor with the spider story. I stood with my back against the door after she'd gone back downstairs. None of this made any sense. How did Sam get in here? And why? Did he want his necklace back? Was this some sort of a trick?

Back to the bathroom I went. Sam was still gone or invisible or whatever. It hurt to think about what that meant.

I studied myself in the mirror. Nope, nothing different. Eyes a little wild, but that's to be expected in crazy people. And that damn necklace. Perfectly round, glass beads lay on either side of my neck. They looked clear to me, but hadn't Jess said they were blue or purple or something? "Freakin' Frankenstein looking things."

They pulsated pink. I raised an eyebrow. "Useless cockamamie glass shooters on a thrown away slip of leather."

Red. Ow, damnit. Hot, too. Okay, so I couldn't insult the nice piece of jewelry or it bit back. It was time to take it off, once and for all.

But not right now. My wonderful long, hot shower had swelled the rawhide and my stubby fingers were no match for it. Figured.

I held up one finger, mad scientist style. I had scissors. I'd admit it scared me, putting something that sharp against my neck, but—*Ow, Ow, Ow!* I swore I had to have two hickey-looking marks on my throat from the heat they emitted. Okay, so no scissors. These beads didn't like the idea of scissors.

The wall clock struck a chord. Half past what? I wondered, just knowing I was a good two hours late for work already. I hadn't even managed to put my watch on yet. I was really slipping.

The alarm clock said eight-thirty. I retrieved my watch and confirmed it. Wow. I could have sworn it was later. That meant I still had a half-hour to brush my hair and coat my lashes with mascara. Perhaps even dig out my lip gloss. Maybe it was going to be a better day than yesterday.

ᘓ ᘓ ᘓ

My illustrious job was with the travel agency around the corner and three doors down from the antique shop. I refused to even look at the sign above door promising "Treasures of the Past" as I drove by and signaled my turn. Parking was a cinch, and I strolled into the office with a big smile plastered on my face.

Everyone there, all of two girls, stopped to stare at me.

"What?" Did I get dressed? Did my hair turn purple or fall out on the drive in? "What?"

"It's Saturday, Ella. Since when do you work Saturdays?"

Flippin' fleepin' phooey. Slap me and tell me to dance a jig. I paused and toed the carpet. "I...uh...just forgot I told this client I'd deliver his tickets to him. I left them here last night."

Breathing with a bit more confidence, I sat behind my desk. "B, B, B," I recited, zipping through the envelopes in my file. "Got it. Thanks, gals."

I headed back out before I managed to make a fool of myself. Funny how I had been at the job the longest and still felt like the new girl. Or maybe just the poor, pitiful Ella whose life was stuck in a rut, financially, socially...everyway.

Screw that. I had something Sara and Althea didn't. A day off. Maybe I should see if I could do something about it, something that would give my life more purpose.

Feeling generous, I held the door for a man in a Chicago Bears sweatshirt.

"Thanks. Ah, wait," he said.

I paused, leaning forward to see what this guy wanted. Okay, really eager to see what this guy wanted. I hadn't seen one this live in a coon's age. "Yeeesss?"

"You're Ella, Ella Mansfield, right?" And he was asking for me. My toes tingled.

"Yeeesss," I answered again, blinking. "You are?" *Only the most handsome man in the universe alive today and I want to jump your bones, cook your dinners and have your babies.*

Okay, I'd admit to thinking the first thought, but added the last two just to make it not-so-cheap. My God, he looked good. In a bad boy kind of way. Hair that looked like it intentionally fell into his eyes—and those eyes. Vivid green framed by dark lashes, enhanced by thick eyebrows. Strong jaw lined with stubble. He looked the type to wear black leather or even ripped up denim. Thank God he didn't, because I don't think I'd be able to breathe faced with that vision.

"Who are you?" I repeated, desperate to get my bearing and stop ogling the customer.

"Quentin Paige." He hooked a thumb in the general direction of the corner. "Sam down the street said to talk to you."

"Oh, no, sorry. Don't want anything else Sam has to share with me."

"So you can't sell me a trip to Denver?"

I'd put my hand out, nearly touching his chest to push him back away from me, but at the word "sell" I reached a little farther and bunched my fist in the material above the Bear's logo. No sense ruining a sale. In fact, after scaring me this morning Sam owed me. "Right in here, what was your name again?" I released his shirt once I was sure he'd follow me back to my desk.

"Quentin. I know. Different. My parents were hippies, what can I say."

I nodded. "Mine were rednecks. Still are. Have a seat."

He was silent after that. I totally ignored Sara and Althea despite the holes they were drilling in the back of my head with their eyes.

They were the Saturday regulars who usually managed to make the bulk of their paycheck from those who wandered in on Saturdays. Most of their clients were the working people needing a quick escape. We were good at those.

Marnie, the boss, had taken a mini-vacation herself just this weekend. I'd get tattled on for snatching customers when she got back. Yeah, so I wasn't scheduled to work, but it's not like I just *stole* the customer. He asked for me. Worst that would happen was I'd have to surrender any commission I made on this one. Or ship the boss back off to Vegas for another weekend. And this time, I just might accompany her. And if I was lucky, never return. No one would miss me, at least for awhile.

"Will you be traveling alone?" I asked in my sweetest professional voice.

He glanced around and nodded. Was this a secret?

"Travel dates?"

"Now."

"What?"

"As soon as I can get on a plane and fly."

I leaned over, a mistake because I caught a load of the heavenly lure he wore as cologne. "Did you try the airport? It's a little faster to get a ticket that way on this short notice."

"They want ID. I don't have any." I studied him. He had to be at least my age, but he dressed more like a footloose college student. Must be it, I figured. Emergency run home.

"And you think I can get you a ticket without ID?"

"I know you'll help me get where I need to go."

I stood up. I needed my job. Wanted Mr. Tall, Dark and Handsome who was sitting in front of me, but he wasn't gonna cover my rent when it came due in two weeks. "Sorry. No ID, no ticket."

Quentin grabbed my hand and hauled himself to his feet. The toes of his shiny new Nikes touched the tip of my boring black ankle boots. Must be a lot of static in the air. I felt the tingles of it up and down the front of my body.

He grabbed both my hands and flipped those deadly emerald eyes in my direction. "Holy—" I said before his mouth landed on mine. I love roller coasters, but saying that's what his kiss felt like would be an understatement. Maybe I could liken it to being the roller coaster, not just riding it. When I drew back, his eyes had turned dark.

I caught my breath and tried to step back. He had my hands tightly in his. "Hey, you're hurting me." What in the heck were Sara and Althea doing anyway, charging admission? "Help me here."

"Looks like you're doing fine all by yourself," Sara jeered.

"You're doing just fine," Quentin repeated, his breath fanning against my cheek in a way that cooled my skin and set my blood on fire. That was not good. Men weren't any more abundant in my life than money, so of course I'd react this way. I drew in a breath. "I'm still not going to sell you a ticket."

"I don't want a ticket. I need you to help me in another way."

"I—"

"Shhh," he crooned. I felt like the rats in the Pied Piper, mesmerized by the spell of his once again green eyes. He lifted our joined hands to my chest. Whoa, danger zone. His eyes met mine. His stare was so intense, I couldn't look away. I tried, trust me.

The high neck of my sweater had hidden the necklace. Until now. He pulled the collar down just a bit until he could see it, and sighed, almost a lusty sound. His eyes were black again. I wanted to rip my gaze from his and check his mouth to see if he had fangs. I expected his next move to be Dracula style, leaving me drained of blood on the floor of the office. Talk about a gruesome death. Sara and Althea would *really* charge admission to see that.

His head didn't move closer, but his hands reached higher. He touched the bared skin just above my pulse and electricity coursed through me. From the necklace? I wanted those beads to freakin' electrocute him for scaring me this way. I held my breath.

He was smarter than that. He made me touch them, his fingers closed over mine. "Move them together."

"What?"

"Push them together. They'll slide."

He jerked my fingers toward the center. I half-expected the rope to break on the back of my neck. Or sever my head.

"Break it up, you two. There's a customer here," Althea ordered.

The spell was broken. I stepped back, shaking and feeling like I'd run a marathon. Backwards. While wearing scuba gear.

"Quentin."

The voice snagged my attention. Sam was here.

I tugged my collar back over the necklace and slid into my chair. Let Sam handle this.

"Can I help you, sir?" Althea, in her long, tight skirt, walked toward Sam, her behind twitching. I groaned and rolled my gaze back toward her intended victim. At least he was ignoring her.

"He's come after this one." I pointed at Quentin, trying to let Althea know Sam wasn't a potential customer.

"You stay out of this Ella-Mae. This one's mine."

I raised an eyebrow, but realized she was nothing. The action was happening right in front of me.

"What are you doing in here? I told you to stay away from her."

Sam walked right past my co-worker and launched into Quentin.

"I need to get out of this town, man. You need to give me my stuff back."

Sam's finger tapped the still smiling Bears' logo. "What are you going to do, call the police? You've been identity diving all over the place. You realize you're causing more havoc than you've helped to avert. I may have to replace you."

"You wouldn't do that. I've got the power now."

"Not without the gems." Sam looked my way.

Quentin dove at me, landing right on me, on my chair. The chair wasn't prepared either and tipped right over.

"Blasted!" I yelped and pushed upward. Quentin popped three feet in the air above me and hung there like a side of beef in a meat locker.

I laughed at the expletive that emitted from his nicely shaped mouth.

And once I realized I could think and keep him afloat, I checked out the rest of him too. I'm one to like longer hair, but his was just plain messy. I was totally convinced those weren't his clothes. The baggy sweatshirt belonged on someone about a dozen years his junior or thirty years his senior. I wondered if I could undress him while he hung there. I leaned back, still positioned in my tipped chair, and waggled my pinky. His sweatshirt rose to show off a nicely defined set of abs. "Nice," I murmured.

"Cut it out, you bitch."

"Tsk, tsk," I warned him. "You don't want me to just drop you like the worthless sack of potatoes you are, do you?"

Sam stepped around the corner of the desk, leaned on one leg and smiled. "Doesn't look like I need have worried about Quentin here taking advantage of you."

"Yes, you do need to worry. He kissed me and tried to strangle me with this rope around my neck. What's with the pull them closer thing?"

Sam snapped his fingers and Quentin collapsed in a heap on the floor beside the desk. Good thing, because I wasn't sure how to get him down. Someone behind me muffled a gasp, but I wasn't going to look at Sara. Althea was in my line of sight, and she was already crossing herself and backing away from the little circle we made.

Sam held up a finger to me. What? Wait?

I waited, only because Sam grabbed Quentin by the shirt and hauled him to his feet. I eyed both of them while biting my lip. What now? I felt helpless—and I wasn't a fan of helpless. But I knew nothing about either of these men except that one gave me a magical necklace and the other one wanted it. I was a pawn it seemed, suckered into the middle of some fight for power. My life wasn't exactly excitement central, but I didn't ask for this to liven it up.

Neither of them, I figured, was truly safe. I didn't know who to trust, then decided I didn't *have* to trust either. While they were otherwise occupied, I could make my escape.

Or so I thought.

As soon as I started sprinting toward the door Sam had me running in place about three inches above the ground. Quentin had the audacity to laugh.

"Chill out, punk. You started this," I warned Quentin.

"How's it feel to hang in mid air?" he teased back.

"Not nice," I shot back at him. Then I pointed at Sam. "Put me down."

Sam intervened. "I can see you two are going to get along just fine. Now stop. You aren't ten years old. If I had wanted ten year olds, I would have recruited them."

This got more preposterous the longer it went on. I stopped air jogging. "Recruit? You call floating over a table and attaching the electric fence around my neck recruiting?"

Quentin glared at Sam. "At least you got yours. He took mine away."

I could see by the blackness of Sam's eyes he wanted to make like the Three Stooges and bash our heads together. I however, wasn't interested in experiencing such a thing.

"Well, now you've done it. He'll probably take mine away too. Until you learn to keep your hands to yourself." Of course, as soon as the words were out of my mouth I remembered I *did* want the beads off. But this very moment wasn't the time. I was still concerned what I had been recruited *for.* Until I figured out why I had been blessed with the magic, I wasn't giving it up. It made me feel a wee bit safer.

I heard talking. Sara was on the phone. Police? I whirled to find out. At least that range of motion wasn't stripped from me. "Sara, what are you doing?"

She looked up at me as if I'd grown horns and a tail. "Sara," I hissed again. "Hang up the phone. I don't know what these two are capable of. Look at me!"

That worked. The phone dropped in the cradle.

I spun, still in mid-air and waved at Sam. "Hello? Can you put me down now? The police are coming."

When the cops walked in, hands on their guns, Sara, Althea and I were intently working. Well, okay, I was playing computer solitaire, but it looked good from their side of the counter. I didn't know what Sara was going to say, but my lips were sealed. Again.

I wondered what it took to learn the art of invisibility. Sam had done it earlier—I'd watched him disappear in a snap. But I quit stressing about parlor tricks when I heard Sara telling the truth. I was as good as in jail. And Althea sat there and agreed. I wondered if sliding onto the floor and under the desk was more than just a temporary option. I clicked the game off, leaving the main menu to glare at me. I bet this was my last day on the job. But I knew just what I was going to do. Walk into that antique shop and demand a position there. Maybe then I could find out what the hell was going on and why I was involved.

I had zoned out, imagining what I'd say when I pounded my fist on Sam's mahogany table. The cops were leaving. Exiting the building without so much as saying "boo" to me. I could swear Sara said stuff about me being suspended mid-air.

"Where did she go?" Althea muttered, wrapping her arms around her chest.

Sara shrugged and perched on the end of Althea's desk. "Maybe we shouldn't talk about it, huh? They don't believe the first word we said."

I glanced down. Yep, purple sweater, black leggings, right there. I poked my leg. Flesh, I felt it. How could I be invisible? I walked up to Sara and waved my hand in front of her face.

Damn, now this could be dangerous. She couldn't see me.

But then she got up and walked square into me.

“Shit, Ella, you scared me. Where’d you go? The police were just here.”

“I, uh, felt sick to my stomach. Had to run to the ladies room.”

Althea eyed me warily. I circled her desk with a tight smile and went back to grab my purse.

Things were not getting better. Weirder definitely. I walked out to my car, fighting the urge to laugh hysterically at it all. Life hadn’t been perfect before yesterday, but at least I’d known what was happening to me.

This was going to be one heck of a story to tell—if I ever got to the bottom of it.

Chapter Three

Quentin was sitting on my doorstep. I was tempted to drive on by, but that would have been obvious. I gunned the engine. Obvious schmovious, who cares? But the little soft spot in my heart, damn it anyway, forced the U-turn.

"You're not coming in."

He followed me anyway.

"Quiggle, you can't—"

"It's Quentin."

"Yeah, yeah, whatever. It doesn't matter; I don't intend to have you in my house or in my life. So take your silly name and have a nice life. After you help me get these gems off."

"It's too late for that you know."

"Nah, you're still within punting distance of the door."

He tilted his head. I really wished he wouldn't do that. "The gems, Ella. They aren't coming off."

"Why are you here?"

"I need your help. Your power."

So take it already. Maybe my little rut wasn't so bad. Predictable at least. "I'd want nothing more than to rip this forsaken—OW!"

"Don't do that. The magic doesn't like you to insult it."

I know what I wanted to call it. "If I thought any harder about it I just might say to hell with it and figure out how to get it off. But somehow, I think Sam would hunt me down and make me pay."

He stuck out his bottom lip and nodded. I grinned and pulled a Sprite from the fridge. I didn't offer one to Quentin, but he followed my steps and helped himself.

"Did I say you could have that?"

"No."

"Then?"

Another shrug. I was tempted to buy fifty pound dumbbells and tie them to his wrists so he'd be forced to answer to me. "Talk to me or get out. I am so *not* in the mood for games."

"Life's a game, Ella."

"Yeah, and so is Chutes and Ladders. So find one already and exit my apartment."

"I really need to understand why Sam chose you."

"Because I walked into his store and bought a gypsy's belt and a few scarves."

He shook his head this time. At least it was different. And it made his hair fall into his eyes. That was almost cute. "Try again."

"Because I'm cute and funny and available. I don't know." I threw my arms out, managing to forget I had a can of soda in one hand and liberally sprinkling my counter and floor with it.

"Well, it's certainly not for your grace."

He pissed me off. I slammed the can on the table, ignoring the additional soda that bubbled over the top. So there we were, toe to toe, nearly nose to nose. I stabbed a finger into his chest. Hard. Tight. Why did I have to remember that glimpse of his toned body I'd seen earlier?

Focus, Ella. "You. You are not welcome in my house."

"You said that already." He had the balls not to look the least bit worried.

"You will not question what Sam does or says in relation to me."

"A bit protective of a man who's basically using you, aren't you?"

"Shut up," I snapped. Fury brought my hand up and caused it to make fiery contact with his cheek. That, I think, got his attention. I know I saw sparks when I hit him. My hand was a bit red and stung. He held his hand over his cheek.

"Sorry," I muttered, pulling his hand away. "Let me look."

There wasn't a mark on his cheek. Can't say I wasn't tempted to try again, but I did worry about that power thing.

He gripped both my wrists.

Oh no, we weren't trying that again. "Let go of me," I demanded. Last time he'd gotten this close to the beads he'd tried to move them or something—I don't know what but I didn't trust him.

"Maybe," he started, "since you're such a violent wench you

should weaken the necklace until we're ready to use it."

"Weaken it?" I jerked a hand free and covered my throat. "How?"

He nodded his head toward the hallway leading into the rest of my apartment. "Go to the bathroom mirror. Slide the gems back apart to where they were."

"And why do I want to weaken them? So you can overpower me?"

"So you don't kill the both of us. You have no idea what you're doing with the magic."

He was right. Still, I would rather trust Sam about this. Sam hadn't tackled me or demanded I use my magic. He'd told me not to. I sucked in a deep breath. Magic. Yep. I was really having this conversation, rationalizing like a magical necklace is something gotten from the antique store any day. "Fine. Just leave it alone for now. Maybe you'll keep your distance if you don't trust me. I need Sam." What I needed was answers.

I should never have remained standing toe-to-toe with this man for so long. He leaned in and nibbled on my neck right under the jaw line. Who knew that would be so sensitive.

"Quentin?"

"Hmmm."

"I am not going to allow you to seduce me."

"I'm flattered you think that way, I was just...tasting."

"Tasting?" *That's so not enough.* "I don't know you. Don't think I want to know anything about you." *Just the feel of your body against mine.*

He stepped back and rubbed his hands together. "Good, it went from 'get out of my house' to 'I don't *think* I want to know you better.'"

I couldn't do anything but stare at him.

I heard footsteps on the wood floor behind me. From Quentin's crooked smile I guessed who it was.

"Hi, Sam." I whirled. "We have to talk."

"Yes, we do." Sam walked calmly across the floor and ultimately leaned against my kitchen counter.

"Here?" I had to voice it. I was still trying to understand how these men had made themselves at home in my kitchen.

"Why not—we're all here. Now."

"Too bad I didn't call Popeye's Chicken to cater the affair."

To my surprise, Sam turned to Quentin, "Don't you just appreciate her?"

Quentin's weary sigh was his answer.

I threw my arms up. "Thanks. Talk about respect. Where's mine?"

Sam pointed to my neck. "It's all right there."

"Yeah, in this case the flea collar is more important than the mutt wearing it."

Quentin snorted, but Sam remained with his hands on his hips. "I did not expect this to be a circus show." Sam squeezed the bridge of his nose and closed his eyes.

"What? I didn't say anything. It was her." Quentin was kind enough to point square at me.

I opened my mouth to answer. And it was going to be a doozy. Sam beat me to the punch. Not that it was as good as mine would have been.

"Well, I could say it was your fault, Quentin. If you hadn't abused your power, you would get to do this alone."

"So what am I, the babysitter?" I expected Quentin, who I determined had the body of a god and the mentality of a ten year old, to stick his tongue out at that quip.

He flipped me off instead.

"Hey, that's not nice." I was tempted to revert in age and hurl the teakettle at his head. Then I realized I could do it without walking over to the stove.

"No magic in fighting. Not among ourselves." Sam held up a hand and stopped me cold. I really hated it when he did that. "Might we have a civil conversation?"

I cast a glance toward Quentin, who wore a smile that was begging to be wiped from his face. I'd get him. Sometime or another. For Sam I plastered on a cheesy grin and waited for him to speak.

"What we need to focus on will require your maturity, common sense and quick thinking. And the proper use of your powers to keep you safe. Bergestein," Sam directed his comment at Quentin, "has the third set of gems. My set. There are only four gems he does not control. Mine and yours." Sam shifted his gaze to me.

"The ones you stole from me?" Quentin cleared my telephone stand with a sweep of his arm.

"Hey!" I shouted, ready to do damage to him right here. The punk.

"Ella, get back. None of this will matter. We must leave immediately. He already has a good lead on us."

"No way. I'm not going *anywhere* without an explanation to whatever it was you babbled off about just now."

"I'll explain when we get there," Sam said with a sigh.

I shook my head. "What's this about sets of gems?" I demanded while shifting my weight and crossing my hands over my arms. "Your set, his set, stolen sets. I'm so lost."

"There are five sets of original gems, ten total. I—my family—used to have them all. They've been stolen. I've got one set and you've got one set. Now let's go."

"Hold on, hold on. I want to understand. Quentin used to have gems but you took them away? Why can't you take mine away and leave me out of this?"

"Can't. Won't. Doesn't matter." Sam was in hurry. But so was I. For answers.

"So this...Booger guy has a set, right? Still two more left."

"Bergestein has three sets total. Quentin here didn't know that. But since he's been such a—"

"At least I didn't lose my set." Quentin bristled.

They weren't helping. Much. Ten gems, divided into five sets. Still a million more questions. "Who's Bergestein?"

"Bad guy," Sam answered. "Honestly, Ella, that's all you need to know right now. I'll tell you more once we get out of here."

"What about this recruiting thing?"

Sam rubbed his hand over his hair. "Huh?"

Quentin at least was nice enough to start picking some of the things off the floor and putting them back on the table. He, for the most part, was ignoring this part of the conversation. "You said earlier you'd recruited us."

"There's little rhyme or reason to the recruiting. I needed someone right away. You were lucky enough to fit the profile. You have few ties here and you are open to magic—I tested you by flashing some magical visions at you when you came into the shop."

"So I hung myself by walking in for costume jewelry." I couldn't believe it. But had to when Sam shrugged at me. Quentin didn't seem surprised by the news either. Unbelievable. I was already a sucker for people in need, but there was something...frustrating about not having a say in my own destiny.

"Listen, we've got to get those gems back from Bergestein."

"Wait." My turn to hold up my hand. Sam raised an eyebrow. Yeah, buddy, you had better listen to me. "You are sending Quentin the Wonder Boy with me to find this Booger guy and steal the necklace back?"

Sam leaned back and smiled. "Precisely. Though not one necklace. Three. Six gems. They might not be on necklaces, you understand."

"And you are doing what?"

"Coming with you."

I looked from one to the other. Both had wide eyes and raised eyebrows. "I am feeling so not with the program here, men. Does one of you want to share some details with me?"

"Details?" Sam ran a hand over his neatly styled hair. "Like?"

"How do I work this damn thing?" I pulled down the neckline of my sweater and exposed the necklace. The beads felt like an extension of my pulse, throbbing against my neck.

"You're doing great." Sam winked at me. "But you should move them apart a bit. You might do a little more damage than you think with them like that."

He walked over to help me. "Don't you even think about laying your hands on me," I warned, backing up against the table. I would climb it if I had to.

He stepped back. I bit my tongue before I could make some sarcastic comment about him retreating back to his corner. I glowered at Quentin, who looked above it all and quite amused.

"Just tell me what I need to do." I sighed. They weren't going to go away, were they?

"No, not leaving." Sam smiled. He enjoyed showing off he knew what I was thinking. I couldn't help it. I glanced at Quentin and thought of his earlier kiss. "Ella, did you have to do that?"

Two could play at that game.

"Wha?" came Quentin's delayed reaction when he caught us both smiling at him.

I turned back to Sam, feeling a little more in control. "Okay. I'm ready. Make this weaker."

Gritting my teeth, I lifted my fingers to the beads and braced for the shock. Wouldn't Quentin enjoy the sight of me writhing with the impact of an electric jolt? Too bad he failed to realize he was the one capable of doing just that.

I listened as if my life depended on it while Sam spoke. Who knows, it might come to that. It was more difficult than I expected, but the necklace did little more than pulsate when I slid the beads to the sides of my neck.

My powers suitably weakened, Sam left to make arrangements for our trip. Quentin stayed behind to help me "practice the magic."

Yippee, just what I wanted. I even clapped my hands in sarcastic glee.

"Yeah, well, it's not my cup of tea, either."

"We really should try to get along."

"I bet I know how we could." His eyes did that mystical green to black to green again fade. "Oh, you know what I'm thinking. Don't think your face doesn't reflect the idea."

I quickly thought of something distasteful. Scrubbing the toilet. That would change my mood in a hurry.

He just laughed at me. "It's inevitable you know. That's why Sam took you on."

"Took me on." I wanted to spit. "He would have grabbed the next customer who walked in. It just happened to be me.

"I guess it makes me the lucky one, then, huh?" Quentin pushed past me and walked into my living room. "What a place you got here."

"Sorry, Park Place was too much of a commute." I forbid myself from feeling self conscious about the state of my home. It was mine. I hadn't invited them over. So tough. They ought to know what they were getting themselves into.

Quentin didn't seem as turned off by the yellow velveteen couch as I had been at first sight. Ugly as it was, it was the most comfortable thing I'd ever fallen into. And the price had been right. Still, I probably would've brought it home even if it had felt like you were sitting on a log.

"So..." I surveyed the room, "...where do we start?"

"Turn the TV on." That was easy. I reached over and picked up the remote. Pressed power and viola, picture and sound.

"You are an idiot, aren't you?"

"Huh?" He'd told me to turn it on. I bunched my fists together, imagining how one would feel pummeling his pretty face.

He just spread his arms wide. And he wasn't inviting me in for a hug. "What are we supposed to be studying here? The mating habits of pigeons?"

I glanced over at the twenty inch screen. Horny little gray birds flapped their wings as they chased one another out of camera range. "Looks like they are a bit shy," I responded.

"Oh, duh, Ella." He shook his head at me.

The remote whacked the wall right next to Quentin's left ear. "Damn bitch! What'd you try to hit me for?"

"Bad freakin' aim. I was envisioning the imprint of those buttons on your forehead."

He grabbed the remote and turned it over. "Great. You broke the back off. The batteries have run away."

I envisioned them lying under the couch. "Here batt'ry, batt'ry, batt'ry," I crooned. All four of them rolled to my feet. "Good little batteries. Now, where's the lid?"

"I got it," Quentin muttered. He retrieved it from the back of the couch. "Thank God we're not stuck watching those damn birds all day."

I pointed at the TV, squinting to see the tiny buttons at the bottom of the set. The channel flickered up, finding some fat woman in a sausage tight Viking outfit belting out an opera. In Italian. "They got Vikings in Italy?"

"Nice one, Ella. Think you can find the mute button?"

I really wanted to tell him to jump in a lake. One full of sadistic, horny pigeons floating in camel spit. With opera playing in the background.

Okay, that sounded more evil than was necessary. So I imagined Quentin tied to a chair and forced to watch live opera. See, for me, it wouldn't be a chore. But Quentin? Ha. He was already squirming as if his underwear had been invaded by a curious squid. Ewww.

"Ella? Can you mute the TV already?"

I tried. I knew the mute button must somewhere in that

smorgasboard of menu buttons. Zing. Oops. Nope, that was the volume button. The up volume. I covered my mouth to keep from giggling. Then my ears when Old Mathilda there hit a high C note. I swore I could hear every glass in my wine cabinet shattering.

"Ella!" Quentin screamed.

"Just a second. Don't get your panties in a twist." I aimed for the button on the end.

Mathilda disappeared behind a screen of blissfully silent blackness. "Ah." Quentin lowered his hands. "I don't think we need to worry about power. Just aim."

That sounded positive. "Whoo hooo!" I pumped one fist in the air.

"What I meant was, it's good you didn't have to scrunch up your nose and concentrate just to do that piddly trick."

"Oh."

"You need a lot more practice."

"Oh."

I, however, was not willing to practice destructive type exercises in my apartment. Do I need to explain why? Ask Quentin. He'd be more than pleased to tell you. My aim sucked.

I think I heard it at least fifty times on the drive there. I drove. Which I think irritated him into repeating my shortcomings over and over. But I wasn't giving up the keys. Even if it was a cream and rust Oldsmobile from seventeen years ago. Didn't matter the right taillight was actually red tape and the bumper was held on with a bungee cord. It was mine—and paid for. He wasn't driving.

Quentin directed me to a landfill. That's right. A landfill. I had to admit, it was the ideal place—if you could stomach the smell. And don't even point out the fact there were probably maggots in there. Vile, nasty creatures. Nothing worse in the world. But, it was October. Hopefully that meant they had all grown up to be pesky flies. Those weren't much higher on my list. After watching the movie *The Fly* I couldn't handle having winged things land on me. Could just picture them projectile puking on me and my skin dissolving. Okay, all together now...ewww.

"Here." Quentin stopped my mental rant. "See you if can pick up the half-smashed can over there and throw it into that box."

I almost, but not quite, reached for it with my hand. Quentin's eyes flickered. I swear those things glowed at times.

And of course, my mental pitching arm was three feet off.

"Again." Quentin braced his feet wide and leaned back on his heels, then rose to his toes. I was tempted to give him a push while he was moving. But then he'd carry the stench into my car. Nope, not worth it.

I settled on picking up an old tire and flattening the TV sized box.

"Nice idea, but not what we were looking for." He shook his head. "Not what I expected from a girl. I might have believed it if you wanted to grow daisies in an old coffee can. But sure hadn't counted on you going for violent overkill."

I offered a tight-lipped smile and sprang a daffodil from a pile of diapers.

"Cute, El. I'm beginning to think you're a woman after my own heart." Oh, that scared me. More than maggots.

"What did you do to get your gems yanked, anyway?" I started concentrating. The dump was starting to irritate my sinuses. And it was creepy.

"Used violent overkill."

"Oh." I glanced over at the flattened cardboard.

"I hurt someone. Someone innocent." He raked his hand through his hair and I saw something new in his eyes. Something real. And raw.

Damn, the guy had a heart. But I didn't feel like laughing.

"So Sam came and got me and said I needed someone to straighten me out."

"Me?" I squeaked. "He chose *me* to straighten you out?" What did I look like, a psychologist?

"I believe he said you were supposed to keep an eye on me." But Quentin rolled his eyes as if he doubted I could do even that.

I nodded. Shift subject before someone pissed off the magic girl. I had blissfully forgotten about all the purpose for this magic and was enjoying the ride until he had to go and call me his glorified babysitter. I didn't like not having a say in this—even though I'd probably go along with it now, because playing with magic was a lot more fun than booking the seniors flights for their southern migration. Still...

I took a deep breath and changed the subject. "So, where ya

from?"

"Anchorage."

"Alaska?"

"Is there another one?"

My aim was improving. Slowly. I was getting within a foot of the target. Much better than the yard when I'd started. There'd be a pile of tin cans to heaven at the rate I was stacking them. "How'd you get here?"

"Sam. He gets around."

"Guess so."

I knew he was getting bored. Alternated between heavy sighs and checking his watch.

"So what's the deal with the necklace?"

He tilted his head in a curious puppy dog look. My turn to say duh?

"The beads, gems, whatever. I get moving them closer equals more power. But this seems to be pretty potent for having them at the North and South poles."

I picked up another can and easily tossed it into the center of the tire. "I didn't even have to say abracadabra," I called. "Let's go home."

"The beads," he said, stomping through the mess, "have some sort of magnetism, I guess you'd say. When they're closer together, they produce more potential power. Can you imagine what it's like to have all ten together?"

I couldn't see his face when he spoke, but the concept had me speechless. Then I remember Sam saying this bad guy had six gems. What had I gotten suckered into?

☙ ☙ ☙

"Where do I need to drop you?" I queried. Quentin stared straight ahead. A muscle in his jaw twitched.

"Don't have anyplace."

"But—"

"And I'm *not* staying at Sam's." Wow, vicious. I'd assumed that's where he'd come from.

"I just got into town today. Forgot how cold it is here."

"Where were you? Obviously not Anchorage."

"Hahaha. Panama."

"Why there?"

"I got in trouble remember? What's in Panama?"

"I dunno. Drugs are what I think of."

"There's a lot more than that. You're close, though. I was involved in firearm movement. Made a bit of dough too. Until our boy yanked me out."

"Can't use the magic like that, huh?"

"Nope. No lottery numbers, no casinos and no illegal sales of firearms."

I raised an eyebrow. Guess that's where the nice tan came from. "And what were you supposed to be doing?"

"In Panama?"

"Where else?"

His sheepish grin was my undoing. I couldn't regret this whole thing because whether I wanted to or not, I liked Quentin. He avoided answering my question, I noticed. My mind was already romanticizing the reasons why. If Quentin smiled at me like that again, I might even be willing to admit I had fun at the stinky landfill.

Instead of tempting fate, I parked in front of my apartment building. "Let's find us something to eat. It won't hurt for you to sleep on my couch." I was such a pushover.

Groucho Marx he was not. But he tried to mimic the elevator eyebrows and fake cigar movement. "Why thank you. Yes, yes indeed."

"Don't push it, buddy. You're here to train me to baby-sit you. This is insane." I unlocked the door and he followed me up the stairs.

Once inside he took up residence on my couch again. "Training, right. You asked me this before. Right now you really are pretty limited on what you can do. Probably a fifty pound weight limit to lift and move. No fire power. Hardly any electrical power."

"Elect—"

"Whoa, Nellie."

"El-la," I pronounced.

"Yeah, I know. Just playing with ya. Geesh."

I wasn't going to let him get under my skin. No sirree, it wasn't going to happen. "So." I smiled nice. While planning how I could drop him from my second story window as he slept. “Tell me more.”

He was busy putting the batteries back in the remote. Guess he didn’t trust me to change channels for him. I tried again. “So, if the gems were ninety degrees from each other instead of at one eighty, I could snap my fingers and we’d be eating prime rib right now?”

“At someone else’s expense, of course.”

“You had to go and ruin it for me, didn’t you?”

“Nothing is free. Remember the rule in science class? For every action there is an equal and opposite reaction.”

“Hello? You memorized that crap?” I shook my head and stared at him.

“Remember it and live by it.”

“Holy smokes, there’s homework to this stuff?”

“Guess you’re not gonna like the geography part.”

I couldn’t help it. I squealed like a pig.

“Well then, smarty pants,” I struggled with the idea of school work, but Quentin was kind enough to point out I used geography every day at the travel agency. “How did I manage to disappear?”

“That,” Quentin advised, “was pure magic.”

“There’s a difference?” I gave up trying to keep my distance. I was cold and not going to sit on the floor. So I perched on the opposite arm of the couch.

“Fine line.” He drew his brows together and frowned. “How do I say this?”

“Out loud?”

“It’s all magic really. There’s the displacement thing, like with the meal you were talking about. You can’t make something from nothing. You move objects. You will learn to manipulate electricity and fire, but the energy to start it will come from you.”

I nodded. Made a world of sense to me. And I wanted to try it right now.

“You’ll start to hear other people’s thoughts. Not necessarily thoughts, but, hmmm, I guess it’s what you say out loud in your head. That’s what you’ll hear.”

“How does Sam do that even though he doesn’t wear a necklace?”

“Just say wear the gems. Necklace sounds so...feminine.”

“Not too in touch with your feminine side, are ya, Quen?”

"No." He leaned over and hauled me onto the couch. "But I could sure handle touching your feminine sides."

I untangled myself from the octopus man and strode into the kitchen. "Well, mister, are you going to answer me?"

"Sam? Yeah, well. He draws on your strength. If none of us had a necklace he couldn't read minds."

"You just called it a necklace." I couldn't help but point that out. "Besides, I want to know more about this mind reading thing."

"Shut up and feed me, okay."

Oh, no. Things didn't work that way in my house. "You want to eat you have to either cook or clean up."

He was right behind me, his voice hot against the back of my neck. "We could really cook together, baby."

I should have been turned off by this punk. Wanted to feel nothing but disdain. Certainly not experience the vibrations that had nothing to do with magic. I whirled around, not expecting him to remain so close after scaring me like that. But there he was, and I was practically in his arms. My heart pounded, my breath caught. So close I could smell his cologne, feel his breath.

He looked surprised as well, his forest green eyes darkened, reminding me of an uncharted row of woods. I was afraid and intrigued, curious about what lay behind the surface.

Did I mention I was a daredevil? Couldn't manage to be afraid of much. At least not until I tried it once. Discovered I didn't like bungee jumping. But this? This scared me.

Quentin yanked me back from my tangent much too quickly. I can't get into trouble when I'm lost in thought. But enveloped in the warmth Quentin offered, knowing there was more heat available if I just dared. Well, that spells trouble.

"No." I gripped his forearms and pushed his hands back between us. The ripple of his muscles beneath my fingertips caused shockwaves in my senses. "You really need to stop distracting me. I can't think."

"There's no thinking to it. You just do."

"Oh, I know how it works. But that's what we need to practice right now—logical, practical thinking. A lot of it. And you've got questions to answer. Seems to me, if I'm the one that is supposed to be keeping an eye on you and keeping you out of trouble, the last thing we need to do is indulge in a little lust party."

"You're tempted?"

"If you need to stroke your ego, yes. It's been awhile, okay?"

He laughed and ran a hand down my cheek. Damn it, my knees were instant spaghetti noodles. Fully cooked.

"How about Italian?" I turned and dug a jar of pre-made pasta sauce from the cabinet.

"That's cheap."

"It's just me. I don't home cook spaghetti sauce for dinner for one."

"Still."

"Listen. It's this or, um, there might be a frozen pizza in there. I haven't exactly gone grocery shopping. I do that on Sunday mornings."

"Anyone deliver a good pie around here?"

"You got money?"

His face fell. "No."

"Then I don't think we're gonna get more delivery than freezer to oven to coffee table."

"I suppose that would work."

I put the pasta sauce back and stood up, right into his arms again. "We can't keep doing this."

"Am I wearing you down yet?"

"My patience it getting thin. And I have the power, remember."

"Sam said no magic used against us."

"He ain't here."

Sam opened the door and walked through.

"I thought you locked that." I slapped Quentin on the arm.

"Hey," he slapped me back, "I did."

"You two are so busy arguing you didn't hear me. That won't work out there when we're sneaking up on Bergestein and his spawn."

I looked at Quentin and he looked at me. Sam had a point. I wondered if I could tolerate this guy. In silence.

His eyebrow lifted. I heard it, as plain as if he said it out loud. "*I can think of a good way to keep our mouths occupied.*"

"Hey!" I turned to him, too shocked over the fact I had heard his thoughts to register what he had said. "I heard you."

Quentin groaned. "Brilliant, Sam. You got me a live one that can read my head even with the gems at one eighty. "

I touched the beads, which rested on opposite sides of my neck, still hiding under the turtleneck I wore. Sam winked at me. Since I wasn't hearing any more mental conversations, I had a good idea I hadn't heard a thing he hadn't put in my head. So I winked back.

"We were just going to have pizza. Care to join us?" See? I could be a generous hostess. "And since you're here, can you tell me about this mind reading thing? Or talking to one another in your head? I've got to learn that."

"You will. Just tune in. Takes concentration. You can also block it out, but that takes even more skill." Sam frowned at Quentin, who was clearly saying something mentally I wouldn't want to hear. But try as I might, I couldn't "tune in". Maybe I was on the wrong channel.

"I can't hear anything. Do I have to be closer, or stare into your eyes or something?"

Quentin groaned. Sam shot him a look and nodded at me. "You'll get it. You more or less need to be in the same room, or if outside, within reasonable vicinity. I think I told Quentin if you could hear them if they spoke normal, then you should be able to detect their thoughts."

"So no listening through walls and stuff?" I tried to be hopeful. Otherwise I would feel spied on, constantly.

"Not unless they're paper thin and you're both very close to the wall. Now come here." Sam hooked a finger in my direction. It felt odd to get the "c'mere" signal from a man at least fifteen years my senior.

"I'm flattered," he grinned. "Try twenty-two."

"You're fifty?" I blurted. "No freakin' way. You're pretty hot for an old guy."

Quentin snorted. I wanted to go hide under the couch. Sam just smiled. I had a feeling this was going to hurt.

"Now that we've got that clear, I need to see you. Come here."

Baby steps, baby steps. Don't step on the cracks. I tiptoed across the linoleum. Hard to miss the cracks in a floor older than me.

I stopped in front of Sam. Afraid to pay the consequences for calling him an old guy. I glanced up through my eyelashes, figuring they had to be good for something. I'd rather gotten caught up in the circus-like fun of doing magic all afternoon and temporarily forgotten Sam's serious agenda. It probably wasn't a good idea to have insulted him, even playfully.

Quentin stepped behind me and slid his hands around my waist. I shivered. "Hey now. I ain't no hugging machine."

"Nope." I heard Quentin's voice in my hair. "Tonight, you're the rocket ship."

Sam grabbed my hands and led them to my throat. He repeated the steps Quentin had started at the travel agency. At his bidding, my fingers closed over the beads and slid them closer together.

For the love of God, get me out of here.

Chapter Four

Disneyland. California

"I didn't mean it, really I didn't." But, by golly, there I stood, looking up into the permanently grinning face of Mickey Mouse.

"Uh, Sam?" I looked around. This wasn't where I wanted to be. "Quen?"

Mickey held out his hand. I shook it. Then he held out his other hand. Okay. I shook with my left while searching for a familiar face. Then the big mouse held out both arms in an I-wanna-hug gesture.

"Uh, *no*." I walked away. Poor Mickey, I bet he'd never been turned down like that before.

All right. Think, Ella. Use that brain before atrophy sets in and you're trapped in an amusement park. I was totally caught off guard with this new development. All I remembered was Sam moving the gems closer, then wham, we were gone. No one told me it was time to fly. Zapped literally. From point A to point B without so much as the chance to grab my purse. I had no money, no credit cards. Well, okay, so they were maxed out, but I still felt a little better with them in my wallet.

Maybe Sam and Quentin were invisible.

"*Took you long enough.*"

"*Why don't you guys tell me anything?*" I shouted mentally. Almost did it out loud. But getting picked up by the mouse patrol would not have been amusing. "*Am I invisible now?*"

"*Watch out! You shouldn't just stand there in the middle of the walkway, have some respect for cripe's sake.*"

"*Someone want to tell me what a cripe was? And while you're at it, how the heck do I become invisible? Someone? Anyone? Are you out there?*"

All I could see was a sea of people. And no one looked familiar.

"Well, lookee here. A pretty girl with a frown. Can't have that happen in a nice place like Disneyland, can we boys?"

Oh God. I didn't like the looks of the *boys* who fanned out around their leader, a skinny Hispanic who stood in front of me with his hands on his hips. I had no way out.

My initial thought was this was a group of thugs who preyed on tourists. Then I saw the beads. Just like mine, two crystal looking round gems on a length of rawhide. Magic. He had magic. And if he had any sort of skill, he could probably read my mind, perhaps had heard my little mental conversation with Sam and...I was in trouble.

"You look lost, princess. D'ya wanna head up to the top of Cinderella's castle and see if we can find our own magic?"

"I don't think so, buster." I stepped back. I wasn't going anywhere with him. Wouldn't have under any condition. His hair didn't appear to have been washed in days, maybe weeks. He wore what had probably once been a white tank top, and it was two sizes too small for his scrawny body. His jeans were nearly black, again, likely from lack of laundering rather than the color the manufacturer intended. Head to toe, there was zero appealing about this guy.

And there were...one, two, three, *four* of them. Another one had a necklace, too. And they got uglier and dirtier as I counted down the line. It was little ole me with limited magic versus the gang-looking magic squad.

With little left to hope for I clicked my heels together twice. *I wish I were invisible, I wish I were invisible.*

"Sheeeeet. Where'd she go?" One of them gasped.

"Why didn't you grab her before she had a chance to get away?" another asked.

Duh. And thank goodness. Thank you, Dorothy. Maybe I didn't have ruby red shoes, but that was all right. I glanced down. I still could see myself okay.

I realized I was still in the clothes I'd worn to the dump. And in this California heat, all these layers weren't making me feel any better about the way I probably smelled. Well, at least walking around invisible could be fun. I imagined people turning around and sniffing, "Who farted?"

"Now I know you're the woman for me." I knew that voice. And couldn't deny those hands that slipped so easily around my waist. And I'd known the guy less than a day. My morals were slipping. Bad.

"Tie me to you or something. This is ridiculous."

"I saw you try to pick up those men."

"Oh, yeah, luckily I managed to find the invisible switch and fake them out."

"You really shouldn't do that."

"They really shouldn't have tried to scare a lone woman. You should have heard what they were suggesting."

"They're magic too. Bad guys."

"Why didn't they disappear?"

"They know better. It's not a good idea to do it plain sight. Tends to freak people out."

"Why are we here, anyway?" I glanced over my shoulder. Still couldn't see him. "How'd you find me?"

"I never left. And after you went invisible I just stayed tuned in to your thoughts and well, your smell."

I lifted a foot. "Do you think it's my shoes?"

"It's our clothes."

"What do we do for lodging, clothes, a shower?" Good Lord I was not going to go without a shower.

"Sam makes those arrangements. Some sort of deal with the other magic people. It's like a world within a world. You're not going to believe it."

His voice still held a little awe. "You haven't been doing this long, have you?"

"About a year."

"Where's Sam now?"

"Hunting Mr. B. He's supposed to be here. Big meeting of magic tonight. At the castle."

"With all these people here?"

"It's not like we sit around and do tricks. It'll be discussions, advancements, and who's doing what." Great. Stuffy boardroom chat. Just what I wanted.

He got real quiet. I glanced around, half my brain realizing he'd gone and shut up for good reason. With the other half I watched some kids twirl around on a nearby ride. I wished I was five again and the biggest worry I had was the length of the line in front of my favorite ride.

"Move." Quentin pushed up against me. Uh, move how? Ok, I'm not mentally five anymore. Is it possible for your mental voice to go into falsetto? Mine did.

Quentin stepped in front of me and reached back for my hand. I didn't think we should be going to first base yet, but considering the circumstance I didn't *not* want to hold his hand. Getting lost would mean danger.

He pulled me into a jungle-like recess next to a little log cabin. From the sounds, it was wheels and chains and grease that occupied it. "What?"

He covered his mouth with mine when I started to talk. Darn near swallowed my words and my tongue in one motion. I really had no choice. I whipped my arms around his neck and hung on. He hadn't meant it to be anything more than diversion. His garbled thoughts were on me and the thugs walking by. But then—then...well, let's just say I wasn't sure what turned me on more, his racy thoughts or prolific tongue.

He was really good at kissing. Usually I could take or leave the making out part. Hmm. Not with Quentin. Shame this wasn't the place or time.

"Release invisible now."

"How do I do that?" I mumbled against his lips.

"How'd you disappear?"

"Pretended I was Dorothy from the Wizard of Oz."

He muttered something. I was probably lucky I didn't hear it. "Then do it again."

I opened my eyes. It was definitely Quen standing in front of me. We were still half lip-locked. Well, it could be worse. Then I realized his green eyes were laughing at me.

"What?"

"Say 'you can see me'."

"You can see me?" I asked.

"There. You did it."

I stepped back and looked down. "Yeah, I can see me. And you."

He just shook his head. I started to leave the much too cozy little hideaway. "Wait." He stopped me.

I pivoted. He mussed my hair. "Now you look like you've been making out."

"But I was."

He closed his eyes. And counted to five.

What? It wasn't good enough I had kissed him back, but I had to look the part?

"Now," he hissed in my ear, "we pretend we're normal."

"Hey, you got your necklace back." I hadn't seen him since we landed. "How'd that happen?"

"Sam had it with him—well, it's really his. He's strong enough to use everyone else's gems to do tricks. I need my own."

"I thought he didn't trust you." We were walking with the crowd now, although I bet we were an unlikely pair of tourists.

"He doesn't, but figures I wouldn't desert you or try to take you with me."

With narrowed eyes I cast a sidelong glance. "You wouldn't, would you?"

"No."

"Where are we going?"

"Right now? The water slide. It'll do for a temporary shower."

"You're kidding."

He wasn't. I might have been less soaked if I'd have just jumped into the blue tinted pool. At least I wasn't wearing a white t-shirt. That would have been disastrous.

"Food, clothes. Especially dry clothes would be nice about now." I glanced around the exit to the ride. "They should have Q-tip dispensers here."

"And I supposed you have a quarter."

I patted my pockets. "Nope."

"Then be glad there isn't one. You got a watch?"

I glanced at my water soaked Timex. "It's almost seven."

"Then we need to go meet Sam."

I hadn't thought it was cold, but the heavy, damp clothes sure made the seventy degrees a bit chilly. "Quen, please tell me we'll get something decent to wear before this lovely meeting."

"Oh, sure. You didn't figure it out? Remember the prime rib example?"

I glared at him with one eyebrow hiked to the sky. "That was food. I'm talking clothes. Jeans, shirt. Dry underwear."

"Yep. Think of what I said about you wanting prime rib."

"That it would be taking something from someone else?"

"Uh-huh."

This wasn't making sense. "I don't want someone else's clothes." I could just imagine my clothes being suddenly swapped with the woman who stood next to me. Not!

"Not someone else's. Yours. You have clean clothes hanging in the closet at home, right?"

"How many thousand miles away is that?"

Quentin reached over and fondled my beads and finished with a chuck to the chin. "Ella. You are panicking. Stop. Don't do it here, it'll leave you, uh, naked for an instant. And personally, I'd rather see that for myself in private."

I slugged him. Then sighed. "How am I doing this?"

"You are going to envision your closet, choose an outfit and then picture yourself in the clean clothes. The same way you pictured the remote smashing me in the face."

I chewed my bottom lip. I thought I got it. "Where?"

"Go in the women's bathroom. Preferably one that's empty or has an empty stall."

As if finding a moment of privacy was going to happen at Disneyland. There'd probably be a fifteen minute wait at any bathroom.

"Fine, then, go anywhere," he responded when I pointed that out. "Someplace secret, where you're not going to be real obvious walking out wearing something different than what you had on going in."

I smiled. Up ahead was the stage where Snow White and her Seven Dwarves were dancing about in a larger than life forest. "Dressing room?"

"Hey, pretty good."

Cha-ching. I got credit for something. Yee-haw. "Should I go invisible?"

"No, I told you you're not supposed to do that in public." So much for feeling good about myself.

"Just pretend you know what you're doing."

Three steps in, there was someone designed to keep out people like me. "Hey, what are you doing back here?"

So I screamed and pointed over the big, burly man's shoulder. And disappeared. As in invisible and around the corner. I bet Quentin would have been proud of me.

I didn't really trust this magic to hide my bare butt. So I was being choosy. The dressing rooms weren't locked. Why in the heck did Snow White's have a big silly star on it and the dwarfs all have knee high doorknobs?

Eventually, I found one that looked like it was nothing but storage and ducked in behind a tri-color block tower. The gems burned my throat. My pulse was their rhythm. I closed my eyes and saw my closet. Jeans were on the shelf. Next, a long sleeve blue tee. Dry bra...should I get the purple lace one with the matching panties? I passed over it and went for functional. Same with the socks and underwear. *Okay, let's see what there is to this.*

I clicked my heels for good measure. It was like a dry whirlwind settling over me as I imagined myself undressing and redressing in the new clothes.

When the breeze died down, I collapsed. Delayed jet lag? Overwhelming desire to fall asleep and wake up to find it was all a dream?

"*I told you magic like that would drain you.*"

I clutched my hands over my chest in case the shirt wasn't there. "Quen, what are you doing here? And where are you?"

"Standing next to the pervert who followed you in here."

I slapped my hand over my mouth to keep myself from screaming, then felt to make sure I *did* have clothes on. Sweat, the cold kind, dripped past my Downy fresh cotton bra and slid down my stomach. Another drop trickled down my back. "Did you— Were you... *Did he...*?"

"Yeah. Was worth it."

"Where is he?" I'd given up trying to communicate mentally. Took too much energy. I was trying to grasp the fact some asshole had seen me naked.

"I've got him. He's not going anywhere," Quentin reassured. At least he didn't make any more comments about my state of undress.

I slumped against the half-open trunk of satin gowns. “This really bites.”

“I can take my clothes off if you want to be on the same level.”

“No.” But I had to laugh at the sharp intake of breath that came from the vicinity of Quentin’s voice.

“So what do we do with the peeping Tom?”

“I say we dress him in the Cinderella suit and send him on his way,” I said, already laughing at the visual.

“He’d just switch back.” Quentin snorted. “But not without getting naked.”

“I’ll pass on witnessing that.”

There was a hand at my waist. I jumped out of my skin and clothes both. Well, not literally. His breath was hot against my cheek. Still, I froze, fearful my senses deceived me and it was yet another visitor to the room.

His teeth snagged my earlobe and pulled, tenderly. My body reacted way too easily. I sighed and reached out for him.

“You gonna just stick her right here with me watching, man? Untie me, I don’t wanna see nothin’ like that, man.” A whiny voice with a heavy accent drifted from the corner. A chair rocked with no one in it. At least no one visible.

“What did you do to your prisoner?” I leaned my forehead against Quentin’s chest.

His hand slid up under my hair and grazed my hairline. I flinched as a shiver raced down my spine.

“What?” Quentin jumped back. The hand didn’t move.

Oh God, Oh God, there’s someone else. Should I scream? I bit my lip. He was trying to untie the necklace. I couldn’t feel the tell-tale cold blade of metal. Without another thought I spun and jammed my knee upward.

Thump, bump, crash.

Satin and silk flipped through the air. The lid to the crate I’d been leaning on crashed closed. I heard a low moan.

Chills shook my body. Quentin, in full color, stood beside me. I don’t think he was any less shocked than I was. *Oh damn, oh damn, oh damn.*

His voice was low and serious. “Ella, listen to me. Now you know.

Now you realize why I followed you, right? Seeing you without clothes was nice, but that wasn't what I was looking for. The creep must have been there, motionless the whole time."

"Get me out of here," I cried, leaning onto his shoulder. "Find Sam and take me home."

"Ella, I hate to tell you this."

"What?" I wasn't going to be able to stomach any more surprises.

"You won't be going home. Ever."

Chapter Five

I didn't care that I was behaving like a spoiled brat. So I jumped up and down and shed a tear or two.

"Sam, you can't mean it. I have to go home. My job, my car, my stuff!"

"You have nothing of real value."

"Speak for yourself. I worked hard to get those things."

"You'll get more."

"I want those."

Sam kicked back on the park bench and tapped his fingers along the seat. He'd obviously been through this drill before. Quentin's pained look must be from his memory of the day he got the news his life would never be the same. "Is that how you stock your antique store? Lure us out here and then clean out our apartments? I've got cash in there. The necklace my grandmother left me. You can't replace things like that."

Sam held out a fist. "Go on," he prodded. "Take it."

I shoved out my hand. There it was, shiny gold in the waning light. "Oh."

"How'd you do that?" I asked him.

"Substituted something for it." He squinted up at me and motioned Quentin over. I imagined a slug from the wetlands crawling through my jewelry box. Wonderful.

"Any other things you can't live without?"

"Money? Food? How are we going to survive with nothing?"

Sam handed over a money clip to each of us. Quentin whistled under his breath. But he didn't hesitate to pocket it.

"I can't take this." I waved it in front of his face.

"You'll need it. You must take it."

"It's not mine."

"It is now." Sam pushed past me and started toward the center of the park.

I jogged up beside him. "At least tell me you didn't get it by doing someone wrong. You didn't steal it?"

"I didn't steal it," Sam muttered. "What do you take me for?"

I fingered the folded wad of bills shoved into my front pocket. The antique business must be doing pretty good. Or he was really Uncle Sam.

Sam stopped me outside the castle and checked the gems, and tightened the knot. Quentin had filled him in on my quick change act and the following caper. Sam was not amused.

ଓ ଓ ଓ

"Bergestein didn't show," Sam noted. I thought what I'd witnessed so far was pretty out there. No, nothing I'd already seen compared to this freak show.

We were at this big meeting Sam had mentioned. This was like settling into an assembly of representatives of every planet in the universe and beyond. My guess was that magic had other uses, such as altering one's appearance. I glanced at octopus man next to me. What did he need two extra arms for anyway? And how the hell did he get into Disneyland looking like that?

And what was up with the woman who looked like a purple Raggedy Ann doll? Still, I think it was the ones who looked totally *normal* that worried me the most. A gray-haired grandma sat next to a librarian looking middle-aged woman, complete with brown skirt and Hush Puppy shoes. Then there was the fat man whose beer belly stuck out against his dirty white shirt. Tufts of matted hair protruded from the pits and the neckline of the tank top. And he carried a cigar. He belonged outside some corner gas station in the hills of Kentucky.

Where did these people come from, really?

Only a few people had visible gems. And way too many of them were eyeing mine with interest.

Some Poindexter stood up and began to extol the importance of practicing good magic. Look what had happened to witchcraft, he pointed out. Yeah, I wanted to answer, they had all been burned at the stake in Salem. But I knew what he meant. I really should listen and keep my sass to myself. Sam laid a hand on my shoulder. I glanced up, and followed his gaze.

A snake. His skin was dark copper, but I couldn't guess a nationality. His eyes were nothing but beady marbles in his head, the only light coming from the reflection of the chandelier. I curbed the comment about him having Minnie Mouse for dinner. This was real. And serious.

"Who is it?" I mouthed, barely daring to breathe the sounds out.

"Bergestein's right hand man. He's got his eye on you."

"Why me?"

"He senses your inexperience. We shouldn't have brought you here."

"We couldn't just leave her somewhere," Quentin piped up, grabbing my arm above the elbow. Funny how his gesture made me feel protected.

I listened. Sam watched. Quentin? Well, I don't know what he did other than bare his teeth at the men who ogled me. Half of me was flattered, the other half felt like a cheap hooker on Valentine's Day.

The meeting adjourned about ten minutes after I gave up and dozed off. "Where's the hotel? I'm too tired to even move."

"No hotel." Sam said as we walked away from Cinderella's castle.

I stopped dragging my stiff legs and twenty pound feet. "What are you talking about, no hotel? Where am I going to sleep?"

Sam glanced at Quentin. Quentin shrugged. "Follow me." Sam turned back toward the exit of the park.

"I ain't moving. I'll sleep on this bench if I have to."

"And you'll be beheaded before morning."

"Is that how they have to kill us? By beheading?" I shuddered. Sounded too much like a sword wielding television show.

"You'll die in many ways, but that's the cleanest way to get the necklace without touching it."

I thought about the built-in protection—the shock factor. "So how did that guy in the dressing room get his hands on me?"

Quentin grabbed my hand and dragged me after Sam. "Because I had my hands on you. You were receptive. It was my fault."

"So I'm vulnerable when you touch me."

"Nice to hear you say that."

I was way too tired to spar with him. "Ha."

Sam ignored our exchange. The man was incredibly patient. "Yes. To answer your question, your guard was down. The necklace is part of you now that you wear it. It will protect you if you feel threatened."

"It zapped me when I tried to take it off."

"That too. Just in case you're being threatened."

"Like with a gun." Quentin piped up.

Sam nodded, grimacing. "It happens."

"I'm scared."

"We'll protect you." Quentin promised and tugged me closer.

"You guys scare me, too." It was dark now, and we had entered the picnic area. Not so many overhead lights or neon signs glaring down on us. I saw the slightest fade to Quentin's necklace. Like the northern lights streaking through the beads. "Does it bother you?" I asked. "That I'm afraid?"

"It bothers me you're saying it and being serious for the first time all day."

"I'm too sleepy to be funny. Or sassy. I feel drunk." I fell against his chest. His heartbeat was calming. Warm. Intoxicating.

I smiled. He'd picked me up. It wasn't real comfortable to bounce against his shoulder with each step he took, but I wasn't going to tell him to put me down. I sniffed, inhaling the deep masculine musk of him. I wondered if he could read my mind. I didn't even try to tap into his. Didn't have the energy. It was easier just to pretend I was a regular girl and this regular guy was carrying me home. Hmm. I snuggled a little closer and wondered what his skin would feel like against mine. Would the magic carry over? I could almost see a trail of color following my finger as I traced it over his shirt.

"Stop." He tilted his head down.

I did. Didn't want him to drop me. Bruises on my backside and my pride weren't necessary. "Are we there yet?" I asked.

"Just a bit farther.

I closed my eyes and leaned in again. It was the closest I'd felt to safe all day.

☙ ☙ ☙

I woke up in my own bed. "Good God, was that really all a dream?" It was. I wanted to cheer. Instead, I felt the pressure behind my eyes. Big headache time. I rolled over and punched my pillow.

I connected with skin.

"Hey now, I haven't touched you all night."

Quentin. And he was in my bed. Without a shirt, I might add. Looking delicious. Much too good. It was one of those moments I didn't know whether to laugh, cry, scream or look under the covers to see what I was wearing and then decide.

I forced myself not to think about the fact I might have missed breathtaking sex with the hottest guy to every say hello to me. I went with asking him the truth outright. "What are you doing in my bed?"

"Sleeping. It was me or Sam. Sam didn't want to be considered a dirty old man. Plus I was more willing to accept a black eye in the morning."

"Guess my aim was a little low."

"Yeah, we established how bad it was yesterday."

Yesterday. Oh God, it was real. The necklace, the junkyard, the horny pigeons. Disneyland? Yes, that had to be too. And the gathering of the odd.

"Having those pinch me thoughts?"

"Did you?" I looked up at him, the intimacy of waking up next to him softening the sarcastic, almost childish banter we normally used to communicate.

"Three days of denial."

"Great. Something to look forward to."

How'd he get the honor of looking so hot in the morning? The shadow along his square jaw emphasized his raw nature. His hair was wild, but that wasn't uncharacteristic. And his eyes were true green. Evergreen.

"Quit staring at me already."

"Never imagined to wake up to a man in my bed without having a rowdy time the night before."

"You weren't the one trying to get your ass through that time-space tunnel while you were sleeping. Sam wasn't sure it could be done."

"Oh," I responded. His half grin had my heart thudding.

"Where is Sam?" I refused to get upset. I needed to stay levelheaded and act like this was all perfectly normal.

"Sleeping on your couch."

"Ah. Well. Isn't that all cozy?"

"But this is it. We leave here today and we won't be able to come back. This was a chance Sam took because we had no other choice with you passed out like you were."

Now I panicked. All my things. I'd have to say goodbye. Tattered border, yellowed blinds. I did have a soft spot for my table lamp, but I could live without it, I guess.

"I do have time for a shower, right? And to get some clothes?"

"You carry what's on your back. Whatever you're wearing when Sam says it's time to fly."

I finally peaked under the covers. Dressed.

"Were you worried?" Quentin's eyes crinkled at the corners with his smile.

"A little."

"Again, my touch would have been unwelcome. You would have been protected if you'd even slightly awakened and fought me."

"So you saved your hide."

"I'd rather undress you when you're begging me to."

"It's good to want." His silent smile did nothing to reassure me that's what was on his mind. "Dibs on shower first. Who's going for breakfast?" Now that knew I was safe I dashed toward the bedroom door.

"Make it quick. Sam and I want to use the hot water, too."

I turned the flimsy lock on the bathroom door. "Like it'll do any good," I told myself as I checked the mirror. Yep. It was still me. The darn magic necklace hadn't given me a face lift. Or a boob job. What good was it? Not, mind you, that I needed a face lift at twenty-eight, but, well, my nose had a funny point and there were already wrinkles at the corners of my eyes.

I felt a little more in control today. Or wait, was that another illusion? No, definitely not a trick. I could see mold in the corner above the tub. In my illusions there is no bad stuff.

"I don't hear water running."

"Chill, I'm plucking my eyebrows." It was Sam. Had it been Quentin I might have been a bit more graphic. I did take it as a hint, however, and twisted the knob to release the waterfall.

I was after the world's record in complete showering. Wow. I hadn't even had a chance to get warm beneath the stinging spray. I just prayed I got all the shampoo out of my hair.

"Okaaaaaay," I called out as I zipped down the hall and slammed the bedroom door shut behind me. I was, after all, wearing nothing but a towel.

ଔ ଔ ଔ

I had to unrelentingly argue the point that I needed a carry-on something. Preferably my purse.

"Don't you have a fanny pack?"

I spared no mercy giving Sam what I though was the evil eye. "Do I look like a fanny pack kind of girl?"

"Okay then, a small backpack?"

I pictured the oversize contraption I used on an ill-fated trip to the caves in Missouri a few summers back. "Nuh-huh."

Sam sighed and held out his hand. "Let me see your purse." Do you believe the man had the indecency to turn it upside down on the kitchen table? And then the lack of scruples to ask me what was in the little pink bag. I swallowed down the urge to show him my tampons and ask if he had a magical solution to make the need for those to disappear. "Girl stuff." I snapped it from his clutches. I needed a drink. Water wasn't strong enough, but at least it was cold. While drinking and thinking about *never* coming back, I hoped there was a store I could replenish my supply when needed. The realization dawned on me, causing a shudder. I was going to have to deal with *that* while fighting magic bad guys. Me...magic...PMS. Oh boy.

"You know there was that one girl who played in Mortal Kombat. Or even the Tomb Raider chick. Aren't they free to participate in this adventure with you?"

Quentin's toothy grin pushed me on.

"Just think, get one who's in top form and knows tae kwon

whatever karate stuff. You'll be set."

"Show me what you're so adamant about taking." Sam was such a no-nonsense kind of guy. Quentin still stood leaning against the fridge eating a snack cake. Probably thinking about those Hollywood hotties, I guessed from the dreamy look on his face.

Decisions, decisions. I couldn't figure it out. I settled on two makeup items, maybe three. How important was lip gloss? More girlie things would be important one day all too soon. The pile was growing quickly. I added a couple of hair ties, a hair pin and a nail file.

"Why?" Quentin tilted his head and looked bored with my frantic shuffling.

"In the movies they're always needing that stuff. Hey!"

Sam was wielding my kitchen shears. "Not my credit cards!" I called.

"Yep. All your ID."

"No."

"Yes." I looked at Quentin for help, remembering his insistence when he had no ID. Come to think of it, I couldn't remember his last name either. My morals were really slipping. I'd never slept with a guy without knowing his last name.

The original bad boy looked at me the way a preschooler watches a cartoon. His face softened with child-like fascination. Although I figured I could mirror that look if Sam cut up my credit card *bills* as well.

"Why?" I stepped over and pulled my wallet from him. He finished the hack job on a thousand dollar Visa as he spoke.

"I can't tell you."

"You're kidnapping me." He technically had already. Taken me to Disneyland against my will, okay, maybe not quite, but at least without my permission.

"Now that's ridiculous."

"I don't have a choice, do I?"

"No." Sam smiled and dropped the remaining pieces of my life in the garbage.

"Then it's—"

"Ella, calm yourself down this instant." Calm? This man was erasing my existence and I was supposed to be calm?

"You're not coming back." Quentin finally joined our gun battle carrying a nuclear warhead.

Nope. No one was sinking my battleship. "Oh, yes I am. I can't leave. People depend on me. Count on me."

"Who?" They asked in unison.

"Well," I paused to consider. "Work. My landlord. My neighbors-they'll know I'm missing. And my parents." Didn't I feel loved?

"Work is easy. You've quit. Landlord and neighbors? They'll figure you've run off with Romeo here."

Quentin flashed a toothy grin and waved.

"And when's the last time you saw your parents?" Sam knew it all, didn't he?

"A month and a half ago. When my uncle remarried."

"Before that?" Damn!

"Mother's Day?"

Sam shook his head.

"Easter dinner then."

"How long do you think it'll take before they realize you're gone?"

"November eighth. My birthday. Mom will call. And then there's my sister."

Sam shrugged and handed me back an empty wallet. I tossed it in the trash. "We can arrange for you to call them first. You'll tell both of them you're taking a vacation for your birthday. Tell your sister you met someone. She'll expect you to be busy."

"Sam, I hate to tell you this. I'm broke. I couldn't afford a vacation. Mom knows that."

"Then you won it, or got it on discount or as a bonus or something. And here I thought you had millions stuffed in your mattress." He sighed. "Of course you're poor. That's how we picked you. I needed someone with few ties, someone whose disappearance would be dismissed."

"You sure know how to make a girl feel loved."

Quentin pushed his hair off his face. It fell right back again. I figured maybe I ought to be nice to him, if he came from the same situation as me.

"Back to the purse. Done?"

My bottom lip stuck out as I ransacked my apartment mentally to see if there was anything else I needed.

"You should go get the money I gave you from your jeans pocket." Oops. Yes, I probably should get that. Instead of leaving it for—Crap, I was getting all choked up at the idea of never seeing this lopsided old apartment again. Maybe it was just the idea that it was mine, leased, not owned, but mine.

On the way, I snagged my toothbrush and deodorant. They'd fit in place of the useless wallet.

Sam was pacing. He zipped my purse closed, checked the tie on my necklace, and then Quentin's. At his prodding we formed a circle. I was wondering how this would work since Quen had the gems again. Sam was still ringleader of this circus show.

I really wasn't doing this, was I? Sam's cowboy boot bumped toe-to-toe with my foot. Quentin shifted his feet the same way.

"Join your gems together," Sam instructed us. I slipped the purse over my neck and one shoulder first. I closed the gap between the beads. My pulse throbbed against the inside of my head like a tribal drum. The heat from the stones bit into my fingers, fighting them just a little before touching. I thought of the repelling of magnets. Odd.

"Hands." Sam and Quentin grabbed mine, forming a circle above our touching feet.

"Together." Quentin's voice was uncharacteristically soft, compelling. I let the men lead, pulling my hands to the center to meet with theirs. A spike of lightning shot up from the floor and into our woven fingers. The room disappeared in a white flash.

Chapter Six

Alone again! Humph. Click. Click. I snapped my heels together. *I'm invisible, dag nab it.*

"Ma'am, for this scene I need you to stand here at the spout and pretend to be pumping water. When Ben walks through here, stop and watch him go by."

Well, so I wasn't invisible. But this was okay. I nodded even as I searched for a familiar face. Pump the lever, stop and stare. I could do that.

"Action!" I ignored the noise behind me and went about pulling the cast iron handle up and down. It wasn't light. Some guy walked by wearing buckskin pants and shirt. A cowboy hat perched on his head. He shielded his face from the fake sun and started talking. It didn't take any acting lessons to learn how to gape. That was—wait, this must mean—we're in Hollywood.

"Cut!" I didn't move. "Clear the stage please." Oh, I guess they meant me. I turned and followed the rest of the extras down the rickety steps to ground level.

"*Not bad for a greenhorn.*" Quentin's voice invaded my thoughts. Instinctively I reached for my throat. The vibration of the gems against my neck coincided with his words. It felt like a speaker turned up too loud.

"*Where are you?*"

"*You won't recognize me. You won't recognize yourself. Stay invisible.*" I caught the eye of a handsome sheriff. He winked at me.

"*Um, I don't think I'm invisible.*"

Quentin groaned. "*You're invisible in the sense that no one can see Ella. You're kind of borrowing someone else's body.*"

I'm what? I reached up and touched my face, then looked down at my hands. Those were not my fingernails. *"Is this safe? This doesn't...kill her or anything?"*

His heavy sighs were frustrating. If I could find him, I was tempted to punch him, then demand answers.

"I guess this is something normal you magic people do. Ride around in stranger's bodies."

"You could say that."

The sheriff walked by again, his eyes fixated on my chest. *"Is that you?"*

"Uh, no. That's the star of this movie. Next to him."

"The wrinkled old Indian man?"

"It's better than being a woman. Or a horse. You will realize you never know what you'll get. Just stay invisible so you don't pop out of her body."

"I am so not understanding this."

"Miss? I need you in another scene." I shrugged at the Indian, and the Sheriff as well. He was cute.

"Where?" I asked. My voice was entirely foreign to me. Quentin had said I wouldn't recognize myself. I glanced down again.

Holy—! Where did they come from? My skin was dark, tan or perhaps Indian as well. The dress I wore was pure prairie get up. Except the plunging neckline. It was way, way down there. And there was a lot of skin between my chin and the white lace. I felt like I should be quoting Laura Ingalls Wilder in this costume. Or maybe not. I glanced down again. Wow.

"The sheriff will come and drag Ben off to prison. I need you to lean out this window and wail. You don't want him to. Pretend he's your secret lover."

"Sam?" I called through the mental walkie talkie. *"Where are you? Is this what you had in mind when you said we had to hurry?"*

"Action!" It was boring to watch the scene unfold in slow motion with cameras and microphones bobbing in and out of everyone's face. I did my big cry scene and went in search of a four-foot Indian.

I so needed a mirror. I knew I looked like a Hooter's girl trapped in a Bonanza rerun. The lusty eyes and drooling mouths of the testosterone bearers made that painfully obvious. Remember my thought about a boob job and touched up face? Erase it, axe it, forget I ever said such a thing. I'll stick with plain 'ole me. This attention wasn't my gig.

"Hey, miss, you got an agent?" Great, they let vermin in this place. The snakeskin coat was much more appropriate than this guy probably ever imagined.

"*Yoohoo, Sam, where are you*?" I looked around for him. "Uh, actually, I do. I was just looking for him."

Sam was Sam. Beaming from behind a safari hat and wild Hawaiian shirt was the face I recognized. The wrinkles around his eyes deepened as he smiled. He recognized me? Or dear God, was he hitting on me, without knowing it was really me? I was ready to throw myself at his feet if he dared to walk past. "I'm Roger Cadlahar. I represent Suzanne here. You were perhaps interested in her for a script you represent?"

The man seemed to shrink a bit and looked from me to Sam to Geronimo Junior who had finally caught up with us. Roger turned on his heel and left. I wanted to shout "Don't come back now, ya'hear?" But I held my tongue. No sense drawing even more attention my way.

"*Where have you been*?" Quentin demanded of Sam. "*We've wasted half the day as actors. Why are we here?*"

"*Don't say anymore. He's here.*"

"*Why aren't you in costume*?" I had to know why Sam could be himself.

"I don't need to be. I want you and Quentin to stay low profile right now. Though you're getting plenty of attention," he said, his eyes dropping to about chin level, then flitting back to meet my gaze. God, I hated that. Understood it, but hated it just the same. Hello, I'm a person here, not breasts on legs.

I was just about to ask when I could be me again. I needed to be me again. But the hand on my shoulder stopped me. It was the one who'd been barking orders at the extras. Oooh. A big shot.

"Good job today, sweetheart. Call me if you're looking for more work."

Humph. Well, if this magic thing didn't pan out I had a place to go. As long as I could find cones like this again. "Thanks, sir." I took his card and suppressed the shudder that threatened. The man's hand lingered near my neck and the gems felt like they were pulsing and growing. Quentin and Sam stood watching. Him, not me. I half expected my dear Indian hero to pull out an arrow.

In sarcastic flair I tucked the man's card between my new found cleavage. The casting director's beady eyes followed it down. I wondered if a trail of grease followed.

So much for that. As soon as he realized I wasn't going to say anything else, and figured out he was not going to get a peep show, he left. I pulled the front of my dress and wriggled, forcing the card to slide straight to the ground. "Eww!" An exaggerated shudder racked my body. "He was gross."

"What next?" Quentin looked so serious standing there with his arms folded across his chest. Any second now someone was going to walk by and mistake him for a cigar store Indian.

"*Clear your mind*," Sam hissed.

I crossed my arms over my chest and looked off into the distance. I figured it was safe to watch the other actors milling around and redoing their takes. Why not, right?

"Bergestein. Long time no see." Sam held out a hand and appeared to be greeting an old friend. I looked the man up and down, trying to imprint his face in my memory. Then watched the cute sheriff cut across the lot. Wow, nice butt.

"Suzanne, I'd like you to me my friend, Mr. Bergestein."

"How do you do." I bowed just slightly.

"Just wonderful after that." He licked his lips. Damn. I'd done it again. I pressed my hand over my chest and forced a smile. Little flames just had to be flickering from my ears.

A big hubbub was going on at the fancy trailer on the other side of a chain link fence. I rose on my tiptoes to catch a glimpse.

"This your new playmate?" Mr. B asked Sam. I was afraid to look at Sam. Oh, I would have been willing to play it up. If I could. I'd probably start laughing or something. "You sure do pick them young."

"But ripe."

I chewed on my bottom lip. Words I usually don't use were threatening to jump out of my mouth.

"You get done with that one, feel free to pass her along to me."

"I'll keep you in mind. If Hugh doesn't get his hands on her," Sam promised.

"What do those women see in him?"

I was tempted to run through the reasons why women would find Mr. B down right disgusting, even compared to Hugh Hefner, but I feared he'd hear me. I winked at Sam and continued to check out the crowd gathering across the way.

Mr. B slid his hand into his jacket pocket slid out some big stogie and lit it up. Sorry, but cigar smoke is nasty. Even out in the open. The snakeskin jacket that other guy had on really would have been better suited for this loser. Blech.

"Sam," I purred. Hey, I never could have pulled that off as plain Ella. "I'm going to walk over there to the fence line and see if I can catch a peek." I waited for his nod and stepped outside their cozy little circle. Quentin still hadn't moved a muscle. He had to be dying to say something.

Mr. B leaned closer to Sam and whispered, "Are you sure you don't want to head over to Switzerland with me? Diamonds and gold. Ours for the taking. Even split, I swear it."

"Sorry, Bergestein, I'm aiming to stay clean this time."

I tuned into the mental side of the conversation. "*Coward*," Mr. B. lashed back. "*Always to scared to take a chance. Can't you see there is no governing body anymore? We took them out. And now the circle of gems is almost complete. Four more until I have enough power to rule all magic. You can be my right hand man.*"

The shiver that ran down my spine had nothing to do with temperature. The crowd let up a scream that drowned out my ability to hear Sam's retort. Whatever it was sent Mr. B off in a huff, the foul smell of his cigar lingering behind him.

Sam snuck up beside me and grabbed my elbow.

"Stop making me jump out of my skin!"

"Speaking of, we'll need to get you into your own again. Poor Quen."

I glanced down at the sour-faced Native American. Mr. B must have felt he was a good candidate for an ashtray. The top of his head was spattered with gray ash.

I nodded. Boy, were there some good comments brewing in my head. But I didn't figure this was the time. I was liable to be the recipient of Quentin's arrow.

Sam led us through the lot. A scantily clad bimbo, a guy who looked like a safari adventurer/beach comber and an incredibly short, mute Indian. We must have looked like the Three Musketeers. Or was that the Three Stooges? I voted for the latter when Sam stopped before a dilapidated trailer. "It's empty."

"How do you know?"

"Just trust me, okay?"

Sam opened the unlocked door and held it. Quentin and I stepped in and nearly ran back out. At least I did. He would have been unable to run on legs that were only two feet long. But it would have been fun to see.

"What is that God-awful smell?" Quentin gasped.

I was more concerned with the sounds that emerged from the shadows. "Sounds like....chickens?"

Quentin pointed to the light switch. I grinned down at him and reached over one of the stacks of boxes that seemed to fill the room to flip it on. Chickens. And Geese. I squinted. Rabbits. A what? Ferret maybe? All in boxes of various sizes stacked on top of one another in the small space. I shuddered.

"I guess we found your smell. Eau de animal toilet."

"Close the door. We'll only take a minute in here anyway."

"Hurry up and tell me how to get out of this body and out of this trailer. What's the deal?

"It's a bit tricky, so watch me first." Quentin reached up with a stubby hand and untied the bone choker that hid his gems. "You need to move them together, but keep a finger between them. Once they are both touching your hand, go to visible. You should pop out of the body you're in and be you again."

I stepped back as I watched Quentin appear next to a wizened old Indian. And the Indian was still alive! "Go ahead," Quentin prodded. He stood in front of me and focused on my fingers. They were all thumbs. Once I had the gems throbbing against the sides of my finger, I clicked my heels.

"Visible," I said out loud. I didn't understand how this visible thing worked when I was visible, just someone else, but I could barely breathe from the stench and didn't want to waste valuable oxygen quizzing him on it.

"Step to the side."

I did. Quentin was there with an arm around my shoulders. I wondered who ran over me with a steamroller? I gasped for breath. Quentin pointed. Standing where I had been was a beautiful girl. Exotic and built just the way Playboy liked 'em. "She's real? Not some cartoon you had conjured up?"

"Well, most of her is real."

I totally understood. She'd found a friend in her plastic surgeon.

"Now what, we just leave them here?"

"Yep, we fly before they see us and realize we've been hitching a ride in their body."

"Will they remember anything?"

"Not this time. But there may be a time you really are just along for the ride. Hiding under their skin."

"That is not cool, man. I don't like it."

"I'm sure it's happened to you before. Ever had a space of time you just know you did something, but for the life of you can't remember the steps you took? I know you've said 'I know I brought it in here, I just don't remember what I did with it.'"

"Well, yeah. But that's just me. I'm a scatterbrain."

"No, you're an easy target for body hoppers. They stop in your body for a few minutes, a few hours, whatever."

"Why?"

"To get revitalized."

"If that's getting revitalized I don't want to know what getting tired feels like. My legs are Jello. Oh, and I'm hungry." I sank against Quentin.

"Unfortunately, that kind of hunger has to wait. Sam's outside, these two will be waking up real soon and," he glanced around, "there's at least forty pair of beady eyes watching us."

"Let's go," I said, forcing my worn out body to move. "Now."

When we stepped out of the trailer it was dark. As dark as Hollywood could get without a major power failure. The set was pretty well emptied. How long had we been in the trailer, anyway?

"We're locking it up here in just a few minutes," the guy who looked ex-football player but sported a Phoenix Suns baseball cap was telling Sam. "Those your two?" He pointed a plastic looking badge in our direction.

Sam nodded.

"How are you feeling?" Sam flipped his movie set visitor pass over and over in his hands.

"Tired and hungry. I don't think I've eaten a real meal in—two days!" It dawned on me that I hadn't even thought about it in terms of time. "When we've tried to get something to eat you've tossed a snack our way and zinged us somewhere else."

Quentin rubbed his tummy and licked his lips. "Steak. Is there a steakhouse around here that won't cost me an arm and a leg?"

Cost. Money. Purse. Oh Sheez. "My purse. What's happened to it?" We were already a good five minute walk from the animal hotel.

Quentin stopped and looked behind him at the trek past the buildings and parking lots. It sucked to be without wheels. "Do you want me to go find it? It's probably right there, where you reappeared."

"No, Quentin," Sam's voice warned.

"Yes, Quentin. Or rather, no, I lost it, I'll go back. Just let me go invisible and I'll hurry."

"Ella." Sam didn't stop walking. He was telling me he wasn't going to wait. Go or stay, go or stay.

"I'm going." I flounced past Quentin and disappeared. There was no way these men were going to push me around. It was mine and I wasn't going to be without it.

Yeah. It was a symbol of my independence. Proof I didn't have to rely on them.

The area where the filming had been done was a darkened maze of fences and trailers. Everything looked different at night. And I hadn't bothered to watch exactly how we'd left the place. Nice one, Ella.

I passed a stable I hadn't remembered seeing before. Actually, I wasn't entirely sure it was a stable, but the whinny of horses and smell of hay and manure clued me in. I was real tempted to peak into the glowing yellow window to see.

Nope, I was in search of a runaway purse. No time for horseplay. What if the actress had snatched it when she came around? Quentin had said something about waking up in a daze. She probably had grabbed it. Or maybe that Indian. My feet pounded on the asphalt in the general direction I expected to find the ratty trailer. The trailers up ahead looked like the ones I had watched the "sheriff" disappear into. Hmm...I wondered if he was there now.

I rubbed my hands up and down my arms. Even with long sleeves, I felt cold. Sure, part of it was the lost feeling. But geez, here I was no ID, no money wandering through a set in Hollywood, surely someplace I had no right to be. It doesn't get much more alone than that. And it seemed like my short term memory had vanished. Over my shoulder were the lights of the city, the lines of the lights that guided the drive to the front gate. Somewhere out there were Sam and Quentin. I could just see Sam powering forward, cursing himself for taking me on and Quentin glancing back over his own shoulder from time to time. At least, I hoped he was. Thinking of me, at least.

Face it, Ella. You're lost.

Something snapped behind me. Surely it was a stick, a squirrel dropping acorn shells or something, right? I took a few more speed walk steps and stole a look over my shoulder. I could see nothing. If I were an animal, say a dog, I could twitch my ears back and listen. Maybe even smell if it was something... I didn't even want to think it was another person. Alas, my barely trained sideshow variety repertoire of magic didn't allow me the ability to pop eyes into the back of my head. And I wasn't going to try. I'd end up stuck that way.

So I treaded as lightly as I could and listened for all I was worth. In the distance I could hear the occasional car horn. The cricket symphony seemed to be playing theme music. It didn't sound like Jaws, but it wasn't exactly soothing to me. Perhaps if there had been a script I might have been forewarned and known to forget about finding my purse. But then again, it was probably all in my head—the fear of the dark, the noises and the fact I was still weirded out from today's travel and body hopping. I shuddered.

Too late now, I chided myself. I'm going in. Wait. I slowed. Was that a footstep? Did I just imagine the rasping sound of someone drawing in a breath?

I shivered and realized it had been this morning when I'd last visited the ladies room. Great timing, bladder o'mine. Not a bathroom in sight. No way was I going to strip and squat, even out here in the middle of nowhere. There were invisible magic people everywhere.

Peeping Toms. That's what we were. Well, I hadn't used that particular skill yet. And why did I leave Sam and Quentin again? For a purse?

Something *was* behind me. Those hairs on the back of my neck were a beacon to danger, necklace or not. I ignored the pressure in my lower stomach and started jogging. Where, I didn't know, but anywhere was better than here.

Wait! I'm invisible right? Then if someone's following me...Duh. How could anyone follow an invisible person? I needed to quit overthinking it. Still, a bit spooked by the noises I kept hearing, I continued to run toward what I hoped was that stinky trailer.

Bam! I stopped abruptly, the wind knocked out of me. Whatever I'd hit, I realized, was big and wide and solid. But not like a brick wall solid. It was also transparent. What was the chance of there being a clear elephant in my path? Yeah, that's what I thought.

There were stars above me, but I wasn't sure if they were really there or just caused by this collision. What the heck had I hit? Could it...he see me? Was I still invisible?

Sam's words had me very gun shy. I had yet to hear him talk about other "good guys" and men walking around invisible in the darkness were likely *not* good. I knocked my heels together hoping they hadn't seen me.

I laid face up on the cool grass obsessing and I hadn't even tuned in on the fact there was another conversation zipping past my ears. I wasn't going to survive my first week on this magic mission.

"*Can you just shut up? Your constant prattle is making me want to rip out your tongue.*"

"*Tongue has nothing to do with it, you idiot. It's her brain. Yak yak yak yak. All the way here, you go on and on. Now you want to review it all again.*"

I winced. There were at least two, and from the low timbre of their voices, they both sounded big, mean. Human bulldogs. I tried not to think about my movements as I forced my body to roll away from the voices. No comment. They didn't see me. "*Well, what did you want me to do, sing to myself?*" I had to get involved in the conversation to keep them from realizing what I was doing.

I moved slow, reaching before me as I half crawled to the left. All I needed was to find my way blocked. Then I'd for sure be stuck.

"*Well, Jonesy, what are we going to do with her? Feel her out for the gems and leave her wandering out here? Someone will find her and no one will believe her story.*"

The other guy replied, "I don't know. I didn't think they wanted us to just leave her. They expected us to kill her."

I crawled a little farther. I made my thoughts stick to the smell of the ground, the chill in the air. Weather was always a good neutral subject. Tiny rocks cut into my palms. My knees would undoubtedly be threadbare. Too bad tore-up denim wasn't the big style right now. I would have fit right in.

That thought must have slipped through the weather. The pursuer, who didn't have a name yet cut in. "*It'll be more than a couple of tears in your clothes that you'll be dealing with when I'm done with you, sister.*"

"*I'm so not your sister.*" God, where was he? He needed a swift kick—

"*Ah ah ah. You forget I can hear you.*"

"*Bite me.*" I jumped up and ran. Something told me he was just about to reach down and realize I'd already put three feet between him and myself. I stumbled and fell once but rolled, got up and continued running. Until I reached a chain link fence. With rings of barbed wire keeping me from climbing over it.

I couldn't hear anything that sounded like a pursuit. But they were there. I knew it.

Now the theme music to Jaws started thudding in my brain. I followed the fence line. There had to be a gate. Damn, damn, damn. All this for a freakin' purse. But who, me? Listen? Yeah.

The thicker bars of silver fencing made me think there was a break in the fence. Yes! I needed a bathroom and warmth. And a phone. I wonder if I called Jeannie if she'd come and get me. I could say my purse was stolen. They'd issue me new ID, right? I could just walk away from this whole magic thing and forget about it.

The warning music turned into a steady pulsing at my neck. The break *was* a gate, but it was locked. Son of a—wait. Sam had walked into my house by moving the tumblers in the lock and letting himself in. Why was I being so ignorant?

"There!" I heard the shout when I pushed the gate open enough to slip through. It would have been pointless to waste time locking it again. I just bolted toward the nearest trailer that still had its lights on.

What would I say? I'd have to become visible again. Could I just ask where that particular animal trailer was, maybe find someone to accompany me there, and then back out to the front of the studio? Ah, sure. That was gonna happen. Right after the aliens came and injected my body with odd shaped metal objects.

Plan B. What the hell was it?

Chapter Seven

I paced in the shadows. If this were the movies, what would happen next? I envisioned an arm slinking around my waist and a second around my face, smothering my scream.

I left the shadows and moved between the small buildings. The ache in my head muffled any sounds I heard. I was scared. Just about to wet myself scared. And my full bladder didn't help any.

The next building was dark, and quite a big bigger than the first. *There's got to be a bathroom in there.* With a little more ease than the last one, I picked the lock. The building appeared to be a storage unit, packed with boxes and chairs and numerous other things I couldn't see from the faint glow of the streetlight.

That was just great. All I wanted was a toilet. Maybe not all. I really wanted to be home, but I'd settle for a bathroom. Then I could go back out and find Quentin and Sam again. I'd even forfeit my purse for a bathroom.

I felt my way through the room. An extension cord tried to wrap itself around my leg like a snake as I walked by. Shudder. I felt my way around the boxes until my hand hit drywall. Rooms. Hallelujah!

But I got no farther. A gloved hand reached around me and covered my mouth and an arm pinned my arms to my body. I tried to scream and kicked like a pissed off donkey at the person who lifted me right off the ground. It didn't matter. My mind reached out through the room and started hurling some of the smaller items at my back. The reverberations of a few hits had my spirits soaring. But it also had the grip on me tightening.

"*I can't breathe,*" I shouted mentally. "*Relax a little or you'll kill me.*"

Thankfully he didn't growl back something about that being his intention. The hand over most of my face shifted so I could suck air through my bruised nostrils.

I couldn't hear any conversations, mental or real. Was this the same person who had been tracking me outside—Jonesy or his counterpart—or a whole new flavor of stalker?

Twisting to try to catch a glimpse didn't work. The slightest pressure had me back off the ground and holding my breath. Unwillingly.

I knew it wasn't Quentin. His heat, his scent would have triggered something, some sort of familiarity. That, I knew, was missing from this confrontation.

But why weren't my gems heating up like an electric fence? What was the problem? Had I shorted them out? No, or I wouldn't be able to throw things. Or be invisible.

I expected a retort considering my rambling thoughts. I was practically talking to myself—mentally. But it was silence that answered. I spoke up, mentally since my spoken word would have been a gasp. "*Listen, who ever you are. I've got to pee. Considering your position, you'll be smelling sweet and feel rather wet if you don't find me a bathroom. Stat.*"

I learned *stat* watching those trauma room shows on the Discovery channel. Apparently, he wasn't impressed. Calling my bluff. I couldn't force myself to willingly wet my pants either. Figured.

Then I remembered Quentin's words. Some electricity. If the beads weren't going to do it on their own, I'd shock him myself. I sucked in a mouth full of air as the leather clad hand was readjusted across my face. I was more or less pinned between this person's body and the wall, so knocking my heels together wasn't going to do it.

Picture lightning bolts. A small arc—something the common person could create by shuffling their feet across the carpet—jumped from my body to his.

I expected to hear him laughing at my weak attempt. He had to be thinking what a piece of cake it was going to be to kill me—or whatever it was he wanted to do with me.

I needed more than a few sparks. It'd be cool if I could breathe fire. I pulled in another leather tasting breath. I figuratively reached down, jerking anything possible from the tips of my toes and fingers. The gems heated up and grew, or at least felt like they did, along with the vortex I sensed twisting in my chest. I closed my eyes. Held it in, let it build. Heat, precious heat flamed up when I thought about my predicament. My throat burned, my tongue was on fire. Anger was its fuel.

It might actually be better than sex, I thought. Then thought again. Nah, not quite. This was intense, a rush, but it was also consuming. I opened my eyes and my mouth and envisioned a fire breathing dragon.

There was a loud yelp in my ear, a bright flash, then an evil sounding laugh.

Arms slid beneath my shoulders and knees. I couldn't muster the strength to think about fighting them. It's all I could do to keep my eyes open. Acrid smell burnt my nose. Bright orange and yellow flames climbed the drywall.

Hands were at my neck, pulling. "Go away," I pushed past my chapped lips. "Stop."

It was too late. In an explosive brilliance I was sucked into a dimension where travel was warp speed. And I dreamed I was a little girl again.

☙ ☙ ☙

New discovery; we didn't just relocate this time. We went backwards in time. Wicked.

"Annabelle, quit dawdling. Get up out of your bed and get ready for your lessons."

"Yes, ma'am," I replied. Initially I was startled by the voice—it wasn't mine! Then I looked down. How fun, I thought after a few deep breaths. I get to be a spoiled rotten child of a wealthy family. I took a moment to absorb the surroundings.

It was warm here, I realized as I stripped off the long sleeping gown and stepped into the muslin dress laid on the foot of the four poster bed. By Nanny. I grinned. There was enough true Annabelle left to guide me through the day. Maybe I could keep from being detected. For a while at least. I might have time to think of a plan.

My hand flew to my neck and connected with lace. Oh, Jeez. What if they stole the necklace? Then I'd really be stuck. No. No. It had to be there. Somewhere. I was Annabelle. I couldn't rightly be Annabelle without it, could I? Not unless those thugs had snatched the gems and cast some sort of witchy spell to turn me into a girl living a hundred years before their time.

"Oh shit, oh shit, oh shit," I cried while clawing at the dress on my throat.

"Annabelle Rockford." Nanny waddled into the room and wound her gnarled hand into my hair. "What would Papa say if he hears you talking like them boys?"

I didn't even know that word was used back then, er, I mean now. I shrugged mentally. I wasn't about to have poor Annabelle shrug and subject her eight-year-old body to any more of Nanny's fierceness. And Papa? I felt Annabelle's tears well up in fright. He wouldn't hesitate to lay down the law.

But Nanny released my hair and was prattling on about the stable boys. "I told your mother not to allow you to watch them boys saddling them horses, cussing and swearing the ways thems do. Ain't no good for a proper little girl's ears."

She jerked me around and deftly buttoned the back of my dress. Those fingers were deceptively strong and nimble. Chalk it up for future reference. No upsetting Nanny.

"Where'd you get such a piece of primitive jewelry?"

"Uncle Charles," I replied. *Who? His name was Sam, Annabelle.* But it was the right answer.

"Uncle Charles, Uncle Charles. It was probably that man, overcome with spirits who taught you such speech."

"Papa would not like you to speak of his brother that way."

Not my ear, no. Not my ear! Nanny yanked me across the room and laid her wide hand to my backside. Ugh...now I'm thinking in this era. She flat-out spanked my butt.

"You'll not disrespect me, young 'un."

I turned, probably red in the face but not broken down. "I will hold my tongue of your talk of dear Uncle Charles and you will breathe no word to he or mother of my own outburst."

Nanny's wrinkles disappeared as her jaw fell open. "Annabelle, you've been listening a far cry too much to your daddy and brother making deals. I swear it. You're too smart for your own britches."

She didn't scold me though. Just pulled the mosquito netting over my bed evenly and set out the water for me to wash my face.

"Hurry, child. No more dawdling out of you this morning. Already too much going on in this house today."

I raised an eyebrow and used the mirror to look back at the heavyset woman behind me. Nanny was humming and pulling frocks from the wardrobe.

I shifted my eyes back to the chocolate ones in the mirror. Wide set they were, set above a perky nose and cupid's bow mouth. Yep. Doomed to be a real debutante in seven or eight more years. But wow, check out those curls—

"Now, quit being prissy. You're getting pretty enough without memorizing every line to your face. Afore long you'll be old like me and no one will see anything that was once beautiful."

I refused to comment and simply walked out of the room and down the hall to the library. I wouldn't slow my pace. I'd already managed to get Nanny on the defensive. Any more odd behavior would surely blow my cover. And I'd gotten here somehow. That meant someone else was here too. Someone probably worth hiding from. Still I gawked inwardly at the finely carved dark wood trim that lined the hallway walls and encircled each doorway. What was this place, a castle?

"Closer to a palace, anyway."

The voice was real, but it wasn't really Ernest, my older brother—Annabelle's older brother. He'd read my thoughts.

"*Who are you?*" I dare not speak out loud—not in the little girl's voice.

"*My name is Jim, Jim Hansen.*"

"*Did you bring me here?*" I could feel the vortex churning in my chest again. Building, building.

"*Whoa, there, Ella, dear. No more flame throwing. Though I have to admit, that was pretty impressive for a novice.*"

I glanced at his hands. "*No.*" He laughed. "*It wasn't me you fried. It was one of Bergestein's goons.*"

Goons. I liked that. "*So, who are you, what were you doing there and why did you whisk us back to this?"*

He didn't have a chance to answer. Nanny came up behind me and tapped my shoulder. "Quit scowling at your brother and let him get on by. Your lessons are waiting."

"Yeah, your lessons are waiting," he teased.

As he pushed past I couldn't help but reach out and zap his arm. Just lightly, I swear it. He turned around with a grin. Not a frown.

What was I in for?

ᘓ ᘓ ᘓ

I let Annabelle lead through the rest of the day. It turned out to be quite dull. Needlework and costume changes. It was no fun to sit while Nanny jerked her way through my thick, wavy hair.

"Well," Nanny spoke as she tapped the silver backed brush on my shoulder. "You didn't utter a peep through all that. Maybe I will take you up on our bargain from this morning."

Annabelle—I—just nodded and fumbled with my fingers on my lap. Nanny must have accepted that, thank goodness, and continued her job of undressing and redressing me like I was a doll.

Ernest was at dinner. So being the good children we are, we ate silently while having an intense mental conversation.

"*So why did you kidnap me*?" I hit him as soon as he had entered the room.

"*To save your ass.*"

"To save the gems, I'm sure."

"It makes me sound like a nicer guy the other way."

I raised an eyebrow.

"Annabelle, don't you act like you're going to throw your food at your brother." Mother was the peacekeeper. Submissive woman that she was. Papa just ate, his features in a permanent scowl thanks to the single eyebrow dividing his eyes from his forehead. I felt no daughterly compassion toward that man. So I ignored him and faced Ernest again.

He chewed his vegetable carefully. "*I used to be Sam's partner.*"

Oh, this had my utmost attention. "*And*?"

"*Let's just say he's stuck to the straight and narrow. Never misused his magic. Not once."*

"He kidnapped me."

"He recruited you. You saw things before he gave you the necklace, did you not?"

The picture of me as an Indian girl flashed into my head. *"That was fake. He made me see the image."*

"Yes, he let you see. You chose to see it."

"That doesn't make sense."

"Doesn't matter now. Magic is a part of you. You can't go back."

"So what's all this with Sam and you and this Mr. B dude?"

Ernest passed the serving platter to Mother. It seemed our bodily hosts were acting perfectly normal while we carried on. This was way too bizarre for me.

"In a nutshell, a very small one, Mr. B needs ten gems to complete a circle and basically control all the magic out there. The council, which has been felled by none other than—"

"Mr. B," I finished.

"Yes, Mr. B. Anyway, the council had passed the rule no men could have more than two. Or wait. I think it was use more than two. He could hold four total while recruiting, as Sam did."

"But wouldn't Sam have had six, mine, his and Quentin's?"

"The ones Quentin wears are Sam's. Quentin lost his and Sam had to go save him."

"Quentin lost his? I could have sworn I heard that Sam lost his."

"It all works out, doesn't it? Sam is strong enough not to need them on. Like me, he can use those belonging to others."

"Then you have none?"

His eyebrow arched. *"I have a pair. Now. Courtesy of the goon you scorched."*

I clapped my hand over my mouth. *"Did he die?"*

"I don't think so."

"Annabelle, are you ill, dear?"

"No, ma'am. Just felt as though I would cough. Pardon me." This little gal had some manners now. I wish I could've thought to be so courteous and precise with my words at that age. I would have said. "No, just had something go down the wrong pipe" and then proceeded to hack it up.

Dessert was being served. I still didn't trust him. There had to be an ulterior motive. "*What now, Jim? Why did we go backwards in time?*"

"It's safe here. Mr. B's men won't be looking for you here."

I touched the collar of my dress, feeling the gems beneath the stiffly starched cotton. *"Why are they looking for me?"*

"Your magic is unpracticed. You're vulnerable."

I shivered. No kidding. Did I trust this person? I didn't even know what he looked like. I sure did want to get a look in his eyes to see if I could detect a lie.

What were my choices? Jim was listening. I could see it by the sleek smile on Ernest's face.

"You like the pie, Ernest, son? The cook made it from gooseberries." Papa scooped up mouthful after mouthful.

Tonight's conversation was over. The little girl had an early bedtime.

Well, I thought the conversation was over. Turned out this Jim guy had some pretty strong magic. We could talk with the wall separating us. Oh joy. I'll never be able to think again without wondering who was honing in on my precious thoughts.

"I can see why Sam chose you."

"Enjoying my wit and charming personality?"

"Well, I was actually referring to your ability to adapt and accept your circumstances while maintaining control. There are many more men in our circle because—"

"Because women get hysterical?"

"Yep."

"Bastard."

"I have been called worse." Jim chuckled. I imagined Ernest lying back on a masculine looking bed, his hands cupped beneath his head. Just like I was.

"Well, being a woman, and since next you'll say something about us asking too many questions, I might as well fit the bill. Why am I safer with you than with Sam and Quentin?"

"It'll only be a matter of time before they lure Quentin back into their mix."

"Quentin?"

"Yeah, he got sucked into that power hungry machismo Bergestein preaches. Ended up in the slammer in Central America. Good ole Sammy-boy snatched him out and brought him home. But I still don't trust him."

Hmmmm. Should I? But why should I believe Jim over Quentin. Or Sam? What made me want to believe any of them? Still...Sam wouldn't be after me to get the gems. If that had been the case, he never would have given them to me in the first place, right?

I had to voice my opinion. *"Why should I trust you, other than the obvious that there's no one else here and you did save me?"*

"Because I will keep you from Bergestein."

"Then why aren't you and Sam working together, if that's your common goal?"

Silence. Deafening quiet. Ah...therein lies the secret. I smiled sweetly at Nanny as she fussed about my wardrobe and urged me to get up and prepare for bed. Maybe Ernest had someone doing the same to him.

"Not on your life, little sister."

Ah...he was there. Just like I thought. *"So why don't you fill me in on your long term plans. Short term too."* I was bluffing my courage. *"You need to tell me why I shouldn't hop out of this body and touch my beads together and take my chances with the next person I might meet."* I could do it if forced to, but I was praying for a different option.

"You'll be dead in an hour out there alone."

"It's that well populated then, with the magic men?"

"Bergestein has enough power to trace all the gems, track them."

His matter-of-fact statement had me scratching my head. *"Then why doesn't he bust through the nice oak front door and kidnap Annabelle?"*

"He's just waiting for us to step out of the bodies. He won't touch the host body. And I told you he won't necessarily be thinking we moved back in time."

So there was another dilemma. As soon as I was to exit, I'd be vulnerable. *"And you intend to figure out where and how and we'll move together and teleport back to..."*

"I know exactly where we're going. And when."

I wasn't sure if I was patient enough to wait for him. What about

Sam, couldn't he find me? He'd found Quentin in a Latin American prison and brought him home. But the time difference worried me.

I cleared my throat, which had Nanny scuttling over to check my face and feel my neck. *"So I should just put up with this for what, another day, another week?"*

"Tonight. I'll wake you. But you must be quick."

Like Speedy Freakin' Gonzalez. I thought. Let me out of this body. Nanny jerked the brush through my hair, emphasizing my reasoning. Never again would I feel deprived because I didn't have someone to wait on me hand and foot. No sirree. This yanking and tugging and ordering and dressing. Yuck.

☙ ☙ ☙

A man stood beside the bed. In the dimness of the light of the moon, I could see the broad shoulders beneath the outline of a hat. "Cowboy?" I ventured, squinting through Annabelle's sleepy eyes to see the figure better.

"I told you to be ready. It's time to fly."

I fumbled with the necklace, pulling it free from the lacy throat of the nightgown. My fingers might have wielded the gems a little easier had it not been for the grogginess of sleep. Finally, I was able to sit up and slide off the bed, leaving a peaceful girl behind. I wondered if she'd have nightmares about this.

"No. I doubt she'll remember. You okay?"

I felt weak, but not uncommonly so for being awakened with my heart pounding through my chest at the thought of an intruder. "Yeah, I'll be just fine." I thrust out my hand. "I'm Ella Mansfield."

"And I'm Superman." He grabbed my hand and held me against his chest. The white lights of a thousand shooting stars blinded me. But I heard the crash of broken glass and the scream of a frightened child as we faded from the room.

☙ ☙ ☙

I reminded myself I hadn't the choice to go with him, and staying locked in the past wasn't an option either. Fate brought me this far, and now it was up to me. Well, it sounded good. I still had this wanna-be cowboy who wouldn't let me out of his sight.

"What are we doing? Circling the island?" I couldn't tell how big this place was. Giant orangish walls rose up straight from the middle of the island, leaving us wandering the narrow beach area. Ahead of us was a wider area with tall grasses and a small area of dunes. No sign of any buildings—or any other people.

"Looking."

"For what, or who, Amelia what's-her-name, the pilot?" I tripped over a piece of driftwood in my effort to get up beside him. I could harass him better if I could look him in the face. "Maybe for Bigfoot? Tell me, Jim, are you just trying to wear me down so you can rip the necklace from me and leave me for the vultures?"

"Now that you mention it."

My heart stuttered in my chest. I glanced upward. No long-beaked ugly birds floated above us. It wasn't the desert. I could still see the crystal blue waters and the pale reefs beneath them. "Where are we, some Caribbean Island?"

"Nope."

"Uh, is this a guessing game? How about Easter Island?" Bet he didn't think I knew that one. I hadn't seen those big head statues, so I knew I was wrong. Oh well, dazzling him with my wit wasn't working.

"There's something here. Look for a cave, well hidden and up about twenty feet into the cliff."

I stared at the yellow-orange stone that seemed to be a fortress around the interior of the island. My weekend plans sure had changed. If I'd even imagined being plunked on a hot, sandy beach, I would have never, ever pictured myself trudging through the sand in jeans and a long sleeve T-shirt. And then to guess I'd follow some Bruce Willis look-alike in a trench coat and cowboy hat? Yeah... I'd have imagined that. And there's a herd of pink horses around the corner.

I hung back and stared at the back of the man who'd supposedly saved me. Sighing, I fingered my gems and thought about jumping. I'd never done it alone, had no idea how to figure out how to choose where I would end up.

Jim growled and waved me up. More afraid of ending up in hell than I was of Jim, and curious on top of it, I clambered onto the rock beside him and shielded my eyes with my hand to follow his pointing finger.

There it was, a tiny pin hole in the side of the sheer cliff. And what were we going to do now that we'd found it?

Jim chuckled beside me. "Guess that means you haven't flown yet."

"Oh sure...just not without a captain flying and a flight attendant watering me like a flower. With vodka that is."

"Well, I'll be your captain, but I'm afraid the vodka isn't an option right now."

I screamed. He hadn't finished talking and I glanced down to see why he'd taken my hand and...oh dear, we were up off the ground and floating toward the wall.

"Ella, Ella, Ella," he chastised me. "This is a piece of cake. I'd expect a complaint had I rocket propelled us toward the hole like a bullet from a gun."

I couldn't see that being any less scary. "I feel like I'm going to drop from the sky."

"We're ten, maybe twelve feet up. It wouldn't hurt you if you did fall."

"Oh." I glanced down again. I guess maybe he was right. It didn't seem much higher than my second story windows.

The thought reminded me of what I had intended to do with Quentin that first night. It seemed like year ago, at least. Crap. I was freakin' homesick.

"It's normal. But don't get too attached to Quentin. I told you. He's on the fence."

I'd rather be on a fence. In fact, just about anywhere other than floating at the phenomenal rate of one-half mile per hour up to the cavern opening. And me, who'd approached the rickety bungee jump deck with the same nonchalance as one walks up to the ice cream counter. You know you're gonna get something good, but you're just not sure what yet.

Although, I wish to dispute the validity of good in that sentence. This cavern opening looked about the size of Annabelle and there were two of us coming at it.

"Uh, Jim. Are we going to fit?" I was quickly becoming more and more convinced he was using me for something. What, I couldn't tell, but I wasn't going to question him hovering two stories up.

"Yep." He snapped his fingers and my perspective changed. I didn't want to know if he shrunk us or if the opening magically increased. This was feeling more and more like I was still in Hollywood and somehow blasted into a warp of all the strange movies I had ever seen.

Then I looked through the narrow opening and saw it wasn't a cave, it was a doorway. There was light on the other side.

Chapter Eight

When my feet were on the rock and I'd caught my balance, Jim announced, "It's safe here. This is the land that exists in dreams and fantasies." The laugh that followed was more evil than comforting.

"And we're here, how?"

"I can't actually enter."

I looked toward the opening at the other end of this tunnel. "What do you mean?" I was so confused. My stomach was in knots that weren't only from the unsupported flight up. There had to be a catch.

"You've never done bad with your magic. Only the pure can enter to learn from the masters."

I envisioned my remote bouncing off the wall near Quentin's head.

"No. That's petty stuff. If that was bad, they'd kick the fairies out of fairyland."

Fairyland? Pinch me.

"Go on." Jim pushed me through the tunnel in the rock and into a world alive with color and laughter and song. I swear I heard him mutter something else before I stopped into the magical land, but I couldn't understand.

I never felt the sensation of falling, yet as soon as I blinked, I was standing on the ground, this time *inside* the giant walls. This was Disneyland, I decided. And I bet it never rained and you didn't have to pay to ride the rides.

A dainty thing the size of a feather reached over and tickled my ear. "Now what?" I asked her. She just giggled in response. Yep. That was going to teach me a lot.

"Lots of secrets." The fairy danced along daisies and the tall grasses. "The magic was created by the folk to keep goodness and peace. Bad men distort it."

"I know," I sighed, "I've met them."

"True magic lies in love and truth. Power is the by-product, not its goal."

No kidding. I thought of the way people had become off-center in their quests in life. Here, in this place, it felt like I was breathing clean air for the first time. Literally and physically speaking. I could get used to this kind of living. Too bad it was a nearly extinct way of life.

In a shallow puddle I saw a face. By now nothing surprised me. An old man, gray beard. Nope, not Santa, but I figured it had to be a relative.

I earned a hearty laugh for my thoughts. The figure moved. "I'm the boss around here. My name's too long and difficult for you to pronounce. So call me Lou."

"Lou?" The father of magic was called Lou? *Hello.* Please *pinch me.* This was a cruel joke.

"Lou," I had to ask this, "are you related to God?" I surely hoped so, because it looked like Lou had a sense of humor.

The water rippled as his chuckle echoed. The fairy slid behind the curtain of my hair. I imagined she was peering around it, waiting for his reaction.

"God's a little farther up the ladder than I am. Like at the top. But I can see you thinking along those lines. You're new to magic."

"Very."

"But not so new to the destruction it is causing."

"No. Not at all." Wasn't that the understatement of the year? I wondered if I should mention Jim, who had brought me here but not told me exactly why. What benefit was there for him if he couldn't get in?

"And what are your thoughts?"

"I'm not sure what to think anymore." Should I mention I was homesick and lost and scared to death of this gigantic world saving mission Sam had supposedly recruited me for? I looked around, trying to think of the right answer to tell Lou. Near the waterfall the rock had been cut—carved into a throne. Gouging holes had been dug into the rock in a circular pattern around the throne. I had a vision of a good and kind leader sitting beneath the glowing aura of the ten stones.

"Yes, they've stripped them all." His hand reached up from the flatness of the puddle. "Lean down here, Ella," he asked.

"No!" I retorted, frowning. Did he think I was stupid? Everyone was after the gems, I wasn't giving them up so easily.

"I don't want them," he said, his voice calm, soothing. "Let me feel their magic."

Still skeptical, but going with my gut Lou really was on the good team, I knelt down and gave him access to the necklace. The water glowed like the sun and then faded.

"Yes. You carry the real gems. Cherish them, girl. Let them not be stripped the way the others have. Do not let power clog the vision you see of love and goodness. It is the only way."

I still thought we should be able to zap the bad men and just go around and collect the gems the way one would collect Easter eggs.

"Sounds simple enough, but are you keeping in mind that to use magic against him makes you no better than he is."

I looked up at the clouds. "Lord, help me." Above me, an ominously dark cloud mixed in with the white bits of floating cotton. Its shadow cast a strip of darkness across the meadow. The fairy curled up behind my ear and held tight. Good old Lou muttered, "Oh dear."

"How did you get in here?"

"Man named Jim," I admitted, backing up from the darkness that approached. "I don't know what he wanted, or why."

"He got in by disguising himself in your goodness. It's the only way. He was within you when you entered."

Which explained why I remembered nothing but that final step and then standing on the floor of the hidden valley. Tears immediately sprang to my eyes. I felt used, manipulated. Why hadn't I known better?

Behind the lead cloud came others. Beneath it, the six-foot shape of a man in western wear charged toward me.

It was absolute chaos. Tiny creatures darted around me like starving mosquitoes. Their high pitched cries of fear echoed those inside me. I shook, waiting for the flow to fall.

"You must go. It follows you." Lou faded into the gray water.

"How?" Jim had said he couldn't come in here, I was sure of it. The air was frigid against my skin. I shivered. "Lou, help me. What do I do? Where do I go?"

The surface of the puddle turned opaque. "Lou, come back. Tell me. Where do I go?"

All the magic beings zipped into their refuges, hollow logs, burrows, and crevices in the sheer, orange cliffs. I'd never felt too big in my life, until now. And it wasn't a good feeling. Especially when something even bigger was hot on my heels.

"Look in the pool. Find your heart's desire and dive in. Dive deep." Lou's baritone resonated in my ears. The wind whipped my hair around, dislodging the pixie that hid there.

"Hide, little Thumbelina!" I was never so scared in my life, so I could only imagine how she felt.

The fairy fought against the gale to hover in front of me with her tiny hands on her tiny hips. She shouted over the rush, "I'm Winzey."

"I know it's windy. You'd better find shelter."

She slid back under my hair. "Winzey," she screamed. Well, if that didn't just blow my eardrums. "My name is my power. Use it."

"Winzey?" I repeated, hunching over when the fierce raindrops started driving into my skin. They'd do serious damage to a tiny thing like her.

"Dive," she commanded. "Before it's too late."

I crawled over and looked into the tempest beneath the waterfall. The once blue water was angry and gray. Dive in there? "*Your heart's desire.*" Lou's voice ran through my head again. In this weather, that was a piece of cake to dream up.

I thought of a warm fire and a mug of hot cocoa. Blankets, too. Lots of blankets.

"Go." Winzey tugged on my ear. The roar of the a thousand train engines thundered up behind me. He wasn't far away now.

I held my nose and jumped.

ଓ ଓ ଓ

The turbulent waters of the pool turned into the beating rain of a storm. It was night. Cold, dark night. "This isn't my hearts desire," I puffed out through foggy breath. My hair hung in stringy ropes and the clothes that had adhered to my body were already stiffening up. I was going to turn into a freaking ice cube if I didn't find shelter.

There was a yellow glow visible, just faintly, through the thick fog. I assumed it was just a streetlight, but it was a goal, nonetheless. I trudged forward, concentrating. Left foot. Right foot. Left foot.

I was so busy looking down as I chanted to my feet, I plowed right into the dark figure holding an umbrella.

"I was expecting you." The low whisper sent shivers that had nothing to do with the temperature down my back.

"Quentin!" I yelped and jumped back, nearly tripping over my own feet and squinting to get a good look. Once I was sure, I threw myself at him. I wasn't going to let go this time. "God, am I glad to see you."

I regretted my overexuberant welcome immediately. He pulled away and smiled, tightlipped, back at me. "Let's get you inside where it's warm."

Back up, Ella. He's not the same Quentin. I declined his offer of the umbrella. I wasn't going to get any wetter. "Where's Sam? Is he here? I can't wait to tell him where I've been."

"Sorry, but Sam had, uh, other business to attend to. He'll catch up with us before too long." He shrugged and started walking away.

I hung back a step. Sam wasn't here? Had he trusted Quentin? I expected it was my fault. Getting sucked away into never-never-land with ex-partners and fairies.

"Bad man," I heard just as I was catching back up to Quentin.

"Bad man?" I repeated.

"Huh?" Quentin turned around. We were in front of a house, a giant, looming two story. I thought I could hear the crash of waves over the pounding of the storm. On the coast somewhere, I guessed. From the rain, I'd guess the Northeastern coast.

"Bad man," the voice came again.

"Did you say something?" I asked Quentin.

"No. I heard you say something, though. I thought you were talking to me." He slid the key into the lock.

"Nuh-huh." I was just hearing things. Must be the wind. My insanity.

"You hear the truth."

I reached up to my ear and felt the culprit. Ah-hah. I jerked my hand down and smiled while allowing Quentin to let me into the room.

He didn't need to know about Winzey yet.

He slid off his heavy wool cloak and hung it next to the umbrella on the wall. There was no light in here, just the filtering of yellow glow from the end of the hall.

I'd expected to want to throw myself at him like I had when I first recognized him. Now I just stood there as if I was stepping into the world of a stranger. He was, though. A stranger, that is. I mean, what did I really know? That he was a helluva kisser and had a great bod? And that I slept with him? Half of me decided it was a shame I hadn't done more than just snore the night away.

The other half? It sided with the pixie who had gotten swept through the vortex of time and space right along with me. Who now had cleverly appointed herself my guardian. Something about Quentin fit in too easily with the darkness. Bad man, indeed.

"You been okay?" I thought he'd never ask what had happened. I mean, really, wasn't it odd I had disappeared from a Hollywood set while searching for the purse that was *really* lost now? Had he worried? Had they come looking for me?

I wanted Sam. Needed his guidance. I hadn't recognized it at first, but I trusted him more than anyone else, including myself.

Dark. It was dark here. Not just the lighting, but I had a feeling it was set that way on purpose. A skittish shiver climbed my spine. I wrapped my arms around myself and finally answered Quentin. "Yeah, I've been okay."

He smiled and I glimpsed a flash of the man who had goaded me on at the dump, the one who had flirted incessantly and made me laugh. Just as quickly, it was gone. Magically gone.

☙ ☙ ☙

For two days I felt like I was living in a tomb. No television, little conversation and absolutely no venturing outside the house. I could roam the sprawling structure, with its high ceiling and modern but medieval-themed decor. My solace was the library-like room and my hushed, brief conversations with Winzey.

Whenever I saw him, his eyes would meet mine, and I'd think he wanted to say something, but then he'd go back to ignoring me. I had tried twice to speak to him mentally, but he'd responded with a hissed, *"No magic,"* and the connection would end.

Only once did Quentin follow me into the kitchen and corner me against the counter. "I know you don't like this. Neither do I, but we are practically in the lion's den here. One misstep and it's over. Hold on for me, Ella. Just hold on for me." He kissed me then, soft and promising. The Quentin I knew. I didn't understand what he meant—not sure I wanted to, but I needed something to believe at this point.

I nodded, catching my breath as his eyes darkened and his gaze flitted down to my lips again. But he pushed back and left the room.

Rufus, who owned the house we were living in, was cordial, and treated me like Quentin's lover. He was full of cute little comments about my figure, immediately turning to Quentin to ask if he'd gotten any sleep the night before. I didn't ask why or how Quentin came to be staying at his house, and he didn't say.

Rarely did our host address me directly, and I knew virtually nothing about him. That was okay, though. I wasn't sure I wouldn't lift something real heavy and use it to wipe the smirk from his face.

I had a feeling Winzey would have a say in that. At least keeping her a secret had been easy. And it was nice to have a friend, even if I dared not think or talk about her much. Especially her name. She'd repeated over and over that her name was the key to her power. Knowing it made her as powerful as one of the gems.

Quentin woke me before dawn the third morning with a curt, "Get up." It was the harshest I'd heard him yet and I wasn't going to cross him. He'd never been deliberately mean, I rationalized, but brooding, almost frustrated.

Whatever had been chewing on his behind must have broken through the skin. He was nothing short of a grizzly bear this morning. And it wasn't going to have a chance to get me.

Quentin's room was next to mine. The sounds of drawers sliding in and out and hangers rattling against each other were unmistakable through the walls. I hadn't used my magic in days, and yes, was tempted to do so now. But I feared what I'd learn from his angry thoughts.

It was ballsy, considering his rush, but I methodically gathered my clothes and padded toward the bathroom.

"What are you doing?" He appeared at his doorway.

"Taking a shower, did you need to get in here? I assumed you were done."

"We don't have time for a shower."

"*We* don't, but I do. If you wanted to leave right away you should have woken me earlier."

I fought back a grin while he narrowed his eyes and tapped his foot. Probably silently cussing me out. I wouldn't turn on the mental walkie-talkie and give him the pleasure of knowing I was listening.

Winzey, curled up in my clean socks, hissed at me to stop antagonizing him. My only retort would have been to ask her how such a little thing could use such big vocabulary.

"Then hurry. We need to leave."

"Where are we going? I really should know so I can dress for the occasion." I couldn't help the sass. It just fell from my mouth. After two days of silence I was just about to come undone.

"Away." His teeth gritted as he spoke. At least I could still strike a nerve. Without a bit of magic either.

"You're cute when you're mad."

That wasn't the right thing to say. His green eyes widened and turned black. His lips curled in a snarl. I stepped backward for each step he took forward. I'd run out of space before he would, making the end result inevitable.

I was half amused but also rather ticked off at the way he pushed. I ignored the tiny bit of fear, only because I was great at self-denial.

The house was quiet, but I doubted Rufus would respond if I were to scream. I turned and ran into the bathroom and tried to push the door closed. When my own strength wouldn't work, I resorted to the muscle of magic.

Quentin already had his hand around the door. The last thing I wanted to do was crush it in the jam. Even if I thought he deserved it for the last few days. I shoved Winzey, socks and all into the cabinet under the sink and relaxed. He'd won this round.

My throat constricted when he locked the door behind him. He was pumped up and seemed bigger than ever. I pretended I wasn't on the verge of peeing my pants and stood my ground. I met him eye to eye. I had to be careful not to flinch when his eyes changed chameleon-like while his gaze stroked my body.

This was it.

The mirror fogged up faster than if I'd been standing in a hot shower. His hand snaked out and grabbed me by the throat. Not in a death grip, but a caress both solid and gentle. My will was crumbling under his touch.

"Listen to me."

"I—" I had to clear my throat. My voice box had already given up the ghost with the tension in the room. "I am listening. You're not talking. You're doing."

His fingers slid over my cheek. His thumb found my temple and pushed with the slightest of pressure. "Listen here."

I quit fighting the mental touch. Even if I had wanted to, I couldn't have kept his thoughts from melding with mine. When he spoke to me mentally, his voice was low, his breathing labored. His erotic thoughts were enough to make me sink to the edge of the bathtub.

"No. It's not right," I said out loud.

"It is. We'll be good together. You know it."

I looked anywhere to keep from falling into the spell of his eyes. It was only postponement, I knew. But I wouldn't surrender. "You were in a hurry. I need to take a shower."

"Undress. Turn on the water."

Being the sucker I am I looked right into his eyes. Just like he had planned. "No," I mumbled with all the fight I had left.

His hand traveled around my face, just grazing my lips. It was amazing how such a small touch left my body pleading for more. He stepped past me and turned the water on. "Undress."

"This isn't a striptease joint. Please. Leave the room and I promise I'll hurry." I barely choked out the last few words. His eyes smoldered like burnt charcoal, his lips parted and advanced much too quickly in my direction. And I wanted it.

It wasn't a lover's kiss. It was desperate, demanding and all the while he filled my head with images of what it would be like. I knew what it would feel like to have his hands on me. And I wanted it.

He'd never separated our lips, but my clothes vanished. His own were finding their way to the tiled floor as well. When his mouth left mine it burned a path down my throat. The beads nestled there hummed and pulsed like an extension of my heart.

My hands slid under the waistband of his cotton pants. Quentin answered my moan with his own as he guided my hand to find the full length of him. He was hot, hard and ready. I wanted it now.

"Not yet," he mumbled in a voice that sounded almost as frantic as I felt. The tremble in his words gave me a boost of power. It wasn't simply a conquest thing in my mind anymore. This was a game of equals. Give and take.

His head dipped lower, finding the rosy peak of my breast that strained for his attention. His hot, wet tongue managed to show me give and take all at the same time.

I slid down his boxer briefs. He released me from his oral assault and freed himself of the rest of his clothes. We stood in the puddles of our garments, flushed, panting and naked. I waited for him to come back to me, to touch me. His mind continued the mental movie of wet flesh, tangled arms and legs and desperate gasps as he pinned me against the shower wall.

I could barely stand. Yet he didn't move.

His eyes finally flitted behind me. I followed his gaze. The shower. "Aren't you going to get in?" he asked, as if he wasn't standing there in full arousal.

"Yeah." It came out a hoarse whisper.

I stepped over the tub and gave the curtain a frustrated tug. Messing with me. He was freaking playing with my head and I fell for it. Now he knew what putty I became at his simple kiss

A flick of the wrist sent the water to an icy stream. My chastisement. I let it pummel my aching breasts and run down to cool the fever between my legs. This wasn't fair. I closed my eyes and tried to think of anything but him. Tried to forget the musky, masculine smell that permeated the room.

Then I felt him behind me. His hands slid up my water slick waist and cupped my breasts. Even the cold water couldn't stop the renewed rush I felt. He teased the back of my neck with his teeth, leaning forward so I could feel him hard against my back.

"Warm the water up, Ella. You don't need to punish yourself for this. How can something so good be bad?"

He had a point. What harm would there be? What if? I readjusted the water and turned to face him.

His hair was wet and slicked back off his face. An outline of stubble darkened his cheeks and chin, making him dangerous looking. And just plain dangerous. Water beaded on his lips; I licked my own, impulsively wondering what he would taste like.

"Taste," he whispered, dipping his head to mine.

That was all it took. Our wet bodies skimmed off each other. I'm surprised the water didn't boil at our feet.

His fingers encouraged my nerve endings to scream with sensitivity, leaving me shuddering and gripping him for balance when they circled my nipples and dipped low on my stomach.

I slid my hand around him. Would I simply go crazy before I felt him inside me? His touch answered that. "Now," I demanded.

"Not yet," he muttered against my lips, his fingers teasing and probing the most vital spot until I thought he'd drive me over the edge before we got to the best part.

He used the magic to hold me up, back against the tile. I didn't care. I might have used my own if I'd been able to control it.

"Tune into me." I did. I felt him hot against me. I writhed to position him, moaning when he didn't fill me immediately. "Feel what it's like," he commanded.

I realized what he meant. I felt his throbbing anticipation against mine when his satiny length finally slid inside. Our minds connected, co-mingling the bursting sensations when we touched in the most intimate way.

His fingers gripped my thighs, waiting, holding, until he pulled back, then pressed forward again. Muddled with my own pleasure, I knew the exact level of his own. I traced my nails down his back, and felt both the exterior and interior tightening reaction.

And like a violin string, the tension wound tighter, until it all broke loose. He caught my final moan in his mouth, finishing the erotic feelings with an immeasurable awareness of each other's satisfaction. I raked his back, knowing I had torn open flesh. His hands would leave their own fingerprints in the flesh of my hips.

ଓ ଓ ଓ

The water was gone. I opened my eyes, expecting to find myself simply moved out of reach of the shower's spray.

What the hell is going on? I sat cross-legged on a blanket with food spread out picnic style. I was dressed. The sun shone overhead, oblivious to my confusion.

"What did you do now?" I demanded of my companion.

"I figured a little exercise would rustle up an appetite. And what's better than a picnic of fried chicken and apple pie?"

I stared for a minute out of the corner of my eyes. Picnic. Yeah. "Were we just, uh, in the shower?" I pointed over my shoulder, but who knows where said bathroom was now.

Quentin winked. "Yeah, but the nice thing about magic is you can skip all the awkward stuff and get right to the good things in life. Like food."

Hello. I just had awesome sex. The best of my life, in fact, and this man was able to snap his fingers and get food ready.

He was reading my thoughts. "It's better than a cigarette, right? Besides, it would've gotten soggy under all that water."

I nodded my head. This was a whole new reality. I still kept expecting the Candid Camera guy. But let's hope they missed taping this morning's episode. Wowza. That would have been embarrassing.

"Bare-assing is the better said term for it."

"Shut up, Quentin. I'm trying to convince myself this is really happening."

"You regretting it?"

Million dollar question. "Should I?"

"No." He took a bite from a chicken leg. His nonchalance did little to ease the butterflies in my stomach. "It was bound to happen. We've been attracted to each other from the beginning."

"But you've been a whole different person these last few days."

"Was. I had Mr. B's people closing in. I was waiting for Sam. He never showed. We had to get the heck out of there. Especially after the shower. We used way too much magic. They'd have found us in a heartbeat if we'd stayed even long enough to get dressed."

So we jumped again and left Sam behind. And...I couldn't think of it. I almost asked if he'd pulled my socks from under the cabinet. No. No reason to cast suspicion. "Now what?"

"Eat your lunch."

I was hungry. I ate and studied Quentin. He was no longer the brooding, dark soul I'd seen the last few days, but he wasn't quite the jokester who'd taken me to the landfill either. While I definitely wished Sam was around to tell me if we were running from something or after something—and all the details that go along with it, I decided it wasn't so bad to be here with Quentin like this. It felt...normal.

"I wish I wouldn't have eaten so much." I leaned back and patted my stomach.

Quentin leaned up against the tree and looked out over the view he had chosen. A few small sailboats bobbed in the bay beneath the hill where we sat. The gentle melody of water lapping against the sand rocked me to sleep. My eyes were just about closed when he spoke.

"You didn't tell me what happened when you went after your purse."

"I was followed. Then cornered. Then rescued." I only opened one eye wide enough to watch his features. Nothing unexpected.

"By who? Where and then who again?"

I reached for my glass of lemonade, lifting it with magic when my arm was too short. "Who ever followed me was invisible. From what I could tell, two guys. I got lost—"

"I figured that was going to happen."

I plucked an ice cube from my glass and tossed it at him. He caught it and raised an eyebrow. "I've heard a lot of nice things about ice cubes and hot bodies. Don't waste these."

I stuck my tongue out. "Do you really want to know this story or do you want to talk dirty?"

"If you're asking—never mind...just tell me."

"Quentin." I rolled my eyes mentally. I was too tired to open them.

"No. Honest. I'd like to hear it." He popped the ice cube in his mouth and smiled with it between his teeth.

"They followed me into this storage building. I thought they were going to kill me. I managed to use some magic and get away. But only temporarily. Then some guy named Jim grabbed me and zapped us off to some island."

Quentin leaned forward then. His hair dropped over his forehead and hid half of his eyes. I almost reached out and brushed away the hair when he spoke. “An island, really?”

“Well, we went to this house first, but then an island. He thought we’d be safer there while we figured out what we were going to do. He said he used to be Sam’s partner. I don’t quite understand how their relationship went. Not even sure what side he was on. He creeped me out. But then a bad storm blew in and it was either get sucked up in it or zap back. I pictured your face and tried the gems.” I shrugged. “They worked.”

Quentin’s left eyebrow was still missing under the dark shock of hair. I didn’t think he believed me much.

“You found me all by yourself?”

“I don’t know how I found you. I wished for a warm fire, blankets and a cup of cocoa and ended up outside your house.”

Quentin stood up and paced the ridge.

“What. What is it?” I brushed the crumbs off my lap and downed the last of my cool drink. “What’s the matter?”

“If you found me so easily, why hasn’t Sam been able to?”

Sam. Damnit. Where was he? I got up and stood beside Quentin. “You don’t think they ah, got a hold of him do you?”

I crossed my arms over my chest and stared at the toy boats on the horizon. Quentin wrapped his arms around mine and tucked his chin on my shoulder. “No. Sam’s a strong magician. Quite trusted. He’s probably carrying out a plan to make sure all goes well.”

“I hope you’re right.” I leaned back against him. I could almost let myself relax like this. I hadn’t really felt comfortable enough to do that since these shenanigans started.

“So now what? Where do we go, what do we do?”

“The big picture is to find a way to bring Mr. B down so the gems can be saved from the hands of evil.”

I had to laugh. “You sound like a commercial for the newest space age movie.”

“I watch too much TV, so sue me.” He nipped at my chin.

“Okay, after you become the savior of the universe, then what?”

“We get married, have little magicians and keep the spirit alive.”

“Well, Quentin, dear,” I did my best Scarlett O’Hara, “are you proposing to me?”

He winced.

"I didn't think so."

"I didn't mean it like that."

"Would it make you feel better to know I'd refuse had you been serious?"

"No."

I practically snorted with laughter. So I'm not very lady-like. "Egotistical male."

"Pompous bitch."

"Damn right." I love having the last word.

Quentin pointed his finger and led the sailboats back toward the harbor.

I narrowed my eyes and watched their journey stop. "Why?"

He shrugged. "Because I can."

"We aren't supposed to use magic like that."

"But everyone does. It didn't hurt anyone."

"I bet someone on that little boat is heaving over the side right now because of you."

Quentin played an invisible violin.

"Jerk." I stomped back toward the picnic and started folding the blanket.

"Leave it."

"I'm not going to leave it." I turned to find Quentin standing right behind me. "That's littering."

"It's not ours."

"That's not right." How could I have eaten someone else's lunch? How could Quentin have let me? "Were you planning to just disappear and pretend Yogi and Boo-Boo had come and raided their picky-nick basket?"

Quentin's serious face relaxed into a wide grin. "C'mere." He crooked his finger at me. I felt a twinge of something primitive in my chest. I wondered on what level he was calling me.

I stepped forward, feeling like I was walking out onto the ledge of a bungee jump rather than just across a small expanse of grass. But this time I knew what the heck I was getting into. Funny, I was still shaking.

He grabbed my hand. Tingles originated from where his skin touched mine. I wanted to hesitate, think about what I was willing to commit to.

I had no choice, no chance to even drag my feet. Only moments after my hand slipped into his he'd zapped us into the strobe brightened travel tunnel. We were off again.

I'd never get used to this.

Chapter Nine

"You could have at least picked someplace warm," I choked out through the shivers that rattled my teeth. We'd landed, if you call it that, in a desert of white. No mountains, no water and no sign of civilization.

Quentin's smart ass response was to wrap me in caveman era fur clothing.

I remembered the exchange rate. "I hope you haven't left some dear woman naked in a compromising position." I lifted my feet to see what suddenly had them oven warm. The fur-lined boots were dry, but way too big for my average sized feet.

"It was a he, and he won't miss them."

"Oh?"

"He's dead."

Dead? I was wearing the coat of a dead man? I wriggled and shrugged until the garments lay like a boneless animal in the snow.

"Put them back on."

"Uh-huh, no way. I'm not wearing a dead man's clothes."

"Fine." Quentin shook his head and picked up the cape like hooded coat. "I will then. I'm not sending it back and I won't leave it laying here."

I kept the boots. The shoes I had beneath them would become solid ice cubes in the deep drifts. Still, these were awkward, threatening to slide off my feet when I struggled to pull them from the deep snow. Each step was a burden. I bet we hadn't gone twenty feet when I called Quentin to stop.

"Why? We want to find camp before nightfall."

"Camp?" As far as I could see it was all white. The horizon blended in with the sky in light shades of gray. "How far away is the camp?" I shivered again. I couldn't believe it would be a little pop-up tent in the middle of this frozen world, but that's exactly the picture that came to mind.

"Several miles."

"Miles?"

"Yep."

"Isn't there a better way to get there?"

Quentin looked the part of prehistoric man in the fur get up. I rubbed my hands up and down my arms and then burrowed them into my pockets. I wouldn't be able to walk miles like this. I'd surely die of—what's it called?

"Hypothermia. Do you want one of these yet?" He pulled away the outer cloak to point to the smaller, thicker one inside.

"Is it gross?" I swear my breath plumed out in front of me, crystallized and fell to the ground. I couldn't believe I was thinking about it.

"No, it's not gross."

"Are you always tuned into my thoughts?"

"No. But I check in on occasion."

"That's not really nice, you know." I accept the fur with great reluctance. It stunk like unwashed skin and spoiled food.

"They don't have washer and dryer hook-ups just anywhere around here." They probably didn't have a department store they could walk in and buy one either.

"Nothing like that. Not even a dry cleaners."

I fisted my hands between the warm folds and vowed to bathe as soon as it was possible. "Where is here, by the way."

"You'll be angry. I'll just say it's a resting place, a spot we can talk, plan and I can help you hone your magic skills."

"I really want to learn fire first."

"Uh, no," he stated flatly.

Damn. I trudged behind him, realizing it was less effort to step into his footsteps than break through the thick icy layer that coated the landscape.

"Go ahead, tell me." I had to know.

"When we get where we're going. I'm not going to debate this with you."

"I won't debate. I promise, Quentin. Puh-lease?"

He sighed. His breath floated like a murky cloud that obscured his features for a moment. I didn't know if he was serious or not. "We're at the North Pole."

"Oh, yeah, right." I looked up in case Santa and his reindeer were circling overhead. I wonder if the reindeer pooped while flying. That'd be really nasty if it landed on your head.

"Ella!" His stern tone was ineffective with the laugh at the end.

"What?" Innocent me.

"I really didn't need that mental picture."

"Hey, well, anything to entertain us. It's not like there's much in the way of sightseeing."

I glanced in all four directions. Absolutely nothing out there to tell me which way was which. The only clue to show where we'd been was the snake-like trail of footprints.

"Which direction are we walking?"

"South."

"Where are we going?"

"Someplace safe."

"Quentin, damn you. I'm cold, tired and my feet ache. I smell and I'm getting very hungry. I'd like to know a little about my fate."

"Ok," his voice was calmer, quieter. "Listen, I think common sense will tell you I have no desire to sleep out here in the cold. Can you just trust me for once?"

"Bite me," I shot back.

"No thanks, but the polar bears or artic wolves might be interested."

My eyes widened and searched out every possible place for such creatures to hide. They'd have to be buried under the snow. I relaxed. I was safe. For now.

He pushed forward, and I followed. I tried counting our steps, but soon got depressed by how few we made per minute. I pictured life on the equator.

"Tell me about Central America," I prompted Quentin after I thought I wouldn't get the "I know more than you" attitude.

"It's hot."

"Lovely," I responded. Even I knew that. "Continue."

He described the oppressing heat and clouds of dust. He was trying to make it sound like a miserable place. I thought it sounded like heaven itself.

The temporary vision did help me through a good fifteen minutes of steady walking.

Finally I saw something in the distance. Something colorful. My stomach growled and my shivers turned to trembles of excitement. Shelter. Warmth. Fire. Yesssss.

"Is that a mirage?"

Quentin stopped. I was so intent on squinting into the white haze to make out what I thought I could see, I plowed right into the back of him. Then fell backwards.

Since I weigh more than a hundred pounds, I sank butt first through the icy crust and became helplessly lodged.

Under the shadow of the furry hood he'd drawn over his head, I could detect the twinkle in Quentin's green eyes.

"Wanna help me up or are you going to just gape at me?" I made a snowball, using magic, not my bare hands, and hurled it at him.

"Obviously you haven't practiced much," he jeered when the flying snow zinged past him. "Nice pitch, though, if this had been a baseball game."

"My pants are soaked, my legs and backside are numb."

"Then don't waste your parlor tricks on me, Wonder Woman. Get yourself out of there."

"How?" When I pushed against the snow to propel myself upwards my arms sank deep. A million tiny pin pricks assaulted my arms. That was cold!

"You look like a frog. Or a grasshopper. All knees and elbows."

"Damn it, Quentin. I'm a human freakin' ice cube here. Show some mercy."

"Then get up. You want me to feel sorry for you, walk over there and pick you up?" He acted as if I asked for a ride to the moon.

"Yes. A little help would be nice." I gritted my teeth in an attempt to be civil.

"So would a warm fire and hot cocoa, or coffee even. Unfortunately, we have neither."

"Quentin!"

Was I attracted to this punk? Was he the same man who'd breathlessly seduced me? Talk about a change of attitude. Yeah, well, maybe I did egg him on a bit, but for crying out loud, he was getting his kicks at my expense. I could swear frostbite was already setting in on my upper legs. If I could get up, I'd find a way to kick his ass.

"Ella, be serious." He rolled his eyes at me.

He must have read my thoughts again.

"I did."

"Figures. Not an ounce of privacy around you."

"That's not true."

"Yeah." After he'd admitted he "checked in" from time to time I can't say those three words were real convincing.

"Cut the sarcasm and I'll tell you how to escape your predicament."

I stared at him, waiting.

"Remember the first time we met?"

Oh, yes indeed. The kiss that rocked my world. Did he want to melt the snow around me?

"After that. When you tossed me in the air."

I shrugged. That wasn't as exciting. "Yeah."

"Toss yourself in the air."

"Huh?"

"Push up and imagine yourself floating."

"You've got to be kidding me."

"Try it." Funny, it sounded like he was talking through gritted teeth.

Fine. I'd try. What was it going to hurt?

I thought about it. Magic, huh? I could push myself above the surface? I closed my eyes and pictured a giant hand reaching up under my derriere and lifting me above the surface of the snow.

"Good!" Quentin shouted.

I opened my eyes, realized I was about ten feet above the snow and prompted tumbled back toward the ground. I just knew I was going to end up worse off than the first time.

Something stopped me. "Hey!" I tried to face Quentin, but my jerky movement in that direction had me pivoting. What was I, a marionette?

"I got you, but only for a moment. Pretend there are giant soles on your shoes, walk on air."

If I was going to do that, why couldn't I simply fly?

"No control."

It dawned on me. "You mean we could have floated toward this camp site rather than trudge through miles of miserable snow? What are you, a glutton for punishment? Do you like being miserable?"

"Get down here. Save your strength."

"You said this was a resting place. Why should I worry about saving it?"

"You never know." He reached up and took my hand, tugging me back down to earth. He lifted my chin with the crook of his finger. "Ella, you have to trust me. Please. Sometimes you won't be able to question me, or see the why behind what I say. Just trust me, okay?"

"I don't get it, Quen. I just don't get this at all."

"You don't have to. Just promise me you'll behave."

"You're treating me like a twelve-year-old."

His face was suddenly close, too close. "I wouldn't do this if you were twelve." His warm lips met mine, pressing, kneading, coaxing them apart. I leaned into him, letting his tongue graze past my teeth and inject a new kind of heat into my body.

I felt much colder when he stepped back. But at least it seemed what had happened this morning, or whenever it was, hadn't been a fluke.

"No. It wasn't a fluke. Don't even think it."

The words worked like fuel on the fire that had started somewhere in my chest. I didn't analyze it, just reveled in it. It got me through the last leg of the journey without another peep about the temperature or aches in my bones.

Camp was a deserted building just as cold as the barren fields outside it. Thank God the wind didn't slice through the walls. It tried, howling through all the invisible crevices. Did I mention it was dark? Black as pitch inside.

"I just bet there's no electricity here is there, brain child?" I wasn't sure where Quentin was in the room, but he was undoubtedly in hearing range.

"Nope. I'm trying to find matches."

Matches? Wasn't this a man who could do magic? Couldn't he make fire?

"Found 'em!" he cried triumphantly. Guess he wasn't listening to me.

I listened for the scrape of the match and the flare of light. Quentin had found an oil lamp.

The inside of the building came to life in a flicker of orange. It was divided in half, one part a cold, empty laboratory area, the other a less than cozy living area. At least there was a fireplace.

"You are going to light a fire, right?"

"Of course." He strode toward the wood piled beside it. I was way confused. Why wasn't he using magic to get it done faster? With little thought I lifted a log and set it on the half charred pieces that had been left in the fireplace. Quentin sat back on his heels, but didn't turn around.

Something was definitely going on. My gems, now a fixture around my neck, throbbed with the use of power. Other than the little push in the snow, I hadn't used them much.

Was he waiting to see if I could start it? Could I? If I could, did I want him to know? He didn't answer. I had to guess he wasn't reading my mind.

I had done it before, hadn't I? Breathed fire. Well, that's not exactly the effect I needed now, unless I wanted to be the human torch. I thought it best I keep that little trick a secret.

I crossed my fingers and reached. Deep, deep down into the energy that was bundled in my cramped toes, aching calves, and stiff fingers. I drew in breath after breath and willed it to a central spot in my chest. It was time.

I pointed my finger at the center of the log. With knowledge that must have been the most primitive, because *I* certainly don't know how I did it, I transferred the power to my shaking fist.

I didn't trust myself. "Quentin, you wanna move?"

No comment, no glance in my direction, but he got up and stood against the adjoining wall.

"All right." I took a deep breath. "Here goes."

I swear it was the rise and fall of my chest and the shivers that still pulsed through my body that caused me to miss. And the recoil. I could blame the recoil.

The fireball bounced off the brick wall and landed just about where Quentin had been. Of course.

He jumped over and stomped out the red embers on the carpet. I expected something along the lines of “Nicely done, Ella.” Purely sarcastic, of course. But he backed up against the wall again.

Concentrate, I told myself. I found the strength easier this time, still smoldering. I stoked it up and let it roll down my arm, puddle like lava in my fist.

I pointed my finger as if it were a long range rifle. I stepped forward, bent my knees and braced myself. Ready. *It’s now or never.* Aim. *Fingers still crossed.* Fire.

I ducked behind the couch when the log exploded into splinters. *Well, I guess we have kindling wood now.*

The oil lamp was on the ground, a figure curled next to it. Had I hit him? Had those flying pieces flown into him like a hundred tiny wooden stakes?

He didn’t move when I stood over him. I nudged him with my foot. “Quentin?” I was scared he wouldn’t answer.

“Are we dead yet?”

“No. But it’s cold and if we don’t get the fire lit, we might have the option of freezing to death.”

“I thought you were trying to blow this place up.”

I shrugged. Sorry wasn’t really an option, was it? I was too exhilarated with the power I had found to feel very remorseful. “No...I just um, atomized the log. Shall I put another one—?”

“No,” he cut in, waving his hands, and the light, above his head. “I’ll do it already. The old fashioned way.”

He doubted me, did he? I snapped around and tossed another piece of split wood where the other one had sat. For good measure I commanded all the tiny pieces to pile themselves around it. To my surprise, that all worked without a glitch.

I was physically exhausted. It had been a long day. Great sex, two travels and a trek through the tundra had drained me. The two previous fireballs hadn’t helped. But I was closer. I might be able to make this one happen.

There wasn’t much fire left in me. I let it swirl around while I chewed on the idea of Quentin thinking I couldn't do it. Wow. That helped.

I concentrated on the small slivers that surrounded the log. They would light easily. They only need a gentle touch. I squinted in the pale light and ran my fingers over the picture of the hearth I had in my head. Spark, I commanded. The light of a match.

The heat burned my fingertips. I held steady despite the pain. I envisioned the flames catching, growing. The heat was beautiful. The sun on my face.

"Shit, Ella. Holy Shit!" Quentin tackled me, grabbed me under one arm and dragged me outside.

"Quentin, the fire, I lit the fire. Why—"

He grabbed my wrist and shoved my hand deep in the snow.

I wanted to howl from the agony of it. "Damn it. That...it effing hurts!" I shouted.

Laughter bubbled up out of Quentin.

"It's not freaking funny," I tried to slap at him with my uninjured hand, but he scooted out of the way.

"Effing? Effing? Ella, if you're gonna say it, go for the gusto."

Oh, I was saying it all right, over and over. Mentally. I couldn't push it past my lips.

"You a coward? Think your Sunday school teacher is going to hear you? There's nothing but a few polar bears for hundreds of miles and you can't bring yourself to say a simple word?"

"It doesn't matter what I say, Quentin. It's not going to take the pain away."

I thought he was going to fall back in the snow laughing so hard. And if he did, I just might feel enough compassion to bury him up to his chin and let him worry about frostbite in his delicate areas. All I wanted was to sit with my hand buried deep in the snow and writhe in the pain. I could almost envision the tips of those digits tearing open and peeling like a boiled tomato. I bet that's what they looked like too.

Chapter Ten

Quentin's patch job on my hand made it look like I was holding a balloon creation of Mickey Mouse's white glove. I wondered if he'd find a black marker and draw the little knuckle dimples on it for me, just because.

So this is what I get for trying some great magic trick. Turning my fingers into matchsticks wasn't such a great idea, but at least we had heat.

But I was still perplexed. Quentin hadn't done an ounce of magic since we'd left the picnic site. Other than the traveling, but I couldn't remember if he'd reached up for my gems. Something was wrong.

Sigh. For the first time in a while I had time to relax and think. My first concern was Sam. Quentin had said something about meeting him at the big house on the coast. Rufus's house. But something had chased us out of there. I wondered if it was Mr. B's people. I hadn't thought about Mr. B and his mob-like magicians lately. That had been nice.

Shit. I hoped they hadn't gotten to Sam. He was a powerful man. He could have avoided it, I convinced myself. Still, they wanted our gems and they knew of our loyalty to Sam. He could be the bait. We were the mice and Mr. B was the cat.

I shivered. *Oh, Ella. Get over it girl. You don't know what happened.* Sam could be out there single handedly eliminating creep after creep while Quentin trained me. The idea of being a magic driven warrior wasn't any more comforting.

I rolled over and clutched the blanket under my chin. I slept.

☙ ☙ ☙

The voices were hushed. The oil lamp had been turned off. I knew what they said was meant to be a secret. When my ears couldn't decipher the mumbled words, I turned my magical mental radar in the direction of the conversation.

"No, Mr. B can't know we're here. She needs protection. Trust me. We're nearly untraceable here."

"We picked up the vibrations of magic from this area last night. That's how we found you." I didn't recognize the second voice. The first was Quentin. No doubt there.

I rolled over and pushed my head under the blanket. I didn't want to know more. This was scaring me.

"I'll keep her from doing anything further, at least until we get into the underground tunnels. There we can practice undetected."

I realized now Quentin was saying I led this person to us. My fireballs must have been one heck of a powerful flare.

"You should've taken her somewhere you would blend in. There are many places magic is normal, expected. Las Vegas for example. Or back to Hollywood."

"You forget, Frederique, she escaped me there. I've got keep her with me until she trusts me."

"Ah, Quentin. She did not escape as much as you lost her." The laugh crawled over my skin like giant bugs. I hate bugs.

"It won't happen again."

God, the formality of this conversation. I lifted the covers and turned to gaze at the fire. It was the only light in the room, and definitely not bright enough to allow me to see their silhouettes, much less any of their features.

I willed the flames to die down. Quentin swore. A chair scraped the floor. I had hoped the visitor would follow him to the hearth and give me the chance to see his features.

I studied Quentin's broad back. The edges of the silhouette blurred as he tossed another log on the ashes. The glowing embers spilled to the floor of the hearth like neon lit sands. The conversation was over. Or else I was too tired to eavesdrop any longer. I let my eyelashes fall closed. I would learn no more tonight.

Quentin was up and banging dishes around. Intentionally, I guessed. He'd wanted to wake me.

"Do you think you could keep it down?" I muttered, yanking the covers up over my eyes.

"Rise and shine, little one. We've got a big practice day ahead of us."

"Oh?" I queried. "After coffee and breakfast I hope."

"You've got to get up and come over here if you're going to eat."

I moaned, more for the sake of protest, and got up. I bypassed the table and headed to the bathroom first. It reminded me of the tiny toilets most camping trailers had. Except this one had a coffee can full of water sitting on the tank. Melted snow, I assumed. For flushing. "Not much better than a tent," I muttered.

I ate alone. Quentin said he'd eaten hours ago and had given up on me waking on my own. I told him how much I appreciated his kindness. He retreated outside.

I scraped the plate clean. There was no telling when my next meal would be. Well, there was always the furniture. It wouldn't really taste too much different, now would it?

"I heard that!"

"Ah, so you're listening!"

Quentin dropped a load of frost covered firewood next to the diminishing stash. He huffed and brushed the snow from his hair. "It's snowing again and blowing. There's a lower level, two if I read the notes correctly. Looks like a fireplace down there as well."

I sat in front of the fire and pulled the blanket around me. "Why are you bringing in more wood then?"

"So we have it. This storm may just blow hard enough we won't be able to open the door tomorrow morning."

I could hear the gale force winds. I did not want to venture outside. "So what do I do?"

"Gee, Ella, don't sound so excited."

"You're telling me there wasn't some empty gymnasium in Oklahoma we could have used for this practice?"

"The last thing we need is for someone to find us."

Was I mistaken? Hadn't we had a visitor last night? Did I want to know? I decided I'd wait for Quentin to tell me. No sense making him suspicious before I knew more. "You sure made certain that wasn't going to happen, didn't you, genius?"

He ignored me and looked over my shoulder. "Grab everything you can find that will hold snow. Carry them over near the fire. Keep filling them until they're full of water."

The task sounded easy enough. I held my breath as I shrugged on the heavy fur. I really would have killed for a pair of gloves. Quentin had found a pair, or imported a pair, but he really did need them more than I. I wasn't that cruel.

After my fifteenth trip from the door to the giant tub I'd dragged over to the hearth, I was really to spit nails. After twenty I was cursing under my breath at every step I took. My fingers on my good hand had long since gone numb. They'd fall right off my hands any second now. My other hand throbbed. It might have been cold, but I couldn't feel it for the incessant pain.

Quentin just hauled in a forest worth of logs and stood thawing himself as I paced back and forth. I had no previous knowledge that snow melts down to water that is only a fraction of its original volume. There are so many things that I knew had to have been created just to make me miserable. God, if he was up there, was laughing his butt off at me, I just knew it.

Then I thought about Noah. If this snow were water, we'd be sunk. Literally.

"What!" I screeched when I walked in with my self-declared final bucket and saw Quentin had taken my perfectly good, clean blanket and piled the dry logs on it. I was not going to be able to sleep amongst the splinters. No way, no how.

"It's better than making a dozen trips."

"What, like you made me do?"

He shrugged. But that's good. That's okay. Really. The last straw would have been to listen to him tell me what I *should* have done to make the job easier.

"Damn, I'm cold," I announced as I held my hands in front of the fire. The flame nearly touched the bandages on my hand. They were soaked.

Quentin must have noticed them. "Let me help you get those off.

Wet, right?"

"Like a baby's diaper after a four hour nap."

"God, Ella, couldn't you have been a little less graphic? I don't want to imagine you used your hand instead of the toilet paper this morning."

I watched as he unwound the cloth, revealing red, wrinkled skin. "You call that stuff toilet paper? Well, paper yes, tissue, no. Closer to sand paper."

"It's probably been here for years."

"That makes me feel better."

Wriggle your fingers, El."

I obeyed. I still felt like the top of my fingers were missing. They were there, I could see. Stretched, shiny, with blisters dotting the perimeter of the angry red skin. Nothing could be prettier.

"Sam would heal these for you. I'm not sure I can. So let's stick to real life and dress them back up when we get downstairs. There's another first aid kit under the sink. I found it this morning."

"They must have known I was coming."

So Sam could heal. I wondered if he could heal himself. Then I wouldn't stress about his disappearance. Hell, who was I kidding? I was worried. Mr. B was out there with control of nearly all the stones. Sam was missing and I'd been kidnapped and buried under a ton of snow in Santa's Village. What a save the world crusade this was turning out to be.

At least I'd have a heck of a story to tell my sister when I made it home. And Jesse. She'd never believe it.

"Are you going to stand there in your daydreams or are we heading down?"

Uh, couldn't I just tap the gems together and land in Maui or something? "I'm right behind you."

It seemed warmer down there. Maybe because the walls weren't being pummeled with sub-zero winds. The fireplace was smaller, certainly less than cozy.

"Get the fire going already. I'll go back up. What else do we need?"

He shook his head. "You'll be starting the fire."

I waggled my fingers at him. "I don't think I've fully recovered from the last one. You can use the matches. It's okay."

He lodged a log in the opening. “Go on, give it your best shot.”

I was shaking, and it wasn’t just from the temperature. I was not going to burn myself again. I folded my hands beneath my armpits to protect them and narrowed my eyes at the log. I couldn’t feel anything in my chest, and I didn’t reach for any reserves. I pictured the tongues of the flame in the hearth one level up. I imagined them devouring this log.

“Was that smoke?” I jumped up and down and bounced closer. “Did I really make it smoke?”

“I think it was the log sighing at you.”

“Stop it. I did.” I stared at the hearth with my best threatening look. I normally would imagine myself throwing daggers at the object. This time, I threw little matches worth of fire.

“Hey!” Quentin yelped.

I thought maybe my aim was really off again. But he was okay. Smart boy. He was behind me. And in front of me? Well, it wasn’t a blazing fire worthy of toasted marshmallows, but the corner of the log was glowing orange.

“Don’t stop now, Madame Flame Thrower.”

I let the matches grow to little flares. It only took two of those to catch a flame on the peeling bark. I had done it. And managed not to hurt myself or Quentin.

“I did it!” I jumped up and threw myself straight into Quentin’s arms. I didn’t stop jumping, despite the fact his feet seemed glued to the floor. “I made fire, I made fire.”

“You controlled the fire, dear. But with all your bouncing against the front of me, I think you started more than one fire in here.”

“I…what?” I pulled back, but he stopped me. His hips ground against mine. Even with the layers of smelly fur between us I could feel exactly what he was talking about. He was hot. And my temperature was rising too.

“You make me crazy. In more than one way,” he muttered against my throat.

I didn’t respond. I could only think of one way to make him crazy. And I was working on seeing if I could fan the flames of insanity.

My good hand slid through the opening of his coat and slid over the roughened denim. He moaned when I cupped the center of his madness.

I couldn't help the wicked smile that pulled at my face when he leaned into my palm. Power.

My control slipped when he turned his mouth to capture mine in an intensely erotic kiss. I have to say, Quentin didn't waste any time using his tongue to make the rest of my body ache. I imagined the damage his mouth could do on the rest of my body.

"Remember when I said you were a girl after my own heart?"

"Um."

"You keep thinking thoughts like that and I'll swear you were made for me."

"Um...oh!" Quentin's hand slid up under my shirt and found one of the places where all the nerve endings met. I tilted my head back to his onslaught. If his intention was to make a wet trail of kisses on every piece of exposed flesh then start with the unexposed bits, I was all for it. I just wished he'd hurry it up.

"This isn't what I had in mind when I said we were going to practice magic, you know." He nuzzled a sensitive spot just below my earlobe. My knees were becoming mush. I was not going to remain standing for much longer. Clothed either, if I had my way.

Quentin growled and pushed the fur off my shoulders. His sparkling eyes met mine. He was listening to my rambling thoughts. Connection on all those levels had me absolutely amazed.

"Lift your arms," he commanded. His voice was more like a caress. Like a marionette, my hands lifted, out of my control. "Beautiful." His voice was hot breath against my skin. It was scorching where he touched. Icy cold where he left behind his trail of moisture.

"Quentin, you..."

He slipped from the cape, kicking it next to mine. I helped him pull up his sweatshirt, my fingers gliding over the bumps and planes of long, well-formed muscles. His skin rippled under my hands. That just heightened the intensity.

Then he did the most amazing thing. A strobe light started flashing in my head. Slowly at first, building up speed just as his hands were driving me to a fury. The flashes were of me, then him, me, then him. It was like I bounced awareness back and forth between us. The rhythm was equal. I was only half aware of the rest of my clothes pulled from my body. The fire-warmed fur tickled my back as Quentin's weight sent me blessedly close to the edge.

The erotic images in my head made my body ache with want. I touched every inch of skin I could reach, pulling him close, needing him inside me.

Sparks that had nothing to do with magic and everything to do with the pleasure of being fulfilled sexually rocked through my body. I closed my eyes and held Quentin still as I tried to absorb the perfection of the moment.

He began to move, slowly at first, but then harder, faster, keeping time with the flashes of light he put in my head.

"Wait for me."

"I don't think I can." The images went by so quickly it became one movie, one heartbeat. One body. I didn't know anymore if my eyes were opened or closed.

I gasped out his name, begging him to take me higher. His answering growl left me shaking with sensual overload. My body shuddered with his, and all sensation slipped from my control. Nothing mattered right now, except this man and the beautiful feelings he was giving my body. I pulled his mouth down to mine as I felt it coming.

We reached the summit together. Then began our glorious, out of control descent. The strobe stopped, becoming one giant white streak. The trail of a falling star. Glorious. Powerful.

Magic.

☙ ☙ ☙

I rolled over and pushed the breath from my chest. Wow. And here I was, all twisted into a pretzel with a sweaty, muscled man who made me feel like, well, doing that, and more, all over again.

A shiver erupted like an aftershock of an earthquake. Echoes of the orgasm, I figured.

Until I heard the voice.

"*Dammit, Ella*!"

My eyes darted around the room, I crossed my legs and covered each breast with my palms. This was the first time in my life I think I was glad I could do that. Having Sam see me like this would be like...like my own father seeing me in bed with someone. Another shiver, this time I knew its source—repulsion.

"Shhh. Don't say my name. Quentin doesn't know I'm here. I don't want him to know."

How could I converse? Where was he? Invisible. That's it. He must have gotten some gems and hopped in unseen. *Oh.* I didn't dare wonder how much he had seen.

Quentin rolled over and slid an arm over me. Great. Now I was stuck under Casanova with the Pope standing over me. I certainly wasn't feeling very Mother Theresa-like right now.

"I can hear your thoughts, even the ones you don't vocalize in your head. I see the ones Quentin can't find. I'm in you, Ella."

I wriggled away, ignoring Quentin's mumbled protest. I danced the dance of the squeamish. It probably wouldn't have been worse if someone had just poured a bucket of maggots on me.

"Ella, please. You make it sound so bad."

"But, you...you—"

"I know, I know," the voice echoed in my head. *"I'm like your father. But not quite. Right now I am your protector, your hidden spy, your secret weapon. You need to go about your daily business. I will be here, listening, learning. There is much you don't know."*

"But..."

"Ella. Please. Don't have any more sex with Quentin while I'm here, okay? I really am not attracted to him."

Now I wanted to barf. Was there a bucket down here? Anything? There had to be a toilet. Where the hell was the goddamn toilet? I pulled on clothes. I hopped on one foot while trying to yank my jeans up over my thighs, which were still sticky with sweat. Nothing could be easy, could it?

I went through the doorway. It was dark, very dark. I couldn't toss my cookies into something I couldn't see. What if there was something already in the toilet? Something that had crawled in there and died or... I felt sicker just thinking about it.

"Ella, I will take over this body in a minute if you don't get a grip. Other than your purse episode, you've been the pillar of strength."

"Who, me?"

"I know what you've done. Choosing you was right. Winzey found

me."

"Winzey!" I gulped, almost fearful I had yelped out loud.

Quentin was reclined, still naked, in front of the fire. "Ella, where are you going?"

"Uh, bathroom?"

"It's rather dark in there."

"What gave you that clue, Sherlock? Is there a lamp or something I can use? A bowl of dried grass, anything?"

Quentin rose, and strolled over to the white closet doors along the opposite wall. Nice ass.

"*Ella*?" It was a growl I could feel in my own throat.

Come on now, I'm a hormone-ridden woman who just had another taste of some real fine male-flesh.

"Stop right there. Do not remember, reminisce or even plan your next encounter until I'm safely out of radar range."

"Then you'll be leaving...tonight?"

"Nope."

Sam was a real party pooper.

Quentin hadn't a freaking clue. That in itself was mighty hilarious. I let my eyes rove up and down his body. It landed on his smug face.

"You like what you see?"

I shrugged, waiting for my hand to involuntarily smack me in the forehead. "I did like what I felt."

He handed over an old-fashioned looking oil lamp.

"Does it work?" I asked, eyeing the smoke stained globe. I couldn't make out the wick. I hated how dark it was down in this basement.

"Imagine so."

"Will you find out?" I sloshed it and heard the liquid inside.

"You got magic, light it yourself."

I was tempted to reach out and grab him by the...*arm*. Hey, that's not what I was thinking. I was going to make it a little more painful.

I narrowed my eyes and blew out a puff. The lamp flickered to life. Not bad.

"*Thank you,*" came from inside my head.

I stared at the wall over Quentin's head. Sam hadn't been there five minutes—at least that I'd known about—and I was already contemplating a long walk outside.

I was surprised Quentin didn't hear Sam's laughter rolling out my ears. I smiled sweetly at Quentin, who still was alternating his gaping between the fire and me. "Hey," I told him. "When you're good, you're good."

He grumbled something I couldn't hear and went to retrieve the fur jackets from the floor.

Walking into a dark room with a pale yellow oil lamp was unnerving. I jumped at every wavering shadow or looming shape. It didn't help that nothing had solid lines. Electricity was so much kinder to the nervous system. I couldn't have lived in an era before modern amenities.

I thought of my stint as Annabelle. Yep, definitely glad I had been born in the twentieth century.

"Sorry I missed you as Annabelle."

"No, you're not."

"I heard you ran into one of my, ahem, friends."

"Jim? He wasn't too friendly after all."

"No, but Winzey's home has dealt with tropical storms now and again. Hurricane James did minimal damage before it grounded in Cuba."

I felt a smile. Justice felt good.

" What's his deal? Jim's, I mean?"

"He has his own agenda. He thinks he can take over the island and therefore rule magic. He's desperate and careless. Bergestein will eventually take him down, I believe. Best to stay away from him."

Brilliant plan. Now, about the reason I was here...

I glanced down at the white toilet. There was no water down here. What was in the bowl was one of those weird colors between brown and green. At least as far as I could tell with the lamp. I wasn't getting any closer to investigate.

"I don't suppose I have any magic to make that all better?"

Talking to yourself was one thing, I reminded myself. But this getting an answer is really making a white rubber room sound like home.

"And how do you think little Annabelle felt? I hope you weren't fantasizing about lover boy out there while you were in her head."

I couldn't remember if I did or not. Now, about the toilet situation? *"I can't do this, Sam. I can't handle a man hitchhiking around in my body."*

"How do you think I feel? I'm stuck in a woman's body."

"Well, this woman's got to pee. You're going to know exactly how it feels to piss your pants if you don't do something about that water."

"Point your finger," Sam commanded.

I listened. And waited. And waited. "*Well?*" I finally asked.

"*Toss the water outside and bring in a lump of fresh snow. I know you can do that.*"

I crossed my legs and concentrated on Sam's command. Sure enough, I had snow to pee on. Wheee. I always wanted to make yellow snow. Men always had all the fun with that.

"You are demented, Ella. Now I know why Quentin likes you."

"You ever been in Quentin's body?"

"No. That would scare me."

I laughed.

"*Ella*?" Quentin was on the other side of the door. "*What's so funny*?"

"Uh, nothing. The toilet was gross so I did a switcheroo with snow. I'm just finding it funny to finally get to make yellow snow."

"You would."

"Is the fire still going? It's frigid in here."

"Yep, and I'll warm you back up. No worry there."

No toilet paper. Piece of cake. I pictured an empty hotel room and snatched what I needed. So someone would walk in to an unflushed toilet and no paper. It was only pee, right?

Sam was silent. I think he was in there bribing my conscience.

For Sam's sake, I settled on sitting beside Quentin. He had his arm around my shoulders. Sam had better not say a word about it.

☙ ☙ ☙

I would have thought someone else would have gotten bored in a place like this and left Monopoly or something behind. I needed entertainment. And sex was out of the question.

I spent an hour juggling objects, learning the "preciseness" I needed. Problem was I didn't know if I was getting any better or if Sam was just humoring me by adding his skills. He had to be just as bored.

"Can you leave from in there?"

"Only by stepping out and then hopping."

"What about me? Could I leave with you still...uh, attached?"

"Nope."

"Oh." Well, as long as he was hitching a ride, I knew he wasn't rescuing me from this place. *"Then why are you here?"*

"Quentin's up to something. He followed you from the movie set, invisible of course. I actually assumed you'd been with him the whole time. I was not very relieved to find you were with Jim, but getting to the island was a benefit. I learned immediately you were there. Those fairies have a way of making sure information gets to me."

"I didn't realize you were so...important." Was that the right word?

"Lou was my father."

"Oh." OH! That made things real new and interesting in the world. *"Are you...human, then?"*

"As much as you. Lou was as well, until the body he occupied was killed by another's magic."

"I don't understand. How did he live?"

"He was unable to step out before the host died. So he became a soul without a body. The body ended up in a small pond. So did my father."

"Then what?" I leaned against the wall, my feet curled up to my chin, my arms wrapped around my legs. I closed my eyes and snuggled further into the blanket. Quentin had gone upstairs. He sounded like he was pacing up there.

"My mother followed his cries. She could find him anywhere, even if he didn't have his gems."

"And?" I could picture a woman standing before the pond that held the face of her husband instead of her own reflection. How devastating it would be to know he'd never be flesh and blood again.

"Yes. She was torn with grief. She dove in, planning, I am told, to take her own life to remain forever with my father. He, of course, didn't let her. He tossed her, and his gems, ashore."

"Oh!"

"You wear the gems of my mother."

I disengaged my hand and touched the necklace. It responded with a warm pulsation. *"Did she leave then?"*

"Yes and no. She found a large bucket and scooped up the water, insisting Lou should fill it. He did, never expecting she would transport him to the magical island, the one you saw. In hopes of bringing him back, she poured him over the waterfall. As he spilled into the rainbow waters, the fairies chanted, 'Free the gems, free the gems'."

Sam cleared his throat. My throat. I felt the tears at the corners of my eyes. The next part of the story was sad. *"My mother would not release the gems. She carried her own, as well as my father's."*

"Why?"

"What else is there, except power?"

I could feel the thundering of the waterfall as my blood coursed through my body. I could hear it, feel its vibrations, and smell its fresh tang. But on that day, I knew it hadn't been calm and sweet. It had raged with the anger of a man betrayed.

"Yes. That's exactly how he felt. You get that from the gems, as well as my story. Your gifts are strong, Ella. Use them well."

I nodded. The gems pounded the rhythm of the water against the flesh of my neck. *"What happened?"*

"She gripped the gems and tried to flee the edge of the falls. They say a hand, larger than life, and the power of pure water snatched her before she could hop. She plunged to the bottom of the waterfall."

I caught my breath. That sounded violent. *"It was violent. Perhaps before Lou had done that, the king of the fairies would have granted him wholeness. His punishment was to be cursed to the water forever. But my mother, she died, taking all four gems to the bottom."*

"How did you get them?"

"I expected you to ask where I was during all this."

I hadn't thought about it. Surely Sam had been born.

"Yes, born and nearly grown. And oblivious to all that was magic. To me, my father had gotten killed and my mother was vacationing in the Caribbean. Everyone thought she was taking the first steps to reclaiming her life."

"She never came back."

"No. It was just a few years later that I went to the scene of the accident that killed my father. You can imagine how shocked I was

when I heard his voice from the lake."

"Lake? I thought she got him out?"

"Not all. He exists in two places. Obviously the island is where he is strongest."

My head didn't comprehend this well. I pressed my eye sockets into the points of my knees until tiny white spots glittered like the stars on a clear night. I'd never been stoned in my life, but I think I needed something to understand all this. Exist in two places? Talk about a split personality.

"Ella!"

"Sorry, Sam, I guess I tend to joke when I can't react in any other way. It's a tragic story. And I know exactly what you mean about being bugged out. You continue to do it to me."

I heard footsteps on the stairs. Damn! I wanted to know how Sam had reacted and then found the island. But he had. That was important. I wondered if the gems Quentin wore were Sam's father's.

"Yes."

I didn't reply. Quentin was in the room.

He'd said Quentin was up to something. "Hey." I squinted up at the lamp he carried. "What're you up to?"

He handed me a plate. "Food. I thought cooking was supposed to be the chick's job."

"And lighting fire is the man's."

One eyebrow disappeared beneath the brown fringe, but he remained silent.

He didn't flirt. In fact, he barely talked at all while we ate. I wondered if he knew.

"Quentin," my voice cracked. Shit. I cleared my throat. "Quentin. You seem distracted. Something wrong?"

"Distracted? Is that really an Ella word?"

I rolled my eyes to check for an answer on the ceiling. Nope. No dunce cap ready to fall into place. "What other words would I have used?"

"I could see something like, 'Quentin, you've got your head in the clouds' or, I don't know. Distracted seems too sophisticated for you."

I just knew he knew. "Who does it sound like?"

He dropped his fork to his plate. "An English professor I once had.

Constantly accused me of the exact thing." He picked up my plate from my lap with one hand and knocked on my forehead with the other. "Hello, Mr. Casey, are you in there?"

I blinked innocently and rubbed where his knuckles had hit. "Ow! Just me. Lots of empty space, yes. But just me."

He growled, low in his throat. For a split second I thought he saw right through my little white lie. But then he pressed his lips to mine. Surprise hit me like a bolt of lightning. I struggled to step back, but my balance was unsteady. I had no choice, I had to grab his shoulders. Quentin took it as encouragement.

In the cold room, his lips were white hot coals against my mouth, face and neck. I leaned, only a little bit, into him. And my fingernails nearly tore into his shirt.

I slid back a little, not because of me, I was sure. I had a feeling Sam *hadn't* dozed off. And he wasn't keen on kissing another man.

That did it. I broke away contact with a heaving breath. I knew it was just a kiss, but what it promised had me steaming under the collar already.

Quentin dropped a kiss on the tip of my nose and went upstairs. I still thought he knew.

"He hasn't a clue."

"How would you know?" I demanded to the inner voice that had a name, and a big attitude.

"I tuned in. You don't bother to. He knows you don't. But he has no clue about me, yet. Just keep doing what you're doing. Except the kissing part. Yuck."

"I figured you'd say that. What am I supposed to tell him when I wasn't quite so hesitant this morning?"

"Leave it up to me."

The hell I would. I unwrapped the bandages on my hand, wondering how bad the blisters looked now. I hadn't felt pain in a long time. Probably numbness from this place. Even with the fire, it couldn't have reached more than fifty degrees in here. It'd be nice if there was a fireplace on every wall.

"I fixed those for you." Sam's voice startled me into dropping the white gauze on the floor. But sure enough, my fingers looked as good as new.

"How—"

"Don't ask. There's a sacrifice involved."

Ugh. I didn't want to know. If Sam took it upon himself, then I certainly hoped it would have healed by the time he reclaimed his physical self.

"I just get to keep the scars."

"Forever?"

"As long as I live."

That sounded drastic. "*Why, Sam? Why would you do that?"*

"*You'll need your hands, your wits and every ounce of your power before this is over."*

"What is over?"

"The Magic Wars."

Chapter Eleven

It didn't matter that I begged, pleaded, promised him a hot fudge brownie sundae with a cherry on top. Quentin would not let me go upstairs. "Why?" I asked, hands on hips, blocking the doorway.

"Because."

"You sound like my mother."

"You sound like you needed more mothering."

"This constant nitpicking is making me feel like I'm living with my brother." I was bored. Stir-crazy. Had a very serious case of cabin fever and he was not helping by confining me underground.

"You have a brother? And you do..." He waved his hand around toward the blanket in front of the fire.

"No and no, you sick pervert. No brother and I wouldn't even think of...doing, ugh...that's just wrong. I can't believe you said that."

He laughed and started to climb the stairs. I sidestepped to prevent him from getting around me. Juvenile behavior, but the best way to beat one was to join him. He pushed around me anyway.

"What's going to prevent me from following you up?"

"I lock the door."

"I'm magic, ding-a-ling. I can undo the lock."

"*That's* why you can't come up. You'll try some fancy trick. No magic upstairs."

"Why?" I drug it out and managed to sound quite frustrated. Well, I was!

"They can track you and find you if you perform tricks. So keep them all in the lower level."

"Who? Who are you worried about?"

"*Me,*" came the little voice inside my head.

I dropped my arms and walked back over in front of the fire.

"Hey," Quentin called. He stood on the second step and scratched his head.

"What?" I turned and gave my best wide-eyed look.

He shook his head and growled. My eyes would pop out if I opened them any farther. Aren't women supposed to be able to change their minds?

He retreated upstairs. His thoughts went something like this: "*Psycho-brain-dead wench.*" It didn't hurt my feelings one bit. I'd been called worse. By him, even.

Too tired to use magic, I tossed another log on the fading flames. Wherever I went next, it was going to have to be warm.

"*Are your bags packed*?" Sam asked.

"*Huh*?" I had nothing with me.

"*While he's upstairs, I'm going to step out. Then we're out of here.*"

"We're leaving?" What about Quentin? And why didn't this prospect make me feel like doing cartwheels?

"*Fear of the unknown.*"

"Huh?"

God, he was confusing.

"The unknown. That's why you're apprehensive about leaving."

Actually, no. I was sad to miss more incredible sex with Quentin.

"Sit down. This will be draining for both of us."

Great. No strength to fight it. With my luck and memory of my constant gripes about the temperature, Sam would drop us at the gates of hell. And we'd promptly go up in smoke.

"Not quite."

Oh, that was reassuring.

"*On the count of three,*" he commanded. I was reminded of the Lethal Weapon movie where Mel Gibson argued with Danny Glover about whether it was one-two-three and then go, or just one-two-go.

Sam didn't wait. He just went.

Was the marathon over? And why couldn't I lift my arms? I felt the strangest pull. Did someone just remove all my bones? It was too tough to think. I slid toward the darkness that beckoned me.

"Ella," Quentin's worried voice echoed through my head. Hangover? Did he have to yell? "Sorry, I guess you're finally awake.

You must have been really tired. I've been calling you for almost ten minutes."

"Really?" I forced myself to check out the log I'd hoisted onto the fire. It was in the same place and barely charred. The fire was crackling right along. How long had I been out?

Quentin settled down next to me and stretched his long legs in front of him. Any second now his toes would catch fire. Ten little candles all in a row.

"Hey, don't you think about it. You still trying to get even with me for not letting you upstairs?" He pulled his feet back.

"Not really."

"I don't believe it."

"That makes two of us."

His laughter warmed me much more effectively than the fire. It went right to the core. He tilted my chin upwards with one searing touch. His lips claimed mine and the cold disappeared.

I'd never get tired of tasting this man. I swore he could bring me to the edge of insanity with just his mouth. His hand slid down my throat and rubbed my breast through the thin material of my shirt. I clawed at my clothing, wanting his hands on me. The through-the-shirt cop-a-feel was for high school. I needed skin on skin.

He smiled against my lips. "I love—"

I nearly peed my pants.

"—your imagination."

I breathed a sigh of relief. I could handle it if he loved my body or my imagination. Even though I didn't think Quentin was the type to love anyone's brain. I was *not* ready for him to love me.

Especially when I know I didn't, per se, love him back. Oh, I liked, and I lusted. But nope, no undying devotion. There was this little element of mistrust that got in the way.

Thank God he wasn't tuning into that broadcast of true confession radio. I just wondered if the other visitor was.

Shit!

I pushed Quentin back. His hands slid from my skin. It was almost painful.

"Ella?" Quentin looked straight into my eyes. The green was clear and bright like wonderfully fertilized grass. And probably just as fake.

"I, uh, thought I heard something upstairs."

Quentin held a finger to my lips. I was all set to launch into a spiel about having sex without protection and not wanting to take any more chances.

Something was up there. The loud metallic crash caused me to jump two feet to the right. Quentin was just as startled. I nearly laughed at his shocked expression. If he'd have been a cat his tail would have been fluffed to the size of his body.

He held a finger to his own lips, but bypassed the "shh." Then he pretended to zip his lips. *Yes, Quentin. I get the picture.*

He looked ridiculous tiptoeing up the steps. I should have shushed him when he slid the bolt on the door. I just smiled to myself. Although it was unexpected, I knew exactly who had caused the noise.

A hand clamped over my mouth and spun me around. I knew better than to scream.

"*Close your eyes and hold on.*" I wrapped my arms around his neck. It felt like I was once again seven years old and had fallen asleep on the couch. Daddy carried me to bed. I was safe.

"*I'm not your father.*"

"Shh. Close enough."

There was no ceremony, no bright lights or colorful flashes. He put one hand to my throat and we were gone.

ᘓ ᘓ ᘓ

I sniffed. What was that? Expensive perfume stung my nose. And a faint scent of flowers. I hid my nose against his chest to ward off the sharp odor. Only Sam didn't smell the same.

I opened one eye and looked at the chest from mere inches. White dress shirt. Black bowtie. Tuxedo?

I looked down at my own self. I was covered in white lace.

This magic stuff was threatening the integrity of my underwear. There had been just way too many instances where I had been on the verge of needing Depends. I needed a drink. I wasn't a drinker, but God, did I need one now.

I lifted my left hand and admired the rock. Not bad. The guy apparently had money. And muscle. He was climbing the stairs like I didn't weigh more than a feather.

It was a shame, though, the long fingers and pastel pink nails didn't belong to me. Sam didn't look much like Sam either. But hmmmm, he was younger and quite handsome, in a clean-shaven executive-type sort of way. I mean, if one was into that type.

I guess it could have been worse. *"Sam, what the heck, did we crash the wedding party?"*

"Ah, yes. I believe that's the correct terminology."

"And where are we going?" The bodies we inhabited were entirely being controlled by the people who owned them. We were just along for the ride.

"Looks like the bridal suite."

"No way."

Sam groaned. *"It's not us, Ella. It's them. It's their wedding night."*

"I'm not sticking around for the fireworks."

Sam deep booming laugh filled my head.

"Follow my lead."

Sigh. I gritted my teeth, but not the bride's, and let the newlyweds talk. When she giggled with a hideous high-pitched sound, I told Sam I was out of there.

"Let her go into the bathroom and get dressed up for her husband. As soon as she comes out, we'll leave."

What a plan.

ଓ ଓ ଓ

It must have been the overwhelming stress of the day, I decided. We stood over the sleeping figures. We were invisible, of course.

"Poor suckers. Didn't get much of a wedding night," I relayed to Sam via our wonderful mental telepathy.

"They'll make up for it. He's one horny bastard."

I clamped my hand over my mouth to keep from laughing. *"So what's the plan?"*

"Get out of here and find Bergestein's suite."

I gasped. What would we want to do that for?

"See if we can find where he's keeping the gems. Maybe get to them. Take his, relieve his employees of theirs. Save the world type of

thing."

"That sounded like a Quentin answer."

"I'm afraid I wouldn't trust Quentin to save the world."

Me either. Just himself. I glanced toward the door. *"So, do we just open it and walk out?"*

Sam gripped my shoulders. *"Let me see you."*

I did the heel click thing. Why change? It worked. I couldn't see Sam, but I just *knew* he'd rolled his eyes back in his head.

His hand was warm on my neck. He moved the gems. The heat was gone. I felt very alone for that moment.

I heard a rustling, then felt his breath on my cheek. I was curious, but not afraid. "Sam?" I whispered.

"You'll need your magic strength at maximum. I've got the beads almost touching. Just to prevent an accidental meeting of the gems, I'm going to tie a piece of ribbon between them."

"To prevent me from hopping?" Yeah, I was suspicious.

"No, to prevent the others from sending you to someplace you don't want to be." His voice lowered. "Trust me. There are places on this earth that would make hell seem like a trip to Mexico in the dead of summer."

"Oh." I lifted my chin. *Save me from that, by all means.*

"Are you going to teach me to jump? You know, in case I get separated or end up in a bad situation?" I figured going in without this knowledge would be like a cop on a stake-out without his gun.

"All you need to know is this. Since you're fond of the Wizard moves, touch the gems, click your heels and say, 'I want to go home.'"

"Where will I go?" I just knew my apartment had been emptied and re-rented already. I glanced at the sleeping couple. I sure didn't want to find myself in another "oops" like this one.

"Nope. That's not your home anymore. As long as you stay true to the cause and don't let greed dirty your heart, you'll be safe on the island."

"Where Lou—your father, is?"

"Affirmative."

"Does this island have a name?"

"Fairyland."

"You've got to be kidding me."

"I am."

"Dang it, Sam." But I realized what he was giving me. A one way ticket to safety. "And thanks."

"One other thing," he said.

"Huh?"

"Stay invisible." I faded into transparency. I still thought that trick alone was the best magic.

His fingers closed over mine, like a father leading a child.

"Stop thinking that way."

"I can't help it!" I followed him to the door. And waited. He was going to open it, wasn't he?

"Come on."

"Where?"

My fingers were pulled until they rapped against the door. I immediately checked to make sure the couple was still out cold. They were, thankfully.

"Sam?"

I felt his touch on my forearm. "What happened, Ella?"

C'mon, really. We both knew what happened. *Walk through walls?* Who'd have thought?

"So Quentin didn't teach you anything new?"

"Apparently not," I replied. "I just worked on what I already know. And made fire."

He groaned. His fingers cut into my arm. "Think of yourself as water and pour yourself through the door." He tugged me forward until I was staring directly at the intimidating piece of wood.

I was air and it was a screen. I took a step, and never let go of my vise grip on Sam's hand. The transition felt like an involuntary shudder. I shook if off and found I was in the hall.

Color me pink. I did it.

But just like all the other amazing magic I'd been taught, it had vicious side effects. This feat made me feel like I'd been run over. No, not by a Mac truck, although that cliché was easy and my brain was tired. Besides, if I'd have settled on the big semi, it would mean I felt dead. It had to be something more like a snowmobile. Something that would come around for another shot at me.

"*Don't let your guard down,*" Sam's mental command invaded my vision of a single headlight and lots of white stuff. Then I realized that was the point.

"*Now what?*" I knew the hallway wasn't our final destination. That would be too easy.

"*Listen for Bergestein's thoughts.*"

I strained to hear, but hadn't heard so much as a cricket chirp when Sam pushed my shoulder. "*This way.*"

He must have had his tuned in better. Off on a new adventure, I thought. Cops and Robbers. Or wait, maybe it was Cowboys and Indians. It didn't matter. I just wanted to be on the winning side.

Sam had resumed his lead position, and I followed by no choice of my own. He had my wrist to keep me from getting lost. It is a little tricky to follow an invisible man.

We used hallways and doorless walls for our marathon run. All I could hope for was that we got there fast. I was a car out of gas.

"Hold on," I gasped to Sam, dropping my free hand to my knees. I bent double to catch my breath.

We were in the pool area. I could hear the high-pitched screams of laughter and see the dancing reflections of the pool lights on the ceiling. The strong chlorine smell burned my nose and made my sinuses rebel. My breathing passages closed up faster than a nun's knees. I was gasping for air from acute sinusitis compounded by running far more than my body could handle at one time. I needed to rest. Just for a moment.

Blinding lights and a sharp pain on the back of my head knocked every bit of the precious oxygen from my lungs. As I gasped I struggled to form a rational thought. Sam hadn't hit me. Someone else was behind me. Someone who wasn't our friend.

In the splash of the water I heard a voice, more like the echo of one. "One gem."

Lou?

I gritted my teeth and swung my elbow back, surprising my attacker enough for him to emit a loud "oomph" and step backwards. Unfortunately for me, he still had my hair wound around his hand.

He was going to decapitate me for my gems. I felt the blood rush from my face. I yanked my fingers from Sam's and clawed at my neck. White hot, the gems burned my fingers and my throat. I could handle the pain. I wasn't ready to die.

Please, please, dear God, save me. For one who hid from organized religion as an adult, I sure knew where to turn when I needed help. I just hoped *He* could see me.

The leather snapped. I mouthed a thank you and grabbed for the gem that had been twisted to the front of my throat. It scorched my hand. I gritted my teeth. It was going to burn right through my palm. I could tell.

Whoever it was must have decided I wasn't worth killing. He grabbed for the leather strap. Somewhere during the scuffle I had either lost the invisibility or he was able to see through the magic. Then again, as hot as the gems were, he probably found the strap by heat alone.

I held tight as he jerked. The gems were designed to slide on the thin leather. I winced as the strap cut into my fingers, but held tight.

I didn't know whether he pushed me or I fell. He'd let go, at least. The fading footsteps meant he thought he'd gotten what he wanted.

"Sam," I whispered. My voice sounded foreign. And it hurt to swallow. All I wanted to do was curl up into a ball under one of the tables in the darkened area and cry. I didn't want to follow bad guys who followed me. And then tried to kill me.

A thick shape knelt before me. I blinked, but could only see his silhouette. I shrank away. What if he'd come back, realizing he only had one?

Sam's soothing voice came through like salve on the wound. I relaxed against him. "Did he get them?" His fingers traced the tender skin of my neck.

"One."

I opened my fist and heard the tiny ball of crystal roll onto the ceramic tile. The darkness took over.

ଓ ଓ ଓ

I faded back to life. And it wasn't pretty. My head had grown to at least five times its normal size. Beyond the ringing in my ears, I heard thumps. Footsteps, maybe? They sounded hollow.

I was afraid to open my eyes. Scared of what I would see. The cold chills torturing me were not the first clue I wasn't where I wanted to be. The air was stale, oily smelling.

"I thought you said she had the other gem." The voice was sandpaper.

"It wasn't on the rope. Just the one." His voice grated on my nerves. It was high and whiney. I pictured some scar-faced coward hunched in the corner as the boss-man stood over him. Served his ass right for trying to kill me.

"You should have finished her off and cleaned the area. How could you not see the gem glow?"

I tried not to smile, but I pictured the little worm wetting his pants. "I...uh, well, maybe she fell on it. Or something. I—I...I didn't see it."

Meant Sam got it. I hoped.

"You didn't see it? Did you notice you only had one? Did you even look?" A loud thump preceded a louder crash. Oops, one less goon to worry about.

"What are you smiling about, there, missy?"

I swallowed, hoping the bitter pill in my throat was just fear. Then I choked. I coughed until I nearly retched. I must have aspirated enough spit to fill half my lungs.

I'd made it alive through all this and I was going to die from *this?* My hands were tied above my head. I was flat on my back. It wasn't so funny anymore. My eyes watered. The tears streamed down my face and into my hair. I couldn't sit up, I couldn't breathe.

"Fools," Sandpaper Voice muttered. "Going to let her live when I say die and let her die when I say keep her alive for bait." He yanked at the rope around my wrists. It was obvious he didn't care if I had permanent burns on my flesh from the friction of his actions. It was equally clear he wasn't worried about me for more than the bait he mentioned. He slapped me on the back and I thought surely I'd cough up a lung, or two, maybe my spleen. And gee, what else? A pancreas? Don't I need that?

"You are a sassy wench, aren't you?" The hint of an old, ineffectively hidden accent emerged. British? Something European, but I wasn't sure. I knew who I was dealing with. This guy must be the torture king.

I almost asked him for a glass of water. Almost. But he'd probably get a bucket and douse me with it, just to prove he was the one in charge. Little dick syndrome. I hated men who had to go to such violent lengths to prove their point.

I blinked and opened my eyes wide. I waited, expecting nothing less than a backhand across the face. Nothing. Hadn't he read my mind? I sucked in a breath, slowly this time. Didn't want to tempt fate again.

Where was Sam? Where was Quentin? Winzey? Anyone out there?

Silence. Except for the hollow metallic footsteps as my captor paced on the catwalks beside me.

"Where am I?" I asked. What's the worst he could do, tell me it was none of my business?

"This is one of the vast properties owned by Bergestein."

"Ah." I really didn't get an answer, now did I? I *knew* that much already.

"Are you going to kill me?" I squeaked out.

The man was of average height, but had shoulders wider than any linebacker I'd seen. And I had a feeling the man before me wasn't wearing any padding. His neck was about the size of my waist. His ears stuck out like handles on my soup kettle.

"I will kill you if you keep thinking like that."

"Oops."

"Oops?" He laughed at me. "You insult me and then say oops? I could kill you right now."

"You could whether or not I insulted you and whether or not I said oops." I squeezed my bladder muscles tight. I would not lose control of my bodily functions. There was no compromise of power in this body.

"Do you think I could use the bathroom?" I was still sitting up. My hands were tied together, but at least not bound above my head. I glanced down. Open grates with just darkness below. "I'd hate to pee on something important down there."

He smiled, his lips displaying rows of perfect teeth that were totally wrong for the unkempt look of his beard and hair. "I think something can be arranged."

Suddenly I was a sack of potatoes thrown over this guy's shoulder. The pressure on my bladder wasn't real nice, but I figured relieving myself right now wasn't the best of ideas.

He deposited me in front of a stall in a public style bathroom. "Go."

I held up my hands. "Uh, could you? It makes getting the pants down a little easier."

With a sigh reminiscent of my own impatience he slid out a pocket knife that looked a lot like its owner. Thick, rough and sharp.

He pushed open the stall and gave me a shove. I took my time. I hated to think, knowing he could delve into my head and snatch any plans I had. I was going to have to trust Sam on this one. He'd come after me. I just had to stay alive.

There was a quarter on the floor. Wish I could call someone who cared. But there wasn't a soul out there who could rescue me from this who was also accessible by phone.

I stared at it and held out my hand. It floated and landed heads up in my palm. Well, I'll be. Magic.

Maybe it was the fact my eyeballs weren't swimming in yellow stuff anymore. Maybe it was the adrenaline kicking in. The realization that I was a helpless female stuck in some political, magical fight between good and evil. Whatever it was, I still had power.

The guard stopped in front of the stall. "I know you're done. Let's go."

I stared at his shoe laces, untying them and retying them together. "There's no paper in here. Could you get me a paper towel or something?"

"Damn!" he muttered and took a step back. A stream of much worse curses streamed from his mouth. His feet must have both flown up in the air, because I could see nothing from my vantage point.

When he finally crashed back to earth, I peeked through the space on the side of the door. He lay motionless on the floor.

Wouldn't Quentin be proud of me now? I jumped over him and stood at the doorway. I wish I knew if he had a weapon. Wait. He did.

I took a careful step toward him. The knife was clipped to his belt.

Was that a flicker of his eyelashes? Was he really out cold? The glint of the overhead fluorescents caught on the gems at his neck. They were much smaller than mine had been and not nearly as lustrous. They looked like smoky beads. Glass. But there was power there, perhaps a weaker version, but I had nothing. Nothing but fear and an intense desire to get away from this place.

I took a deep breath and exhaled it quickly. Like an athlete preparing for the Olympics I shook my hands, stretched my neck and focused on my goal.

I eyed the snap on the leather that covered the knife but reached for the necklace. I'd walk away with one or the other. That was the plan.

The snap came loose. It sounded like a cannon in the empty room. I watched his face. No twitches, no flickering of his eyelashes. A good actor or still unconscious. I was wasting time.

My fingers slid along the cold tiled floor toward his neck. I concentrated on lifting the cover and making the knife peek out over the cheap leather sheath. Just like a snake charmer.

But sometimes the snake charmers get bit.

His hand reached out and snagged mine. I screamed and jerked.

My hand slid free. Invisible, I commanded myself. I turned toward the mirror. *It worked!*

"Bitch! I'll find you. Where did you go?"

I glanced toward the door. I had a clean exit, but had the sinking feeling it'd be easy to be caught there. My heart was thundering so loud I just knew the noise of it would give me away.

If I got caught would I be any worse off than if I had never tried? They were going to kill me, right? No matter what? Spurred on by the realization this might just be my only chance, I dropped to the ground and kicked back with my foot. It connected with the door, shoving it open enough. Then I scrambled back to the dark, mildew infested space under the row of sinks.

He grunted, patted his side and half-jogged out of the room. I sighed. I was free. Why did I know it wouldn't last for long?

So now what was the plan? I had no weapon, and I'd failed to get close to the gems. I rolled out of my hiding place. The mirror told me the truth. Invisibility was gone. Apparently it'd walked out the door with the mean guy.

Now wasn't that just ducky.

"*Sam!*" I shouted mentally. "*Sam, where are you?*"

I figured this was about as effective as dressing like a clown and riding around on a tricycle with a red flashing light. But it wasn't going to be any worse than walking out into something I didn't know.

"Invisible," I said out loud.

I faded.

Oh, damn. Oh, shit! I wasn't alone.

Dare I crawl back under the sink? What if I walked out and the person didn't follow me? I'd certainly fade back into full blooming color and get nabbed in a heartbeat.

Decisions, decisions.

Something tickled the back of my neck. Cold sweat dripped down my sides and between my breasts. My heart flipped over. Breathing was no longer automatic.

I closed my eyes and took a shaky step forward. I expected a hand to close on my hair and jerk me back, in the least.

Nothing.

Had he moved with me? The blood pounding through my ears was a runaway steam train. I wouldn't have heard a footstep if I'd listened for it.

I dropped into a crouched position.

There was a bit of change in the pressure on my neck, a slight pull, a bit of weight. Added though. Not lifted.

I stood back up. It was much too vulnerable to stay on the ground.

"Yeow." Reflex jerked my hand up to the pull at the back of my neck. If I'd had to think about it, I would have just run away.

But there was nothing touching my hair. It was full of tangles, but no hand had it bunched like the reins of a horse.

A shiver coursed through me. A cockroach? A spider? I glanced back under the sinks and followed up the first one with an even more spastic willy nilly shake. I started slapping my hair, my shoulders, my neck, my face-

"Ouch!" something squeaked.

I stopped. Only my eyes moved as I glanced around. "Who said that?"

A giggle.

My eyes shot open wider than I thought physically possible. I whispered, "Winzey?"

Another giggle.

God, I hope this wasn't a trap. I slid my skeptical fingers along my neck toward the source of the pressure. I just knew any second they'd be bitten off and some hideous monster would jump out and proceed to kill me.

Hey! It could happen.

I found her. At least it felt like her. She was invisible, too.

"How'd you—"

"Shh. Hide!"

Hot damn.

She must be magic. She could take the place of the gems. "Can I go through walls?" I asked quickly in a hushed voice.

"Yessssss."

"Did you hear something, Frank?" I backed against the wall next to the paper towel rack. Two men walked in. It was like Abbott and Costello, but they were not funny. Good thing I'd just emptied my bladder.

The man named Frank started banging open all the stall doors. The tall one peered over the top of the stalls. "She still has one gem. She might have enough power to be invisible. But she'll be weak."

He walked straight for me. His neck was bare. I couldn't see Frank. Did they have power?

Winzey, what do we do? I tried to ask her mentally. She didn't respond.

I smelled the stale cigarettes and coffee of the tall one's breath. He was leaning against the last sink, effectively pinning me between the towels and him.

I felt a tug.

What?

I heard a toilet flush. Another tug on my hair.

Both men had gone running toward the far stall. "Back," Winzey's voice in my ear was like a gust of wind. I stepped backward. Sand through the colander.

The cold breeze whipped around me. Where was I?

"Climb," Winzey's tiny fingers clung to my ear lobe. I opened the neck of my shirt. The last thing I needed was for my little friend to get blown away.

I felt the fairy duck under the collar and sit with my bra strap across her lap like a seatbelt. Her tiny wings tickled, but at least I knew she'd be safer there.

We were back on the grates. Below me I could see an endless spiral of stairs. Above, it continued and above it, the gray light of a dismal day.

My legs felt like spaghetti. I remembered the last time they felt like that. Quentin. My pulse raced in answer to the memories of his kiss.

"Bad," Winzey said. Her voice wasn't sing-song as it usually was, even in warning.

"Bad? Where?" I looked all around, trying to see if someone was watching us.

"Quentin is bad."

My heart stopped, my throat sealed closed and I sat on the step. "How bad?"

"Climb."

Winzey had become incredibly short on conversation. Then again, I suppose she needed to keep me invisible, and that would take some serious energy. And while I was tired, the wall wasn't nearly the obstacle I had expected.

The steps, of open gray framework, whistled and rattled on their own. I did my best to remain quiet and tread lightly. Thank goodness for the heavy winds. They disguised the chatter caused by my shaking hands.

"Be air," Winzey commanded.

I didn't know what she meant, but didn't dare question when I felt her pinching my ear. I pressed myself back into the corner of the landing, closed my eyes and followed her mental cue—imagining what it would feel like to fly.

I imagined myself streamlined, dancing circles around the flagpole at the top of the stairway, playing hide and seek with the flag. Then I dove down the side of the building, following the stone that was only a shade darker than the dreary sky, swooping up like a bird at the last moment to rustle some leaves that lay dormant at the base of an old gnarled tree.

I circled the tree, diving in and out of branches the way a slalom skier avoids the flags.

"Careful." Winzey's momentum slowed me and I delicately tickled a clinging leaf until it shuddered and fell. At this speed I could see the courtyard. It was a square within the confines of the building. Castle, actually. The gray stone walls were several stories high, with decorative columns and lookouts. I imagined an invisible guard at every one of those stations.

"Be a light breeze." It was a command, not a request. I became wind again, swooping down along the base of the courtyard. As I passed each window I glanced inside. All seemed empty. Seemed being the operative word. There was no doubt this was the land of invisibility. And I knew there was a way for them to find me.

"Quit thinking." Her sing-song voice didn't go with the death grip on my ear. I was starting to wonder if she'd shoved a forearm through my piercing and just tugged to get my attention.

Air. I am air.

Air just hit a brick wall. And it wasn't the castle.

Quentin stood in a doorway, looking upwards.

"Air, wind, breeze!" Winzey was tugging and screaming at me.

I was crash landing and there wasn't a thing I could do about it.

Quentin was here.

In the house of Bergestein. And he wasn't a captive.

He was bad.

Chapter Twelve

"...don't know what happened. They said she just fell out of the sky."

"There's something fishy going on at that place. I always thought so."

"I had a call there once, a ride along with the local paramedics. I could swear I felt I was being watched, no matter where I went or what I did. It was downright creepy."

I kept my eyes closed. These weren't Mr. B's men. From the sharp ammonia smell, to the pull of the needle at my arm, I suspected a hospital or clinic.

"Crap!" I sat up, eyes wide. Winzey? What if they found her?

"Whoa, honey," the soothing deep voice accompanied a push against my shoulder. My vision was filled with white flashes. Perfectly coinciding with the white hot pain behind them.

"That was a wake up if I ever saw one." The comment came from whoever was standing behind me.

I felt a hand on my head, then my neck. I almost jerked away. He was just checking me, doctor-like.

"What happened?" I moaned. And I didn't even have to act that one out.

"You were brought in by one of the groundskeepers up at the training facility. At least that's what he's calling it. Anyway, he said you fell right out of the sky." Both men laughed. It was obvious they knew nothing of magic or being air. And if I told them? The psych ward for me.

I mulled my options. I chose to lie. "Close. I was pushed from the second story window."

The doctor closest to me sat up abruptly. His chair slid on the floor like fingernails on a chalk board. "Pushed?"

They exchanged a glance. "You involved in that cult?"

I couldn't strain my head back to the man behind me. Cult? How fitting of a description. "No, they sort of...drafted me. I was trying to escape. One of the goons lunged at me, tripped and the momentum shoved me through the window."

Doctor picked up my arm and examined it for cuts. "It's amazing you didn't bleed to death from the glass."

"It was a screen." I frowned. "It tore. Probably still hanging from the window."

"Ah," they said in unison.

I wondered if my original thought was way off. Maybe this was just another set of goons. The room looked authentic enough, but creating atmosphere would be a piece of cake to do with control of the most powerful magic in the world.

Regardless, I didn't see reason to fear them any more than anyone else I'd met.

"Now what? Am I hurt? Is anything broken?"

He shook his head. "I'll go get your boyfriend and he can take you home." I laid back and stared at the ceiling, wondering why I'd had to go get Jess that darn gypsy stuff at the antique shop.

Both men walked past and left the room.

Boyfriend? Damn. There was little place to hide in here. "*Winzey? Are you around here anywhere?*" The little fairy was probably really ticked off at me right now.

I closed my eyes and tried to be invisible. I got up and looked for my reflection in the glass of the cabinet door. I was gone.

So there was magic in this room, in this building. But no windows. Only one door.

The footsteps echoed down the hall. I felt the tell-tale brush against my ear and didn't know whether to panic or cry with relief. Winzey was here. But what if they discovered her? What if *Quentin* discovered her?

"It's Quentin, isn't it?" I quizzed the figure that clung to my hair like a nasty thistle.

"Bad man. Bad man."

There was no time for this nonsense. I took a deep breath. Then another. No magical doors opened. Walking through the wall wasn't going to save me.

"Can I jump?" I asked Winzey. "Can you help me hop somewhere else?"

"No. Bad men will come."

The door slammed open and I covered my face with my arms. If I hadn't been leaning on the far wall, I might have sunk to the floor and begged for mercy.

Hard soled shoes slapped the tiled floor. I peeked out beneath my hand. A brown coat nearly skimmed the floor.

He took my hand. I gasped a cry of protest. I just knew this was the end for me. Instead, he dropped a marble into my open palm and closed my fingers over it.

"Hide it well." It was the voice from behind me when I had come to. The face I hadn't seen.

I jerked my head up. But the features meant nothing. The eyes sparkled, a brown so dark they were nearly black. They seemed rather young for the wrinkled face with heavy jowls. And I had pictured a tall skinny guy. I was way off.

The gem in my hand thumped against my tightened fingers. There was no doubt what it was. "Thank you," I whispered. I opened my hand to see my treasure. When I looked up. He was gone.

If it weren't for the gem in my hand, I'd think I was losing my mind. "Am I nuts?" I asked Winzey, hoping she was still hanging around. What was going on here? Why didn't it make sense to me? Was I missing something? But maybe that was the answer.

After all, I'd fallen head over heels for Quentin. Big problem, though. He was on the same side as the guys who were following me around and trying to kill me. Yeah, I was definitely going insane.

☙ ☙ ☙

I tied the gem around my ankle and tucked it inside my sock. Wasn't the most comfortable thing, but it worked.

Quentin, or whoever was posing as my boyfriend, hadn't bothered to fetch me just yet. Was I going to stay? No sirree.

I opened the door to the room and walked right into a misplaced football player. "Uh, don't you have a game this weekend?" I squinted up at him. "You play for that New York team, don't you?"

He grunted. I suppose that was the extent of his vocabulary. Not much more is necessary for someone of his size.

"I need to get by, I'm looking for someone."

Grunt. Arms, no those were tree stumps, blocked my path. "Uh, no really," I told him. "I have to meet someone. I'm running late."

No matter how many times it happened, I would never get used to the thrown-over-the-shoulder carry technique.

"Where are we going?" I asked my captor. "I'd be happy to walk nicely if you'd just put me down."

We rounded a corner. From my view, which was more of the label on this guy's jeans and the floor than anything else, it still looked like a hospital. We rounded a corner and I saw a gurney. And the guy laying there didn't look like he needed a doctor. He needed the coroner.

I was deposited, literally dropped, on the black and white tiles of a long hallway. The dark wooden double doors in front of me were closed. A butler-looking guy stood beside them. Any second now he'd lean forward and open one of them, rows of toy soldiers would then lift their long trumpets and salute my entrance.

That dream bubble popped when Mr. Hercules handcuffed my hands behind my back. I was not to be received as royalty.

Oh darn.

The butler did admit me the way I imagined. And then I got a punt kick in the tush that left me nearly sprawling along the shiny floor. Not even a red carpet for me to follow.

I recognized the snake known as Mr. B immediately. He held out a hand to me as I approached, but I knew he wasn't asking for a dance.

"What do you want with me? I don't have the gems. I'm nobody. You send me back home and I swear I'll forget any of this..." I looked around the room and expected the Mad Hatter to emerge and seat himself at the long dining room table, "...mayhem."

"I have a better plan."

I rolled my eyes up to look at the ceiling. It was as fancy as the floor. Cathedral style with garish chandeliers and stained glass windows.

"You like what you see?" He swept his hand around the room. "This can be yours. I need an heir."

I nearly fainted.

He laughed, a belly laugh that creeped me out. "I don't want you to mother a child for me. Although I can't say the idea isn't tempting."

His eyes were roaches and they crawled over my skin. I wanted to rip at my body with my nails. I shuddered.

"I know what you think of me. I couldn't trust you to be a good mother to *my* child. But, you wouldn't harm or destroy Quentin's child, would you?"

I glanced down at my stomach. Oh, it better not be true.

"No. Not yet anyway, so say the doctors who checked you out. But your dear boyfriend expressed his desire not to see you killed. So I will save your life, in exchange for your firstborn son."

"Never," I hissed.

He reached over and cupped my chin in his greasy hands. "I know your worst nightmares and I can make them come true. The only way is my way."

Tears stung my eyes, but I refused to let him break me. I couldn't be reduced to a quivering puddle of female flesh. How would that look? "Then I will have gems. You will give me a set of gems and allow me my magic. I will not be unarmed." I was rather in shock I had the nerve to ask, but I didn't think it was wrong to try to bargain.

His head fell back like a Pez dispenser and another round of laughter bubbled out. "You are a sassy one. I can see why Quentin likes you. He's a strong one, himself. Quite willing to go to great lengths to get what he wants."

My heart had finished its gymnastics routine and had landed, belly-flop style, in what used to be my stomach. That particular organ was up around my throat and threatening to alter the perfection of the formally set dining table.

"C-Could you untie my hands? I'm not feeling so well." It would serve him right if I puked on his shiny black shoes.

He patted my cheek. "There's a bathroom in the corner there. Don't be long. First course is ready to be served."

I choked it back. My legs couldn't move fast enough to get me to the bathroom. Then nothing.

Well, how long had it been since I'd last eaten? The Arctic Circle adventure? It had to have been.

It felt like all that happened days ago. Time had a freaky way of sneaking off from me. And now, it seemed, so did my dignity.

I splashed cold water on my face. All it did was make me look like a drowned rat. I needed a shower. Clean clothes would be nice, but I'd shower *in* my clothes if that wasn't an option. Actually, the idea of food didn't sound half bad. It was the company and his idiotic proposal that had me gulping down bile.

Either Winzey had abandoned me or was just as shocked by the recent events. I prayed for the second. I wasn't going to be able to do this alone.

I scooped up a handful of water and sucked it in, swished it around and spit it out. I felt sufficiently sure I would be able to swallow my food and keep it there. *I think.*

Bergestein nodded to me and rose to pull out the chair at the opposite end of the eight-foot table. It had been set with a white lace table cloth and elegant, creamy china.

A bowl of soup had already been placed at my station. I stirred it, almost afraid to ask.

"Simply vegetable barley, my dear. I wouldn't poison you. I've been quite honest with my intentions."

I raised an eyebrow but lifted the spoon to my lips and sipped. I realized just how hungry I was.

Mr. B's only comments were to the staff, and when the empty plate that had held roast potatoes and steamed chicken was removed, he pulled me from the table.

"You've learned much magic in a short time. Quentin said your command of fire is amazing for such a novice."

I nodded, looking out the window. The courtyard was below us. Four or five stories below.

"What is this place?" I asked. It seemed like it housed a factory, a hospital and then, this...ballroom?

"It is ever changing. The magic here is strong. You know that. Your tricks have all been rooted from the power in the original gems."

So they were here! I turned back toward the table and used magic to bring my goblet to my outstretched fingers. "You tell the truth," I said. I wondered how he liked being accused of honesty.

One of his overgrown eyebrows shot skyward. I felt like saluting.

"So humor me, why is it you don't have a wife or mistress to give you an heir, surely with your wealth and power—"

"Exactly, my dear. A wife, even a mistress would make demands of me, of my wealth, my power, my life. I've thought this through and am not making this barter lightly. I'm on the cusp of joining all the gems, but no amount of magic will give me immortality. I need an heir. I think that's truth enough, don't you?"

I gulped, unable to believe he'd throw it all out there just like that. I was too freaked out to suggest maybe he couldn't have children. Plus, he was bargaining my life here—and I really believed I meant it. "You don't have a second-in-command? What would a mere infant do for you?"

"Can you imagine the skill he would learn, growing up with the most powerful magic at hand? Those at my right hand would also be at his. I require loyalty. Require, not request."

The food was not settling well on my stomach at all. I needed out of here. How could he suggest—no never mind, Mr. B could suggest, even demand anything he wanted. "I'm still quite unsure of this...p-p-plan. I'd like to talk to Quentin, of course." I took a deep breath and felt a little of the old Ella slipping back. "But not tonight. You *must* know what I've gone through recently. Will you offer me a room, a bed, shower?"

Mr. B's eyes shot open, then glittered with what I hoped was amusement. "Of course I will. I would not be considered inhospitable. Crank?" The burly man who'd treated me like an oversize football was at his right hand. Invisible. He'd followed me in and been invisible. I cringed when I wondered if he'd followed me into the bathroom.

"Crank, see Ms. Ella to her room. I think we should give her the suite on Floor Four of the new wing."

Mr. B. even got a grunt in return. At least I wasn't delivered to my lodgings in the same manner I had gone to dinner. My full stomach would have surely rebelled.

ଓ ଓ ଓ

Quentin sat in the recliner. He was either asleep or staring out the window. If he hadn't heard mine, I'm sure he couldn't have missed Crank's heavy footfalls on the polished wood floors of the hallway.

Once the shock of seeing him faded, I did a quick survey of the room. It was plush. Definitely hotel-like, but homey. Whether I wanted to admit it or not, I could get used to this.

The décor was rich plum and a deep green. If I'd tried it in my apartment, it would have looked like sour grapes. This, however, looked amazing.

A sitting room was adjoined by the bedroom. The color scheme matched throughout. A light peaked out of a doorway just out of my line of sight. I assumed the bathroom. My first stop. After Quentin and the football player left.

I ignored Crank and approached Quentin.

"I'm not liking this."

"I know. I lied to you. I wanted to protect you. That's why we were up there at the North Pole. But then you left and, of course, Mr. B has the ability to trace anyone who's using their magic. It was best for me to come here and wait. We knew you'd get here sooner or later."

"Why, Quentin. Why are you on his side?"

"Can't you feel the power?" Quentin's green eyes flared bright for a moment, startling me. "This place is magic in and of itself. Bergestein isn't all bad. His ideas aren't the cultish, fanatical, rule-the-world schemes at all. Done right, it could lead us to a controlled, peaceful way of life."

"Done correctly," I repeated, wanting to spit on the idea of control.

"And that's where I come in. I can't prevent him from taking over. It's inevitable. He's willing to kill anyone who has an original gem. He has nine now. There's just one remaining. *One*."

I swallowed and gazed over his shoulder. "What are you going to do?"

"I'm going to continue to prove to Mr. B. that I want to help him, stand beside him and ease the load of responsibility. I can be at peace by gaining some control."

"That sounds noble, but what about the island? What about the natural scope of things? This place, you, me—I just bet we're all simply figments of our imagination at this point. I don't know what's real and what isn't anymore. He's creating illusions."

"And isn't the idea of living in a world you can control so much better than facing the polluted life of a nobody the world just pushes around? Do you really want to rejoin the rat race of those millions of people out there who'll never believe magic is possible? What kind of life is that?"

"A real one." I stomped. How could he say this, believe this?

"Reality bites."

I didn't want to even think it, but I did. He was right. Reality, for me anyway, was no bed of roses. I stood there for a minute, looking down at the set jaw and sparkling eyes. The memory of Winzey's voice echoed in my ear, "*Bad.*"

Oh, he wasn't bad. He was good. Very, very good.

The bright green of his stare darkened to a forest shade and his eyelids slid part way closed. He reached up his hand and pulled me onto his lap. It was like coming home.

I could have resisted a kiss. But he didn't offer me one. Instead he folded me against his fishermen's sweater and rested his forehead against my shoulder.

That's all it took. If I'd have dared look, I probably would have seen my heart scurry across our intertwined arms and leap fearlessly into his chest.

"Why did you leave me?" His voice sounded the part of a deserted lover.

I opened my mouth, but closed it again. *A half-truth really wasn't a lie, it was it?* "I was scared," I finally relented. That was the truth.

"Of me? I was trying to protect you."

"I'm still scared of you."

He tugged me away from his chest and framed my face with his hands. "One thing I wouldn't do is hurt you."

I shook my head. "There's too much going on. Too much I don't know. It's not a clear good versus bad out there, is it?"

"No." He chewed his lip. "It isn't."

"And you're somewhere in the gray."

I had to smile when his eyebrows turned downward.

My heart melted. "You look the villain when you frown like that." I tried to mimic his expression.

He laughed and pulled me close. I turned my head at the last minute to avoid the kiss.

"Why?" His voice tickled my cheek and sent a shock wave of awareness through my entire body. That was why. He could turn me into putty with a touch.

"I want to stay in control. The last thing I need to do is complicate this with sex."

"For a minute there I wondered if you'd gotten over me that quickly."

"I see your ego survived the trip." I got up off his lap and stared out the window. "Where the heck are we? It looks old here...England?"

Quentin nodded and reclined in the chair.

"Then why no accents? Everything, and everyone, here is...Americanized."

"It's safe here. The castle's real, but everything inside it was brought by magic. Remember the exchange rate," he said and grinned with his teasing, crooked smile. "This stuff is real, but it doesn't belong here. And it could be gone tomorrow, replaced with something completely different." He patted the padded arm of the chair in emphasis. "But there's no one around who's going to say a thing about this place or what's going on here."

My mind was boggled. If the events weren't enough to make me question my sanity, the idea of an ever changing castle/hospital/factory whatever this place was—it was too much for me to comprehend. "I don't like all this stuff."

"You don't have to. You just have to accept it. Don't make waves. Just stay in the rooms assigned to you and read, watch TV." He shrugged. "Mr. B will only notice you when you're a thorn in his side."

"And I guess he doesn't care that he's a thorn in mine."

His half-laugh caused the burgundy chair to bounce. He used the momentum to stand and stretch. "Don't you worry, Ella. I'll be around to take care of you. Promise me you won't try anything funny. It's best you stay away from any magic whatsoever."

I twirled the chair around to me and took Quentin's vacated spot. I used magic to rotate it back.

He frowned and tilted his head. "I guess you can do that kind of stuff. Just no walking through walls or starting fires. And don't even *try* to jump. Not that you could without gems."

"No flying, then, huh?"

His eyes widened. "That *was* rather impressive. Especially without your own gems."

I waved my hand, hoping my feeling of panic didn't reflect on my face. "Everyone seems to think I have the ability to pick up the wavelengths or something. Didn't Sam even say my...adaptation to magic was one of the reasons he picked me? Anyway, I didn't even realize I was flying. I just was enjoying the wind on my face and suddenly opened my eyes and I was floating." I watched him, praying he bought it.

He shook his head. "And once you realized what was happening you lost concentration and fell like a ton of bricks."

"Quite." *I don't believe it. He bought it.*

He continued shaking his head until he'd left the room. I looked back toward the window and stared at the gray sky through the trees. For asking me to behave they'd sure given me a room with a chance to escape, magic or not. The tree branches held out their limbs like helping hands. All I had to do was climb down and walk away.

I turned back around. I just didn't have the strength to do it tonight. The room's glory hadn't faded in Quentin's absence. One night won't hurt. One bath, a good night's sleep. Then I could plan.

☙ ☙ ☙

I figured either Mr. B or Quentin arranged for meals to be brought to my door like clockwork at eight and noon the next day. I'd woken startled, but golly, it was so comfortable I didn't care there was a stranger standing at the doorway calling my name. "Breakfast, Ms. Ella."

I nodded. I hope there's a room account. Ha. Even if there was I'd never be able to settle it.

Just because I could, I'd filled the oversize tub with hot water and pink bubbles and lounged until lunch arrived. I could get used to this, I had thought. Life of luxury. Nothing to do.

Nothing to do, I muttered again. It was scarcely two o'clock and I'd found myself going stark raving mad.

Maid service never showed up, so I made my own bed. There were no books, no paper, and the TV was on the fritz.

I had managed to sit for a half an hour and watch out the window, but that had grown old, too. What was I going to do? The big grand scheme of getting the gems from Mr. B certainly didn't seem to be coming to fruition here. I had no plan, hadn't heard from Sam and Quentin's admission of his intentions left me without help on the inside. What could little ole me do? Nada. Nothing. Just wait.

I was still trying to decide if this was prison or a hotel. My current bored-out-of-my-mind consensus was hotel disguised as a prison. I was actually ready to admit my first priority was to escape. Defeating this evil man was a little farther down my list of things to do at the moment.

When I heard the knock I nearly pitched myself into the arms of whoever dared to rescue me from the madness. Thank goodness it was Quentin.

I didn't even let him speak. "Do you know what it's like to be cooped up in there?" I pointed back over my shoulder. "There's nothing to do. Nothing."

He glanced over my shoulder without a change in expression. "Did you check the closet? You could have picked out what you wanted to wear to the gala tonight."

Oh, that just bites the big one. "Clothes? In the closet?" And God only knows what else I could have found. I tried to reassure myself I would have resorted to that sooner or later.

Quentin slid past me, pausing as our bodies rubbed. I didn't step back, enjoying the static. His eyes darkened, just enough for me to know he was well aware of my reaction.

He crossed the room and pulled open the double doors. My jaw hit the floor at the colors and fabrics I could see from here. I had to run over and get a close up look. Amazing.

"You didn't even open it?" Quentin looked at me like I'd grown antlers. Or maybe "Here's my sign" had appeared on my forehead.

I shook my head. Maybe it'd fall off. I didn't need anything confirming what I feared he thought already.

"What's this about a gala? Isn't that quite contrived? I arrive, there's a closet full of formal dresses, which I'm sure are just perfectly fitted for me." I waved down my body, disgusted by the filthy clothes I'd slid back on after my bath. "And then, and *then* there's a gala?"

Quentin tilted his head and stared at me some more. I felt my head and face to see if there was something amusing there. It must have been my own ignorance shining through. Or else. Wait! I had it! This was all planned, it was all part of this mastermind plot to make me think I really was losing my mind. So I wouldn't try to get to the jewels or stop Quentin or even try to warn anyone about what was to happen. That had to be it.

Quentin had turned back to the closet. His shoulders were shaking. It looked uncontrollable.

"What?" I placed my hands on my hips. "What in God's green creation is so funny?"

"You," he sputtered and fell into another peal of laughter.

I threw up my arms with a sigh. Another part of the plan, I told myself, nodding my head. I was too smart for this. I could stay on top of things. Of course, I'd play along. After the day I'd had, I wasn't staying in this room when there was a gala somewhere.

"You're a fruit." Quentin sat on the bed. The spasms had stopped, but occasionally a half-cough, half-laugh emerged from his lips. His eyes sparkled with the danger that he might go over the edge with hysterics again.

"Just call me Anna Banana. Or wait. Mary Strawberry. No, I've got it..."

He held up a hand. I set my lips in a tight line and pulled a blue satin gown from the closet. Uh, no. There was no back to speak of in that dress.

I slid it back in and pulled out the dark purple shimmering material. It was long, and had a halter top, but it looked like it covered all the right things.

"Can you live with purple?"

"Try it on."

The mirror made me look...good. I strained to look over my shoulder and judge the size of my butt. The clingy material of the dress was bad enough, but the glittery thread woven throughout would accent any extra bulges. And I had a feeling I might have a few of those. Especially since I wasn't one to dash off to the gym at five every morning.

I hiked my boobs up one more time and surveyed the faux cleavage. I'd need duct tape if they were ever going to stay there, but hey, it was fun imagining.

Quentin knocked at the bedroom door.

"Just a minute."

I slid my hands down my sides and decided he'd seen me naked. It's not like he'd laugh. At least not if he ever wanted to see me naked again.

But it wasn't Quentin who was the recipient of my pose in the doorway. I shrieked and immediately covered my chest with my arms.

Bergestein laughed and clucked his tongue. "You do look dashing, dear. I'm sure Quentin would find himself quite enamored with you in that dress. But it's a little more flashy than I had in mind."

I looked up, one eyebrow nearly scraping the ceiling, as Mr. B fingered the dresses on the other side of the bed.

"Here." He handed me a fuller, old fashioned gown in a deep rose color. It was satin, with off-the-shoulder puffed sleeves, a sweetheart neckline and full long skirt. I swear it was a cross between my prom dress and Cinderella's gown. It was not something a woman in her late twenties would pull over her head.

"Are you sure? It's kind of..."

"High school?"

"Uh, yeah."

He winked and took it back to the closet. The next one he pulled out was a little better. I could actually wear it if I had to.

I took it from his hands. "I'll try it on." I ran to the bathroom and locked the door.

It made me look fat and short. With no chest and no waist.

"I don't think the tight oriental dress thing works for me."

To my relief, Mr. B wrinkled his nose and nodded his head.

"Anything in green?" I asked when I saw his fingers pause over a bright yellow garment. I was not going to be Shelly Sunshine. No freaking way. It totally would clash with my skin tone.

"Wear the one you had on. But you can't keep your hands crossed over your chest the whole time."

I narrowed my eyes. So what was the point of all this? Some kind of test?

If he was thought reading, he ignored my puzzled questions. “Quentin will be back to fetch you at six. You’ll have a private dinner and he’ll fill you in on the details of the rest of the night.”

“Uh, sir?” I didn’t think I should call him Mr. B to his face, but Bergestein seemed like such a mouthful.

He stopped near the doorway.

“Shoes? Stockings? Are they all in the closet?”

“You’ll find everything you need here. Cosmetics are in the drawers of the vanity.”

The problem with that dress, I soon realized was the inability to hide the gem. The solution? I threaded a piece of dental floss through it and attached it to the charm bracelet I’d chosen for my wrist. Too bad there wasn’t a matching one for my ankle. Then it’d really be out of the limelight.

ଓ ଓ ଓ

Quentin’s eyes shone like dark emeralds. We stood on either side of the doorway and devoured each other with our eyes. He looked dashing in the black tuxedo. He hadn’t shaved, but I was glad. The hint of shadow gave him just enough bad boy appeal to have my mind rethinking the no sex clause I’d added to our relationship.

I mean, what would one fling mean? It’s not like we hadn’t done it already.

I licked my lips and invited him in. His eyes remained on my mouth, but he shook his head. If he came in, we’d never make it to the gala. We weren’t fooling each other for a moment.

“Let’s go.” His deep voice was husky. In the room? Pshaw, I was ready to pounce on him in the hallway.

I didn’t taste dinner. I declined to drink any of the wine. I needed my head clear. Or at least as clear as possible. I still had reservations about Quentin’s part in this. Mr. B had me puzzled. I still couldn’t make heads or tails from his earlier visit.

And being a gala it guaranteed I’d rub shoulders with all the other big shots from the darkside. A chance to take notes and...

I didn't know the *and* part of it. But I knew I'd need the notes later.

I really had expected something right out of the movies. Boy was I failing to give credit. This was larger and more intense than any ballroom full of beautiful people waltzing together.

"My God," I whispered to Quentin. "There has to be three hundred people here."

He just frowned and nodded. "Probably."

We circled the room and greeted the people Quentin knew. I'd need a notebook to remember everyone's name. Even magic couldn't help my brain.

Mr. B. stood on the stage where a big brass band was assembled and did the perfunctory thank you for coming speech. I tuned out his monotone voice and instead listened to the conversation behind me.

"All the money from the bank is wired through my service. I can get you whatever you need. Adjusting the interest rate and holding fees won't be problem."

"Let's start with two and go from there. I think that should be enough to keep the FBI from investigating."

It might as well have been Greek, but I understood this party was full of very powerful, very bad people. I shuddered.

"...Enjoy." Bergestein bowed and stepped off the stage. As the band started, dozens of couples stepped out onto the dance floor. What was this, ballroom dance competition? I didn't know these steps! Try the electric slide or the YMCA and I might be able to keep up.

"We have to." Quentin pinched the nerve in my elbow when I ignored his efforts to lead me to the circling throng.

Says who?

"I can't," I hissed back even as I gave in. "I don't know how."

"Just follow my lead."

Did I say, anywhere, I could dance? Was it in my contract? No and no. What this was could be described only as ankle torture. Step back then forward, no side, side, wait—back? I was crossing my ankles and stumbling like I was walking on marbles. Quentin, on the other hand, moved smoothly and gracefully. Quentin totally didn't seem to be the type who could dance, much less would want to. It might have been my jaw I was tripping over. Just something about a man who could dance...

Unfortunately, I couldn't master it, no matter how hard I tried. Before the song was half over, I think even Quentin was ready to admit I had been right. But it was too late. Mr. B himself walked up and held out his hand to me. I gripped it, and nearly fell when he lifted mine to his grossly full lips and kissed the back of it. "Shall we waltz?"

Quentin snickered and stepped back.

"Oh, I couldn't. You see, I don't—"

"Nonsense, darling, you were doing wonderfully. I suggest you just imagine a layer of air between your feet and the floor and let me lead."

I guess that's why he was the mastermind of this whole thing. I didn't have the brain cells to think of using magic to save Quentin's toes.

I still held back.

"Go on. You can't deny the host a dance. It would look bad. He could have had you killed you know."

And the downside was?

I stepped onto the polished wood floor and pretended to know what I was doing. Everyone look at Ella, Mr. B's marionette, I felt like shouting.

When the dance was over, we faced the band and clapped. I turned without so much as a curtsy, eager to hide behind the congregation that lined the dance floor.

"Just a moment. I thought we might talk."

Mr. B's plump fingers bit into my arm. I jerked away. His finger slid down my arm and caught on my bracelet. The strain broke the rope and chain that held it together and sent charms and beads scattering on the shiny floor.

"Oh!" I exclaimed, my eyes searching for one bead in particular. Damn, Shit! *Why me? Why?*

Chapter Thirteen

I put my hand down and used magic to pull all the pieces toward my hand as if it were a magnet. The guests around me had retrieved some of the pieces but stopped and stared in awe when the pieces moved on the floor.

"Cease!" Bergestein clapped his hands. Everything stopped. Including my breath.

A gentlemen cleared his throat and rose from his kneeling position. His hand was in his pocket. He turned his face before I could see his features. I just knew he'd snatched something from the floor. And I still hadn't found the gem.

"Ella?" Mr. B's eyes had sunk in his head and shrunk. I was looking at a vile creature, a snake, poised to strike

"Yes, sir?" My voice quivered. I didn't try to hide it.

"Your parlor tricks have no place at my party. I told you that you must stop practicing the optical illusions you are so fascinated with. Look at the scene you've caused. Someone could trip on these trinkets."

Pig. Asshole. I bowed my head. "I'm sorry, sir." So magic was a secret? I nudged the pile with my toes. "I'll clean it up and be off to my room then."

"Negative."

The tips of my ears were ready to spontaneously combust. "I need a drink." One was pushed into my hand.

I downed the contents and grunted. Wow. That was strong. I used the empty glass to hold what was left of the charm bracelet and found Quentin.

"This was his fault, you know."

His tight lipped smile curved upwards. “No one will believe you. Mr. B’s more powerful than the President.”

“With all these people around, I’m surprised the Prez isn’t here tonight.”

Quentin just winked and slipped my hand through his arm. I left the cup of mangled bracelet on the table. It was truly worthless to me. The gem was gone and so was my party spirit.

ઔ ઔ ઔ

I did realize I’d learned something in Hollywood. No, not how to vamp, after all I didn’t have the figure for it. I could act, though. I smiled and laughed and pretended it was the best night of my life. And I wanted to puke.

Mr. B’s influence was huge. And since I’d managed to make a fool of myself on the dance floor, I was practically a celebrity. More than once I’d threatened Quentin with various forms of castration or other torture if he didn’t get me out of there. He didn’t believe a word I said.

I got my second wind the instant Quentin caved and agreed to take me back to my room.

“Now? Really?” I could barely refrain from throwing my arms around his neck.

“Yeah, I think we’ve done enough socializing. I know you must want out of those heels and fancy clothes.”

I shrugged. My feet had gone numb hours ago and I found I was dressed quite modestly in comparison to some of the other guests. I’d have looked pretty silly walking around trying to hide the hint of cleavage in the deep V of my dress front when there was one woman wearing a dress cut to the navel...and beyond.

He opened the unlocked door and waited for me to enter. I stopped and twirled at the telltale sound of the deadbolt sliding home. “Why? We left it unlocked while we were out, why lock it now?”

“Because we don’t have a do not disturb sign to put on the knob.”

“Why would—”

He shook his head and crossed over to me. His eyes were black and worked their magic, freezing me in place. “Quentin,” I breathed.

“Ella. I’ve missed you.”

I snapped my head back and blinked. “I can’t do this, Quentin. I won’t.”

“Shhh. This is the safest place you could be. I won’t let anything happen to you.”

“But—” He silenced me with his lips on mine.

I gasped as his flesh sizzled against mine. That just gave him more room to maneuver. His tongue plunged into my mouth, stirring my senses until I couldn’t remember why I had said no.

He tasted of sweet cream frosting and uncut scotch. I was drunk already. His hands slid up and braced either side of my face, but the room didn’t stop spinning. “Crazy,” he murmured. “You make a man crazy in that dress.”

I put a hand out to steady myself and met with the contradiction of his clothes. Sleek lapels, starched cotton and a rock solid foundation that radiated heat through the layers. I wanted to claw the clothes out of the way and get my hands against flesh.

I shouldn’t be doing this, my sanity reminded me when he paused to allow us a breath. I stepped back. His mouth claimed mine again. I fisted his shirt, but continued to walk.

His hands skimmed down the bare skin of my neck and traced the dip of my dress with the touch of butterfly wings. I shivered.

“Quentin, no. This isn’t a good idea right now. I really can’t.”

“Yes, you can. Your body says so. Your mind is tired, confused. This will relax you.”

“No.”

I jerked my mouth away from his and fell back onto the couch. “No.” I stated again with more emphasis.

His crooked grin did nothing to help the frantic beating of my heart. He smoothed his shirt and ran a hand through his hair. “I can’t believe you’re turning me down like this.”

Poor baby. “I am. Things have changed, I’ve changed.”

“The only thing that’s changed is the place. This isn’t the North Pole.”

“And you’re not the only man in five hundred square miles.”

“I really wasn’t—”

“Shut up. Just...” I squeezed my fingers so hard my nails dented my palms. “Go. Please. You don’t understand what I’ve been through.”

"You're doing that female analogy thing. Trying to make order and sense of things."

"What's so wrong with a little order?" I stood toe-to-toe with him again, this time pulling myself up to my full height in my heels and pressing my fists onto my hips. Even if I wasn't anything threatening, I *felt* bigger.

"You can't categorize the magic."

"Magic?" I pointed at the candleholder on the side table and held it above Quentin's head. It was heavy brass with lots of sharp edges. Real damage potential with that one.

"I think you should put that back where you got it."

"Make me."

He dove at me just as I let go. It fell with a thud to the carpet. In the meantime I was trapped under Quentin on the sofa. The draft tickling my thighs meant my skirt had crossed the line of decency. I had a feeling border patrol was on its way to investigate.

Quentin's deep gaze connected with mine. There was something paralyzing about it. Isn't there a snake that has the same technique—?

"Oh."

His fingers rested mid-calf and stroked the sensitive skin there until shivers chased one another up to my core. I knew where I wanted his hand to go.

"Quentin." Why was it so much more of a struggle to push his name past my clenched teeth?

His hand never rose above my knee. He hadn't done anything that would have evoked an "R" rating if it had been in the movies. But I still felt as though he'd flicked the switch for the most intimate parts of me to wake up and scream for attention.

He pushed off and let his fingers trail to my ankle. With gentle hands he loosened the strap of my shoe and let it drop to the floor.

I couldn't help it. I moaned in appreciation of the thumbs he pushed deep into the center of my aching foot. His leaned over and kissed the top of my big toe and then lifted my other foot for the same attention.

My nerves were playing a crazed game of ping pong. I thought I'd gotten used to my ears ringing. I pulled myself upright on the sofa and stared at him. My heart pounded. I could say no to sex, but not to loving him. Even when I knew the bad things he was involved in. Even when I knew he was using me.

"Good night, El—"

"Wait."

He turned and waited. He's lucky. If he would have so much as raised an eyebrow, my rejuvenated foot would have assisted him to the door. "Uh. I'm sorry."

He shook his head, his hair coming loose from the gel that had kept it slicked back. I liked the messy look better, I realized. It dipped onto his forehead and nearly covered his eyes. He was dangerously sexy looking out from under the dark tips of the fringe. "I should be the one apologizing, Ella. I didn't mean to push myself on you."

"I—" I stood, not sure how to reassure him I didn't think worse of him. I mean, it's not like we hadn't already gone down that road.

The little devil on my shoulder started showing my mind souvenir photos of the fireworks I'd seen on the last trip. I took a deep breath. To thine own self be true, right? There was always tomorrow.

I stood and slid my hands around his neck. The kiss was chaste. "I don't need a lover," I told him with my head against his shoulder. "I need a friend."

His arms tightened. "I told you nothing would happen-"

"A friend, Quentin." I pushed him an arm's length away. "Not a bodyguard."

He licked his lips. I felt his eyes travel up and down my body before meeting mine again. The dark passion was gone. But I thought I caught a glimpse of something warm, inviting.

"I need some sleep. You want to help me out of this dress?"

"Not tonight," he sighed. "I think I've got a headache."

I laughed and snatched my shoes up. "Good night."

"Sweet dreams, Ella. I hope you dream of what we could have had tonight."

"Undoubtedly, I will."

The door clicked behind him. I threw my shoes as hard as I could at the closet door. Doing the right thing totally sucked.

ଔ ଔ ଔ

My dreams were tortured facsimiles of the grand ball. I imagined every bad thing that could have happened and then exaggerated it tenfold. The fate of the last gem haunted me. What if Mr. B. had found it? Would he come around to question me? What if Quentin had it and was waiting for me to admit losing it? What if—

I stopped tossing and turning at the sound of someone pounding on the door. I had no clock beside my bed. All I knew is that dawn hadn't broken.

I shrugged the heavy robe over my shoulders and pushed a hand through my hair. Whoever dared knock at this hour deserved to see me looking like a witch.

"Quentin!" I exclaimed when I pulled open the door. His lip was bloody and his eyelid swelling. "What happened?"

He nearly fell into my arms as I tugged him into the room. I latched every lock and slid the bench over to block the entrance.

"Won't help," his words were slurred. "They'll walk through the wall."

It was back to magic then. Who had done this to Quentin? Why?

I pulled the sweatshirt over his head. Grass stains tainted the elbows of the white shirt and the knees of his jeans. One leg was torn. I was worried what I might find beneath the ragged denim.

"Quentin, talk to me. What happened?"

"Chasing a fairy. Big man.

"Say what?" I unzipped his pants. He put his hand over mine and held it there.

"I wish you'd have tried that earlier this evening."

"Me, too," I admitted. But now there wasn't even a drop of romantic foreplay in the motions we took to free him of his clothes. Not all of them, mind you. Just the ones that hid the bruised ribs and bloody shin.

I had to guess the damage to his leg had been the result of a fall, not a knife wound. The jeans were neatly cut, though. I pushed against the edge of the angry red flesh. A drip of blood seeped out and traced through the dark hairs.

"Okay," I breathed out. "That's enough for me."

"What?" I could tell Quentin's eyes weren't focusing well at all. His head bobbed as he stared at his leg. "Where is it?"

"You lost a fight with something here." I poked the leg a good two inches above the damage.

"Oh, yeah." His voice went high for a moment. Then he sighed and took the pillow I offered him and stretched out on the floor between my bed and the bathroom. "That does hurt." He was fading.

"I'll be right back." Shit. What now? What if he should have stitches? What if it was an animal bite? I turned around and looked at it again. It could be. Could he be exposed to rabies?

I knocked over a stack of towels. Muttering curses under my breath, I threw one in the sink and twisted on the cold water.

The first splash of the icy water against my cheeks just about sent me screeching back to bed. Deep breath. I did it again. I had to wake up in order to deal with this properly. Last thing *I* needed to do was pass out. Seeing oozing wounds wasn't exactly my idea of fun, and didn't make my stomach feel real stable. Anything that could be considered a crisis was on my list of most avoidable things.

"Quentin?" He'd either passed out or fallen asleep. "Bleeping, blaring bunghole." I threw the rag at his leg and sat on the edge of my bed. I held my head in my hands to keep it from spinning around like in the exorcist movie. I just knew that's what had to be next. Why me?

Sleep was out of the question. Now what? Quentin wasn't complaining so I let him be and paced the floor. The fairy? Probably Winzey. And here I'd been hoping she'd either flown home or was hiding up in my closet. Why was Quentin chasing her? Who had gotten in his way and done this to him?

The tenderized man of my dreams moaned and rolled onto his side. "C'mon, Quentin. You're killing me here." I leaned over and pressed the damp rag to his shin.

He sat up with a garbled scream. I couldn't help the laugh that rose in my throat.

It faded quickly enough. Quentin was spooked. Those expressive green eyes darted around the room. Their luminescence spoke volumes.

I knelt beside him and smoothed the hair off his forehead. He winced. He'd taken a good hit to the head. Who ever this big man was, he must have been a monster. Quentin was no slouch. He might not have been a linebacker for the NFL, but I could almost see him as bouncer material. In this case, he was the one who was bounced. Dribbled, in fact.

And just where had these maternal feelings come from? I'd never really escaped Disneyland, had I? I was really starting to hate roller coasters.

ଓ ଓ ଓ

I woke up with a heavy feeling of dread in my stomach. The lights were still blazing. I must not have turned off the water all the way. How'd I sleep through the annoying sound of drip, drip, drip?

I reached up to push the hair out of my eyes. It was stuck. I pulled, and realized someone was sleeping on it. "Good Lord, Quentin, get off me!"

He rolled over and grinned.

I pushed out of bed and high tailed it to the bathroom. "*No* following me," I ordered Mr. Cheshire Cat.

The panic of last night hadn't really faded. I scrubbed my teeth while studying my hairline in the mirror. I just knew gray hair would be taking over the dark strands prematurely. If I lived that long.

My hand shook as I slid the mirrored cabinet aside. My silent prayer was answered when I saw the bottle of pain relievers perched on the second shelf. "Thank you, God."

I popped the top and tossed the cotton aside.

"Bring me about four of those." Quentin's voice sounded like a scratched vinyl record.

I poured out two more. "I'm not your maid." Then I thought about it. "And I'm not a nurse." But I gave in and delivered the meds anyway.

"Wanna play doctor?"

If he wasn't in my bed I would have tossed the glass of cold water at him. The problem was I did want to nurse him, take care of him. That's what a fool like me gets for falling in love.

I thought about what he'd told me the night before. Getting all sappy was not going to help this situation. "Did you say you saw a fairy?"

He tossed back the water like it was a shot of whiskey, and grimaced as if it tasted that way. "Damn head feels like it's been used as a hockey puck."

I hated to tell him it looked the same way. "Well?"

"Yeah. It was peeking in the windows. I went out through the French doors to follow it. I called to it, her, whatever it was, but it flew off."

"How big was it? Are fairies common?"

"I'd never seen one before. Bergestein mentioned them at one point in a conversation I'd overheard. I think he said their power was greater than the gemstones, but then he said they never leave their home."

"But one did, right?"

"Sure looked that way to me."

I walked to the balcony and opened the door. The damp breeze ruffled the sheer curtains that obscured the view from his side of the room. I'd never be able to spot a figure the size of my forefinger.

"So you followed this fairy outside and then what?" I didn't look back at him. I slid the door closed and twisted the lock. Habit.

"Someone bulldozed me and chased the little thing. I think it went up into the tree. Anyway, Brutus was too big to climb it, so he came after me to vent his frustration, I guess."

His story sounded preposterous. "Why would he do something like that?"

I turned back from the window and leaned against the door. Quentin sat up in bed, the blankets pulled away and exposing his chest. Why did he have to look so damn good? Even in the morning with darkening shadows around his middle and the raccoon eyes? He swept his hair off his face, exposing a bright red knot.

"Looks like your attacker had a lot of frustration," I commented. Nothing like a few hours to make everything look worse. At least his eyes were clear.

Quentin shrugged and stared at the lump his toes made under the bedspread. There was something else, I felt it raise the hairs on the back of my neck. I wanted to trust him. I needed to trust someone.

And where the heck was Sam? He'd been the one to pull me into this mess. I shivered and looked at the bathroom door. I was almost afraid to know the answer to that question.

"I think I'm going to see about breakfast. I'll have something sent up here for you."

"You're not going anywhere without me."

I raised an eyebrow. "Something you're not telling me? Do you think I need a babysitter?"

"A bodyguard, maybe."

That was a tickle. The man was beaten and bruised, lying in my bed and *I* needed someone to protect me? "You're...kidding...me," I gasped between peals of laughter.

He crossed his arms. My gaze fell to his chest and I sucked in air. "Yeah, okay. You can be my bodyguard." I closed the door to the bathroom. Whatever he wanted to hear.

I opened it up and peaked out at his grinning face. "After breakfast."

ଓ ଓ ଓ

I really had no idea where I was going. Quentin had dozed off while I was showering. Which was good, since I'd forgotten to take clean clothes in the bathroom with me. I wasn't favorable to being his entertainment as I dressed.

I stuck to the corridors I'd traveled before. Mainly to make sure I could find my little suite again. Nothing like having food and nowhere to go. I doubted I would want to sit at a formal table with strangers for a long, long time.

"Ah, good morning, Ella." Mr. B's booming voice glued me in place.

I flashed my teeth in a portrait-style smile. "Good morning to you, sir. Could you tell me where I might find some food for breakfast? Quentin and I would like to share a meal in my room."

This was his idea, right? I figured he'd be thrilled with that news.

Wrong move. His face instantly flamed red and his eye widened so big I thought I might have to dive and catch them as they popped out. His voice was eerily calm. "Oh. I see. I had hoped to meet with Quentin this morning and discuss business. I was just on my way to his room. You have saved me some trouble."

I forced myself to stand still as his gaze stripped me of my clothes. Perverted geezer. "I can let him know, he'll look for you later then?" I didn't wait for a nod. "About breakfast?"

He pointed to the hallway and stomped off in the opposite direction. I gave myself a mental pat on the back and found my way to what I initially thought was a school-type cafeteria.

My first impression of the place wasn't exactly right on. It was more like a restaurant, a fancy one set up buffet style. I found a woman in an apron. "Can I make up a couple of plates and take them up to my room?"

She looked at me like I'd threatened her life. The loosely pinned bun on top of her head bobbled with her vigorous nod. Yeah. Okay. This was weird.

I almost expected to find a cash register at the end of the line. No one screamed at me or yelled "thief" when I carried the tray laden with enough breakfast food to feed five people.

Dilemma. How was I going to open the door? I had locked it behind me, sort of as a precaution for Quentin. But I was *not* coordinated enough to pull off a one-handed tray hold while I turned the knob. I guess that killed the idea of knocking as well.

I did the next best thing. I kicked the door, just lightly, with the toe of my sneaker. I expected it to sound like a midget knocking. The door squeaked open instead.

I stared at it for a moment. I really didn't want to believe this. What was I gone, twenty minutes? I used my foot to nudge the door the entire way open. If someone was there, they were going to get a new version of pie in the face. Pancake style.

And it'd be a shame because I really was looking forward to the extra helping of whipped cream.

Lucky for my stomach, the room was empty. Maybe the door hadn't latched when I pulled it closed behind me. I couldn't recall the telltale snap.

"Quentin, breakfast. Can you get up?"

No answer.

I pushed the lamp over with the edge of the tray. I gave the precariously balanced plates the palm out "stay" signal and walked around the corner.

The bed was rumpled, but empty.

"Quentin?" I called. He must be in the bathroom.

But the door was open. Crap. I strode over to the door and looked around. My towel was still on the floor near the tub. The toilet seat was still down. No Quentin.

I rushed back out to the bedroom and checked both sides of the bed. He hadn't fallen off. Balcony! I tried the door. Locked. Behind the sheers was nothing but empty gray skies. Dead end.

I turned around, one hand on my hip and a frown on my face. I could believe he left of his own accord, but something just wasn't right.

"Looking for someone?"

I jerked my head up. Mr. B stood in the doorway.

I tried to act nonchalant. I knew he didn't buy it, but it made me feel better. "I guess Quentin didn't want breakfast."

His smile told me he wasn't surprised.

This man was not going to get under my skin. No way, no how. He held out a cup to me. "I was just returning your bracelet from last night. I don't know if all the pieces were found."

Now I felt sheepish. He wasn't here to intimidate me. Still, he probably got pleasure from watching me squirm in embarrassment.

"I'm sorry about using magic. I didn't know."

He sat the cup down when I didn't cross the room to take it from him. Then he waved his hand to clear the air. "It's not your fault. It's one of the things I wanted to talk to Quentin about. You see, not everyone here knows about the magic. Even fewer of them can perform it."

I nodded. That much was clear. The why part still bothered me, but well, it wasn't my mystery to solve.

"I wanted to thank you for playing along with the explanation."

"Believe me, Mr. Bergestein. The last thing I want is to be in the limelight."

His eyes twinkled. I supposed he thought he was breaking down the barriers. Not a chance. They were double insulated walls of something space-aged and indestructible. Except for the little rust spot Quentin had found.

"Uh, you're welcome, I guess. I think I'll have my breakfast now, before it gets cold."

"Of course, of course. Enjoy."

He left the room. I heard it click closed. My appetite was gone. So much for my bravado. That man just made me quiver like a beaten dog with my tail between my legs.

I passed the overloaded plates and plopped down on the edge of the bed.

"Damn you, Quentin. Where the fu—" He would have been proud of me for almost saying that without hesitation. But I got distracted by the twinkle on my pillow. It flashed like a diamond catching the light.

"What the heck?" I dropped my hands and squinted at it. My guess was that Quentin had left something.

But what? A tooth that had gotten knocked out? My stomach turned over as my gruesome mind pictured his eyeball laying there on my pristine white pillow. But after all I've been through, would it surprise me? Heck, no!

I got to the foot of the bed when I realized what it was. A gem. Perhaps even the one I dropped in the ballroom. I released my pent-up breath and stepped around the side of the bed to lift the small round bead from the pillow.

I shrieked and jogged in place when an invisible hand covered mine. I jerked back as quickly as I could. The gem was tightly held in my fist and was burning the tarnation out of me. "Hot damn!" I cried. The combination of the heart-stopping surprise and the pain in my palm was enough to make me beg to go home. I didn't care. I was even tempted to move in with Mom and Dad. I could plead insanity. Once I told this story to a doctor, he'd surely offer up this week's variety of nerve-calming drugs and ship me off to be babied by my parents.

"*Don't even think like that, Ella.*"

He was invisible, but his voice invaded my mind.

"Was that you?" I asked out loud. I didn't trust my head. It was deceiving me too much already.

"Yes," Quentin laughed. "I figured invisible was safe. And I saw you had a visitor. So it was best to stay this way."

"Then you know he left. You could have appeared and not cut twenty years off my life with these stunts of yours. I can't do this, Quentin. All this fuss over gems and magic and mind reading and who to trust. And you. You play these games with my head and games with my heart and you tease my body and—"

Gentle arms wrapped around my shoulders. A hug. My God, I needed this hug. "Even if I wanted to deceive you, Ella, I couldn't."

"I don't know that," I sobbed into his arm. "I don't know what, or who to believe." I was truly breaking down, wasn't I? This was it. "I don't know who I can trust. Certainly not Mr. B. But what happened to Sam? I never wanted to trust him either, but he's never put me in danger."

"Sam is doing what he thinks is right. I have my own ideas about saving the world. Which is literally what we have to do. So yes, little mind games are involved. You're stronger than that. I know you. The first big trick you did was to toss me upside down over you and hold me there. It was amazing. You are not going to back down now."

He faded back into to the room. I think I'd forgotten how bad he looked. Those bruises really told the story. It was a serious matter, not some high school scheme to make sure the girl you wanted won homecoming queen. This was about the integrity of people everywhere.

I let him pull me down so I was sitting beside him. He still had his arm slung protectively around my shoulders. He must have sensed I needed it.

I said, "I need some honesty. I need answers and plans and most of all, I need to know where I can be safe." I turned to him, praying I wasn't wrong to trust. "I need to know."

Quentin lifted his hands to my cheeks and locked his eyes with mine. "I promise I will do everything I can to protect you. When I'm with you, you will be safe. But I can't be here every single minute of the day."

I nodded. Asking that would be too much. And I didn't want a bodyguard.

"Let me figure something out and I'll see if you can grasp it all. But I need the same from you."

Fair was fair. Here goes.

"First," he started, tapping me on the nose. I smiled. "I need to know where you got the gem."

I opened my fist. "This gem?"

"That one."

"Dime store?"

His nose wrinkled and he shook his head. "I don't think so."

"Would you believe I lost a tooth and that's what the tooth fairy brought?"

"Nuh-uh."

I sighed. "You are hard to please, you know? All right. Then the truth. Some man was in the room where I was examined after I fell from the sky. He gave it to me."

"Who was he?" Funny how Quentin managed to know when I wasn't lying.

"I don't know."

"Would you recognize him again?"

"Don't know." At least my words were partly true. I could forget pretty easily.

"Ella?"

"Hmmm?" I was enjoying the texture of his thumb against my cheekbone.

"About the falling from the sky thing?"

I opened my eyes wide. "Yes?"

"Even with magic, we can't fly."

"We can't?" I chewed my lip after asking. Surely he was joking.

"Nope."

What about the hovering thing? What about Jim and I floating up to the tiny little passageway on the island? Did I know something Quentin didn't? Ammunition. "Darn. Guess that's why I fell when I jumped off the building."

"Yeah. Right." We had a thirty second stare down.

He gave in first. "Why don't you just confess and save us the grief of discovering your secrets later."

Hello, Quentin. Who jumped *your* body?

I stopped, frozen. What if? Had I been entirely sure it was Quentin I was talking to all the way through this ridiculous adventure? The answer scared me.

"Confess to what?" I hoped my voice didn't portray my nervousness.

My handsome, if bruised, lover leaned against the headboard. Gulp. Could I say he was my lover? Did I want to be able to say it? I slid from the bed and stood more than an arm's length away.

That part of the adventure and the idea of body hopping had me shaking in my panties. And it wasn't from desire.

"You know the fairy, don't you?" The gentle voice had hardened into something accusing.

"The one you were chasing?" Hey, it could be another.

"Is there more than one?"

"I don't know any. Isn't it possible?"

"None?" This question war was getting old. I couldn't stay sharp with his bantering.

"Tinkerbell? Maybe she followed you from Disneyland. Quentin, why is this so important?"

His smile was weak, at best. "So tell me instead where this gem *really* came from."

"I'm not saying another word. You were supposed to be sharing information with me. I feel like I'm on trial. And I am seriously not liking it!" I was trying to keep my temper intact. I was failing miserably.

I tucked the gem inside my pocket.

"I thought you were going to trust me. You accuse me of having secrets and I know you're keeping things from me. I know there's something about that fairy that you know. Like her name." This was a side to Quentin I didn't like. The hairs on the back of my neck stood at attention. I felt like a cat puffing up and ready to pounce.

"No. Quentin, no." The desperate shake in my voice made the tone more pleading than a definitive negative.

Show him a loose string and he'll pull it to unravel my cover. I felt naked. My feet were glued in place as he rose from the bed. My breath caught when the covers slid down.

I tore my eyes from his boxer shorts. I ignored the fear that hummed just beneath the surface of my skin and took a moment to admire the very masculine body as he walked toward me.

If I were a man I might have said "Down boy," to myself. The memory of his past lovemaking had my body shifting my fear into anticipation. *Touch me.*

All it took was the back of his fingers grazing against my cheek. God, I would have told him anything he wanted to know. But he didn't stop his assault there.

"Don't throw any remotes at me. I'm going to kiss you."

Quentin. I sighed. It was him. I wouldn't have thought of doing anything to distract him from his task at hand. I closed my eyes and waited.

Instead of his mouth, the pad of his thumb stroked and pulled at my bottom lip. His hand wrapped possessively around my cheek and jaw. I leaned into it.

I dared not open my eyes. I licked my lips. Still waiting, wanting...needing him to kiss me.

"Mm, nice," he muttered, breathing heavy against my ear. He held his body away from mine, purposely torturing me. It wasn't going to work.

I snaked my hand out and tucked my fingertips in the waistband of his shorts. A slight tug was all the invitation he needed to shift his body against mine. Perfect fit. *Oh yeah, just like that.*

His mouth danced against my cheek. The day old beard scraped my cheek—all the more erotic. I could smell him, the faintest whiff of his cologne still lingering. My entire body sighed.

He leaned against me. There was proof in the hard lines of his body he wanted me, too. My heart slammed against my chest with the knowledge of it.

Quentin had the ability to send me over the edge with his lips. And he knew it. Just when he had turned my knees to the consistency of butter, he did. He slid a knee between my legs.

I pushed against him. His mouth left mine and created a path of hot kisses to my ear. And then he asked me the fairy's name in the deepest whisper I'd heard from him yet.

I gripped his shoulders and answered back, my mouth once again meeting his. "Winzey."

He froze. The icy blast turned my ultra sensitive skin into a breeding ground for goose bumps. *System shut down in four-three-two...*

"Nicely done, Quentin, son."

...one. I released my grip on Quentin's shoulders and started sliding backwards. Out of the corner of my eye, I saw Mr. B stepping through the still solidly locked door.

I stepped back quickly. No. I wasn't going to faint. Passing out would be too cliché and I didn't need Mr. B to see me so off balance. I took a deep breath and stared at Quentin. Poor boy, he had the gall to look surprised, and hurt even. I reached up and patted his cheek.

"It's okay, Quentin, you do what you have to do. As will I. Do you gentlemen mind giving me a little privacy? I'm feeling a little under the weather and well, I think I'd like a nap."

Bravo, Ella, you just made Broadway collapse with that pathetic acting job.

Quentin looked at me as if I'd grown wings. Or horns. Heck, maybe both. I could be an angel and the devil himself if I tried, right? Almost. But we won't tell him that, will we?

We? I stayed silent for a minute. Had I been body hopped? Had Quentin?

I felt like an old lady herding her chickens across the yard as I followed the men to the door and bolted it tight. Not that anything I did would keep them from walking back in, but just the same...

I threw myself head first and face down on the bed. Thank God it was empty. I might just sleep like this.

When I pulled my knees up, I felt it. I still had the gem.

ଓ ଓ ଓ

"*Ella, wake up.*"

"Huh?" The sound was the most welcome thing I could have wished for. "Sam?"

"*Shhh. I'm here. Listen to me for a minute.*"

I nodded. But I sat up and searched the room. I needed to see him. Know it was really him. "*Where are you?*"

"*Here. That's enough for you to know. I'll be here as much as I dare. It's too easy for them to pick up on my magic. I won't be able to watch over you. Trust your instinct. Do the* right *thing.* "

I felt duly scolded. That's what I get for giving away secrets. The memory forced me back against the pillows. Damn. How could I have betrayed my little friend so easily?

"*You love him. You clung to him and trusted him because there was no one else.*"

"*Thanks. You know how to make a girl feel good.*"

"*It doesn't matter. We need to take a walk. You never know who will just pop in.*"

"*You got that right.*"

I knew my face was smeared with tears and my eyes undoubtedly not far off from matching the red of Quentin's. At least his boxing match had been physical. I felt like I'd been gutted. This emotional stuff wasn't really supposed to hurt, was it? Like as in physical pain?

Well, it did.

"Ella, go brush your hair and wipe your eyes. Is he really worth crying over?"

If I could have seen him I would have gifted him with an evil stare. "*You're messing with a heartbroken female here, mister. What's the saying about a woman scorned?"*

"I could leave, you know. I've learned quite a lot about this operation here. Enough to spot a few weaknesses. I don't really need you, but I hate to see you killed when it all collapses upon itself."

"*Sam Nelson, you wouldn't dare do that to me."* I tried to make my mental voice reflect humor, but it came out scared of its own shadow.

☙ ☙ ☙

"So how, exactly, do you intend for this to work? Mr. B. has nine gems. I have one. And Quentin knows it. What if he asks for it back?"

Sam's voice was low, rough. His eyes glinted and one eyebrow arched, just slightly. "My father's here."

"Lou?" I breathed. "How?"

Sam slung his hand out. "The ocean has carried him here, and even now, a storm is brewing."

I squinted up past the bare tree branches and into what seemed like a permanently colorless sky. Still I didn't see anything foreboding in the emptiness.

"Not today. Perhaps not for a few days. Storms need time to gather, to strengthen. Find Winzey and be ready."

"You mean she's not with you?"

Sam's head tilted and he gave me one of those parental you-had-better-be-kidding-me looks.

"I haven't seen her since..." Heck, even I couldn't remember. I didn't even know how long I'd been in this place. We walked past the courtyard and away from the giant structure. It was the only fathomable place to hold a conversation, and even then, not having eavesdroppers wasn't guaranteed.

"You must find her, before Bergestein does. She could easily substitute for the missing gem and make our job much, *much* more difficult."

I cringed at that second "much." One was too many for my liking. I wanted it easy, like my life had been before this. That's it, my life now had a BM and a AM. Before Magic and After Magic.

I was afraid to find out just what I was going to have to face AM.

It made me think of my parents. I walked to the edge of the yard and stared over the bluff at the waves below. Did they know I was gone? Did they worry? And what about Jeannie? I couldn't help but guess she figured I'd up and taken off with some guy. Or else she'd had Jessie remind her I was talking to the TV Guide and she just chalked it up to needing a vacation.

This was not a vacation.

"Well, of course it is, Ella. Aren't you enjoying your stay?"

Somehow I turned around and managed to keep my balance. "You startled me." I slapped my hand over my chest and took a deep breath. "Just feeling homesick is all."

"Your family is okay. They've received a postcard from you and think you are vacationing with the man of your dreams."

I closed my eyes and shook my head. I felt so helpless. "What would you have sent if your men had killed me?"

"The same thing. And then news of a terrible boating accident and word that unidentifiable remains were located in a well-known shark-infested area. Poor Ella."

I shuddered. And there wasn't an ounce of emotion apparent in Mr. B's voice. The pure emptiness was the most frightening part.

"So is this your headquarters?" I waved to the house that sat back a hundred or so yards behind us. "Or do you have places like this everywhere?"

He laughed and flipped up the collar on his jacket. The wind had picked up.

"I never stay in one place for long. And I think it's nearing time to move someplace warm. I hear there are some nice, uninhabited Caribbean islands. I should check them out."

With that, he left.

I bunched my hands into my pockets and turned back to the

ocean. The water rushed toward the base of the cliff about a story below me with the energy of a raging bull and then locked horns with the rocks, only to back up and try it again. Over and over.

I smiled down. "*Don't let it give you a headache, Lou.*" I winked down as I hit send on my mental thought. I searched for an answer in the gray vastness. Then decided that was about as fruitful as counting the blades of grass. Which were growing much too quickly under my feet. The time had come to mow. I turned and walked straight into Quentin's arms.

I was tempted to turn and leap from the cliff. He was going to be the dandelion that kept coming back, no matter what. Since I couldn't guarantee Lou would save me, I hesitated. And, well, I was a coward deep down inside.

"What?" I pushed past him and stomped toward the castle.

"Wait a minute, Ella, I'm sorry."

"Sorry for what, Quentin, being yourself? For worrying about power and not giving a damn about other people's loyalty and feelings? The idea of "us" obviously didn't mean anything to you, because you threw it all away."

"You don't understand. I didn't want to. I was supposed to make you lure the fairy in. When I didn't deliver I got my ass kicked. Do you think that was fun?"

"Step back, Quentin. You made the bed, sleep in it. *I'm* not pretending to be a partner to this guy. I have my morals and ethics. Don't try to blame this on me."

I stood up on my tiptoes and got right into his face. *Atta girl, Ella*! "Leave me alone," I warned him. "I'm not sorry for what you did. I'm sorry I let it happen."

Wow. Someone had just opened me up from sternum to belly button. And then liberally salted me and stuck me over an open fire. But from the look on Quentin's face, the shock, the open mouth and glassy-eyed stare...he felt the same way. *Good for you, buddy. Enjoy the sensation.*

I just knew something was going on I had no control over. It vibrated the air. I studied the building as I walked back, alone. It dawned on me I'd been allowed outside without handcuffs or at least a leash. Of course, Quentin's appearance might have just been that, a bloodhound on a trail. Maybe he was checking to see if I had some secret rendezvous planned with Winzey or something. Stranger things have happened.

Today, I decided after realizing I barely knew my way around this...this...asylum, I needed to explore. I knew what I hoped to find, was completely aware of what I didn't want to find and...

Ow!

I felt a flash of heat at my ankle. I leaned over to rub the spot.

I jerked up when I heard an unmistakable, yet dreaded voice bid me good day.

"Sorry, I...uh, had an itch." I twisted my ankle, hoping my secret was still hidden. I put my hand over my chest. "And you scared me!"

"Ah, I see."

Damn, I hope not. I forced out what I hoped sounded like a nervous giggle. It worked, after all, I was nervous.

"I'm going to go lie down...I'm tired." I gestured madly with my hands, likely managing to look more like a rabid marionette than a person indicating the need to excuse themselves.

He frowned. His eyebrows tilted downward in synch with the corners of his mouth. It creeped me out. He asked, "Are you eating enough? Keeping yourself healthy?"

My own eyebrows became one. "Why?" Did he suspect what I was starting to fear? I swallowed and barely kept from putting my hand over my stomach. How many days...weeks since this adventure started? Did I need to worry?

"You and Quentin will need to kiss and make up. You need to keep up your portion of the bargain."

I wanted to throw up. And it had nothing to do with hormones.

He laughed. "Take a nap, Ella. Quentin will be in later. Oh, and we're downsizing. He'll be sharing your suite with you from now on."

I don't think so.

Chapter Fourteen

"Hey, it wasn't my idea." Quentin stood staring at the line I'd drawn across the carpet with talcum powder. "And what about the bathroom?"

"You control the outside door, I control the bathroom. Ask first. I said I didn't like you and don't trust you. I'm not that cruel."

"The hell you aren't."

I fisted my hands in my hair. "Why me? What have I done? I just want to be left alone and now you're accusing me of being cruel? It was you who betrayed me here, Quentin, boy. And if you don't get a grip it'll be a bit more than a remote you're dodging."

I sidestepped into the bathroom. Cold water, yeah. Maybe diving head first into an icy lake would help me wash away the unexplained guilt I felt for talking to him like that.

A bath sounded nice. Warm, no, hot water would work better. I flipped on the faucet and stripped down. I could hear Quentin fooling with the television. "Good luck," I muttered.

The smile on my face faded as I noticed the strap around my ankle. Now what? Last thing I needed was to tempt him with it. Would he take it and use it if he had free access? I didn't know.

With an eye on the door, I slid the gem off and tossed the string in the trash. Hmm. I rolled the gem between my fingers as my eyes darted around the room like a hummingbird with a sugar high. Where would I hide it?

Quentin pushed open the door.

The gem squirted from my hand like a slippery grape.

"What was that?" he asked, leaning against the doorframe with arms folded across his chest.

I swallowed, trying to force down the thoughts of being enveloped in those arms. "Uh...my...uh." I spied the blue semi-transparent bath beads on the shelf. "It was one of those...I squirt them into the tub. They're filled with bath oil."

"Uh, sure."

"Do you mind? I'm trying to take a bath here. I told you to ask if you needed to use the bathroom, not just waltz in when you felt like it."

I took a deep breath and tried not to flinch while his eyes took a walk all over my body. Thank God he was a horny male. My nakedness seemed to distract him from the gem. I thought *I* was going to melt under those smoldering green eyes. *And I don't like this man, remember*?

"Hello? Done staring? I want to bathe here."

His eyes crept back up to mine and he winked. "Go ahead, get into the bath."

I reached up to the container of bath beads. I knocked it over. I hope it looked like I did it accidentally. "Oh crap."

Little blue orbs scattered like ants at a picnic. No, wait—didn't ants do the single file thing?

Didn't matter.

"Go on," I shooed him out and pushed the door closed. "I'll get this."

I picked them all up, including the real McCoy. It should be safe amidst a bunch of "Spring Rain" scented bath balls, right?

The hot water was heavenly. I sank to my shoulders and tried to remember how peaceful real life had been. I tried not to ask myself what the heck I was going to do. Could I just go along with this and wait for a way out? I felt so...useless. But Sam had said Lou was coming. A storm was on its way.

My pickling was almost complete. I was almost ready to call it a success when I heard the footsteps approaching. And damn, the bubbles were gone. Not that it mattered.

The knob turned slowly. Guess he hadn't expected me to hear him coming. I pushed against the door mentally.

"Ella?"

"Go away. Can't I relax in peace?"

"Bergestein dropped off something for you."

"I don't want it."

"From my understanding, it wasn't an option."

"So *you* take it, I won't tell."

"Damn it, Ella." Quentin gave the door a good shove. I wasn't expecting him to be so forceful. I fell back into the water as the door banged open.

Quentin had changed. Clothes that is. I still couldn't and wouldn't trust him enough to believe anything that came out of his mouth. But he stood before me in neat black trousers, a charcoal mock turtleneck and a black blazer. I nearly whistled.

Good thing I wasn't a man or he'd be able to see my physical reaction to him. Of course, if I *was* a man, I wouldn't react like that, now would I?

What really made me catch my breath and forget all my modesty was the black tether necklace in his left hand.

Gems.

"What are those for?"

"A gift," he said. "But you have to keep up your part of the bargain."

He repeated it. It wasn't said in any realm of enticement. No twinkle in his eye.

"Are you aware of the bargain?" I narrowed my eyes. I had to be sure. Oh, the conspiracy of it all.

"No, though I find it quite amusing *you've* gotten to bargaining with our leader."

"He's not *our* leader and I haven't agreed to anything." I had a feeling Mr. B created this little bargain because he wanted to see how high and far he could get his minions to jump. Clearly having an heir wasn't so important he'd tell Quentin about it. Not that I was in a hurry to make it happen, either.

"Oh?" His eyebrows shot up. I started shivering. He'd better not be reading my mind.

"It's time you leave. I need to get dressed."

The gems lay sparkling on the counter, winking at me as I slid up my panties. How did I know they weren't tiny cameras?

I didn't. But at this stage of the game, there was little I did know.

Suddenly Ella the captive has been provided with magic. Go figure.

I reached for my bra and started hooking it when I remembered I hadn't been wearing a black one. I glanced at my underwear. Matching black. Great, now someone was pulling a clothing switcheroo. Would have been nice if they'd have brought the entire outfit in. Now I had to go let Quentin watch me get dressed. This had to be Mr. B's doing. He wanted me to tempt Quentin.

As I expected, Quentin was sitting on my bed. He had totally ignored the dividing line, but at least he'd made my bed. Magic probably.

"Where's my clothes?"

Without as much as a peep he pointed to the chair. I lifted the outfit that matched Quentin's. It was tailored a little more feminine, but it still looked way too gangsterish to me.

"Where's my jeans?"

He shrugged.

"I'm not into dressing like twins. Where's *my* clothes?" I stomped over to the closet and flung it open.

Empty.

Completely empty. Bare. Nothing. Nil.

"What's going on?

Another shrug. "Orders are getting passed down, I haven't gotten to talk to Bergestein."

"But...he gave you the gems for me. Why?"

"Messenger. He said we'd need them. I got some too."

"I thought you were some kind of right-hand-man, what gives?" I put my hands on my hips. My bare hips. I looked down. Here I was doing an underwear commercial for him after vowing to tease him with just a glance. Forehead slapping time. Only I was more interested in what was going on.

I pulled on the clothes. "Well?"

"I guess he didn't need my extra input for this decision."

Translation, Mr B. knows Quentin's not entirely on his side. Interesting.

Gems meant I could jump. I could leave. Go. I fingered the beads and looked toward the window.

"Ella, I can't let you do that. Don't even think about it."

"Why?"

"It was part of my orders."

"Orders? You're taking orders? You just said you didn't know anything."

"I was just told that you have to use your magic sparingly and I should keep an eye on you."

"How do you intend to make sure I abide by these ridiculous rules?"

He smiled. A sexy, twinkle-in-his-eyes grin that had me buttoning my blazer.

This was torture. *Thank you, Mr. B.*

I went back into the bathroom and surveyed the clothes. Why I continued to be surprised they fit well and were actually flattering, I'll never know.

The beads, I realized, were knock-offs. They were smaller, and cloudy. Generic all right. Obviously there had to be more than ten gems in the world...even the guys at Disneyland had some. So clones like these were very readily available. I should've added two plus two a long time ago.

I tied the tether around my neck as snug as I could. I debated on the spacing. Crap. I was a basket case over nothing. I gave them full power and tucked them beneath the turtleneck.

Then I glanced up at the bath beads. Decision, decisions.

"Ella, are you okay? We've got things to do."

Things to do? Well, it'd save this gal from dying of boredom. "Give me a minute."

I slid out the cosmetics and tried to look the part. What part, I didn't know, but certainly the dramatic outfit deserved a little mascara. Once my lips were pouting and wine-colored, I snapped off the lipstick and stuck the faux bath bead—the legitimate gem—into the tube. Mission accomplished.

A big sigh and I was ready. I opened the door talking, "Quentin, where are—"

He was gone.

"Quentin?"

Fine. Something was going on and I was going to figure it out. And then maybe jump the sinking ship. Hmm. Ship. Cruise. *Why wait?*

I glanced from side to side from the corners of my eyes. Quentin could be invisible, reading my thoughts. Heck, so could a half a dozen other magic men.

Too bad.

I jumped.

ଔ ଔ ଔ

For my first solo flight, it wasn't bad. Of course, I hadn't really mapped out a destination, so I did have some trepidation as to my luck. But it held.

I was securely hidden in the body of a middle aged woman on the sun deck of a giant floating city. Wow. I'd booked a few dozen cruises a year, but had never expected the majestic size of this place.

This was like an Annabelle, I wasn't controlling anything, although I could influence my host to react. She didn't need to react right now. I was absorbing enough of her sensation of warm sun beating against my flesh. The breeze was wonderful. It was cool, fresh, but made the temperature perfect. I eyed the waiter as he walked by with a colorful arrangement of frozen drinks on his tray. Strawberry Daiquiri. Yeah.

So maybe I did plant the seed, but she raised her hand and summoned the hot little Love Boat character to bring her, "One of those red drinks with an umbrella."

I did a mental eye roll. Hey, at least I wasn't stuck in the waiter's body. The last thing I wanted to do was work on my vacation.

It took three hours and the lobster look to realize the error of my ways. Now, even the wonderful breeze hurt.

I was lonely. Dot, short for Dorothy, I imagined, was having a blast, despite the burn. I think she liked it when the fifty-something spare-tire carrying steward offered to coat her body with something soothing. I pretended it was Quentin's hands.

I missed him. I couldn't trust him, really didn't know him, but I'd managed to defy all I knew and fall in love with him. Since I had time to think, I tried to rationalize it.

Sure, sex was great. But it wasn't everything. It was the attention. Like I mattered to him. He made sure to include me and never really put me down. Sure, he joked—a lot, but it was almost as if...he respected me.

And truth was I was kind of impressed with his drive. Whether I agreed, he was going after what he wanted. He always did. And it didn't seem to matter what price he had to pay.

Apparently my rambling had tired out my host. Lulled her into sleepy-land. When her dreams turned R-rated and involved the steward and the drink boy, I had to get out.

So I did.

My black penny loafers clicked together, just to insure my invisibility. I was still in the black mobster looking uniform. And the gems, all three of them, were still in place.

Not bad for a novice alone in the world, I decided. Not bad at all.

I slid into the hallway and found my way up on deck. The nighttime blanket above me had been inset with thousands of diamonds. The air was clean, fresh, with only the slightest hint of salt. Paradise.

A perfect place for a honeymoon. The piped-in music was muted, but expertly chosen. A light tinkling of piano and horn, bluesy without being sad. Mood music, and me without a date.

A shifting shadow had me jerking my head over my shoulder. I realized I would always be on the run. My magic left me traceable. I wasn't safe, even here.

"Lou?" I hummed, walking toward the guardrail. "Lou?"

A porpoise jumped and squeaked. A few other people who'd chosen to enjoy the night gasped and pointed.

It was stupid to think he'd answer me. Not here, not like this.

My best bet was to find a place to sleep and think when the magic of the night wasn't so thick.

I turned back toward the empty chairs the sunbathers used. And ran smack into a wall of invisible bodies.

"Son of a bitch," I swore. "What now?"

I didn't recognize the voice that soured a lovely evening. "Bergestein isn't real happy with you."

Was I supposed to care? "Why, did he want to come along? I'm sorry, but you see, it was a last minute flight, I couldn't pass up the price for the tickets." I couldn't help it; I wasn't going back without a fight. And what better way to slip on the boxing gloves but with a bit of sass.

I failed miserably.

"Pick her up," Mr. Voice ordered one of the men.

Something flashed in my head. Something amidst the store of cold sweat that was being pumped to my armpits and the mush I call brain. Something about home. Something about...

I grabbed my neck and clicked my heels. "Home!"

Chapter Fifteen

I floated up to the beach on the gentle waves. My hair was encrusted with sand and seaweed and I just knew there were creatures sharing my clothes. Relieving myself of them was first priority. Then I could figure out where I had washed ashore.

I shuddered when a small sized lobster-looking character fell out of my shirt as I shook it out. Ewww. Those pincers would have hurt if it had wanted to hold on to something. I peered down the neckline to make sure his brothers weren't hanging on for dear life.

Nope. The coast was clear.

Now what? I looked up to the pin prick high on the orange rock wall.

I tried to push myself up off the sand. No go. Hovering about eight inches up and being able to hold myself there for mere seconds was not going to get me up there.

I trudged over to the base of the sheer cliff. It was smooth as marble. So climbing wasn't an option unless I developed suction cup feet. Nope, wasn't wishing that on myself. I didn't trust my magic to work well enough.

Well, could I go through? I really wasn't good at it, but at least I'd know. Air through a screen, water through a colander. I pushed my hands in before me. Hmm. So far, so good. They tingled like the feeling you get when your foot starts getting the circulation back after falling asleep.

I was up to my shoulders. I stuck my face in, eyes open wide. Oh. My. God.

"Ella? Ella?" I felt a slap against my cheek and an echo. The voice came from heaven. I'd died. I knew it. I'd gone too far into the wall and shed my human skin.

"Wake up. Open your eyes, move already!" The voice was frantic. "Shit, Ella, please!"

Shit? Cuss words weren't allowed in heaven, were they? Goodness gracious, I was...*there*. I wasn't that bad, was I? Mr. B belonged there. Maybe even Jim. But surely I didn't.

I lifted one eyelid, barely. Quentin stood over me. His wet hair still hung in his face and lay glued to his cheeks. The jacket was gone. The once gray shirt outlined his well-defined chest in solid black.

I jerked open both eyes. "Not you, too!" I exclaimed. Hell would be spending eternity with this man and finding out he'd switched sides. And I'm not talking political parties.

"Quentin?" I lifted a hand to touch his face. He wasn't a mirage. My heart raced with that realization. He was here with me.

The weight of his head was supported by my hand for a moment as he closed his eyes and breathed, "Thank God."

Well now, how could he get away with that in Hell?

"Wh-where are we?"

"On the island. On the beach. Ella, why did you try something so stupid?"

"What?"

"You can't go through those walls. The spirit of all the men and women before you who tried the same thing are now trapped in the rock."

I locked eyes with him, praying it wasn't so. The thought had flitted through my mind, but how would I have guessed that to be the case. "Honest?"

"Honest." He leaned and touched his lips to my cheek. "Oh, Ella, I couldn't bear to know you were forever lost to me."

It was a dream. I was unconscious and imagined Quentin had just said something so...sappy and un-Quentin like. Wishful thinking had put the vision in my head. I sighed and relaxed, defeated by the realization of the error of my ways. Not heaven, not hell, just some blank, empty place in between. A soul lost in the abyss of the walls surrounding Fairyland.

"Ella, come back to me, Ella. I know it must be tough to fight back. God, I hope you didn't lose anything in that rock." He slapped my face, then shook me. The accuracy of my imagination surprised me.

I could feel it, the sting on my cheek, the ache in my head.

I slid my fingers higher, reaching up with my other hand as well and entangling them in his hair. My vision was fading. And I wasn't going to let him go anywhere, least of all out of my dreams.

ଔ ଔ ଔ

It was humming that woke me.

A weathered, old gentleman pushed a broom around the lounge chair where I lay. "Ma'am, so sorry. Would you be wanting to go back to your cabin?"

Cabin? I looked up at the huge stack thrusting upwards from the deck. In the artificial daylight, I could see blue and white banners outlining the upper viewing area. I was back on the ship.

"Um, I don't know." I rubbed my eyes, hoping he'd just walk on by. What was I going to do now? They didn't toss castaways overboard anymore did they? Or make them walk the plank?

The trip to the island must have been a dream. A horrid nightmare. Especially the Quentin part. I closed my eyes to bring back the image of his worried face. In my dreams, he cared. He had pleaded with me to wake up. He'd touched my face with the caress of someone who loved, not someone who was just a lover.

"Ma'am? Your husband told me to escort you to your cabin when you awoke. He took your purse, said he didn't want to leave it here for just anyone to pick up."

Purse? Husband? I sucked in a deep breath. I'd already checked. I was myself.

I gave myself a mental pep talk. The tube of lipstick was still in my pocket. Only now they were shorts. And I still had gems around my neck. So I wasn't stranded.

I pulled myself up, feeling about as old as this fellow looked and followed him and his broom down the hall.

Everything down the corridor screamed first class. The trim along the top was most certainly teak, the carpet a thick plush royal blue. Wonders will never cease.

The steward knocked on the door, winked at me, and retreated as fast as his little legs would carry him. I was still watching his lopsided gait when the door opened.

"About time."

Quentin stood in the doorway. Actually, he leaned against the doorframe. The door was open about four inches, allowing me a clear view of his bare chest. A pair of black satin pajama bottoms hid the rest of him from sight.

"What?" I was speechless. Stunned. And relieved.

But he hadn't opened the door.

"Are you going to run again?"

I shook my head. Not for a long while. Not if I had a warm bed to sleep in and the promise of food when I woke up.

He opened the door wider and let me walk in under the tunnel of his arm.

I dropped immediately into the nearest chair. "Thank you," I whispered. "Thank you, Quentin." My eyes closed of their own accord.

My fanciful dreams had influenced it, I know, but the illusion of feeling loved was once again tangible when Quentin scooped me up and carried me to bed.

I felt pulled from deep sleep just a few times. The cabin was dark and quiet. My heart would race for just a few seconds before Quentin's even breathing and warm body would come back into focus. I'd wrap an arm or leg around him and slide back into nothingness.

But I awoke alone.

It was bright. We had a giant window on the wall opposite the door and the brilliant sunshine had chosen to peek in through the glass at me.

Did I have a hangover? I couldn't remember drinking, but there was no telling what had happened during my lapses in memory. "Crap!" I grabbed at my neck. Yes. Gems were still there. But my clothes were gone. That meant...

I jumped up and jerked until the starched sheet came loose from the military style tucks at the foot. Toga clad, I searched the room. The shorts and top I'd been wearing had been folded on the chair just outside the bathroom. The pockets were empty.

I sank to the floor in horror. What if Quentin had taken it back? What if it had been all a ploy to get me to trust him? If I had it, he could basically control it without having possession of it. He could have been waiting for the perfect moment to walk in and use that gem as the ultimate bargaining tool.

What if right now he was back at headquarters fitting it into the final spot, creating the circle of power and proving to Mr. B his worth and claiming his place into right hand man? What if the island had already crumbled and I was stuck on a cruise ship, far from being of any help?

"Please, God, no. Please don't let him have taken it. Please give me one more chance, I'll dump it in the ocean, anything."

I heard a throat clear behind me. Quentin stood with his hands on his hips and a lost puppy dog look on his face. I guess he hadn't expected to find me wrapped in a king size sheet, crumpled on the floor and crying.

"Go away," I told him. Of course I meant the exact opposite. I just prayed that he hadn't already.

"You were so glad to see me last night, too. I had hoped you might learn to trust me, Ella."

"But..." I motioned at my shorts.

"You shouldn't leave it lying around, Ella. It could fall into the wrong hands." He pulled the lipstick from his pocket and tossed it at me.

I stared at the dark tube against the white sheet. Disbelieving. And afraid to open it.

He must have figured it out. "I wouldn't steal it, Ella. For crying out loud, I'm the one who gave it back to you. Or did you forget that already?"

My mind flashed back to the scene where I learned he was betraying me to get to Winzey. I narrowed my eyes as the pain returned like a fresh knife to my chest.

Quentin had tuned into my channel 3 reruns. "Before that, Ella, before Bergestein was there."

I saw the pillow and its glittering treasure and Quentin's hand coming out of invisibility to grab my arm. I nearly jumped when he touched my shoulder.

"Easy now. Go on, check to make sure it's there. Then we'll have to figure out a way for you to wear it."

"Wear it? Can I do that? But I thought there was some rule about having more than two?"

"Just be careful with fire, okay? You'll be pretty powerful." He winked. His dimple winked too.

"Now, I bet you'd like a shower, a toothbrush and some clean clothes?"

"Oh yes." I couldn't convey how much.

Quentin excused himself. He had other matters to attend to, which of course, just raised the hackles on the back of my neck. It was a creepy feeling even the hot, pounding shower couldn't wash away.

A ham sandwich was waiting for me when I stepped out of the fully steamed bathroom. The only thing missing was a razor. The poor patrons of the boat would have to deal with Queen Hairy Legs until I could get to the convenience store. That is, if I had any money.

"What's the chances of getting a razor for my next bath?"

Quentin's sideways grin said it all. "You finished faster than I thought." He held up a brown sack. Make-up and deodorant? I certainly hoped so.

The deepening creases around Quentin's eyes told me yes. I wanted to cheer as if the Cubbies had just clinched the World Series. Hey, I live in a magic world. It really could happen.

"What am I wearing?"

"One heck of a sexy blue towel." Quentin raised an eyebrow and tossed a glance at the still messed up bed.

"Later," I whispered. I wasn't much of a seductress, but I could play a good flirt. "I'm interested in food. I hear cruise ship food is the best in the world."

"It certainly ranks near the top."

"So what are we waiting for?"

He looked down at my towel. Oh. Yeah.

"Clothes?"

He stepped back and showed off two fancy suitcases. "Tell me these aren't someone's luggage?"

"Hey, suitcases go missing all the time. No one here on this cruise. Do you have any idea how hard it was to mentally scan all the outgoing suitcases at the airport to find one that had our sizes?"

I didn't want to know. Really. "This doesn't sound ethical."

"Unethical would be to let you go have brunch in your towel.

You'd get plenty of attention, but I bet a few husbands would have to be tossed overboard to cool them off."

I didn't believe his comments, except perhaps the attention comment. Regardless of a woman's build, if she went to a public meal dressed like this there'd be talk.

"So what's in the suitcase?"

He held out a strappy sundress. With big sunflowers on it. He was kidding, right?

"No."

"No?" He asked. I think he'd liked it.

"Well... Is there a white t-shirt in there to wear under it?" I was caving in.

He frowned. "It ruins the cleavage."

"Tough!"

He laughed and pitched the t-shirt at my face. The owner of the suitcase had obviously just bought herself a new set of clothes for her ill-fated trip. I hope she was wealthy enough to replace the items. And of course, Quentin would return these bags, slightly worn, to the airport when we were done.

"I will?"

I nodded. "Yup."

He rolled his eyes at me. If I wasn't afraid my towel would fall I'd reach out to slap him. I ducked back into the bathroom instead.

He followed. "Here's your supplies."

I didn't even want to think where they came from. "If you must know, I used the money I had left and managed to do pretty well at the casino downstairs. Those items were bought honestly."

"Money you had left?" I queried, lifting an eyebrow.

He simply smiled.

Quentin gambled with what could only be stolen money and called the gains honest. You just gotta love the man for his warped sense of right and wrong.

I figured any minute now the pirate police would arrive to cart us off to that area below deck prepared for just such offenders. The shock was, just the opposite happened. We were greeted as royalty and pulled into the midst of an overflowing food extravaganza.

"Wow," I exclaimed, pointing to my near empty plate with a fork full of Belgian waffle. I smiled as I licked the frosting off. "I've heard the fastest way to a man's heart is through his stomach, but on a place like this, I think I'd fit that category as well."

I meant it as a jest, not even slightly serious. I wasn't even fishing for a comment back, perhaps a laugh, a smile at least. What I got was stony silence.

I replayed my words. Had I gone too far? Did he think I was being pushy, even smothering? Dear God, what did I say to counteract that?

"You should try the waffle," was the best I could think of.

"I think I'm full."

"I'm sorry," I blurted. I couldn't have him getting all distant on me. Not after the warm comfort of the bed we'd shared. Not after I thought I'd gone and lost it all. I might be holding on by my fingernail, but this little hangnail wasn't going to get rid of me.

"For what?"

"For saying what I did. I think we should leave our hearts out of it, don't you? I was just, you know, using a cliché to mention how good the food was."

He waved me off like I was a bothersome fly. The tight-lipped smile contradicted his creased forehead. I could tell the difference, because the captain got the honor of a full dimpled smile when he walked by and clapped Quentin on the shoulder.

It was too late.

I was the cola someone had drained the caffeine from. And the carbon dioxide. I was flat and without energy. I feigned a headache and sought refuge on the sundeck, alternating between a seat with an umbrella and one without.

The whole time I stared up at the crisp white lines and festive colors. Why should I have even entertained the idea that an illusion of harmony was possible for me? I chewed on my tongue, the perpetrator of this new mess.

I sat up on my elbows and studied the bodies around me. Well, not actually the bodies themselves, just the people. The nice thing about a cruise ship, I realized, is the diversity. Quentin stood at the railing. His conversation with the forty-something mid-life crisis in a polo shirt was full of sharp animated hand gestures.

"Hey, look at him," I heard the breathy voice of a Hollywood vixen.

I looked. There was more than one of them. Great. And they were looking in Quentin's general direction.

Please let them be thinking of the older fellow as a potential sugar daddy.

"Wouldn't you love to run your fingers through his hair?" Bimbo One said to Bimbo Two. Nope. It was Quentin. So while I was doing a wonderful job of pushing him away, these chicks were doing there best to land a lasso around him and lure into the silicone valleys.

I faked looking at something over their heads to take in their fake tan and fake hair color and fake breasts. While I could almost stifle a laugh, I felt no less substandard.

What a fun vacation I was having. I think I'd almost rather have my toenails plucked by a homicidal maniac. Well. I said almost.

I did the next best thing. I walked away. Of course, the little green man sent me directly in Quentin's direction. I stuck out a hip and touched his arm. "Honey, I'm going to lie down for a bit. I don't have my key, can I use yours?"

He looked straight through me, but relinquished the door card. I felt like sulking away. But that would defeat the purpose.

"Thanks, sugar," I cooed, loudly. And then turned heel and sashayed, at least I hope I sashayed, to the upper deck and the hallway to our room.

The idea of a hot bath was tempting. But impractical. *Duh, Ella, as if.* I didn't need to finish that. I turned on the faucet and plugged the drain. It was my bath and I would enjoy it.

I shouldn't have looked at myself in the full length mirror while I slipped out of my clothes. My thighs were heavier than the current designers had intended a woman's to be and my stomach had nothing in common with a washboard. The sun obviously wasn't interested in mutating my melanin, for there wasn't even the slightest tan line to be found.

And I wondered why I was still single?

I piled the stick straight, dark hair on my head and contemplated my features. Sure, I could paint my eyes just so and look more oriental. Or maybe pull off an American Indian look. Too bad the lithe body that accompanies a face like that had abandoned me at birth.

"Ugh," I told the mirror.

So I lowered myself into hot water, yelping little curses as my skin turned the color of sunburn. See? I felt like yelling to the orb of fire, water can change the color, why can't you?

But my tension dissolved like a bitter pill and I didn't have the energy to even mouth the words. I didn't bother to fix my hair when it rebelled against the bobby pins. I didn't even care when the phone rang.

Tough. Quentin, eat your heart out. I'm on a date with Neptune.

I was too lazy to even wonder if Neptune was even close to the right name to give a god of water. Hey, in my world it was right, just for that moment. Bliss.

"Ella?"

I hadn't even heard the door open.

"In the tub."

The way we kept meeting in the bathroom was uncanny. "What do you want?" I hollered, hoping beyond hope he'd just answer me and not have to invade my false sense of peacefulness.

I should have known better.

He'd changed into his swimsuit. I groaned. Yeah, that's all I needed. A distraction. He leaned against the bathroom counter with his long, tanned legs and arms crossed.

My water suddenly went tepid. I guess he had something to do with it.

"What-"

"You ran away," he accused.

"How could I have run? I was sitting in the sun and decided I'd had enough."

"Yeah."

"What do you mean, yeah?" I reached over and gave the hot water tap a quick flick of the wrist. His muttered answer was drowned in the gurgle of the water starting to drain.

"What are you doing now, running away again?" His louder comment managed to reach over the noise. I stood up and pulled the shower door closed.

"No. Just showering."

"Helluva avoidance technique. Maybe I wanted to talk to you now."

"What's there to talk about?" Soap ran into my mouth. Ugh. I hadn't even said the "f" word. Yet.

"About why we're here and what we're going to do."

I was too busy gargling hot water and scrubbing my tongue with my finger to answer.

I spat out the last of the sudsy water. "What time is it?" I was technically done. My hair was washed and conditioned and my body squeaky clean.

"Time for you to come out before you start looking like one of those senior citizens. Though you might fit in on this particular cruise."

I glanced at my crocodilian fingers. "Hey," I called back, "my breasts aren't big enough to sag like theirs."

That earned a laugh.

"Besides," I continued. "You just said you wanted me to stay in the bath so you could talk to me."

I flipped off the water as he forced an exaggerated groan. "I'm going to get dressed now. You can leave." I made the little pushy motion toward the door by sticking one hand out of the opaque door.

"Okay."

He agreed too easily. But I heard him walk toward the door and it opened and closed.

I stuck my head out. It looked like the coast was clear. "Well, fine then." I got out and immediately clicked my heels to go invisible.

"Hey!"

I knew it.

"Quentin, when I said leave, I meant really leave." All the while I yanked a shirt over my still wet body. Once sufficiently covered, I popped back into visibility.

He appeared with a chocolate-dipped strawberry held inches in front of my lips.

"Oh," I gasped. He slid the blunt point of the fruit against my semi-parted lips. His green eyes darkened as mine widened in surprise.

My eyes remained locked on his. They had nowhere else to go. The chocolate on the fruit had softened and melted against my tongue.

"Oh."

I let him push a little harder and fill my mouth with the drug-like taste of chocolate.

"Bite it," he whispered. I did.

The sweet juice squirted against the inside of my cheeks, bubbling on my tongue and running out. This was edible ecstasy.

My body felt a million miles away yet zinged with the lightning bolts of every nerve ending. Taste had become the most important sensation. I felt enslaved by it, but didn't care.

He slid the sweetness from between my lips. It was a lover leaving me, its warmth replaced with coldness.

"Chew." He whispered. I never would have guessed that word could be sexy. But the continued flavor and texture of the berry had my mind burning with the images of Quentin and me together. Naked, in a chocolate bath.

But then the thought froze as he lifted the strawberry to his own mouth and took a bite. I licked my lips, finding more chocolate and juice left behind.

"Don't." He stopped me. Then his lips were on mine and I tasted the way the juice mixed with his natural flavor. My knees weakened. My chest was being pummeled by my reckless heart as it tried to escape.

My hands slid up Quentin's chest, driven by some animalistic need. I could feel his reaction, which was as intense as my own. I drew in a ragged breath as he kissed the juice from my chin.

I ached to feel the rest of him, his hardness against my body. The need was almost frantic. But he resisted me.

He reclaimed my mouth and plunged his tongue deep inside. I moaned with him and laced my hands in his hair, holding his mouth there as he continued to ignite blazing fires throughout my body. Touch me, my mind screamed at him.

Instead, he stepped back,

"What?"

The light of the brightly decorated bathroom blinded me, killing the mood almost instantly. Quentin's eyes were half-closed. His chest still heaved, but he blew out a few breaths and raked his hand through his hair.

"I guess it is true."

"What's true?" I rose on my toes and clenched my fists. No way did I want to hear I was some kind of experiment. That single strawberry had me on the edge, and willing to step off.

"The way to your heart is through your stomach."

He had heard me. The breath was pushed out of my chest as if I'd taken that step and landed flat on my back. "Did you need to know? And—"

"Yes."

"And for your information, the little treat you brought me wasn't affecting my heart at all. Heart rate maybe, but don't for one minute confuse lust and love."

"Who was talking love here, Ella?"

I almost wished there had been a sarcastic smirk on his face so I could slap it off. But the look was that of a curious child.

And my heart was busy jumping up and down with its hand in the air screaming, "Me, me, me."

I finally unfroze my vocal chords and explained it to him. "The phrase is supposed to relate to the idea of making a man fall in love with you by showing him what a good wife you'd make, i.e. cooking."

His bottom lip protruded and I ached to nibble on it. "Oh."

"But what you proved is food can also be a really interesting item for foreplay."

He nodded, not taking the hint I was offering myself up in some sad sacrifice. If I couldn't have his love, I knew I could have his body. And now that was denied me.

He looked me up and down before turning to leave the room. I could hear him talking. "Cruise like this...make someone mix up love and lust easily enough..."

I was tempted to pitch the pink lotion bottle on the counter at his back. Not sure why I didn't. Maybe because it was baby lotion. I squeezed until a dollop fell onto the carpeted floor.

Baby lotion. Baby. Pregnant. Oh God. With the panic rising in my throat like bile, I followed Quentin back into the main room. Maybe it was true and the runaway hormones were making me see things I shouldn't. "Hey!"

He ignored me. He stood in front of the bed and scratched his head.

I grabbed his arm and spun him around. "Hey," I repeated. "What are we doing? What should I wear? Where are we going?"

"We're on a boat in the heart of the Caribbean, we're not going far."

It was hard to feel dignified in a t-shirt and thong panties. But I ignored the sad state of undress. "No, kidding." I chewed on the thought. Should I? I opened my big mouth and hurled the question at him before I could swallow it along with my fear. "Can I have some money to go to the drug store?"

"Why?" I hated the tilt of his eyebrow. I was tempted to shave it off. I was going to do it too, as soon as I got my hands on him.

"Because I need something."

He looked me up and down. "What? What did I forget?"

The bathroom was stocked better than Tammy Fay Baker's dressing room. But I highly doubted it had what I needed. And as far as answering him? "You don't want to know."

"Well, finish getting dressed and we'll take a walk down there."

"No." The word shot out like a misfired bullet. *Way to go, Ella, get him suspicious.*

The only thing left to do was get dressed. My hair had naturally dried in the only style it would hold. Straight. Makeup wasn't necessary for this trip. Chances are I'd ruin it with tears anyway.

I zipped my jean shorts and slid my feet into sandals that were at least a size too small. I'd need to visit the boutique, too. Maybe trade these in.

My hand was on the doorknob when he finally spoke again. "Wait."

It wasn't a request. It was an order. Well, la-de-da. I stepped into the hall with my chin a little higher in the air. I could do this alone.

Of course, finding the dang shop was my first priority. Once around the corner of the room I let my chest deflate a bit. Didn't want to seem haughty when I had to stoop to ask for directions.

But I was feeling pretty good. The bath really had revitalized me. And of course, Quentin was there to get the blood flowing. The smell of tanning lotion had to be the single most visible scent there is. Palm trees and soothing surf. White beaches and gentle breezes.

Crash!

I sucked in a deep breath and let it out slowly. The grunt that followed the jumble of breaking glass sounded too familiar. Does disaster just follow me?

I tried to resist. Really I did. But I had to look back.

Here I was expecting Quentin and the room service waiter I had just passed tangled together on the carpet with pieces of discarded food and drink dressing them up like a pair of clowns. Nada. That guy had made it past. Quentin had collided with a different waiter. A tray with a plate and a glass lay on the floor. The two men stared at it like they'd never seen spilled...soda before. I squinted, but it was just a dark spot on the floor. The glass had cleanly broken in two pieces.

Darn it. Nothing dramatic to distract me from making it to my destination. Dread was still alive and living as a tapeworm on my confidence.

I ignored the sound of my name ricocheting down the hallway. I was intent on getting to the drug store and back and perhaps putting the fear to rest. It consumed me now that I had given in to its ugliness.

The hand baskets were wicker and painted with the logo of the cruise liner. I felt like a little old lady at the grocery store as I roamed the aisles while it dangled from my arm. I have to say, I was impressed. The selections ranged from generic to top brand name. Of course, all the prices had my heart in my chest. They wanted *what* for a bottle of aspirin?

I found the kit I needed. Not that there was much of a choice. Obviously pregnancy tests weren't high priority on a cruise. Just in case, I bought a box of tampons. Yeah, I wanted to be hopeful and have the checkout girl dying to ask me.

I was three feet from the counter when I froze. The cold, wet sweat of dread dripped down my back. How *was* I going to pay for this?

"Uh, can I just charge this to my room?" I lifted my arm and the basket and tried to look hopeful.

"I need your card."

"My door card?"

She nodded. Damn. Where was it? I patted the pockets of my shorts. I wanted to drop down and wail with my legs and feet kicking.

It was in the room.

"Looking for this?" Quentin strolled in with the piece of white plastic in his hand.

"Yep." I walked over, grabbed it and surged forward. Of course my progress was cut short. I might have stopped dead in my tracks if I'd have thought he'd use magic so blatantly. My forward steps were suddenly reversed.

"Why are you doing this to me?" I growled when he released me from the spell.

"Why are you running? I told you'd I'd..."

His eyes must have met with the words on the box. "Ella?"

Chapter Sixteen

Funny how Quentin's voice went from accusing to suddenly soft and full of wonder. I had a sudden image of him as a boy, tugging his mother's sleeve. "When we gonna see it, huh? When?" and then the gasp and "Oooh."

I took the opportunity to snatch the card and walk up to the cashier.

"Ella, use cash."

I passed the card back over my shoulder. I closed my fingers when I felt a bill touch them. I wouldn't, couldn't look him in the eye. This false brave act would crumble.

I wrapped the brown sack around itself and tucked it under my arm. My march back to the room was just as purposeful as the one on the initial trip. Maybe even more frantic since he was behind me. And gaining fast.

He spun me at the door. I was ready for the accusing eyes and third degree. Instead I was folded into a protective hug. "Ella, why didn't you say anything?"

The tears fell then. Whatever reserve I had melted in the warmth of his arms.

When I my eyes were suitably swollen and my nose running, he pulled back to meet my gaze. "What? What is it?"

"Quentin, I'm so scared." My body shook. I wanted to run away, away from magic and the long arm of Mr. B and his stupid power. I wanted to be Ella Mansfield, the nobody from nowhere. And if I was, indeed, pregnant, then so be it. It's not really a rare occurrence anymore.

"Stop it, Ella."

I jerked my eyes open and ran my hand across my nose. "What?"

"Stop beating yourself up. I am not going to desert you if you're pregnant."

Oh yeah, just what I wanted to hear. "We don't know anything yet. It could be the stress, the food or lack of, it could be..."

"Let's go see." Quentin took my elbow and led me to the bathroom. Every step was taken as if there were eggshells beneath our feet instead of a forest of carpet fibers.

"I can't."

"What do you mean, you can't?"

"I-I can't do it with you standing over me. I've got to read the instructions."

He opened the box and passed it over to me. I sat on the closed toilet seat as if it were a throne. "Please, Quentin. Just give me a minute or two. I mean, how would you feel?"

"How do you think I feel? It's not just your baby."

No. If it's there, it's Mr. B's. "Please?"

His hand traced the side of my cheek. For a moment, a brief flitting moment, I thought I saw something deeper in his eyes.

But he turned and walked out of the room.

I muttered and moaned and turned the box over and over in my hands. Now what? I mean, I knew I had to go ahead and pee on the stick, but really, then what?

"Ella? You okay in there?"

I breathed out and tore the box open. "Just getting started. I'm okay."

I couldn't help but smile when I imagined him pacing. He really was taking this better than I had imagined. But that just made it worse. My rambling mind was getting the best of me. I needed to concentrate.

Of course, it had to be complicated. I should have known that. I never was one to have the ability to pee on command. I drank at least three tumblers of water in an effort to get the message to my bladder.

I followed the directions and then put the kit on the back of the toilet and commenced my own pacing. The water finally got through my kidneys and I used the toilet again, keeping my eyes from everything but the indicator.

Another knock. "Ella? Is everything okay?"

"Uh, yeah," I fibbed. "I'm just waiting for the results."

"Can I come in and wait with you?"

"No."

Why did I think he would listen? He didn't bother opening the door. I suppose he knew I'd locked it.

"Why?"

He spied the indicator and detoured toward the pink piece of plastic. I scampered over as well. He wasn't going to know before me. Nope.

Negative.

I sighed in relief and looked again. Clearly it stated I was simply late, but not pregnant. I let out a whoop of joy and grabbed Quentin around the neck and started jumping up and down.

"You're happy?"

I nearly fell on the white tile. "What, you *wanted* me to be pregnant?"

"I was kind of having fun entertaining the idea of a little tyke who looked like me."

I couldn't believe what I was hearing. I wasn't going to. "Get out of here, really?" *Hurry up, Ella, push the smile back down into a frown. He's using this as a ploy toward working on making it for real this time. Can't you see that?*

I shucked the plastic indicator into the box and dropped them both in the trash. "Ah, well, party's over. Did you say something about a casino on board?"

ᘓ ᘓ ᘓ

I'd expected to find the carnival atmosphere would work like helium and keep my spirits up. They might have if Quentin's heavy weight wasn't dragging me down at the other end. His lackluster "Yeah," when I asked his opinion on the number of the roulette wheel had me second guessing my choices. I turned to slots. Nickel slots. Cheap, no thought needed. But I couldn't get him involved.

Finally I stood up and hit the cash out button. "What's with you?"

"Huh?" He looked up, dazed. "Oh, nothing."

"Quentin, you've been acting bizarre all evening. Are you still hung up on the pregnancy thing?"

"No. Just have some...other stuff on my mind. The smoke in here is killing my sinuses. Can we head up to fresh air or back to the room?"

"Yeah." I followed him. His feet rubbed the carpet as he shuffled along. That little old man with the broom had more spring in his step than Quentin. And he should be ecstatic, he wasn't bound to me by a child created out of a huge mistake.

He whirled on me. Before I jerked back I could have sworn his eyes were red and reminiscent of a charging bull. "It wasn't a mistake, Ella."

I'd forgotten he could read my mind. Well, maybe not forgotten, but rather gotten accustomed to the fact he didn't eavesdrop on my rambling thoughts as often as he used to.

"Well, it certainly wasn't planned, Quentin. That is, unless you were in cahoots with Bergestein on that regard as well."

Maybe it was the relief of knowing. Maybe it was the pent up hormones that were starting the ritual PMS after a couple weeks delay. I rose to the challenge, devil may care.

Several people in the hallway gasped and stopped to stare. I ignored the horrified looks and hand-covered mouths I could see out of the corner of my eye and let loose. "I'm just a game to you, Quentin, a stepping stone. You've used me from the beginning to get the power you needed. A pawn, that's all I am, and that's all our kid would have been. Another pawn, a freaking token you could take to the bargaining table."

"Ella, no—"

"You tricked me, just like you did to get Winzey's name. You knew Mr. B bargained my freedom for a child, that's why you set about seducing me every moment you could. To plant your seed."

His face fell ashen. The freight train was now a runaway. There was no stopping it now. "You gave me the gem, knowing I could hold it and you'd still control it, because you controlled me."

"I didn't—"

"Shut up!" I screamed.

I felt hands on my arms, murmurs in my ear. "How dare you do this to me, Quentin? I trusted you. You're all I have and you continue to betray me. Why?"

I sank to my knees, pulling against those who were trying to hold me. I suppose I would have tried to claw his eyes out, or at least scar him for life if I'd been free. The sobs shook my chest, tore through my body like a dull knife. He'd known. I just knew he had been in on it all along. It made sense. Perfect sense.

The fight faded as quickly as it had come. I felt stupid. Foolish. And not just for my outburst, but for being strung along the way I had. "I want to go back to my room now." I told the woman who approached me with the face of an upset school teacher. "I'm sorry." I turned to all the people behind me. "I'm so sorry you had to witness that."

I wasn't going to apologize to Quentin. But it didn't matter. He was gone.

I noticed I was silently escorted by a trailing steward. Guess he needed to make sure I made it back without any more problems. I figured having a referee was a good idea in case I ran into Quentin again.

He wasn't in the suite. Nothing indicated he'd been back. Fine, I thought, go out and find yourself one of those bikini clad chicks who was eyeing you up earlier.

See if I care. I'll just... I took a gander at the king size bed. Then the lazy-boy. Yep, that's it. I'll just see what there is to drink in the bar and drown a few sorrows. Maybe a couple of regrets, too.

The bottle of vodka was less than half the size of the cans of soda that were its neighbors. But it was my name on the label, plain as could be.

Of course, it went down with a little more bite than cola, and certainly had me gasping for a drink to sooth my raw throat. Paint thinner is what it was.

So while my intestines were being cauterized by the straight liquor I gulped half the contents of the red cola can and stumbled back to my chair.

And I stumbled because I tripped over my shoes. I wasn't drunk or anything.

But the chair was nice. I'd have to tell my sister about it. And the room. She wouldn't believe what first class was like. Chances are neither of us would ever see such a thing in our lives. I tried to memorize each detail. My already fuzzy brain was having trouble committing the details to long term memory, so I closed my eyes. Just for a moment.

Too bad I'd forgotten a camera. That would have been the ultimate. But who would ever see the pictures? Chances are they'd get left behind just like everything else has been. I still held on to a strand of hope I'd find a way to see my sister and parents again. If only to let them know I was all right.

Now that was a lie.

I pried open an eyelid. The room was mimicking the motion of the sea. My stomach decided to chime in.

I leaned back and covered my face with my cold hands. What had I done?

"Ella, Ella, damn it, wake up."

"Huh?" Was the boat sinking? *Oh, ow! If it was, let me go down with it.*

"Wake up."

"Yeah" I gripped the arm of the chair. Now who'd gone and displaced me to the Tilt-A-Whirl? *Stop the Ride!*

"Ella?" Quentin stood up. I heard him, didn't see him. I had my eyes closed tight. As if creating a vacuum. If no light could come in, nothing could go out, either. Namely my stomach contents.

"Are you sick?"

"You could say that."

I heard the rattle of glass and a disgruntled curse. "You got drunk?"

"No, I fell asleep before I got to feel the alcohol's potency."

"Sweet Jesus, Ella."

"Whatsa matter, Quentin, never had a gal drown herself in liquor over you before?"

"Are you still drunk now?"

"What time is it? I don't feel drunk, I just feel sick."

"We've got to go, we have to jump, tonight. Do you want to go make yourself throw up?"

"Wha?"

"Vomit, hurl, toss-cookies. Go shove your finger down your throat so you don't do it all over me during the jump."

The idea of stale vomit, especially revisited alcohol had my stomach revolting. "Get me up."

Maybe I'd turned green. Maybe he'd heard the panic in my croaked order. But I was carried, at a run, to the bathroom. I arrived faster than I would have been able to get out of my recliner. And it would have been too late.

"Go away," I muttered as I leaned against the sink. This willing myself not to be ill wasn't working. The metallic taste was evidence of my upcoming humility. And I wasn't in the mood to share this particularly low point of my life with *anyone*.

"Get the hell out of here!" I yelled and lunged for the toilet.

"Son of a bitch."

It was at least six hours later. Quentin insisted it was morning. So did my raging headache. I would be tucked into bed and doing little more than praying for dry land if my stomach hadn't gone through phase two of the revolution.

But I had no clue what Quentin was cursing at, except perhaps me. My stomach was inside out and superglued to the back of my throat. The convulsions had stopped, hopefully for good. I was considering whether or not I could tolerate the minty freshness of toothpaste when he'd cursed. He'd already held my head when my neck had become about the consistency of an egg noodle.

"What?" I moaned at him when he repeated it again. Quentin reached over me and into the garbage. A pregnancy test lay on top. And it read positive. A big pink plus sign.

"No," I said. "It's not mine. I shoved mine back into the box. And I haven't touched it."

Quentin pulled out the empty box and shook it. Then narrowed his eyes at me. A cold sweat washed over me again.

"Damn it, Quentin. You saw it as well as I did last night. It was not positive when we left."

"So you're just denying this? Did you read the instructions thoroughly? Did you let it sit long enough before reading it?"

"Yes," I yelled back at his accusations. "For God's sake, you think

I was just careless? That's a big freaking deal!"

"And it also is why someone's hot on our heels. We should have jumped last night. We need to go now."

"Let me brush my teeth. You get the gem." I hauled myself up to my feet with the aide of the counter top.

"The gem?"

His shin was an easy target for a swift kick. He'd forgotten, even *lost*, the gem? I had to do everything didn't I? "The one in my lipstick case? Remember?"

"Shit."

"Move, Quentin. I think I've got to throw up again."

He scuttled from his seat on the closed toilet lid. I had really been joking. But I'm sure if I thought about losing that gem long enough I could certainly feel sick.

I patted my pockets. Empty.

"Where did you have it last?"

"I don't know. I guess around the time I took a bath yesterday."

"Damn it. Find it!"

"It's gone. Whoever came in here, messed with the test and then saw it." I wanted to slap myself square in the forehead, but knew the repercussions of that the loss. If Quentin was closer I might have substituted, though. He still needed a slap from last night.

His face was pale and stony. I'd have almost thought he'd become a zombie if his green eyes weren't neon lights. "Now we've got a problem."

"While you figure it out, I'm going to go back to bed and sleep this headache off."

"No you're not."

"I've just ripped out my guts, through my nose no less, been faced with the idea maybe I am pregnant and have now flooded my unborn child's system with straight vodka-"

"Straight?" Fire flashed behind green. For the first time I saw his gems glow. Red.

"With a Coke chaser."

"Ella."

"Shut up." I leaned against the counter. I no longer felt out of control of my body, but totally out of control of the whole situation.

"Just shut up." I repeated, more to my conscience than to Quentin.

I closed my eyes. Get a grip, Ella. This was all so, so wrong. When I opened my eyes I had planned to ask Quentin where it was he was so keen on jumping to. But I saw it. It lay glittering beside the tub.

My hand clenched the necklace around my neck as I crept up to the twinkling in the small crevice. Quentin must have followed my gaze. He got there before me and palmed the precious piece of magic before I'd had a chance.

Magic, you stupid. You could have used magic and snatched it right up.

My eyes followed as he stuffed his hand, and the gem, into his pocket.

"Come here." I could tell. He had the gem now. He was ready to fly.

I pushed past him and flung myself on to the bed. "No. I'm not going." I knew my adamant proclamation was muted by the feathers of the pillow. I didn't care.

I half-expected to hear something. Maybe even catch a flash of light. Nope. Not Quentin.

"I can't leave without you. What would you do? They'd come after you, thinking you had the gem anyway." He patted my head and pushed my hair back. It was nice in the sort of way a dog must feel when its owner pets it.

It was enough to make me fall asleep.

"Ella. Wake up now. You've slept through lunch and it's almost dinner. You've got to eat. What if..."

I woke up enough to hear the end of his tirade. He paced back and forth at the end of the bed. Sometime during my extended nap he'd had the decency to throw the blanket over me.

But my headache was duller than this morning. I felt nasty. My stomach growled. And hungry.

"I heard that, Ella, even your body is talking to you. I've gone damn near stir crazy in here waiting for you to wake up. We can't be alone. I saw them on the ship earlier." Quentin stopped and pulled the blanket off me. "Come on."

It was bright. My eyes protested against it via my mouth. "Uh."

I couldn't believe how sluggishly my body moved. I'd been invaded by a giant snail. And it was one heck of a shell on my back.

The bathroom seemed father away, too. Quentin followed me. I guess he didn't trust I wouldn't collapse under my imaginary burden. I'd feel much better as soon as I could toss some cold water on my face.

The phone rang.

"I'm not moving, Quentin. Go get it."

My blood was flowing again. I could stand up. I could walk. And I'd found my voice.

"Screw the phone. I'm getting you dressed and we're leaving."

"I'm sick of constantly jumping around. And I'm sick, period."

"That isn't my fault."

"Oh no?" I was feeling brave. "You'd think I'd have gone through all that puking in a first class bathroom on a cruise ship without your influence? Answer the damn phone."

I pushed the door closed and started the process to revive Ella. It was going to take time and effort and a little help from Max Factor to get it right.

"Ella, get to feeling better in a hurry. We're on in an hour." I heard the phone rattle against the desk. I don't think whatever news he got over the phone sat any better with him.

"What exactly does 'we're on' mean?" I flipped on the water and held my toothbrush like a weapon.

"There's a costume in the closet. You're my assistant in the magic show tonight."

My head jerked up from the basin. I looked like a mad dog with foam around my mouth. Felt nearly the same way. "Magic? I thought we were leaving."

Silence. I scrubbed and spit.

"Are you saying we have to put on magic show?"

He stood at the doorway holding a skimpy sequined and mesh outfit. It was little more than a black bikini held together with fishnet. And a boa.

"I blame you. You made me answer the phone. We're a husband and wife team and we're on the schedule. You oughta jump into the shower, my dear."

I laughed. Oh it was funny. How had Quentin managed to pull

this one off? My peals of painful laughter faded when I saw his straight face. Not even a dimple gave him away. "Uh, sorry to break it to you, but you'll be performing alone tonight, sweetheart. Just tell them your *wife* is sick."

"That's not going to work. You see, tonight's our opening night."

"I thought you wanted to jump."

Yep, those were darts flying from his eyes.

"How noble." I rinsed my mouth and turned off the water.

"Get your ass moving."

I turned my back and crossed my hands over my chest. That wasn't going to stop him. He lifted me up and floated me right to the bathtub. Hot water cascaded down the minute my feet hit the non-skid surface. "Quentin!" I shouted, my fists clenched. My clothes were soaked. I had no shampoo, no soap.

I dodged the bottles he hurtled over the top of the door.

"You're wasting valuable time, Ella. You're going to need the stage makeup tonight. I don't want all those people out there thinking I married a sunken-eyed mad woman."

The water was helping me come alive. I stripped and kicked the sodden clothes to the back of the tub. It took everything I had to ignore his description. He was right, but dammit, that hurt. "Magic show?" I was still incredulous. "How did that happen?"

"Don't think. Your costume's on the counter. I'm going to get dressed."

I bet he didn't have fishnet.

I scrubbed the shampoo into my hair. My fingers connected to the knot of leather that held the gems around my neck and a cold chill raced down my spine. Just like the first time, I remembered. When I thought it was a spider.

But now I know better. I could jump. Leave. Run. But he had the trump card, the last original gem.

Fine. I flipped off the water. Magic show it is. Warming up would probably be a good idea. I had the hair dryer floating over me as I waggled my fingers at the towel. It rose, spun and pirouetted on its journey to me. Then it opened and circled my body in a warm hug.

Energy soared through my veins, warming me even more. We could do this. I could do this. While I wasn't real happy with Quentin, my options weren't very appealing. The least I could do was go along with it and use magic to get the gem back.

"I'm not wearing this," I shouted a few moments later.

"I heard you. And I think you look smashing." Quentin materialized beside me.

"This is more suitable for a boudoir than on stage."

"Hey, we could be in Vegas. Performing topless, or even nude is considered normal there."

"Not me."

"I think you perform well in the nude." His eyes twinkled as he met mine in the mirror.

"You're influenced by this scrap of black lace."

"Mm."

"Why do you get to remained fully clothed?" He looked like royalty in purple and gold. I half-expected to find a sword hidden between the layers of satin.

"I'm not as beautiful as you."

"There'll be some ladies in the crowd who'll beg to differ. Give me the cape and turn around."

"No."

"Do we have time to argue?" I struck a pose and then returned to puckering my lips for another coat of wine colored lipstick. My head started pounding again.

I stuck my hip and my hand out. "Cape."

He rolled his eyes but tugged on the gold braid. I snatched it and tossed it over my shoulders. The cloak was heavy and fell nearly to my ankles. Thank goodness.

"Now. Let me see your butt," I ordered.

"What?" Quentin's eyes shot open wide.

"Turn around. I want to make sure you give those single girls a good show."

He sighed with utmost dramatics and pirouetted. Even held his hands in the air like a ballerina. I was too busy admiring to laugh. Those shiny gold pants were snug in all the right places.

Was it hot in here?

I picked up the make-up sponge and patted my forehead. Yep, I was sweating already. I glanced over one last time. “Cute tights.”

His answering growl tugged at the corners of my mouth. I wanted badly to be able to hate him. Or at least feel nothing but lust. But here he was, being sexy as hell, sweet as could be and I was putty. How else could I explain the fact I was going to face a few hundred people in something less than a bathing suit?

Chapter Seventeen

We were hustled into a cramped dressing room about ten minutes before showtime. "I guess this is why they had us dress in our suite," I told Quentin.

He nodded. The room was tinier than our bathroom. And the space was stuffed with every imaginable magic prop. Certainly not a place for the claustrophobic.

I eyed the saw-the-lady-in-half box. "Wanna do a twist on that routine and let me cut you?"

He nodded with a crooked smile. "Ah, no."

"Five minutes," accompanied a staccato rap on the door.

"Here's the deal. You go first, do some simple stuff—tear up a napkin, turn a scarf into the bird, etc. Use mental displacement. Remember the prime rib of your first lesson?"

"The one I didn't get?" It felt like those first lessons happened years ago. If I only knew then, I might have been a little more skeptical about finding adventure. *This* certainly qualified as adventure. I knew precious little about putting on a freaking magic show.

I hadn't quit yet, so I took a mental photograph of the room. A ball, a dove and a pile of scarves. And there on the makeup table was a box of tissues. Check. I could do this.

"I got it," I told him while straightening my spine. My voice still betrayed me with a quiver.

"I believe in you." Quentin winked and blew me a kiss. For once, I trusted he did.

I nearly floated onstage. But I thought maybe that would be pushing the magic envelope a little far.

Music...lights...applause? Obviously we had a warm up act. I hoped like hell we were worth it.

I wished I'd added a streak of red glitter to my hair. I'd left it down, of course, there wasn't much choice in the matter. Oh well, maybe I looked exotic enough.

"Introducing Mr. Thunder, the magician, with his lovely assistant, Dancing Rain." I jerked my mouth from a giggle to a wide smile and did my best to glide on stage.

Dancing Rain? What was that, something Native American? Not that I minded, of course, but whoa, the surprises were getting old.

I'd tied a string of scarves together and led them behind me as I ran along the lights that bordered the stage. The music swelled and the spotlights narrowed.

I held up one arm and let the multiple colors coil around my wrist and down my entire body like a giant snake. With a snap of a finger, they dropped.

I wadded the scarves into a ball and tossed them skyward, spinning until it was the red rubber ball that fell back into my hands.

A pair of hula hoops were rolled across the stage at me. Dare I? Did I remember how to do it? Uh, not with Quentin's heavy cloak. This was going to be humiliating and challenging.

Here I was, half-naked and dancing with a hula hoop. At least it wasn't a pole. I swore I'd never stoop to that. But the catcalls were the same. I hoped the stage makeup kept my face from looking as red as it felt.

I swallowed, hoping that lump was my pride going back down. I twirled one, and then both of the glittery pink hoops. Now what?

A poof of smoke and the pair of hoops became one. My smile was no longer forced. The crowd was going nuts. I could see the enthralled faces of youngsters who had come up to the front row. That made it all worthwhile right there.

I encouraged one little girl up on the stage. Boy, was she a sweetie. I still didn't want to speak. I guess I was pretending it added to my aura. So I handed her a wand and led her to where I'd dropped the cloak.

I lifted it the center of it about two feet up so it created a little tent and pointed so she would touch it with the wand.

A bolt of lightning flew out of it, scaring both of us. That *was* not in the script. But after I swallowed, my heart this time, I mimed, "Oh, no." and pointed to the lump beneath the cape.

I took the wand away. Didn't need the precious little thing with eyes as big as her fists to torch the place.

Motioning her over, I peeked under the edge of the cloak. Her giggle went all the way to my heart. Having a child wouldn't be all that bad, would it?

She nodded and smiled, out-glowing me and my sequins. We stepped back and I tugged on the cape to expose what we'd found. The audience gasped when they saw the birdcage holding a white, folded paper bird.

I was having fun. My cheeks hurt and I couldn't remember why I'd been afraid. The crowd was supportive, encouraging my adrenaline to reach heart-pounding levels.

My little helper was no less excited. She jumped up and down and squealed with glee when I lifted the birdcage to a stool that was at her eye level.

How to do this... I tapped my foot and my finger against my lips in tune. The little girl should get the paper bird. Souvenir.

I passed it to her. "Open," I mouthed. At first she pounded a foot and shook her head. The audience laughed. I played along but repeated my instructions. Her hands fisted into her pockets.

Once more she shook her head. I had to laugh with the crowd this time. What was she, six? Sassy little thing. Okay, okay, I mimed. I pointed at the pocket on the girl's pinafore and held out my palm.

She had a tissue there. One I'd put there. That, she was willing to give up. I wadded it up, walked around the cage, opened the door and tossed it inside.

Of course, by then, it was a live dove.

And I was tired. Exhausted.

"You did good," Quentin whispered in my ear. I'd had a feeling he was around, invisible during this. It was our ace in the hole, since we knew nothing about this illusion bit.

I dared not answer, but tuned in to his thoughts. The crowd's cheers faded, and all there was left was a stage and two lovers.

I lifted the cape. This was Quentin's grand entrance.

The stage darkened. Those lighting people were good, almost as if they knew what we were thinking. Uh-oh.

I didn't let it force me to miss a beat. I followed Quentin's lead as the music shifted to something darkly romantic. We danced.

Around and around, my feet barely touched the floor. The cloak billowed like wings in a breeze before pulling tightly around us. The faintest puff of smoke added to the atmosphere. For me as well as the audience. I was in another world with Quentin, one in which we were touching. Heart to heart. Soul to soul.

"Invisible." His command broke the spell. He gathered the corners of the cloak and circled until I was gone and he stood alone in the center of the stage. To the crowd, I had become Quentin and the dance had never taken place.

I backed away in the frenzy of a standing ovation. Exhaustion weighted me down. From my seat on the side of the stage, I watched Quentin bow and wave.

It was hard not to be jealous. Not of Quentin, for he deserved the thunderous applause for his fanciful tricks. But I was jealous of the crowd, who had his undivided attention. He wanted to please them, share with them the things that would make them happy. Too bad he wouldn't glance behind him and wink, just once.

"*Ready, darling?*"

The mental query jerked me to alert status. I hate it when he startled me like that.

"*For?*" I asked while rising to my feet. Did someone add lead to my shoes? This magic stuff wasn't unlike a sport. Wow.

I watched as the saw-the-lady-in-half box was rolled on stage. Quentin even invited three people to inspect the saw and the box. No trapdoors. No secret passages.

This was it. He intended to do away with me once and for all. Fine.

I'd seen enough magic shows to know how I was expected to vamp it up. I smiled and pointed my fishnet clad toes as I circled the box.

"*Talk to me, Quentin.*"

"*You don't have to do anything. Save your magic. I'll use mine.*"

Trust him? My hands shook as I stroked the sleek black wood.

"*Trust me,*" he reaffirmed.

And I'm a dancing bear.

"*Say chicken loud enough for the audience to hear when I ask you a question."*

"*Chicken?*"

The box was open and I was being helped inside. A little reluctantly.

"Dancing Rain, are you afraid?"

Ready to hurl, I wanted to say. But I didn't ruin it for him. "Chicken," I stated evenly.

The crowd howled. I was mortified. The box closed over my head and I heard the lock snap.

"*Lord, I haven't meant all the bad things I've done, I—*"

I was back in the closet-like dressing room after only the slightest jostle.

I went invisible and ran back to the corner of the stage. Quentin was gritting his teeth and acting like he was cutting through bone. I checked my waist. No blood. Not even a run in the hose. Amazing.

"Honey?" Quentin knocked on the top portion of the box. "Are you in there?"

Of course I didn't answer.

"She said it tickles," Quentin announced.

The crowed cheered.

Quentin resumed his sawing until he was all the way through. The lights emphasized the sheen of sweat on his forehead and upper lip. Faintly defined muscles bulged against the tightness of his costume.

My own mouth watered at the truly masculine sight of him. Any jealous feelings left when he arched an eyebrow toward me. A fountain of hope spouted from my chest. *And for now he's mine. Good or bad, angry or mad, I'm with him.*

"*What about happy?*" he chimed in. "*Don't I make you happy*?"

His routine never missed a beat. He stood back while his audience members unlocked the box and fell away laughing. At Quentin's insistence one man went back to lift what they'd found in the foot of the box.

A live chicken.

"*Touché.*" I strolled around the box and came up behind him. I figured a nice pinch on the rear when he bowed for the audience wasn't exactly out of line.

"Hey now, no touching unless you're serious."

"Serious? I won't deny you're a seriously nice looking piece of flesh. Is that enough?"

"For now." He wouldn't look at me. *"Get in the box. Invisible, of course. Can you pull your feet up to fit in half?"*

I eyed the box. *"I suppose."* While the men goofed and chased the chicken around the stage and Quentin thanked his two helpers I stepped into the death trap. Watch, he'd want to saw me in half now.

The spotlights followed them around the stage and gave me glimpses of the audience members. I could see faces, features and laughter. And on one face, utter hate.

I was glad to wrap myself in a hidden ball. That man's eyes were black. Not even a reflection of light in them. And his gaze never wavered from Quentin. Even when the spotlight did.

"You in there?" He closed the lid to the box and walked around it. Funny how the mental voice moved when the speaker did, just as if it was carried on sound waves.

"Yeah, did you see that creep in the audience?"

"Which one?"

The box was rolling. In a circle. *"Can I stretch out yet?"*

"Just wait."

"This guy—he wore all black, maybe navy. Sat about three tables back along the left wall. Black creepy eyes." I shivered.

"Ten-Four. Straighten and find a smile, Ella." Quentin's voice held little inflection.

I obeyed and found myself not only being shown to the crowd as reappearing, but also floating at waist level.

"Aren't you cute?" I dodged at him. *"How much longer of this show?"*

"Couple more tricks. Aren't you having fun?"

"I was. That creep made me nervous."

"He should. But don't look too hard. There are bunch of them in the crowd."

"Great."

"Is that why you wanted to jump?"

"Mmm. Yeah, and we're going to—it's our finale."

"You got the gem?" I couldn't imagine him hiding it under those skintight clothes.

"I looped it into the back of my necklace. So guard my back."

His chuckle curdled the contents of my stomach. What if I had to?

Our banter continued for the next half-hour. I didn't ask where the white tiger came from. I didn't want to know. But when Quentin took his final bows I knew he was using the final gem as his ace in the hole. The sweat was dripping, darkening his clothes, and I watched his chest rise and fall faster. He was tired.

"Whatever you do, don't let go."

"Are you going to fill me in on this trick?"

"Follow my lead. And trust me."

Easier said than done. *"Where are we going, by the way?"*

"I though we'd check out Venice."

"Venice?" As in Italy? As in canals and old architecture? *"Okay."*

"On the count of three."

We stood hand in hand, side by side. I felt safe, secure and worthy of the cheesy grin plastered on my face. If I could escape the political mess and keep the gems I might give Copperfield a run for his money. Vegas was warm, right?

"One." Quentin squeezed my hand as we bowed again.

—but I'd sure miss him.

"Two." He held the cape out like bat wings. I moved within them.

"Three!" He shouted, picking me up, twirling and making us disappear into a cloud of smoke.

Venice was cold.

Especially for this half of the would-be figure-skating couple. Well, that's what we'd been mistaken as. The gondola driver had shouted at us when Quentin indicated he had no money to pay him. We were "cheap American ice-dancers."

It made me wonder if the canals froze in the winter and if so, what did those glorified cabbies do for a living then? Play hockey?

"We need to get to Frederique's hotel." Quentin's hand pushed me along. Normally I would have enjoyed his attentive touch on the small of my back. It felt...possessive. But now it was demanding I pass up the sights I'd waited a lifetime to see.

"But-but..."

"You'll get to drool over crumbly buildings from the hotel window. Frederique will have secured clothes and money for us."

I know I'd heard his name before. The hairs on the back of my neck prickled a little with the fleeting memory. Had he been one of Bergestein's men? Maybe he'd been at the meeting in Disneyland oh-so long ago.

"Do I know him?"

Quentin was still a half-step behind me so I couldn't see his face. "I don't think so."

His disinterested tone did little to quell the nervous tick that threatened to surface.

Vegas was sounding awfully nice. And warm, considering my barely there clothes.

"He *will* have clothes?"

"He said he would."

My eyebrow lifted on its own. Must have been the natural reaction to my wondering just when Quentin had talked to Frederique last. What plan did they devise?

I glanced back across the square at the dark water. I just hoped I wasn't going to end up feeding fish.

Quentin gave me a push that nearly sent me and my three-inch heels skidding across the mosaic looking tiles.

"Is that how you intend to kill me, by making it look like an accident?"

"Who said anything about killing you?" His warm fingers wrapped around my upper arm and steadied me.

A flick of his wrist sent me spinning into his arms like an intricate dance move. Mamba, samba, ooh.

When my body stopped with his arms around me, my head continued the dance. I let it spin across the square. I didn't need it. I had hot breath against my temple and a lean, hard body melting into mine.

"*Stop.*"

"What?"

"Quentin, stop. Just take me to where I can get some real clothes on and find a place to rest."

"We're going."

I leaned my head sideways against his shoulder. Why couldn't I just accept the attraction, the friendship? Neither of us had a future, much less the ability to plan one together. But I kept finding myself realizing that it was exactly what I wanted.

I rested my weight on him.

"Ella?"

"Hmm?"

"I promise I'll let you lean on me once we find ourselves a private room."

"Quentin?" The idea of being alone and safe was fading. "What are the chances we're being followed?"

His body tightened and he stepped back. Grabbing my hand, he pulled me toward the door to the bakery.

Quentin turned around once he closed the glass door behind him and surveyed the plaza. It was all store fronts and hotels with tiny slivers that looked like they must be alleyways. Not the kind of place nice girls go.

The bursting smell of blueberries beckoned like a mirage in the desert. I gaped through the glass while a wrinkled, gray-haired lady stared at me with the same intensity.

It took her sharp rap on the glass to jerk me from the smell-induced stupor. She rattled something off in a foreign language. It took a minute to figure out what it was—Italian. Certainly nothing I could understand.

Quentin let me out of the little shop. Either he understood or the woman's tsking gave him a clue. Quentin wouldn't let me turn around and give her the evil eye when I heard the laugh follow us out the door.

"Let me guess, she kicked us out because we didn't buy anything."

"Yeppers."

"Then I'm not going back even when I have money."

I got a chuck under the chin for that. "Figures. I wanted one of those eclairs for breakfast."

Did he know me that well already?

"Frederique's hotel should be about another block. Lose the shoes and we'll step into the alley and go invisible."

"Is that smart? Wasn't there something to them detecting magic?"

"If they're already here, it doesn't matter, now does it?"

Quentin swept me up. My breath caught as he sidestepped down an alley where sunlight couldn't reach. He almost made it feel like we were two lovers stepping into the shadows for... I shook my head.

Must be the romantic vision I had of Venice.

"Well, we could do that, too." His voice dropped an octave, and he laughed softly.

So he was reading my mind again, eh? I shrugged in response and disappeared.

He already had his hands on me though, so my chance of escaping anything more than his vision was hopeless.

"Quentin, please, let's go." His grip was strong, and almost cruel. "Haven't the events of the past two days been crazy enough?"

No answer, not even via mental telephone.

"Can we go to the hotel now?"

Silence.

It wasn't Quentin's hand that dug like leeches into my skin. Someone jerked me half off my feet and to the right. I landed against Quentin's chest. His breath and lips grazed my cheek as his shaky hand plunged down the front of my costume. Something icy remained when he withdrew it. I reached for him, grazing only the tips of his fingers as we were pulled in separate directions.

Monsters had emerged from the shadows of the alley.

This was going to be no vacation.

I didn't fight him, them, whoever. I mean, what was the point. It was obvious my captor was bigger and stronger and had magic to boot.

A little itch allowed me to position my tiny gift beneath my breast. If they managed to find it there, I'd better be dead already. Kidnapping I could handle, rape was out of the question.

"Quentin?" I cried out a mental beacon one last time. What were they going to do with him? If they suspected him of any wrong doing toward Mr. B they surely wouldn't hesitate to...

I grimaced to imagine life without Quentin. He irritated me to no end but I'd allowed myself to fall in love. Bad, bad Ella.

"He's gone already. You're the one we need. Now get yourself visible before I rip those gems from your pretty little neck."

Didn't have to tell me twice. While I wasn't scared enough to pee my pants, I certainly was shaking enough to know the shoes had to go.

I strained to recognize the voice. Nothing. Not a clue. All I figured was that it had to be just another of Bergestein's guys.

"Guess again," he muttered in my ear. I jerked back from the flash of hot breath. At least he could have had the decency to have eaten a breath mint before the kidnapping attempt. Not that it mattered.

"Ready?"

As if he gave me the time to answer. He twisted me until my back was against his broad chest and the fireworks went off. Visual, not emotional ones. Unless you count my temper.

"Here you are, ma'am, would you like anything else?"

A plate of steaming lobster tickled my nose with its faint garlic, buttery smell.

"No thanks."

This was like being stuck in Annabelle, but worse. I was a leech, a rider. My host was oblivious to me and I had about zero influence on her actions.

What fun.

Now where's the dude who snatched me away? Surely he hadn't morphed into that sweet little old lady who sat across the table.

"Mom, how's your pasta?" The deep but definitely female voice of my host asked.

I listened to their conversation about unsalted potatoes and watered down drinks.

Despite the mild complaints, I felt good about where I was. Middle class America. Probably in the body of a workaholic daughter who was taking her mom to lunch to celebrate a birthday or anniversary.

Mr. B, and even Quentin, seemed miles and years away. I ignored the emptiness in the fleeting thought of Quentin. I had to be strong and get my own self out of Mr. B's control before I could find and rescue him. That's what I was supposed to do, right?

"Mom," I heard the woman interrupt, "Jason and I are getting married."

Good thing I wasn't in the mom's body or I would have toppled right out of the chair. Or spit my drink across the table.

Instead I watched emotion play across the wrinkled, powdered features. Surprise, shock and then deep lines of anger.

"I told you about him."

"I know you think he's after my money. But he said he'd sign a pre-nup. Isn't that enough?"

I mentally rolled my eyes and cursed myself for the thought this could be normal.

Had I lost my mind?

Then again, I imagined breaking the news to my parents I was getting married. To a man with no past and no future. Someone who doesn't even have ID to fly across the States. Yeah, that'd go over about as well as this.

I'd lost my mind. At least, it seemed to be the only viable answer when a dragonfly dive-bombed the water goblet.

"What was that?"

"Too big for a fly. A bird?" Dear old mum waved her hand. "It's gone now. Enjoy your meal, Meredith. You're too uptight."

What if—was it? Winzey?

I definitely wasn't liking this along for the ride thing. Forget any prior ideas that this might be a good place to hide. At least in Annabelle I had control. Even that short stint in the bride, I had influence over her actions. This was nothing but prison. I couldn't even get Meredith to turn her head so I could try to catch another glimpse of the insect looking visitor.

"*Winzey*?" I called mentally, praying it could be heard. "*Come back, Winzey. Get me out of here.*"

The buzzing was behind me, like a mosquito that was much too close. God I hope Meredith didn't have a killer aim.

"Honey, that bug is back."

Shut up, dear mom, don't tell her. To Winzey I begged, *"Please, please, tell me how to jump."*

"*Sam wanted to keep you safe. Unless Meredith reaches up and touches the gems just right, you must stay.*"

"*No.*" I wasn't staying, even it I felt the rush of relief Sam had been behind this. "I'm not staying. I'm not."

The buzzing was gone. And Meredith was wearing the gems? Based on the manicured hands and extravagant jewelry, I had a feeling she wasn't going to like them. I mean, let's face it, they weren't a string of pearls or anything.

"*Winzey? Sam?*" My brain was digesting information slower than Meredith's stomach was processing her seafood dinner.

Sam? I wanted to pound on the windows of her eyes. *Let me out, let me out!*

Where was he? Here? "Winzey? Where are you?"

Is this what a madman feels like? Dementia? Rubber rooms couldn't even keep me safe from myself.

Deep breath. Breathe. You can do this. Think. Think. It's all you can do.

Okay. First things first.

Sam had something to do with me being here. Or had he just found me?

"*Sam?*"

"*Patience, my dear. You're safe and sound in there. Now quit screaming like a banshee or you'll have Bergestein's men all over us.*"

"*Where are you?*" Sam was here. I would have jumped up and down if I could. Sam was here.

Nothing. No answer. Sam wasn't talking. The idea of being hauled from Meredith's body by Bergestein wasn't exactly on the top of my wish list.

"*Fine,*" I muttered. "*Guess I'll just ride along with Miss Priss until you get me out of here. No problem. Fine.*"

Who was I fooling? It couldn't have been fifteen minutes and I was bonkers.

And powerless. Powerless. Me, who didn't want magic to begin with, who would have thrown it all away several times.

I take it back. I take it back!

Meredith drove her flashy Lexus like she was the queen of the street.

"*Sam, is this punishment? Are you finding this totally laughable?*"

I knew I wouldn't get a response. I knew I was alone. Deserted.

Quentin wouldn't have done this to me. Quentin wouldn't leave me...would he?

"*Quentin?*" I whispered, though there was no need. "*Where are you?*"

I didn't anticipate an answer. Now what? *Now what?*

ଔ ଔ ଔ

"*Ella, wake up.*"

I must have dozed off during Meredith's documentary marathon.

Sam was here.

Standing right there, between the TV and Meredith. I wanted to jump up and hug him.

Wait a minute. Why wasn't Meredith screaming about a stranger in her house?

"You have full control now. Just like Hollywood," he said, speaking normally this time.

Damn, wished I would have known that sooner. I missed X-files. I blinked at him a few minutes, still unbelieving.

I reached up and felt my neck. Yep. Beads. I held those fingers out in front of me and wiggled. Still Meredith's perfect manicure. I could move... I could talk!

"Sam?" I pushed out in Meredith's husky voice. I sucked in a deep breath. "Oh, God, Sam, thank you."

He stepped back, his hands behind him. "Are you sure? You're not wishing you were still with Quentin."

Uh-oh, twenty questions. I fired one back. "Would that be wrong?"

"Bad man, bad man." Winzey buzzed up to my ear.

"Still?" I looked from Sam to Winzey. "Why would he have left Bergestein's compound? And given me the gem?" I patted my chest.

Oh no. The gem.

Sam pulled a hand into view and opened his fist. The gem glittered and glowed in the light from the TV.

"Phew, Thank you. For a minute there..."

"You thought he'd gotten it back? He might have if I hadn't gotten to it first. I was tagging along with you, Ella, I jumped during the magic show. Nice presentation, but all that razzle-dazzle was like a flashing neon sign."

I batted myself in the forehead with my fist. I should have known. I really should have.

"Was that you there in the alley?"

"Yeah. But not as myself. And Bergestein's men were hot on my heels."

"So what happened to Quentin?" There was dread again, back to pay another visit as a rock in my stomach. That fueled another thought. My hand went to my middle. "Am I?"

Sam pulled me to my feet. "Quentin is back at Bergestein's. No doubt he's locked up in some underground prison after letting you and his heir go."

"So I am?" That was no rock on my gut. It was a live grenade and it just exploded.

"No."

"But—" Hadn't he just said?

"I rigged it, Ella. I had to."

Air left my body in an exaggerated whoosh and I sat back down. My knees were feeling a bit unstable.

"Don't kid yourself for a moment. Bergestein would have taken the kid. No matter how hard you and Quentin would have fought. Then he would have done away with you, if necessary."

Boy was I glad I was sitting down. "Why?"

"Oh, I doubt he wants an heir, but he knows it would devastate you... and Quentin now."

"Bastard."

"He is who is."

"Would he do something—to Quentin, now?"

Sam's lips pinched together and lines around his eyes deepened. "I don't know."

"We have to save him."

"Bad man, bad man."

I was tempted to flick Winzey off my shoulder.

"No, Ella," Sam pocketed the gem and pulled me on my feet again. "We're not. I've saved him too many times. He's dangerous and untrustworthy. I'm sorry I even thought he'd change because of you."

"Sam, no."

"Let's get you out of there. It's hard to face a middle-aged business woman with her eyes full of tears. Especially over a rebel punk kid."

I didn't need to be told twice. My hand flew up to my neck and I stepped away.

I leaned against Sam for support. Again? Balance was in short supply. This stepping out thing had me all discombobulated. I needed to figure it out.

"Now what?" I looked from Winzey to Sam. I tried to. Things were a little blurry around the edges. "Does this ever get easier?"

Sam's wise face slid into an easy smile. "Think of it as training for a marathon. You're not going to mange to be ready in a month."

Well, I wouldn't even think of tackling a marathon, but I knew what he meant. "Point taken, mister. So where are we headed?"

"We're going home."

Winzey zipped over to Sam and dove into his chest pocket. I lifted an eyebrow then glanced down. Oops.

"Uh, you think I can get some new clothes?"

"When we get there."

Sam took two steps and snapped the beads of my necklace. I clicked my heels. After all, there's no place like home.

Chapter Eighteen

The orange walls looked like the sides of a giant pumpkin reaching out of the sands of the island.

Despite the heat, cold tremors raced up my spine. It was almost as if I could hear the hollow echoes of the lost souls who were imprisoned in the hardened clay.

"Sam?"

The only figure on the beach was the one in the overcoat and cowboy hat.

Damn. And not even a footprint to indicate Sam had landed with me. Where to run? Jim was charging me like a bull seeing red. I was not going to stand here and be trampled. And likely stripped of my gems.

I flashed invisible and leapt toward the sea. Yeah, okay, so I wasn't captain of the diving team, but it temporarily had him scratching his head.

My bare feet left a tell tale path behind me. Too bad I hadn't thought to float. Brilliant me. My sarcastic attitude was fading. My hands trembled as I touched my neck.

Could I hover now? Levitate? How about float? My head pounded while five dozen horses raced through my blood stream. *I can do this. I can.*

Either I was going to float or my teeth were going to crack from the gritting.

"Sam?!?"

I was plucked out of the air by the back of my...suit and carried like a wayward kitten to a half-hidden cave.

This was it. I floundered with the gems, trying to get my hands on them just right.

I don't want to do this, but...

"Bad man." Winzey buzzed around my ear. "Jim very bad man."

I sucked in the humid air. Water lapped at some underground stream behind me. Breezes rustled the tall grasses at the mouth of the cave. So far, no heavy footfalls counted down my doom.

"Oh, Winzey, thank you, thank you." I brushed my fingers through my tangled hair as I followed her back into the cave. I must have looked behind me every fourth step. What if Jim had seen or heard? What if he could sense the magic and trace me down?

I opened my mouth to ask Winzey where we were going, but she put a hand to my upper lip. "Shh."

Her voice was little more than the sound of tissue rattling. I still checked every crevice of the room we had come to.

Dead end.

Winzey flapped out over the glassy pool and pretended to dive.

Who me? I already displayed my inability for this sport. I pointed at my chest and glanced behind me again.

Had I heard something? Someone?

I stood on the edge of the gray rock and peered in. It was like there was some sort of metallic film, or a gas residue floating on the surface.

The light wasn't exactly conducive to cave exploring. Occasional chimneys led to blue sky, offering just enough of the sun's rays to keep an explorer from smacking into a wall headfirst.

At this point I wasn't sure that was a bad idea. I might wake up from this nightmare.

I circled the pool that disappeared under the wall. Three sides gave me three views of the multi-colored shiny water. Dive, eh?

Winzey was getting frantic. Her little wings were approaching hummingbird speed. Something, like a stone crumbling, sent my heart up in my vocal chords. I imagined they were hugging each other for dear life as I finally nodded at Winzey.

I sucked a deep breath into my unwilling lungs and dove.

I had to be dead. That pond was probably only three feet deep and I must have hit my head and broken my neck. Which would explain why I was swimming in the underworld, heading toward a brilliant white light that warmed the chilled water. Dolphins and tiny mermaids swam with me, laughing, encouraging, leading me on.

Heaven was underwater? Then Winzey floundered, her little wings flapping slower. We'd swum down, under rock and the new surface was visible, but still out of reach. I pushed Winzey up, kicking with every ounce of strength. When her little body seemed to give out again, I denied my chest relief from the fire that had started and dove back down for her.

"*No, no, no,*" I screamed mentally and shook my head. Muscles screamed as they pushed and kicked.

I kept reaching for the surface, a mirror-like image that was always just out of reach. The animals danced around me. But when I tried to use them to propel myself upward, they swirled out of my grasp.

It was up to me.

"*I won't fail you, Winzey.*" I pushed the limp fairy ahead of me. The steam was almost gone from my body as well. We were on the verge of sinking to the bottom.

"No," I shouted, sucking putrid water. It gave me enough disgust for one final surge, draining all adrenaline reserves.

My hand and head broke the surface. The air that rushed into my lungs was filled with slivers and something that scored my mouth and throat. I gagged and coughed.

There was nothing left in my muscles to pull myself ashore. I pushed Winzey up on the edge of the grass and dug my fingers into the moist soil, hoping to anchor myself there.

My upper body was nearly numb when I felt the large hands under my arms. I was lifted, feeling about as boneless as a rag doll. I couldn't even pull my chin up to look around me.

The green grass blurred into watercolor.

Oh, look, just like in the fairy tales. I've been saved from certain death by the good guys.

Mr. Senior Good Guy stood back on his heels with arms crossed over a wet splattered blue shirt. He was smiling. My own weak attempt faded before I flashed my teeth.

The smile wasn't because he was happy to see me.

I clenched those teeth together, bracing myself for something I had a feeling I didn't want to hear. "I'm sorry?" I squeaked out.

"Sorry?" My single word was Sam's cue to pace. Back and forth until my head ached from the motion of watching. "Sorry doesn't cut it. Do you know why you almost didn't make it? Do you know why you nearly killed one of my fairies? Do you?"

His voice was thunder that rolled through the valley. I winced, waiting for the inevitable lightning.

"No, I'm not going to strike you. You've done enough damage to yourself. Quentin. That's why you're here on the barest of mercy."

I let my eyes wander from his flushed face. I was inside a dramatically still island. No birds sang; no fairies visited. The waterfall continued to fall, but its volume had been turned to mute. Like a calm before the storm. Or perhaps the storm had already come through. Maybe it was over.

I looked back at Sam, who was slowly shaking his head. No. The storm was still coming. And boy, was it was brewing up a good one.

"Oh, it's all here, the whole island. You just can't see it. You can't see Winzey even though she's floating right in front of your face, and you can't hear the peace and joy of this place because you're not worthy. You're barely worthy of standing on this ground. Count your blessings my father still sees good in you. I see a spoiled rotten, selfish brat who's been worried about herself and her sex life."

Now that I wasn't expecting. It shot through me like a nine millimeter bullet. I expected to look down and see a hole where my heart had been.

"Oh?" It sounded wimpy. I tried again. "Is that what you think?"

"That's exactly what I think. You've been trailed every step of the way. We know you were here and tried to get in. Lucky for you Quentin decided you were worth saving."

I gulped. What would make me think they didn't know? "I was trying to get away from Bergestein." That was one hundred percent God's honest truth.

"After you betrayed Winzey. You remember the one who has come to your rescue time and time again?"

Go ahead, Sam, twist the knife some more.

"But..."

"It's useless, Ella. Just be quiet and listen."

My strength was returning at the speed of maple syrup floating downhill during a Vermont winter. So I wasn't going to argue with him.

"Last chance. And I mean *last* chance. No help—you've got to prove yourself. You've got to stop Bergestein from completing the circle."

"How—"

One raised eyebrow cut my question short. It didn't, however, stop the race of cold through my blood. Me? He expected me to do something of such enormous magnitude when I'd already messed up like I had?

"You didn't mess up, Ella, you just lost focus. You let the enemy too close and made yourself vulnerable. If Quentin isn't totally on our side, consider him the enemy. No compromise. So now we're going to use those facts to turn you into a spy and have you blow up the compound."

"Do what?" My voice echoed through the empty field and sounded remarkably like a wounded bird.

Sam's eyes twinkled. A real smile.

"Quentin doesn't know where you are. He still thinks Bergestein has you somewhere, perhaps even torturing you for the final gem."

Sam winked. "Your lover boy's actually pretty tore up over the idea that you're in danger."

A rush of hot air hit me. *Sam's telling me Quentin's concerned. Worried. He does care. Maybe he does.*

"Oh, I think he does, but, Ella, we're talking Quentin here. He's not some cardboard cut-out of a man who's honest about emotions. To himself, let alone to the woman he loves."

My knees gave way.

He loves me.

The hamsters woke up and got back on their treadmills. Adrenaline kick started my muscles and I started to feel human.

"Why?" Deep breath. "Why are you telling me this?"

He shrugged, that same I-know-something-you-don't-know smile on his face.

"Sam?"

"Maybe I just think you'll work better knowing. Or else you'll go crazy wondering."

I had a feeling Sam knew me better than I knew myself. And it wasn't magic that told him all this.

"So, what's the plan?"

ଔ ଔ ଔ

My legs were stiff, not to mention they felt like Popsicles from sitting on the ground for over an hour. I propped my chin up on my palms, but my arms kept falling asleep as well. I was cold, tired and would never remember all the information Sam was rattling off. I had never been an A student. I didn't even have a way to take notes.

But Sam had kept my attention, reprimanding me the millisecond my brain shouted, "He loves me."

Then he got to the explosion part.

"Isn't the plan a little extreme?"

A baritone voice reached through the stillness. "Extreme?" The laugh that followed rumbled the ground beneath me. And I thought Sam's had been thunder. Whoa. Lou was very intimidating.

I stood up and brushed off my backside. "As exciting as it all sounds I'm still curious of the alternative."

Sam bit his lips and the laughter caused another mini-earthquake. "I'm afraid there is no alternative."

I caught a sour whiff of my own fear. Cold chills followed. I wrapped my arms around myself, wishing I could just disappear. Sam, I knew, was reading my thoughts. My eyes met his as my hand snaked up to feel my throat.

Bare.

"You didn't think I'd give you a way out, did you? You'd jump now if you could, wouldn't you?"

I started nodding then shook my head. Anytime I'd tried to escape I always wanted to come here. Where would I go now? I suddenly felt very alone.

"Alone? You'll never be truly alone where magic exists."

I wasn't clear on what he meant.

"Clarity isn't something easily defined," the baritone voice boomed. "Just know there's always more than meets the eye."

Wind swirled. The ocean's salty tang bit into my nostrils and I could taste it at the back of my throat.

I swallowed and blinked. Back in the sand. Out of the security of those orange walls. Alone. This was alone, I didn't care what Lou and Sam said. I was scared, vulnerable and—

"*Let it happen.*" I heard, as if it were carried on the wind.

"Let what—"

Someone remarkably like the famed Bigfoot tossed me over his shoulder without so much as a grunt. Uh-oh.

This was not the Stone Age and I did not resemble Wilma Flinstone or Betty Rubble. Except the hair color. But that didn't count. I didn't have a bone in mine.

"Who are you and what are you doing with me?" I gasped out.

Without an answer I did what came naturally to a hysterical female.

Screamed and kicked.

The arm around my shoulders tightened until I could scarcely breathe. "Okay," I sputtered, relaxing my limbs and pretending to be Raggedy Ann.

"Umph."

Great conversation. Was that an apology? Because I needed one!

"Where are we going?"

Repeat one syllable grunt.

Ah, yes, that told me a lot.

Since my only view was of a rather wide backside and endless sand, I couldn't have ventured a guess. Looks like it was wait and see time.

Did it matter?

Before I could blink again a flashbulb went off in my face.

We were off.

It was the smell that keyed me in. The strange antiseptic cleanser the compound couldn't seem to cover. Though it did seem an interior decorator had stopped by since my last visit. Or, I realized, this was uncharted territory.

"Welcome back."

I shivered as if a roach had just crawled up my arm. Then I shivered again when I realized how much worse he was.

"We've got a suite all ready for you."

"Why?" I turned on him. "Why?" It was no secret I'd expected to be chained to a wall in a dungeon somewhere. Unless that's what he meant.

His rendition of a belly laugh did little to ease my uncertainty. Can I throw up now?

"No you can't, and no, it's not the dungeon either. It's a room, not so unlike the one you had before. Just a little more surveillance, but that means more protection for you."

"Jail, eh?" My sarcasm had no bounds. I might be on a mission, but I wasn't kissing anyone's ass.

"No, I'll treat you like my own daughter."

Red-headed stepchild maybe.

"You'll have the best of everything during your pregnancy."

That pulled my head up as if it were on a marionette string. What? Who? An admission ran through my mind. "How'd you know?"

I waited for lightning to strike.

I almost thought I heard a peal of Lou's thunderous laughter. But Mr. B didn't flinch. Guess it had been my imagination.

"We've been with you the whole time. You and Quentin are like children to me. My prodigy. And of course, children rebel—they try to spread their wings. But you've come home now." He spread his arms wide.

No, thank you. And moi? A rebel child? *Lord help me, he's talked to my mother.*

"I take it I don't get to use magic?" Crap, I even heard the desperation in my voice.

Mr. B looked surprised. His wide but still beady eyes slid down my neck and back up again. There went another shiver. "Your gems broken?"

Let me sink through the floor. I reached up and touched them. "I-I assumed you would have them stripped from me when I arrived."

"I gave them to you."

Where was the trap door again?

This is what being blind must feel like. I figured it was well into the middle of the night. And silent. I'd fallen asleep after searching every available crevice, nook and cranny of the suite. Not sure what I was looking for, but I didn't find it.

Now all I was searching for was a light switch and couldn't find one of those either. Half of me was terrified I'd jumped in my sleep or been taken somewhere else—or heaven forbid, gone blind. The other half frustrated because it was my own stupidity that put me in this pickle.

"Anyone here?"

I expected, no *hoped,* Quentin would answer. Of course, I could have a row of invisible, and mute, guards standing at the door. I wouldn't know it until I walked into them.

Funny. I'd managed to pull out every dresser drawer and found a lost button on the floor of the empty closet, but I didn't have a clue where the lamps were placed or even where the furniture was.

Guess that indicates I'd be a poor detective. They could have planted a camera, a bug, anything in the lamp and I'd have missed it.

"Oh well," I muttered out loud. "Detective work wasn't next in line on my career choice list after all."

I felt my way back to the bed, then knelt on the floor. While I did remember this room being of the same general layout as the suite I had at the old compound, I wasn't taking anything for granted. Ha! That made it sound like a hotel or bed and breakfast or something. *Prison cell, Ella. Keep that in mind.*

This room didn't have a sliding door. No, then Ella could escape. There was just a window. Hidden behind the heavy draperies I didn't recall closing.

My journey across the room was riddled with bumps and mutters. And one rather loud expletive when I racked my baby toe right into a something harder than it was. Wood, I think. Whose bright idea was it to put a table there, anyway?

It didn't surprise me in the least when I realized the window couldn't open, and had a crisscross of bars. Don't know why I had missed that earlier. Too busy being paranoid, I guess.

"See, Ella," I told myself. "Prison, just like I told you."

I pulled the drapes all the way open and stared up at the starless night. Never a full moon when I needed one.

I sighed and reached up, lifting my heavy hair from the back of my neck. A shower did sound good.

My fingers connected with the leather tie at the base of my skull. Once again it pulled back the memory of Sam and a previous shower. What I wouldn't give to go back to that moment and make a few different decisions. Like not to go.

Quentin's face seemed to loom before me in the night. What would I change there? Anything? Surely I would have to. But would I want to miss a minute of it?

Damn. I was tired of the darkness. My hand flew out as I spun around. Every light flickered to life.

Oh yeah.

Magic.

It couldn't have been fifteen seconds later that someone knocked at the door. Boy, they were watching me, weren't they?

There wasn't much I could do about my appearance, so I opened the door with a sparkling smile in place.

"Good morning," I announced. "Or is it still evening?"

"Morning."

Oh. My. God. A butler?

He ignored my wide-eyed stare, or at least appeared to. Heck, in this place he'd probably seen it all.

"Is everything all right, Miss Ella? Mr. Bergestein said he sensed you were awake, agitated. Can I get you anything?"

"Uh," I pointed behind me over my shoulder. And felt like a human pretzel. "I couldn't find the light switch."

He leaned in and glanced around.

"I, uh, finally found them."

"I see, ma'am. If that'll be all?"

I grabbed his shoulder before he turned and waddled away. "Jeeves, you wouldn't happen to know the way to the kitchen would you?"

"Ma'am?" He scuttled sideways. "Kitchen?"

"I'm a little hungry." I rubbed my stomach for emphasis. "You know, someplace I can raid the pantry, even the fridge?"

"What would you like?" Now he was bowing. I wanted to slap him out of such subservience. Argh. What I wanted was free reign of Oreos and milk. Maybe chips and dip. Ice cream.

I wanted to look, explore, find something for myself.

Damn. There I went, obsessing over nothing. I took a deep breath.

"Are you offering me room service?"

"So to speak. Ma'am?"

The little penguin suit was ready to run. Can't say I was real surprised.

"Okay, do your best with this—" I rattled off the list my mind had created. And then added chicken noodle soup, a turkey sandwich on rye and a bottle of root beer. "Substitute if necessary."

He didn't blink.

Oh but perhaps he'd heard the pregnancy story. Must be it. Even I would have been surprised if someone asked for all that as a three a.m. snack.

Then I realized he hadn't moved. Poor man was in shock. "Please?" I added, smiling.

I dropped back on the bed. Ten to one I wouldn't see a bite to eat. Probably wouldn't get a candy bar out of the deal.

I hoisted myself into the shower. It took effort, yes, to peel off the clothing I'd worn longer than I cared to figure and subject myself to the cold water.

The citrus scent was nice, though. Almost nice enough to eat. My stomach echoed the thought with a growl that mimicked thunder.

"So are you."

Crash.

There went the shampoo bottle.

"Quentin," I shrieked. "Get out!"

He waved an Oreo at me.

"Heard you were hungry."

"Right now I'm cold and pissed off. Out."

He laughed at my pointing finger. I couldn't exactly get out and wrap up in a towel. My soapy hair probably looked like a white afro.

The icy water ran down my shoulders. I ducked my head beneath it and held my breath. Maybe I could freeze my senses. Numb myself to Quentin.

Fat chance.

He'd already pulled the string that left my head spinning like a top.

As the soap trickled down my legs, so did my apprehension. I debated about shaving, but figured finding and transporting a razor in would take too long. And Quentin had Oreos. Hairy legs were fine when there were Oreos.

He had to be reading my thoughts. "I'm eating all these cookies," he taunted. He probably tucked in with my treats and was licking his fingers with delight.

I jumped out of the shower and dried off as fast as possible.

"I'd rather—"

"Cut!" I called out. I smiled at my reflection in the mirror. He hadn't finished. I didn't even want to know. No, too late. I knew what he meant, and my body was already responding.

Be it magic or the wonder of housekeeping, I found a long, white terry cloth robe hanging on the back of the door. Hesitation wasn't part of my genetic make-up, at least when I was cold and there was an alternative option.

"Showtime," I breathed and tied the belt. "Ready or not, Ella's coming for the Oreo's."

I stopped in the doorway. "You had better have saved some fresh milk for me," I warned, running my hand through my wet hair.

My tongue skated across my teeth. Ew. I'd kill for a toothbrush about now.

"Try the cabinet behind the mirror. But you'd better hurry."

"For just one day, Quentin, would you stay out of my head?"

Silence. Glorious silence. Not for one minute did I think he wasn't reading my mind. But I could pretend, couldn't I? Pretend I was back in my apartment in nowhere land. Where my biggest worry was my next date and my next sale.

Okay, so that wasn't heaven, and Quentin wouldn't have come into the picture.

"Face it, Ella, you're a woman so you'll never be satisfied—"

It was a sacrifice, to be sure, but I could always get more. I waggled my finger at the pitcher of milk and provided Quentin with a mini shower.

He stopped mid-chew and glared at me. I expected nothing less than fireballs zipping in my direction once he realized what I'd done.

I waited. Nothing shattered against the wall that separated the bath from the bedroom.

Cautiously, I took a step. He was probably laying in wait, like a cat ready to pounce. The rush of adrenaline hit me like a double latte when I realized I wanted him to pounce. Wanted him to stalk and ultimately capture me.

Here I was feeling all...excited, and I turned the corner to be met, not with my own milk bath, but the sight of Quentin laughing so hard nothing was coming out of his mouth. I do believe milk, however, was spurting from his nose.

"Hey," I shouted, miffed he could relax in such a time like this. "Quentin!"

Gee, I was going to have to store this information away for future reference. Pour milk on Quentin and he giggled like a schoolgirl. Only I didn't want a giggling schoolgirl. Not even a giggling Quentin.

He waved me over. Oh sure, like I was buying into that. I stood there, studying the picture he made against my white bedcovers. Glistening wet cookie crumbs were black diamonds on his lap. His hair was half-plastered against his face, and his tongue shot out to catch the dripping rivulets between peals of laughter. It was almost as if the taste of the milk tickled his tongue.

Aw, shoot. The pre-lecture Ella would have taken her chances for the sake of Oreos. Okay. *Uncle.* I walked, no...sauntered over and helped myself.

"You know," I pointed with my half-eaten cookie. "You really should seek help for this problem."

"Ella," he gasped, reaching up. I stood my ground and ingested another cookie middle.

"Hm?"

I was jealous. Completely envious of his abandon. Why couldn't I let loose and laugh like that?

I ignored the answer. Even if I was asking, I didn't really want to know. It would mean work to change, and I wasn't up to work.

Someone was knocking. I stomped over. But even that didn't sober hyena boy. I think it made him worse.

"Yes?" I answered.

Mr. B. In silk pajamas no less. "Is everything all right, Ella? One of my men indicated there was a ruckus and thought I should check on you."

Let the man see for himself. I stepped back and played butler, since Jeeves hadn't been seen lately. "Right through to the bedroom, sir. You'll find my problem there."

I followed him, flipping off a few of the unnecessary lights. We'd have a 747 landing in here with this luminescence. But I didn't want Mr. B thinking I was getting romantic. No. Not at all.

The lace coverlet looked like cookies and cream ice cream. I guess that's pretty close to what it was.

"Quentin?" I lifted my eyebrows at Mr. B's tone. *Quentin's in trouble. Quentin's in trouble.* "Do you want to explain yourself?"

Quentin extended his index finger and pointed at me. Huh? "Me?" I tapped my breastbone. "I was in the shower. When I got out, he was here, helping himself to my midnight snack."

Silk swished as the head guy stepped over and picked up the empty milk pitcher.

"She did it," Quentin sputtered.

I felt transported back into second grade. Only the teacher didn't hand out demerits. This one snapped his fingers.

With just that, the mess was gone and I was alone.

Now, this was all interesting. I'd been abandoned. Without even a crumb of an Oreo left to show for it.

Yawn.

As much as I wanted chocolate, I didn't want to venture out alone and have Mr. B snap his fingers and turn me into a toad...

Hey. I had magic.

Rather than slap myself in the forehead, I cursed my forgetfulness and shut off the rest of the lights. I didn't deserve any chocolate.

Was I ever going to be able to succeed?

I swore the awful pounding was in my head. But when I shoved a pillow over it, it helped. "Go away. I don't want anything but sleep."

Of course, they wouldn't stop knocking long enough to hear me. Bastards.

Even if the sound didn't come from mini-jackhammers in my brain, the pain surely did. For goodness sakes, a hangover?

I couldn't recall drinking anything and I'd had, what, two cookies? Was this punishment for the milk-over-the-head stunt?

Knocking persisted.

Oh, gee. I was going to have to get up.

"Today, Ella!"

The voice was totally unfamiliar. And not happy.

"I'm coming already. Stop your knocking and get me some aspirin—my head's a ticking time bomb."

"You don't want to know what it would feel like if you're late to Bergestein's table for breakfast."

Magic.

I wasn't going to forget it this time. And in this case, using it for my benefit was wrong, wasn't it? Couldn't risk teeing off the main man, could I?

"Give me just a minute. Promise." I brushed my teeth and hair the old fashioned way, but wiggled my fingers at the closet for the rest.

Had to do it twice. Riding pants didn't work with the floral silk top. It was still faster than if I would have stood there and sighed over my options.

The nondescript butler junior led me to a long hall that had tables set up. Always a different room, a different scene. Oh look, just what I wanted, an audience. Quentin, who refused to meet my eyes but ogled my chest, was not at my table. No. I was sitting at Bergestein's right hand.

"So, Ella," Mr. Bergestein started, "when might I expect to see my heir?"

Water spewed from my mouth. Glistening droplets decorated my black lacquer plate. I counted them, refusing to look up. "I'm not sure. I'd have to consult a calendar."

Snap.

Be careful what you wish for. I really was regretting my decision to answer the door.

I flipped the pages of the newly appeared calendar back. Crap. When was the last time we—

Eyes bore into mine. I searched the table and ended up locked in a gaze with Quentin.

"*Tell him it'll be the end of June. Roughly.*" The mental message printed out in my brain.

"June? Maybe the very beginning of July? I could be wrong. Time has a way of getting away from me." What day *was* it anyway?

Mr. B must not have been monitoring the wavelengths, because he simply nodded. "I shall hope for July then. I do enjoy rubies."

A box appeared on my plate.

"Whoa," I said. A few people at the table caught their breath. Oh yeah. Some people don't know about the magic. Well, folks, you ain't seen nothin' yet.

"For you, Ella. You held up your end of the bargain. Here is a gift for you."

This wasn't in the script.

Since everyone was watching me, including Quentin, I had to play along. My hands shook. The velvet, hinged box opened easily. On the creamy satin lay a beautiful sapphire solitaire necklace.

I picked it up, and received murmurs of admiration.

"Mr. Bergestein, I—"

He held up a hand and my tongue froze. "Of course I expected you to object. But it is simply a token of my deep gratification. No further obligations, no pressure."

I let out a breath. No obligation? I was sweating like a horse on race day.

"Quentin, come help Ella with the necklace, please. I do believe her emotions have overcome her."

He had that right.

Chapter Nineteen

Quentin did look quite debonair as he walked the length of the table. Maybe I should have been nicer to him last night.

The touch of his hands on the back of my neck triggered that familiar stirring. He, unlike Mr. B, was fully attuned to my thoughts. Fingers intentionally lingered at the base of my throat. Want switched gears and became need.

"Later," he whispered and sealed the promise with a kiss.

I'll bet I had the pregnancy glow with the resulting blush from his show of affection.

"Nice. Very nice. Thank you, Quentin." Mr. B nodded and addressed the entire table, droning on about his plans to add on to the complex. To introduce a school so younger recruits could be trained on-site.

This piqued my interest. Recruits? Were we talking about cult-like activities here? Some bizarre religion?

"Shh." Quentin saved me from the backlash of Mr. B's raised eyebrow.

I tuned it out. I couldn't object to what I didn't hear, right? My fingers slid over the generous square-cut pendant. The heat from Quentin's touch was still there, just waiting to spread. I cupped it in my hand, and felt it pulse.

No.

I immediately let the flighty thought of it being a real gem pass. A real sapphire, yes, but a real magic gem in disguise? I don't think so.

Why? The idea still floated in the air. There were no reasons. More than likely it was a beacon, a combination wire and video that recorded my every move.

Sure. That made me feel better.

Finally we were able to eat. Being a pig was expected of me. I couldn't let anyone down, right? Waffles topped with thick whipped cream and fresh melon balls were my favorite. Then I had to have a blueberry scone dripping with real butter, not the oily margarine stuff I used to buy because it was cheap.

I must have heard a hundred wishes of congratulations. I pretended they were offering those words because I'd won the lottery. I'm sure it made my smile more genuine.

Through it all, the mild pounding headache became intense. Pressure increased behind my eyes and sharp stabbing sensations poked at my ears. I was on the verge of begging for mercy. And my stomach was seriously thinking about rebelling.

I wondered if the test was right—or was that wrong? It seemed months ago. But I couldn't concentrate to figure out the exact amount of time.

"Ella? You've gone pale. Is everything okay?"

"Uh, not really. My stomach isn't feeling too great right now. Perhaps I should be excused."

The woman next to me patted my cheek. "Morning sickness, dear. Have you had it long?"

I shrugged and shook my head. "Just a bit queasy now and then. Nothing like this."

"Then late June should be about right. I started my morning sickness when I was six to seven weeks along."

No way was I going to argue with her reasoning. I looked for Quentin, wondering if he'd overheard that prediction. He was gone. Mr. B must have noticed my search.

"Go on, back to the room, Ella. I'll be along to look in on you."

I nodded, stood and bowed. I didn't run until I reached the hallway. I ignored the door and dove straight through the wall.

No doubt. I was sick.

A curse. Witchcraft and black magic. I cursed it all. I didn't care if demons who rode fire breathing dragons flew up from the pits of hell because of it. Magic sucked.

Magic couldn't take away the wrenching sobs and stomach muscles that protested as if they'd endured a couple hundred sit ups.

I met every knock at the door with a terse. “Go away.”

But hey, at least they’d had the decency to knock.

“Ella, you’ve got to come out. You’re not sick anymore. You can’t be. There can’t be anything left in your stomach.”

I couldn’t argue that. Quentin, the know-it-all. Hell, he’d probably perched invisibly on the edge of the tub while I’d dealt with convulsion after convulsion.

“I still feel queasy.” My doubts were now solid. This was not morning sickness. Panic, I think, had given flight to the idea. But after a sip of water had ricocheted upwards and through my nostrils with as much force as Niagara Falls, well, I figured this was just a nice case of the stomach flu. “And I don’t want to come out. I want a shower. And a cold glass of water. But I’m scared.”

I was. Frightened and angry. At me, at Sam, at Quentin and at Mr. B. Hell, I was just mad at the world but too wrapped up in self-pity over my stomach woes to do anything about it.

“Why don’t you come out and I’ll rub your body down with a cold rag?”

Now that was an invitation. I flushed the toilet just to buy myself some time. The cold floor against my face felt good.

“Ella?”

He was at the other side of the door. Probably with his head stuck through. If he was visible, he’d probably look like he was in the guillotine.

Schwack! Off with his head.

I frowned, then bit my lip. No. Beheaded isn’t how I wanted to see Quentin end up. Mr. B maybe, but not Quentin. My heart was already justifying his nagging.

Fingers splayed on my shoulders. Yes. They kneaded, lightly, finding tension knots from weeks of stress. I practically melted the rest of the way onto the floor.

“I just want to go to bed,” I whined, but feeling justified. “I don’t feel strong enough for a shower right now. Help me get to bed”

Considering my lack of sleep the night before, I figured I’d fall asleep immediately. Not so.

Quentin sat in a chair beside me. And watched me.

"Don't you have something to do?" I sounded bitchy. But I really didn't care. "Doesn't Mr. B need you to fetch him coffee or train magical assistants or something?"

I opened one eye and watched him. He lowered the book he was using as a half-fence. "Nope."

"You haven't turned a page in ten minutes. I know you're not reading."

His eyebrow arched above the spine but he relaxed in the chair. "So?"

"Go away. I can't rest with you watching me."

He did the unexpected. He stood, dropped the book and stripped off his shirt. Next he unsnapped his jeans. I sucked in my breath. Dear God. What *was* he doing?

"If you're entertaining me with a strip show, at least hum and shake your hips a little. You won't get good tips otherwise."

Seems I'd thrown up my intestines, but not my sarcastic attitude.

Quentin's sense of humor, on the other hand, had found its way to the sewer. "Move over, Ella. We're taking a nap." I had no choice. Either become Quentin's mattress or move. I moved. Quentin, in just his briefs, slid beneath the covers.

He snapped his fingers. Lights dimmed, but the room was still bright from the sun streaming in the half-opened blinds. He snapped again and it was dark.

I lay there, stiff as the headboard above me until sleep claimed me. Then I slept like the dead. I never felt anything more than the covers shift and the mattress give.

He was gone when I woke up. I hadn't expected anything less.

The inability to think, hash out the plan, was undoubtedly the source of my anxiety and core reason my body rebelled.

Or they could have poisoned the food, tipped off by my mental ramblings.

Valium, anyone?

The note was on my dresser, propped up so I wouldn't miss it, when I came out of the bathroom. I hadn't heard a thing. I was only in there ten minutes.

My thumb brushed over the crisp, heavy bond paper. I smoothed it through my fingers. Prestige. It would hold a demand, not a request. Of that I was sure. My name was printed neatly across the front. Ella Mansfield. My name meant nothing. Nothing. I had been erased, yet here it was, right in front of me.

"Here goes." I snapped the seal. Wax. Gothic, but just Mr. B's style. Three words, in the same elaborate typeset, graced the middle of the page.

Dinner. Six. Formal.

Groan, I added a fourth word to humor my growling stomach. But it wasn't hungry. No way, no how. Pure revulsion.

Now what? I suppose checking the closet would be my first smart step. I thought about the last fiasco involving the fancy ball gown.

Ugh.

The idea of pink frills on yellow lace or purple taffeta made me more nauseous than the prospect of dinner.

"*Don't back down now,*" a voice in my head echoed. "*You're on the right track.*"

I didn't dare name the source, even though it left me sagging in relief. Breathe, I commanded myself. *See? You're not alone. It's okay.*

"Gee, your magic must really be well developed if you were able to sense me come in. I was going to surprise you." Quentin held up a half-gallon of milk and a container of Oreos.

I swallowed hard to squelch the scream and the bitterness that rose in my throat. "No," I sputtered out. "No food. Get out. I'm not well. Go."

"Ella?" He dropped the food on the table and hurdled the bed. Well, almost. I couldn't help but giggle as his foot entangled in the covers and brought him to his knees. He barely let it slow him down. "What's wrong, you're still not feeling better?"

Gulp. "Absolutely not."

"What is it, what do you need?"

I spread my arms wide. He stepped into them, pulled my head to rest on his shoulder. For the first time since this fiasco started I felt warm and safe. Without any doubts clouding my head. Finally. I let the peace wash over me and dreaded for this moment to end.

"Better?" He must have sensed how my body relaxed.

"Yeah, a little."

"A little? It's tough being the sensitive man here. You've got to give a bit."

I laughed into his shirt. "Do I really have to do this formal dinner thing tonight? Can you write a note saying I'm sick or something?"

"I'd bet Mr. B would want to see you for himself. Chances are he'd call a doctor. Do you want that?"

He'd backed up and looked me in the eye. I didn't think I wanted to answer his unspoken question.

Big sigh. "What time is it?" I didn't trust my clock, or my stomach to tell me it was after lunch.

"About two." Well, maybe I should have. Four hours to prepare, eh?

"Okay, okay." I surrendered. I dropped my hands to my side. "But you get to pick out my dress."

The metallic taste of regret coated my tongue. What had I done? I couldn't wait to see my punishment.

Then the idea hit me. It didn't matter what dress he chose. I could make an appearance and then...a disappearance.

It was really a shame. The gown Quentin had picked was actually pretty. Not in a lacy, feminine way, but in a dark, gothic theme. I shouldn't even call it pretty. It was...I fingered the black mesh overlay...medieval. But I don't know anything about historical periods.

Ah heck.

I let the robe drop and I slid the dress over my bare body. Well, if this wasn't the cat's meow. The rose colored panel pushed up cleavage and pushed down on my stomach. It made curves where I didn't think I had any. Now this, if any, would be the costume to take home.

My hands dropped to my sides. Home was a distant memory. Who knows where I'd end up—but the walls of this compound were all I had at the moment. And they wouldn't be around long.

I unlaced the black satin criss-cross tie and pulled the yards of material over my head with a dejected sigh. I was wasting entirely too much time feeling sorry for myself.

I needed something to wear now. Something unobtrusive that would allow me to blend with the decor. The dresser drawers had been adequately filled with a variety of clothes. Something comfortable was the ticket. I passed over the camouflage tank top and Hawaiian print shirts. No, no neon t-shirts, no spandex. Give me denim and a white t-shirt here, people. Where's your fashion sense?

Ugh. I finally gave up and slipped on a kelly green polo and khaki shorts. Just call me a regular old girl scout.

My fingers were a bit rusty, but I managed to secure my hair into a smooth French braid. Screw makeup. It'd serve them right to have to stare at my boring unadorned features. Maybe Quentin wouldn't be so enchanted.

But he was just as inquisitive.

"Where are you going?" He found me in the hall, three steps from my door.

"Out."

"Where?"

"Out."

"Looking for Oreos?"

Looking for a knuckle sandwich? I so wanted to ask him that and in the same breath tell him I didn't care if I never saw another cookie in my life. "No," is what came out instead. Best not to bait him and make him think I was hiding something.

Too late, I realized he was honing in on my thoughts. I could tell. His eyes darkened.

"Hey, can't a girl go exploring?"

"Not here."

"I promise not to enter any room marked employees only, okay? Those four walls have me losing my sanity. And you know I'm on the edge already, don't you, Quentin?" I stood up so my nose touched the tip of his.

"See you at six." I planted a chaste kiss on his stony lips and whirled away.

"Ella!" He grabbed my braid like a horse's rein and nearly ripped me off my feet.

"What the hell!"

"Sorry." He had the decency to look apologetic. "That was a lousy kiss, you know."

His mouth hit mine with all the heat and power of lava from a volcano. His tongue invaded my mouth, tempting, teasing. A strobe light of our first time together flashed in my mind.

Fingers relaxed on my braid and cupped the back of my head, tilting it back for his desperate pillaging. Nerve endings came to life, sending tingles through my body. The pressure of his lips left me hungry for so much more of him—I ached with the want for this man—all of him, body and heart.

"Ella," he breathed. "Let's go back inside your room."

I let him lead me two steps closer to the door and then I stopped him. I had to know. I was too invested in this emotionally to let him take advantage of me. "Why, Quentin?" I muttered against the pulse in his neck. His fingers slid down my body and across my lower back. There, his thumb rubbed erotic circles. I hated the layer of material between my skin and his. He held me tightly against the evidence of his passion. I got a grip on my emotions before they betrayed me. "Why do you want to make love to me? Do you love me, or is this a distraction technique?"

"I don't know, is it working?"

Immediately I thought of icy rain and blustery winds. Mental cold shower. "No," I answered, and backed out of his embrace and put my back to him. Looking at him, seeing those dark green eyes darken with desire would be too much. I knew I'd ache to push his hair off his face, to run my hand over his strong jaw line and pretend I didn't care why he kissed me. I'd just let him. So I didn't look.

"Wait, honey, I was just joking. You know I do."

"Do what?" I stopped but didn't turn around.

I heard his breathing. Felt his heat, smelled the musky soap he'd showered with. And wanted him. But I didn't find the words I needed anywhere.

"Sorry." I continued down the hall. It didn't matter what Sam said. If Quentin couldn't say it, I couldn't do it.

The idea of exploring didn't have the same spark as it had initially. Still, I let my fingers trace the carved wooden trim that lined the hall. Even the air felt better on my lungs. I needed this. The taste of freedom...

...had gone sour.

There was no doubt I wasn't supposed to be here. I didn't cross any yellow tape, or enter any doors with a skull and crossbow signs.

Yet I knew.

"What a surprise, Ella, I expected you to be preparing for tonight's event. Are you lost?"

His voice was nails down a chalkboard. Especially his condescending final sentence.

I inclined my head. "Well, actually, I may be. I expected to find a doorway to the gardens along this hallway."

Mr. B frowned. "We've no gardens here and I'm afraid I can't trust you enough to allow you to leave the walls of this compound anyway, Ella. You're a risk."

I ignored his distrust. I didn't expect for him to plop a crown on my head and anoint me a princess. "No gardens? But I remember an enclosed square of wonderful, colorful blooms. Was it a dream?"

He stared at me as if my hair had faded to pink and I'd popped out an extra eye. "We've no such thing."

I reached up to scratch my head. "But I could've sworn—"

He squeezed my shoulder, turned me back around and led me down the hall. "Why don't you head back and start preparing for tonight's events?"

It wasn't an option.

Chapter Twenty

My curiosity was more than piqued. What was Mr. B hiding that was so important he escorted me all the way back to my room himself? Did he think I'd turn around and retrace my steps? Was he going to stand guard to make sure I didn't? Why?

Quentin, dammit, wasn't in the room. Not that I'd ask him. I wasn't sure if I'd believe what he'd tell me.

"*It's all up to you.*"

"What?" I turned in a complete circle, looking for the source of the voice in my head. "Who's there?"

"*You must go down to come up, the circle should never meet.*"

Sam. Had to be, whispering so softly I could barely understand, much less recognize his voice. Had I missed something? Why was he talking in riddles?

I jammed my hands in my pockets and stomped across the room, mentally pleading for him to tell me what the heck he meant.

I stopped after three steps. My hand was shaking when I withdrew it and turned it over. As I opened my fist, I gasped. There it was. The last gem.

Now what? Goose bumps covered my arms as I remembered the first part of the cryptic message. *Up to me?* Sure. No pressure.

But I wouldn't simply sit here and let things happen around me. Nor did I think I could safely protect the gem. I could...hopefully, figure out a way to use it to stop Mr. B. That thought almost had my half laugh turn to tears.

Now thankful Quentin wasn't around to question or follow me, I went invisible and snuck back into the maze of hallways until I found a staircase leading to the basement.

And I wouldn't have gone down there, really, if I hadn't felt the pull. I could feel the power in the air. A pulsing heartbeat coming from the center of the compound. The life blood.

The gems.

I'll admit it, first curiosity and maybe even greed had me straddling the doorway. I knew it was there, just around the corner.

Quentin called my name. Couldn't tell if it was in my head or in my ears. It was intense. Had to be the magic. The power called to me. I couldn't fight against it. I had to see, to know, to understand what I fought for—to understand why this raw energy couldn't be trusted in the hands of anyone like Mr. B.

My body pulsated, as if my very heartbeat was connected to the power the gems radiated. I followed the invisible lure until I reached a door. It looked like any ordinary door. Yet I knew.

Something icy cold blasted me from behind and sent me sprawling into the room. I could almost feel the chilling, snake-like laughter wrap itself up and around me and stop my heart.

I shook it off and stood.

There it was.

Incredible.

It was like being in a room of pure sunshine and oxygen. Power seeped through every pore on my body. Like a super injection of revitalizing vitamins. I felt whole, powerful, alive.

Funny, though, the circle exuded so much power yet the room wasn't filled with light, Brilliance from such an extreme amount of magic should have spilled out through the doors and windows, desperate to escape and fill the world.

But then I remembered my last visit to the island. I'd been tainted. Couldn't see that. Perhaps an innocent could. But for me, the Technicolor was hidden behind bad intentions and selfish decisions. I was still stuck in black and white, and likely doomed to stay there.

I wondered if Quentin or Mr. B could see anything more than the contraption that centered the room, illuminated only by overhead fluorescents.

These gems were supposed to be the heart of happiness, the soul of goodness, the power of freedom. And they were about to turn off the lights on the good side of things forever.

Enough philosophizing, Ella. That's not going to stop him. Think.

How are you going to do this?

Plan? Why hadn't I engraved notes from my talk with Lou and Sam on my arm? I couldn't remember anything except...something about acting like a magnet and the power turning. I didn't have a magnet. I shook my head and looked around. There had to be a solution here.

The room wasn't ornate. In fact, the walls were nothing more than painted concrete block and the only thing worth seeing in the entire space was its centerpiece.

It rendered me speechless. Thoughtless. I could only stare, mouth agape.

The giant glass-looking circular frame, constructed in metal, stood nearly six feet tall. From what I could tell, it was propped in some oversize contraption that reminded me of a decorative plate holder. But this thing was meant for function, not aesthetic appeal.

And that's not what had me gaping.

It was what decorated the glass that held me in awe.

Gems. Nine of them. Placed around the circle like numbers on the clock, gleaming like diamonds in the plain overhead light.

They radiated the power.

Awesome power.

It took virtually no effort at all to close my eyes and wish to be wearing the ball gown I'd left laying out. An easy finger flick created the perfect hair style. I snapped my fingers and was rewarded with shoes. Now, one last thing.

I held out my hand and mentally reached for the velvet box.

"Looking for this?" Mr. B strode through the door and closed it behind him. "Ah, you sensed it then, the pull to the magic. The sapphire has its own magic—one a little different than these." He gestured to the circle behind him. "It can stand alone, to some extent. Its magic is limited unless paired with one of these."

At the top of the circle, high noon, was a place I could only expect had been created to hold the sapphire Mr. B currently clutched.

He continued, "Combined with the ten gems, the magic created by this circle will be stronger than any that came before it."

"What of the other gems, the copies? Couldn't you, at any time, have put them in the circle with the sapphire?"

He shook his head. He'd tried it, of course, he was too greedy not to. But even one hundred of those fake gems couldn't have the power of ten real ones.

"We're getting close. The labs working day and night to duplicate the power."

"You're making magic?" Preposterous. There had to be something, a link, a draw. Magic wasn't creatable. It just was.

Listen to me. Like this little travel agent from Illinois knows jack about magic.

"Oh yes, we're making magic. Once we can complete this circle, Ella, we anticipate magic will be at our disposal."

I couldn't imagine a life with magic in abundance. Chaos and mayhem would rule. Everything sacred would be replaced. And no one could govern a world in which everyone had so much power. Even if Mr. B thought so.

If he tuned in to my thoughts, he ignored me. Didn't say a word, but walked over to the circle of gems and touched one. It pulsated with color at the contact.

I must have gasped. He laughed.

"Go, on, Ella, dear. Touch one. Feel the exquisite strength in the real gems. But then, I forget, you've worn them, known their power, haven't you? You're quite familiar with the pull they have."

And I did. Much as I wanted to deny it, having known them, I feared being without them. Any of them. And there was a definite difference. Zirconia to diamond. Pyrite to gold.

Mr. B glowered over me. He was not a friendly creature. I took a step backwards, aiming for the general direction of the door. "Why are you doing this to me?" I asked.

Mr. B lifted his hand and the glow faded. "Why?" He ignored my intent to escape as if he didn't think I would, or could. "Why indeed, Ella Mansfield?"

I waited.

"I need you." He smiled like a hypocritical preacher asking for tithes, and slung an arm around my shoulder.

My hands dug deeper into my pockets. I hated this—having my personal space invaded. Especially by a snake.

"Pardon me." He stepped away. "But I should expect you to be repulsed. One of the things I like about you, dear, is your loyal spirit. Soon, however, you will see I am not evil at all. My establishment is run with careful consideration. My intention is not to corrupt the world, but rather to show by example how my ideas can revolutionize the modern globe."

I felt like snorting. He sounded political, and one of the first things my father taught me was politicians will tell anyone what they want to hear.

"Why do you need me?" I knew it wasn't really me he needed. It was something he thought I had.

"No, Ella, I know you don't have what I need. But you're carrying my heir. A child—proof my theory of peace can be successful."

The man was talking in riddles. But I really expected that was what he wanted to do—confuse me. It needed to stop. "I need to get ready for this dinner," I said.

"Why? You look ready now."

I glanced down and growled. That's right. I had played tricks with my clothes to save time. What a stupid move that had been.

Still, I wasn't completely ready. I pointed to my face. "War paint. Make-up. Something to make me appear beautiful. I know I look stressed."

He waved his fingers. I should have expected him to use magic. A feather like touch brushed over my face. I guess he solved that.

An easy snap of his fingers produced a full length mirror. "Smashing." Mr. B nodded and smiled. "Quentin will be pleased. He chose this dress, yes?"

What could I do but nod?

He made the mirror disappear. Lord, I wish I could do that.

"No!" Mr. B stepped toward me, his eyes flashing.

"Don't worry, I'm not going anywhere." I fought to think about not *having* anywhere to go, even if I wanted to. I sighed.

"Good girl. Now let me help you with the necklace."

I stood while he fastened it around my neck. It'd be so easy for him to choke me. Or unhook my gems and leave me defenseless.

"Defense, Ella? They were provided simply to aid you in daily life—"

"It's not what I mean." What did I mean? I could remember a time when I hated the gems, didn't want them. Now I was scared to be without them.

"Ah, Quentin, good of you to finally join us."

A hand rested at my waist. A warm, welcome hand.

"Hi, dear, how was your walk?" He looked down and smiled.

Opaque eyes. I hated the emptiness there. His touch suddenly didn't feel so comfortable.

I didn't squirm, despite the overwhelming urge. Instead I practiced acting and tried to look like the loving partner as I smiled back up at him. "I got lost—caught up in traffic. Can't believe there's so many people down here."

Can't say as I liked the exchange the two men shared. I interpreted it as "piece of cake"—referring to my apparent naïveté. "What?" burst out of my mouth like it had burned my tongue.

"You ask too many questions." Mr. B nodded at Quentin.

Oh, give me a break.

"The dress looks great, Ella. Why don't you come back with me to the room while I get ready?" The whisper I usually found irresistible became irritating

I should have tuned into them. I tried, then, but found nothing. As if I was blocked. Well, that was a new one.

Quentin tugged at the back of my dress. I heard something fall. My hand immediately grabbed at my neck, but both the tight choker containing my knock-off gems and the sapphire were in place.

It could only mean...

I refused to think. Instead I cursed dresses and the lack of secure pockets and even the fact I didn't have ample cleavage to keep my secret...well, secret. All this during the moment we all sort of stared at each other, disbelieving.

Then, on some invisible cue, we all dove toward the sparkling gem. I, of course, might as well have been wearing a straight jacket for the speed and agility in which I reacted. Damn dress.

It was Quentin who came up with it.

The final gem.

"At last," Bergestein gasped and clapped his hands together in evil glee.

I shuddered and choked. "No." I reached for it, but Quentin fisted it and held it to his chest.

He wouldn't meet my eyes.

Now what? I knew. I'd failed. I'd let Quentin in too close and the mission was over.

Lightning, strike me now.

What happened next was considerably worse than the prospect of a few hundred thousand volts of electricity. A giant green vine reached out from the wall. Like a horror movie. A Jack and the Beanstalk horror movie. It snared my legs.

Panic ensued. I kicked, stomped, tried to run. But it held tight and pulled me backwards toward the wall.

Oh. My. God. I was going to die.

I fought with everything I had. And my magic was useless. Even with the supposedly powerful sapphire against my throat, I could do nothing to get free. I wouldn't look up at Bergestein or Quentin, though the passing wonder of why Quentin refused to help me stole some of my strength.

The snake-like vine slithered up my back. I clawed at my neck, reaching for the gems, praying for their power. But the vine was quicker than I, squeezing my neck and keeping my fingers from reaching the gems.

Power. One last chance.

I closed my eyes and relaxed. God, it was hard to relax. But I had to let it build. Easy. Easy. I couldn't use my hands. I had to be sure of what I was doing. I thought of what had transpired, letting the anger, the hate, all flow through me and become a giant ball of power in my gut.

I'd have to use eye contact to direct it. I prayed it was enough.

Fire.

Literally.

Fear must have weakened my ability—or else my gems had been rendered inactive. I gave it all I had. Mr. B should have gone up in smoke and ash. Instead, his sleeve caught fire and his eyebrows got a little singed.

All I'd managed to do was piss him off.

Nice move, Ella.

Quentin echoed the thought, mentally. Finally. I was beginning to think I was powerless. No, I had power, just not enough to do anything with it.

The gem remained tightly in Quentin's grip. And my lover and my friend—the one I'd trusted and run to—had failed to even acknowledge I was becoming dinner for some oversize Venus fly trap.

Since nothing else worked, I tried to save myself the old-fashioned way. "Help!"

And I yelled loud, too. Bergestein laughed. Quentin frowned.

Bad thing was, apart from blinking, my mouth was the only thing I could move. And with the huge vine circling my neck, my jaw was quickly becoming immobile.

I really was going to die.

No.

Not with that creep leaning down to sneer at me. I'd have given anything to wipe the arrogant smile off his face.

"Ella, Ella, Ella. You're a fiery one. It's a shame I have to extinguish your spirit. But you can't go on. You've learned too much. You're too dangerous to me. Surely you understand that."

The limbs tightened. He intended to have me ripped limb from limb. Brain cells exploded, as if finally taking it in. *I don't want to die!*

What of the child? The heir, the whole purpose for my being?

"Sorry dear, but you're not the only fertile woman on this planet. As much as I'd hoped this would work, you're just too much of a liability."

The pain blinded me. The vine circling my stomach had gotten to rib crushing power. How could he?

"Apparently Quentin is as eager to be a father as you are a mother, my dear. He's quite unwilling to save you, or your child."

Mr. B and Quentin stared each other down.

"Quentin, no. Please." My teeth were locked together, but I had to get it out. I could feel the waves of indecision. He was almost ready to give in. Probably afraid of suffering the same fate as I.

He caught my eye, then looked away. I willed him, begged him both vocally and mentally to do the right thing. Mr. B pulled the other way, I knew that without hearing his thoughts. God only knew what he was feeding him. And Quentin's own ego had to be involved in the volley. He'd been power hungry all along.

I choked back a sob as my shoulder popped. I wasn't sure I had legs anymore. Circulation had ceased and even the tingling stopped.

I could only hope my brain would be as numb as my extremities when the skin started tearing.

"Do you want to see her suffer further?"

A drip of sweat rolled down Quentin's cheek as he looked from me to Bergestein.

"No, Quentin. Don't worry about me. Do *not* give him the gem. Please." The room was getting hazy. Blurry.

"Do you want to watch me kill her?" Mr. B's voice was followed by the expected villainous laugh. It was almost funny. Except the pain part. If I didn't have nerve endings I could have pretended I was dreaming this ridiculous stunt.

"This is the one you love, isn't it, lover boy? The one who would give you a son."

I was being severed. Something rolled down my back. Sweat? Blood? Who knew?

"Let her go!" Quention straightened his shoulders and squared off against Bergestein.

I felt limp. "*No! Don't give in. I'm nothing. Save the world, dammit.*"

"Here, take it. Let her go!" Quentin threw the gem at Mr. B., or I assume he did. I heard something skate across the floor. And then I felt fingers at my neck, struggling against the vine.

He touched my gems.

Nothing.

I gasped a hard fought breath. Nothing?

"*I'm so sorry, Sam. I'm so sorry.*" I felt it coming, the tunnel that would take me from this body. Close. So close.

But Quentin was in my way, peering into my eyes.

Close. So close.

"I love you," he whispered.

My eyes closed.

"Heeeeelp!" The dark tunnel took a distinct right turn and jerked me back into bright light. I was being shaken like a rag doll at the same time. But I could move. I really could.

Magical green eyes bore into mine when I forced mine open. I could breathe, too. My lungs screamed their thanks as they filled with oxygen. Quentin. Quentin had saved me.

"Oh, Ella," he said, finally letting go of my shoulders. "Thank God you're okay."

"I'm not," I croaked. My throat burned. And that didn't even describe it well enough. Something told me that once feeling came back to the rest of my body I'd wish I were dead.

The would-be murderer stood before the circle of gems. Totally oblivious to us. His nonchalance surprised me, but I even didn't have the energy to point it out to Quentin.

I watched as he rolled the stone over and over in his hands. But even I understood its importance. That once little marble-looking thing could disturb the balance of the entire planet.

And the wrong man was in control.

I opened my mouth to shout. Tell him he'd be a fool to do it.

Quentin's hand came up and covered my lips to stop the words. He shook his head, his eyes boring into mine. Like he was trying to make me see what he was thinking.

I couldn't.

The magic was gone.

All we could do was watch.

The room took on a purple glow. Each gem became a giant amethyst color. Even the one in his hand.

The sapphire, which I miraculously still had around my neck, burned my neck. It had to have sizzled against my skin. Tears immediately sprang to my eyes. "Get it off, get it off." I reached up and tried to claw at it, but I was so weak, I couldn't make my fingers work the clasp.

Quentin didn't say anything, but the look on his face scared me. Because *he* looked scared. I could only imagine I'd carry around the scar of this, a permanent necklace.

"Please, hurry." Sweat slid down my back and sides. I wanted to escape and find that dark, cool place again. It burned. God, it hurt.

"You lied to me!" Mr. B roared and lunged at us. His eyes had gone black, his lips curled up in a snarl that would frighten a rabid dog. He was evil, through and through. Tangibly evil.

Quentin reached out and grabbed the sapphire, ripping it from my neck. But I knew it was no good. Powerless against the circle of ten. It was, in essence, nothing more than a pretty knock-off gem.

"You *lied.*" Bergestein repeated, his voice lowering to an evil hiss.

I shrank back, expecting him to turn into something dragon-like and attack us with teeth bared.

It sizzled. The sapphire actually sizzled in Quentin's palm. I cringed, feeling his pain and knowing it had done the same to my own skin.

For a moment I thought he'd juggle or drop it, but almost as if he were unaware of the way his hand blistered beneath the gold, he turned and looked at the circle.

Then hurled the stone, necklace and all, into the center of it.

"Quentin!" I screamed, wincing and waiting for the big kaboom. But then I knew I must have mirrored his own unhinged jaw look when the piece of jewelry simply bounced off the circle and lay crumpled on the ground at Mr. B's feet.

Why couldn't it have all been Candid Camera way back that first day? Why couldn't Quentin and I have escaped to live strangely—happily was pushing it, I realized—ever after? Why now, why this? And why did I feel like the weight of the world was on my shoulders, crumbling my knees and stealing the breath from my lungs?

Mr. B growled, and once again the two of them lunged for a gem.

And all I could think of was no one, and I mean *no one* back home would believe this. Even Jeannie. God, I missed her. Much as I hated to admit it, I did. And Jess and Karl and my mom and dad.

If I failed this mission—and I didn't think there was a mission left at this point in the game—I'd never see them again.

Mr. B reached up with the sapphire and placed it in the top of the circle. The sapphire stone was a mystery to me, even now. Sam had never spoken of it.

But then he set the tenth gem into place and things started happening. Fast.

Rainbows scattered on the walls, tiny prisms set off from the spinning gems. Rather pretty for something so evil.

At least Quentin wasn't pleased. He looked downright pissed. His eyes were a storm cloud black, his brows low over them. For some reason, that scared me. Maybe because it wasn't what I expected.

Whose side was he on? His own? I finally realized yes, perhaps, he could be. But where did I fit in on that?

The room started to hum and vibrate from the spinning gems. This had to be what it was like inside an erupting volcano. Maybe not as hot, but one hundred percent as intense.

"Stop it. Stop him!" I gasped. My efforts would probably get me two feet closer and then face down on the floor. I was drained, beat and helpless.

I was yelling at Quentin, but he didn't even twitch.

Someone, however, responded.

My legs gave way, half-exhaustion, half-relief. Quentin noticed that, and scooped me up under my shoulders to prop me back up. His attention was on the circle.

Until Mr. B saw what I had seen.

Quentin gasped, his fingers tightening on my upper arm.

Winzey was here.

Chapter Twenty-One

The tiny fairy flapped and fluttered around Bergestein's head as if daring him to zap her.

When he tried, she darted away. She was too fast.

Thank God.

"Winzey," I breathed. I didn't expect her to stop whatever she was doing and come over to make nice. Especially since I had the feeling she had come to save my ass.

"It's too late, El, it's started already."

Started? What? I looked at the gems. And Winzey, who was flying in and out of the circle so quickly her wings resembled a hummingbird. Then I saw it, a line—not fire, but not something solid either—starting to connect the gems.

"What is she doing?"

Quentin pulled me down to the floor along with him. "Have you written your will?"

I looked down at my torn gown, felt my knotted hair. Besides that, all I had was a pair of useless beads strung around my neck. What would I leave behind anyway? Who would I leave it to? Like it'd get shipped to Jess or anything.

"Wait a minute. Why?" Mr. B wasn't on a suicide mission. And while I doubted he was going to just let us walk away, we weren't strung up on the noose...yet. I squeezed Quentin's arm. What was he saying?

"Either way, it's all over here."

"But this is what he wanted. The ultimate power. The circle is complete."

"It's tainted," he hissed.

I could barely hear him for the rumble that filled the room, the low grade hum that vibrated the very floor where we lay. Surely I had misunderstood him. "Tainted?" Now Quentin wanted to talk in riddles. It was my, albeit meaningless, existence on the line here and the one person I'd trusted all along was playing mind games with me. I came real close to bursting into tears. "How? Talk to me."

He was so calm, as if he hadn't made that comment about the will in his previous breath. "He's not controlling it. She is."

I squinted up at the circle. Winzey looked frantic. Control? I wouldn't believe it.

A low rumbling shook the foundation. Like a far away earthquake. But then I heard it, almost a growl. Lou? I stifled a nervous laugh. He'd probably leave me to die in the rubble for all the good I was to his cause. Chances were the vibrations were from the building power. It filled the room, heavy and thick.

Of course, it could be Mr. B. I had been so busy watching Winzey I hadn't paid any attention to him. I feared for all of us. He looked mad enough to shoot lightning out his eyes and fire from his fingertips.

I couldn't imagine what Winzey was trying to do. The gems were being connected one by one, despite what looked like her attempts to stop it. She flew around and around.

Until Mr. B reached out and grabbed her.

"No!" Quentin and I both shouted.

He dropped her, limp and lifeless to the floor.

"No," I screamed again. I crawled toward her, heedless of Mr. B and Quentin and the circle above me. It didn't matter. The bastard had hurt my friend. Truly, the one who was always faithful to me.

I lifted her, cradled her. She was so tiny. But like a little rag doll. "Please, please, Winzey, come back to me. Help me. Help me."

"*Put her in the circle. Stop the cycle.*"

No one in the room had spoken. No one appeared to have heard it but me.

"Don't let the connection reach the blue stone."

Lou.

I looked up at the circle, so high above me. The connection was moving quicker now. And I had the solution in my hands, a dainty human of the smallest scale, and yet her wings, her glittery hair, it was all so magical, but at that moment so lifeless. My heart was tearing out. And he wanted me to put her in the circle?

Quentin pulled me up. "There's nothing we can do."

The power built. The energy radiating was awesome. And it scared me nearly to death. But I alone could stop it now.

"Lord, forgive me." I didn't know how God felt about fairies. I didn't know how he felt about me, the prodigal's daughter, but I hoped somehow he was listening. Maybe Lou had an in with him.

Her little body trembled in my hand. Maybe if she woke up, her magic could stop it. I was so intently watching her eyelids for a tiny flicker I hadn't realized Mr. B was right behind me until he spoke.

"Give me the fairy."

I tightened my fist at his words. No way was I turning this precious thing over to him. "No."

He put out his hand.

As if. Nothing in the world would make me turn Winzey over to him.

He lunged.

I fell back.

Quentin leapt.

While those two wrestled, my brain tried to get a toe-hold on what I had to do. Seemed a lot like putting your best friend on a set of railroad tracks with the train in sight. But I did it, albeit with a shaking hand.

Bergestein had to go down. Even if Winzey and I had to go with him. It was just the way things worked.

The neon light continued to link gem to gem. The deep roar continued. It was all going to blow. All I could do was hope it came fast and painless.

The grunt and clashes behind me had me at wit's end. Quentin's cry—certainly not a victory cry—had me giving up watching the countdown to doom and awkwardly rushing to him.

Bergestein was fighting like a man without magic—whether he possessed it or not, I'd no way of guessing, but his punches and kicks were nothing more than Quentin's. He just had more weight than Quentin.

Which left my last hope of escaping this room and perhaps the building knocked unconscious against the wall.

"Quentin!" I crawled the few remaining feet to him.

Big mistake.

Huge.

Mr. B went straight for Winzey and plucked her from the circle like a piece of lint from his trousers.

I continued to fail.

Was I just a loser by nature or was this a learned trait? Didn't matter—at least I hadn't passed it on to any children.

And suddenly I was picturing a little boy who looked just like Quentin. Tears couldn't be dammed up any longer. What was the saying about Hell and a woman scorned?

Mr. B had stood up and seemed to be ignoring the two of us. His mistake. I dove, using every bit of momentum I could find, right at his knees.

Of course, he was twice my size and merely took a step backwards from the impact. He did, however, throw his hands up in the air to balance. Which must have freed Winzey.

First I thought she just arced limply across the room.

Then I realized it. She was flying.

"Winzey, help us!" I reached out for her, but she avoided my hand and flew arrow straight at the circle.

I saw why. The circle had become bright red. It was nearly complete.

She screamed. It tore my heart with a certainty that she had sacrificed herself, unselfishly. Something I couldn't have done.

The flash that followed was immediate and intense. What I'd imagine a nuclear bomb to be like. The blinding white light lasted less than a second, then all went black.

ଔ ଔ ଔ

Sam stood over me, shaking his head. He must have sensed I was awake or he'd woken me up himself. He clucked and said, "You really know how to make things happen, don't you?"

I squinted against the most agonizing pain I ever remember feeling. A breath-stealing combination of physical and emotional grief in its purest form. "Am I alive?" Surely there was no pain in heaven, and since Sam was here *and* there weren't any flaming fires or red men with pitchforks, I didn't think I'd gone the other way.

"Yes. Alive. And lucky to say that."

I let out my breath. "Did we, did I..." If I was alive then we had to have achieved something.

"Somehow, yes, the plan was executed. But not without a price."

I slumped down. I'd really hoped it was all a bad, bad dream. That I'd imagined the silly charade. Made it a mental worst case scenerio.

Not so.

"Ella," the voice boomed from the edge of the valley. Not thunder, but a welcome, fatherly tone.

I studied Sam's reaction. Maybe a little surprise. But maybe, then again, welcome wasn't the correct description for the summons.

"Go on, quit analyzing and face the truth, Ella," Sam prodded.

I wasn't feeling up to it. Not up to anything. I should have died. I deserved to have died.

So what had saved me?

"Lou?" I turned to the voice that called me, expecting to see his imagine in the pool.

"Over here, Ella." I followed the sound of his voice. A man sat in the once broken rock throne. Only now it glowed like mother-of-pearl marble and stood majestically at the end of the wide open meadow.

My jaw should have bruised my toes as I gaped. Lou was...awe-inspiring. Certainly wizard-clad, but he looked like a slightly older version of Sam.

Incredible. "Lou?"

As he nodded, the gems that circled the stone behind him shot to life with glittering sparks.

"Come closer, Ella. Do not be afraid."

Yeah, right. But I was more afraid of not listening to his command. I stepped carefully, cautiously, as if walking on eggshells.

"Come here." Lou raised a hand that glittered with a sapphire ring.

He must have seen the expression I couldn't keep off my face. "Yes, Ella, even the ring had been stripped from me. It had been my wife's. The Fairies fashioned it into a ring for me."

He slid it from his finger and let it reflect the glorious sunlight. Pure, like the sky, like the deep sea.

"It's yours."

I couldn't. "No." I put my hand out to stop him.

"It's rightly yours. It holds no power now, only beauty, the way a gem should. Please take it. Without you I would not have it to give."

Riddles, riddles. Without him, I wouldn't be here to accept it. But I didn't say anything out loud. That would be too much. I stepped up to him and knelt before him. It felt right.

"Get up. I'm not a king or a god or a lord. I'm Lou."

Sorry. He'd never be "just" Lou.

The ring was placed in my outstretched hand. It was miles too big for my fingers. Even if I sized it, it was too large to wear on my hand. Perhaps a choker, a brooch. Maybe someday. I couldn't imagine wearing it for a long, long time.

I closed my fingers over it, still feeling undeserving. It warmed my skin, almost pulsed. I looked back up at Lou. He said it had no magic, yet I felt its energy. Warmth. Like a loved one's hug slid up my arm and touched my soul.

"Thank you, Ella, and you presume correctly. The stone itself will always carry something. But you won't be able to use it, only feel it." He winked. "But I can allow this. Guard it, respect it, and it may protect you."

My eyes fell. My knees gave way slightly and I continued their motion with a curtsey. "Thank you, Lou. Thank you. I don't deserve this." Tears threatened. It ached so bad.

"Which is why you'll never have magic again. Never."

Even though I expected it, the words crushed my innards and left me hollow. Where would I go? What would I do? Everything I had, identity, all if it, had been destroyed.

"I'll grant you one wish. You faced some tough decisions. Heart decisions. And I'm proud of you for standing true to yourself and being willing to sacrifice."

"Winzey," I blurted without hesitation. "I want Winzey back. Alive."

"That's your wish? When you could be Ella Mansfield again and have life restored as it was before. I could make this all a dream."

But Winzey would still be dead. I shook my head, shaking out the notion he was telling me exactly what I wanted.

"Winzey," I insisted.

He snapped his fingers and from the base of the waterfall flew the most beautiful sight I'd seen so far. She was glorious, if possible, more vibrant than before.

She buzzed around my head, kissed my cheek and then settled atop Lou's throne.

"That was a noble wish."

I bowed my head. But I knew. For once I was very proud of myself and my decision. No matter what, I'd done the right thing. "It was what I wanted, sir. I could not accept fortune or happiness while carrying the burden of guilt." My mom always told me one day I'd get serious. This was certainly that time. A preview of judgment day, I ventured to guess.

"What will happen to me now? I know I can't stay here. But will you drop me back in my hometown or just outside the island to fend for myself?"

"I wouldn't have asked you to waste your wish on a ride home. Even though I suggested so. Are you ready?"

I clasped my hands behind my back and braced myself. "Yes."

A tear slid down my cheek. My eyes burned. It was over. The adventure to end all adventures had ended. Somehow I'd been involved in defeating the bad guy and saving the world. But I'd made friends—Sam, Lou, Winzey...Quentin.

The pain centered over my chest. The axe of grief cut through skin and bone and left me raw. And I cried—standing there as still as a statue, I silently wept for my lost heart.

I only regretted I'd heard the words from him only once, and had not answered him back. I had truly loved him, despite his issues. Despite my own.

"Ella?"

Even now, I could hear him calling me in gentle concern. *Stop*! I had to get a grip. I sniffed and blinked the dampness out of my eyes. "I'm ready, Lou. Let's do it."

"Ella."

Quentin. It was his voice.

Was this another test? I was so scared to turn, afraid I'd see

Quentin standing there, yet so afraid I wouldn't. I knew I couldn't handle the disappointment.

I didn't have to wait, God bless the procrastinator in me. A warm, gentle hand squeezed my shoulder and spun me into waiting arms.

I sighed, squealed, screamed, I don't know what else. The joy that flooded me was incredible. At least as powerful as the waterfall beside us.

Once I'd leaned back and made sure it *was* him—I knew my heart wouldn't betray me, but I had to make my brain comprehend—I threw my arms around him. The tears returned then. I couldn't help it. I felt on the verge of bursting.

Quentin was alive.

After our overlong embrace, I studied him, memorized each feature in case Sam were to tell me it was just a dream, one of his holograms.

But Quentin's clothes were torn, his face and hands red beneath the layer of soot.

"How?" I asked, of anyone, no one.

Quentin stared up over my shoulder at Lou. With his arm securely holding me closely, I turned to face the only one who could have done it.

"No, no. It was my son's idea." Lou smiled down. "Sam knew without magic you two would need each other. So he went back for Quentin before it was too late. And almost didn't make it."

Sam stepped up to stand beside his father. I expected him to be dwarfed by the presence of Lou, but realized Sam had his own aura, a giant stature that had little to do with physical size. It was all heart.

"Quentin, you're probably as confused."

I felt, rather than saw him, nod.

"A friend of yours named Frederique got in touch with me when the storm blew up. He spilled the plan knowing you weren't going to succeed. Something about your heart getting in the way."

I looked up. Quentin's eyes glittered playfully. He squeezed me a little tighter. "I couldn't leave without Ella."

Lou coughed.

Sam continued, "You see, Ella, Quentin was on the same side, going against orders, yes, but he did work with help and had managed to infiltrate some of Bergestein's secrets. Like word he had the sapphire. The problem was Quentin was so far underground, none of us could trust him. We knew the power of these gems were a giant influence. He'd slipped in the past."

I nodded. I'd learn those stories sometime, I hoped.

"Which is why all the created gems are being deactivated—"

"They're not already?" I interrupted. Magic was still out there? Being used?

"The mission we undertake now is to locate and destroy them. But all the work to finish that will be done from the safety of this island."

I didn't even want to know how. And obviously *that* mission could be done without me. Which meant I got to go home.

I drank in the last view of paradise. The scent, freshness, harmony, they would all be things I'd never forget.

"So, Lou, about a ride home?" I prompted.

"To Alaska, then?" Quentin nudged.

What was it with him and cold, wet places? "Huh?"

"I haven't been home in years."

I countered. "Alaska? What about me? What's wrong with central Illinois?"

"I don't live in Illinois is what's the matter."

"We can vacation in Alaska, right, Lou, Sam?" Help me here. I wasn't a snow lover. And we had snow in Illinois.

The two men at the throne wore smiles the size of the entire United States. "You've got to make a decision. Now, preferably, and seal it with a kiss. You can go anywhere you want."

I had an idea, one I thought he'd buy. "Vegas?" I arched an eyebrow.

His arms locked around my waist as I faced him. "Hey, I can do Vegas." He leaned down and pressed the most gentle, promising, loving kiss to my lips. My toes tingled and my heart swelled to balloon size.

I realized in that moment having a magical power wasn't all it was cracked up to be. If you have love, you have all the real magic you'll ever need.

We opened our eyes to the roar of a crowd.

Even the magician looked surprised to find us there, locked in a kiss, when he'd pulled away the red curtain.

"Evening," I said with a smile and allowed myself to be led from the box. Quentin stepped down onto the stage behind me.

"Who *are* you?" The magician hissed. "And where'd you come from?"

Quentin and I exchanged a look. A knowing look with a promise. I touched the sapphire fisted in my hand.

"Magic," we said in unison. I added, "You just have to believe in magic."

Melani Blazer

To learn more about Melani Blazer, please visit www.melaniblazer.com. Send an email to Melani at melani@melaniblazer.com or join her Yahoo! group to join in the fun with other readers as well as Melani! http://groups.yahoo.com/group/melaniblazersmusings

Enjoy this excerpt from...

The Distressing Damsel

Available now in book from Samhain Publishing.

It was the long tongue on the back of her knee that woke her up. Forcing her eyes open, she looked over her shoulder to see Briec, naked and beautiful, stretched across the enormous bed. His big arms placed on either side of her legs, holding his body over her as he leaned forward and again licked the back of her knee, reveling in it as if someone had spread the finest honey on her skin.

"What are you doing?"

"Waking you up." His voice sounded raw and husky from sleep and sex. She liked it.

Nipping the sensitive flesh, he grinned. "See? You're awake now."

"How long did I sleep?"

"Too long." It didn't feel like too long.

When he'd finally exhausted her in the hot springs, he'd picked her up and carried her back to her bed. After quickly drying her off, he'd set her down and got in behind her, muttering something like, "It's about time you let me in this bed." Too tired to ask what the hell he meant, and enjoying the feel of his strong arm around her as he drifted to sleep, she instead buried her head in the pillow and quickly dropped off.

Now here he was, dragging that gorgeous body up and over hers, his warm, wet tongue leading the way.

"You taste good."

"Coming from a dragon, that compliment can be a little scary."

He nipped one butt cheek, then the other. "Be nice, woman."

She didn't want to be nice. She wanted to play. Especially since she never had before. At least not in bed. "Why should I be nice?" she teased. "You're not nice." And my, but she did enjoy that about him.

He kissed her lower back, right where her spine met her hips, then licked at it. "I don't know how," he murmured against her warm flesh.

"Perhaps I can show you how easy it is to be nice."

Slowly his eyes lifted to look at her face. "Oh, I think I'd like that," he breathed out huskily.

She pulled from his grasp, raising herself on her knees while he leaned back, his hands flat on the bed, propping him up.

Turning, she moved to his side and placed her hand on his chest. She stroked the hard, smooth skin and marveled at how her merest touch caused ripples across his body. And that was only with her hand.

Leaning forward, she used the tip of her tongue to tickle one nipple. He let out a harsh gasp, followed by a moan when she suckled him into her mouth. She slid her mouth to the other side and did the same. He shuddered and moaned again, making Talaith smile.

Who knew she had this kind of power?

Talaith slid her hand down his chest and her lips and tongue followed. Before she even reached his straining erection, he'd lifted his hips as if expecting her to take him in her mouth. Her arrogant dragon.

Instead, she licked it from base to tip and back again. Then she followed the pulsating veins, avoiding the head except to occasionally tickle it with her nose.

"Talaith," he groaned.

"Aye?" Her tongue slithered up the underside of his shaft.

"Don't torture me, woman."

"Torture you? Me? The weak human torturing a dragon of such awesome power and intellect?"

He grinned at her teasing. "Yes, evil witch. You're torturing me. At least have the decency to admit it."

"I'll admit nothing."

"So I noticed," he muttered while his eyes watched her every move.

She ignored his comment, unwilling to ruin the good mood with the reality of her situation. She had no idea how long before the goddess came for her, and she didn't want to waste a second thinking about anything but him and how he made her feel.

Talaith wrapped her hand around the base of his shaft, marveling at its length and width while enjoying the taste of it, of him. She licked fluid off the tip, teasing the slit with the tip of her tongue, forcing another broken moan from him.

His hand slid into her hair, massaging the back of her head with his long fingers. "Talaith..."

"Mhmm?"

He growled and she fought her desire to laugh.

"Stop teasing me, wench. You're being heartless."

"I find using the word 'please' quite effective at these moments." She nipped the base and his body jerked in response. "Begging would be even better."

When he didn't answer, she glanced up to find him staring off, frowning.

Leaning back a bit, she stared at him. "Gods, you've never said please, have you?"

"I'm thinking." He was silent for a few more seconds, then... "No. I never have." He looked down at her, one eyebrow raised. "And I don't plan to start now."

Anyone else—king or peasant, husband or child—she'd feel insulted. Yet she wasn't because she knew he wasn't being cruel or cold hearted. Just a dragon who never had to say "please" and "sorry" before. And if she thought for one moment she would end up spending the rest of her life with him, she'd have some real concerns.

Since that wouldn't happen, as he'd reminded her the day before, she wouldn't worry.

"That's a real shame, dragon." She ran her tongue across the tip, blew on the wetness she left behind. "Because without it..." Her open mouth hovered over his shaft for several seconds and she could hear him swallow in desperation, anticipating her sucking him into his next life. Instead of doing that, she snapped her mouth shut. "I can't help you."

"You evil—"

"Ah, ah, ah. *You* be nice."

Snarling, his hand still tangled in her hair, he pulled her close then pushed her onto her back. He lay across her, his mouth claiming hers.

Wicked, wicked thoughts flowed through her brain while Briec's hands moved across her body, his tongue thrusting against hers.

She moaned and writhed under him, and he pulled back just enough to say, "We both know I can make you beg long before me, sweet Talaith."

"My, my, we are..." she arched into his body as one of his hands slid between her thighs, "...sure of ourselves."

"It's a gift."

"A gift for you. A curse for the rest of us."

He smiled as he teased her hard nipple with his tongue. Digging her hands into his hair, she silently urged him to take it into his mouth, but he only chuckled, opting to blow on it instead.

Bastard!

Printed in the United States
55338LVS00001B/1-102

9 781599 982113